Walla Walla County Libraries

Tropical Heat

A Tom Doherty Associates Book
New York

Tropical Heat

John A. Miller

FIC
MILLER
2002

TROPICAL HEAT

Design by Heidi Eriksen

A Forge Book
Published by Tom Doherty Associates, LLC
175 Fifth Avenue
New York, NY 10010

www.tor.com

Forge® is a registered trademark of Tom Doherty Associates, LLC.

ISBN 0-765-30165-2

First Edition: February 2002

Printed in the United States of America

0 9 8 7 6 5 4 3 2 1

For Gray and Linda

Tropical Heat

Prologue

The thing Roscoe Franklin would always remember, beyond the murder itself, was how quiet it was that night. The almost unbearable heat that had settled over Prince George County, indeed over the entire state of Virginia and all of the eastern seaboard, discouraged even the cicadas from their nocturnal singing. Roscoe had purchased a quart jar of clear corn whiskey and was walking home with it when he decided to stop at Bud Taylor's old feed warehouse for a rest and a drink. A three-quarter moon was rising as he slowly squatted down with a loud sigh, resting his back against the still-warm red bricks of the warehouse. Though it was almost ten o'clock, the temperature remained above ninety degrees with not the slightest hint of a breeze. Perspiring heavily, he struck a kitchen match with a thumbnail, his deeply etched face and rheumy eyes briefly limned in the flare as he lit a cigarette, his features disappearing once again into shadow when he blew it out. He carefully unscrewed the lid of the whiskey jar and took a large drink, shuddering as the almost tasteless liquid burned its way past his esophagus and into his stomach.

Later, much later, when he could think about it without breaking into a cold sweat, he realized that he had heard the automobile, the first one, well before he saw its headlights. At first, he guessed it might be a couple of teenagers, looking for a place to stop and neck, and the thought irritated him, for he had gotten to the quiet, out-of-the-way warehouse first, and had neither anticipated, nor desired, company. He carefully pinched out the half-smoked cigarette, saving it for later, and moved into the deeper moon shadows on one side of the warehouse, hoping that whoever it was would pass without stopping. The automobile, a 1948 Plymouth, slowed down as it approached the warehouse and, to Roscoe's intense annoyance, turned off the road, its headlights sweeping across the facade of the small one-story building as it drove around to the rear and stopped. He listened as the driver set the emergency brake and got out, then heard one pair of leather shoe soles crunching on gravel as the person walked up the opposite side of the building. The footsteps stopped before the person got to the front of the warehouse, and silence once again settled over the otherwise deserted countryside.

Roscoe shivered, an involuntary reaction to the current of fear that coursed suddenly through his body, and he wondered what he should do. While reviewing the limited options open to him, none of which seemed particularly attractive, he heard another automobile approaching, and he unconsciously pushed his body even more tightly against the brick wall of the warehouse. Peering carefully around the corner, Roscoe saw the second car, a 1951 DeSoto, stop in front of the warehouse and turn its lights and motor off. Almost simultaneously the driver of the first car, the Plymouth, stepped from the shadows and softly hailed the driver of the DeSoto. Roscoe couldn't quite make out what they were saying, but it was clear to him that the DeSoto's driver was at first surprised to see the other man. The Plymouth's-driver walked to the DeSoto and stood at the open driver's-side window, assuming a relaxed yet clearly attentive stance. The two men spoke in a conversational tone for several seconds, both clearly visible in the bright moonlight, and at one point shared a laugh about something. The laughter was reassuring to Roscoe, who reasoned that as troubling as the scene might otherwise have been, the comradely laughter meant that there was nothing ominous in the meeting itself, nothing that might pose a threat to an innocent, if clandestine, observer. Suddenly, in the midst of their conversation, the driver of the Plymouth casually reached back with his right hand as if to take out a handkerchief or a billfold. In a movement almost too swift for Roscoe to follow, he pulled a large pistol from his waistband at the small of his back, put it to the other man's head, and pulled the trigger.

Panic-stricken, Roscoe, without conscious thought, stepped away from the shadows as if to flee, the quart jar of whiskey slipping from his hands. At the sound of the jar shattering on the pavement, the shooter whirled about. Roscoe, realizing that he was about to die, stood helplessly, the moon and stars bearing silent witness to the crime about to be compounded. He opened and closed his mouth several times like a fish plucked from the water and thrown onshore, unable to summon forth the words that would surely save him. Frozen in the moonlight, the two men stood silently, the pistol never wavering. In one of those odd twists of the mind that often occur in the face of inevitable doom, Roscoe suddenly realized how quiet the night was, how he could hear the ticking of the DeSoto's motor as it cooled, could hear for the first time in his life the beating of his own heart, and what a sweet, re-assuring sound it made from deep in his chest. Finally, much like a poker player who has just turned over an unbeatable hole card, the shooter smiled, exposing the most perfect teeth Roscoe thought he had ever seen. Barely a second later he lowered the pistol without a word and walked quickly to the Plymouth parked behind the warehouse. Roscoe stood, para-lyzed with fear, until he could no longer hear, much less see, the automobile as it sped away.

Chapter One

The cardboard fans fluttering restlessly throughout the chapel of the Calvary Baptist Church of Hopewell, Virginia, reminded A. G. Farrell of nothing if not the tattered souls of his neighbors struggling to slip their earthly bonds. The fans had been provided to the congregation by the Creech Brothers (Your Friends In Need) Funeral Home and bore, on one side, the image of a gnarled, arthritic pair of hands clasped in prayer and, on the other, a grainy, slightly out-of-focus black-and-white photograph of the Creech brothers themselves, faces set in rictuslike grins. The vigorous, nonstop fanning of the parishioners notwithstanding, the small chapel was fiery hot, and although A. G. was wearing a fine linen suit that had belonged to his father, rivulets of perspiration raced down the small of his back.

A. G. tried and failed to stifle a deep yawn as the Reverend Jimmy Morton labored mightily in the heat, bringing forth a long, disjointed, and exceedingly morose prayer seeking relief from any number of perceived earthly afflictions, including, among others, the extraordinarily hot weather and the specter of postwar racial integration. Roundly corpulent and possessed of a cheerfully optimistic nature when not in the pulpit, the Reverend Morton was prone to serious depression on most Sundays, the more so as he looked out on his copiously perspiring flock from his vantage point in front of the choir. A. G. yawned again, wanting to look at his watch but knowing that to do so would be rude.

"Sheriff."

If the whispered salutation, coming as it did as the Reverend Morton struggled unsuccessfully to tie up the many loose threads of his prayer, surprised A. G., he did not show it. Thirty-four years old and a bachelor, A. G. was a graduate of the University of Virginia, a distinction of some note in a county where fewer than 25 percent of the population could boast of so much as a high school diploma. He was tall, handsome in what his neighbors thought of as a bookish way, and had been born with only one kidney, a defect, if such it could be called, that had kept him out of the army and both the Second World War and the Korean conflict. Appointed sheriff in 1942 when the incumbent officeholder, caught up in the patriotic spirit of the times, enlisted in the Marine Corps, A. G. agreed to serve strictly as a favor to his community, fully intending to return to Charlottesville for graduate studies in philosophy as soon as the war ended. Twelve years later, his predecessor having died storming the beach at Iwo Jima, A. G., much to his own surprise, still held office.

Without taking his eyes off the pulpit, A. G. inclined his head sideways in the direction of Warren Elam, the young man crouched in the aisle next to A. G.'s family pew.

"Sheriff," Warren continued in a loud stage whisper that carried easily to all corners of the chapel, "Mr. Taylor says you got to come right away." Knowing that the entire congregation was now straining to hear his words, Warren paused for dramatic effect. "Mr. Taylor said to tell you that a dead body's done been found."

Warren, who did odd jobs and ran errands for Bud Taylor, badly wanted to relay to A. G., and of course the rest of the congregation, additional details of the exciting discovery, such as the fact that a bullet had passed through the unfortunate decedent's head, but a stern warning from his employer to reveal nothing beyond the existence of a cadaver inhibited him. But only for a second or two.

"Mr. Taylor don't know who found . . ."

A. G., recognizing that Warren would blurt out anything that came to his mind, put a finger to his lips. "Hush, now," he admonished quietly, noticing that even the Reverend Morton had fallen temporarily silent. He carefully replaced the Creech Brothers fan, together with his hymnal, in the rack on the back of the pew in front of him and rose with a barely concealed sigh of relief at the prospect of missing the remaining half of Jimmy Morton's service. Leaving with as much dignity as was possible under the circumstances, he gently shooed Warren Elam down the center aisle as one might coax a child. Outside the church, A. G. asked Warren where the body had been found.

"It's in a car parked in front of Mr. Taylor's feed warehouse," Warren gushed as he climbed hurriedly into Bud's pickup truck. "We better get on over there. Are you going to run the siren?" he asked hopefully, nodding toward the sheriff's car.

"I doubt it's necessary since, according to you, the man is already dead. By the way, who is it?"

"I don't know, but he was wearing a . . ." Warren suddenly paused, remembering Bud Taylor's unambiguous order to keep his mouth shut.

"Wearing what?" A. G. asked impatiently.

"A uniform," Warren blurted, starting the truck. "But don't tell Mr. Taylor I told you, okay?"

A. G. got into the black 1950 Ford sedan the city of Hopewell had purchased, used, two years earlier. It had a single red dome light on the roof and the word *Sheriff* painted in block letters on each side. The lettering had been done by a sign painter serving a three-year state sentence for bigamy who had been loaned to the county for a week's worth of painting. While he was working for the county, A. G. allowed him to take his meals at Francine Baker's boardinghouse. In the course of his week's stay in Hopewell he repainted both the mayor's and A. G.'s offices, lettered the sheriff's car, re-caulked all the windows on the city's small administrative building, and impregnated Francine Baker's thirty-two-year-old daughter.

"Howdy, Bud."

"A. G.," Bud Taylor acknowledged A. G.'s greeting with ill-disguised annoyance. Sixty-one years old and a childless widower, Bud was short, bald-headed, and overweight. In addition to being the owner of the feed warehouse, a large general store on the outskirts of Hopewell, and several hundred acres of prime bottomland, he was the county Democratic Party chairman and, as such, considered himself, not wholly inappropriately, a man of some consequence in that part of the state. The telephone call from Fort Lee alerting him to the presence of a body in Hopewell had awakened him at home from a restless sleep on cotton sheets wet with perspiration. He opened a packet of headache powder, his second in the past hour, and poured the contents on the back of his tongue, washing it down with a drink of lukewarm Coca-Cola. The sweet, syrupy flavor made him grimace, the overall effect of his unpleasant expression heightened by the fact that he hadn't yet shaved.

"What have we got?" A. G. asked, nodding in the direction of the 1951 two-tone DeSoto coupe parked in front of the warehouse Bud had inherited from his father-in-law in 1934. He and Bud were standing in the building, looking out one of the front windows. Warren, who had badly wanted to stay and listen, had been summarily dispatched by A. G. to find Henry Beal, a local army-trained photographer who had a contract with the county to provide whatever photography, crime-related or otherwise, might be needed from time to time.

"The provost marshall's office out at the fort called me about an hour ago," Bud said after he finished the Coke and put the sweating bottle in a wooden crate on the concrete floor. He belched indelicately, not bothering to cover his mouth with his hand. "Some lieutenant, the duty officer, said he had just gotten an anonymous telephone call saying there was a dead body in a car in front of the feed-company warehouse." Bud pointed unnecessarily out toward the DeSoto coupe. "Said he tried to reach the sheriff first," he paused to glare briefly at A. G., "and, since he couldn't, he called me."

The discovery of the body represented something more than an inconvenience, for it came at a time when the county was without the services of a coroner, the previous holder of that office having died unexpectedly, of natural causes, six weeks earlier. Bud, as the county Democratic Party chairman, had reluctantly taken on the newly vacant office until such time as the county could recruit a reasonably competent person for the job. He had obviously not anticipated, in the short time he intended to hold office, having to deal with a homicide.

"Man or woman?" A. G. asked.

"It's a man," Bud grunted, assuming A. G. was asking about the gender of the body in the car.

"No, I meant was the person who called to report the body a man or a woman?"

"How the hell would I know?" Bud took out a handkerchief and mopped his brow. The two headache powders he had taken in the past forty-five minutes clearly had not yet begun to have a positive effect on his disposition.

A. G. smiled, unoffended by Bud's tone of voice. "Let's go take a look," he said, opening the door and stepping out into the harsh sunlight. As hot as it was inside the warehouse, stepping outside was like walking into an oven.

The automobile's two front windows were open, as were the window vents. A man lay slumped against the steering wheel, arms hanging straight down over the front edge of the seat. The head was turned toward the driver's-side window, both eyes frozen open in a stare of profound shock and dismay. The body was that of a Caucasian male, mid-thirties, A. G. guessed, wearing the army uniform and insignia of a captain in the Quartermaster Corps. The man had brown eyes, a close-cropped military haircut, and a five o'clock shadow on flaccid cheeks. An entrance wound was visible on the left temple, slightly forward of, and a little above, the left ear. Because the head was turned, no exit wound was visible. Leaning down and looking through the driver's window, A. G. could see that the headliner and passenger door were splattered with a copious amount of blood and what appeared to be fragments of the decedent's brain.

"Large caliber," A. G. murmured, more to himself than to Bud. He felt surprisingly calm, almost detached, as he looked at the body. *Perhaps it was the war,* he thought. *Perhaps we all got so used to death on a large scale, even those of us who didn't go overseas, that we can now look at something like this without it making us sick.* "If so," he said quietly, "I wish we hadn't."

"What's that?" the older man asked. The hot sun, together with the aftereffects of the better part of a fifth of bourbon he had consumed the night before while playing gin rummy, made him more than a little queasy.

A. G. looked at Bud and realized he had been thinking out loud. "Sorry, Bud, I was just talking to myself." He looked back at the body. "This wound was made by a large-caliber bullet," A. G. explained, pointing at the hole in the man's temple. He held his thumb and forefinger approximately half an inch apart and sighted them over the wound. "I'd guess a .45."

A. G. walked around the front of the car to the passenger side, stopping at the front-quarter panel. The pavement in front of and below the passenger window bore evidence of blood spatter, as well as at least one piece of what he assumed was brain tissue. Before he could examine that side of the car more closely, Warren Elam returned in Bud's pickup followed closely by Henry Beal's 1950 Studebaker.

"Morning, Henry," A. G. called out, motioning for the freelance photographer to join him at the front of the DeSoto. "Sorry to drag you out on a Sunday morning." He nodded back toward the body. "I'm afraid it's not a very pretty sight."

Henry raised a hand to forestall further apology. "Believe me, I need the money. Sally is expecting again. Who was killed?"

"Don't know yet. Before we disturb the body, though, or anything else around the car, I want you to get a good set of shots from every angle, okay? Oh, and Henry," A. G. added, almost as an afterthought, "needless to say, I don't want you touching anything, and," he pointed to the bloodstains and tissue lying on the pavement outside the passenger window, "be real careful about where you step."

The photographer nodded absently, already busy with getting his camera ready. "Yeah, sure, no problem."

"Warren." A. G. walked back around to the driver's side of the car, crooking his finger at Bud's young handyman. "Come here, I want you to look at something." A. G. pointed toward the open window. "Look through there, and tell me what you see."

"See?" Warren asked, obviously confused.

"Look through both windows. This one," A. G. indicated the driver's-side window, "and the passenger window, out toward the vacant lot across the street."

Warren bent down and looked. He straightened up and turned to A. G., fearful that he was about to fail some sort of test. "Trees?" he said, his response more a question than an answer.

"Bingo." A. G. smiled. "Trees. Now, Warren, what I'm hoping is that one of those trees stopped the bullet that obviously passed through this unfortunate soul's head. What I want you to do is go over there and examine all the trees along the probable path of the bullet. Start on a direct line with the two windows and work out from there."

"You want I should dig it out for you if I find it?" Warren pulled out his Barlow pocketknife for A. G.'s inspection.

"No, don't touch anything. Just come get me if you think you've found it." A. G. turned to Bud Taylor as soon as Warren trotted away. "Come on, Bud, let's get you back in the warehouse and out of this sun while Henry takes his pictures."

"Don't you want to check the body for any identification?" Bud asked. "A wallet or something?"

Leading Bud into the relative cool of the high-ceilinged warehouse, A. G. shook his head. "I don't want to disturb anything until Henry gets done. There'll be plenty of time to look then." A. G. paused and fanned himself with his straw hat. "You don't look so good, Bud. It's going to be a while before I've got things wrapped up here. Why don't you head on home, and I'll call you later."

"I just need a little hair of the dog that bit me last night," Bud assured him. "But you're right, there's no use to both of us sweating like field hands out in that hot sun." He mopped his brow one last time before putting on his white Panama hat. "What are you going to do with the body?"

A. G. shrugged. "Not much I can do. We'll have to keep it at least until I can arrange to borrow someone from the state to come do an autopsy. Probably be a day or two before a pathologist can drive over from Richmond." He pointed to the telephone on the desk. "I'll call Bob Creech to come pick up the body and store it in his mortuary for the time being."

"Well, keep me posted," Bud grunted. He opened the door and winced at the sudden blast-furnace heat. "Give Warren a ride home when you're done with him, will you?"

"You don't mind if I store the car"—A. G. nodded toward the dead man's automobile—"here for a day or two while I get it checked for fingerprints, do you?"

Bud took a single key off his key ring and tossed it to A. G. He left without another word.

A. G. made a quick call to the Creech Brothers Funeral Home and then walked out of the warehouse and watched Henry take the last of his photographs. "I appreciate your coming out," he told him.

"Like I said, I can sure enough use the money," Henry assured him, as he stowed his gear in the trunk of the Studebaker. "I swear, it seems that all I have to do anymore is look at that old gal of mine and we've got another young 'un on the way."

A. G. chuckled. "I'm thinking you two must be doing more than just looking at each other."

Henry shook his head good-naturedly and got into his car. "I'll develop these tonight and have prints ready for you in the morning. Or I suppose I could print them up tonight, if you want them badly enough."

A. G. shook his head. "Tomorrow morning's fine, Henry. Call me before you bring them over."

"I found it, Sheriff." Warren's high-pitched, excited voice easily carried across the street and over the sound of Henry's departing Studebaker. He was standing some twenty yards into the overgrown lot, jumping up and down and waving both arms.

A. G. smiled and walked over to join the excited young man. "I believe you have," he told Warren after examining the tree trunk in question. "Good work." A glint of dull, gray metal could be seen at the base of a deep hole in the trunk at the approximate height of the DeSoto's windows. Splinters of wood stood out from the impact site, and a single golden teardrop of sap had already begun to harden an inch or two below the hole. "Tell you what you can do to help me," he said. "Dig out around the bullet so we can get to it easier." Before he could say anything else, Bob Creech drove up in an unmarked panel truck. "Don't touch the bullet or try to get it out, though," he added as he turned to walk back to the warehouse. "Come get me when you get real close to it." In front of the warehouse A. G. watched as the overweight undertaker slid out from behind the truck's wheel. "You would think," he teased, "that as much as you charge the county to pick up a body we could at least get the hearse."

Ignoring A. G.'s banter, Creech went to the rear of the truck and took out a telescoping gurney. "I've got Ida Mae Jones's funeral to set up in one hour," he said tersely, drawing on a pair of surgical rubber gloves with elongated cuffs. He took a second pair out of the truck and handed them to A. G. "You want to give me a hand?"

The two men removed the body from the DeSoto coupe, A. G. taking care not to soil his linen suit. He noted that the decedent's uniform had relatively little blood on it, a fact he attributed to the forward-leaning, seated position the body had assumed after death. They placed the body on the gurney and rolled it over to the Creech Brothers' truck.

"Wait a minute," A. G. said as Bob Creech prepared to swing the gurney into the truck's cab. "I want to check for a billfold." He patted the breast pockets of the uniform blouse and, finding nothing, rolled the body partially onto its right side. He withdrew a leather wallet from the left rear pocket. It contained twenty-three dollars in cash—a ten, a five, and eight ones—and a military identification card. "Captain Martin P. Fitzgerald," A. G. said quietly, comparing the ID photo with the decedent's face.

"That how you want me to list the body?" Creech asked, wiping perspiration from his brow with the sleeve of his shirt.

A. G. shook his head. "Put him down for now as John Doe. Assuming his wife," A. G. nodded toward the plain gold band on the man's left ring finger, "lives at Fort Lee, I expect I'll be over later with her to make a positive identification."

"Anything else?" Creech looked pointedly at his watch.

"Be careful undressing him. Bag the uniform and make a list of any jewelry," A. G. pointed at the Bulova on the decedent's right wrist, "as well as anything else you find in his pockets. If I don't come over later today, I'll call you tomorrow," A. G. said, putting the billfold and ID card into his suit pocket.

"Bud Taylor going to be doing the autopsy?" Creech asked snidely.

A. G. barely smiled. He didn't much care for Bob Creech. "I doubt it."

A. G.'s first-floor, corner office in Hopewell's modest two-story City Hall, though large, was sparingly furnished—a

desk, two filing cabinets, and three chairs. A ceiling fan circulated the air, and a row of double-hung windows opened
out onto Hopewell's two-block–long commercial district.
Waiting for a return call from the provost marshall's office at
Fort Lee, A. G. leaned back in his wooden swivel chair and
took a nearly empty pack of Chesterfields from his desk
drawer. He held one of the cigarettes under his nose, savoring
the sweet smell of the cured, bright-leaf tobacco. Lighting it,
he watched the smoke rise slowly, almost regretfully, as if
struggling against the thick, humid air. Although he had been
expecting it, the sudden ring of the telephone startled him.

"Sheriff Farrell, this is Lieutenant Barry Giles, out at Fort
Lee. I was told that you've been trying to get in touch with
me."

"Yes, sir, I have." A. G. sat up and neatly flipped the ash
off his cigarette onto the wooden floor of his office. He tapped
at it with the toe of his cordovan wing tip. "I understand
you're the weekend military-police duty officer out at the fort.
The one who received an anonymous tip about a body here
in Hopewell."

"That's correct. I had no way of knowing whether the
information was accurate, but I thought I'd better pass it
along."

"The information was indeed accurate," A. G. said. "The
body was right where your caller said it would be."

"Were you able to establish a cause of death?"

"I was," A. G. said as he tapped more ash on the floor
and then placed the cigarette on the edge of his desk. "At least
until such time as an autopsy is completed." Reaching into
his breast pocket, he withdrew the badly misshapen slug he
and Warren had dug out of the sycamore that had absorbed
the last of its malevolent energy. "It would appear to the casual observer that the decedent, a white male, was killed by
a single gunshot wound to the head. Although state law re-

quires us to do an autopsy to establish a definitive cause," A. G. added dryly, "I'm guessing in the meantime that the gunshot wound is a pretty sure bet."

"A homicide." Lieutenant Giles, impressed, whistled a single, low note.

"Perhaps," A. G. conceded. "On the other hand, it could have been a suicide. Suicide is clearly a less likely hypothesis since there was no weapon near the body, but then whoever called your office might have taken it."

"How do you mean?"

"The caller could have innocently happened along and discovered the body, seen the pistol, and, realizing that the decedent had no further use for it, walked off with it. Depending on what kind of pistol it was, a man might could sell it over in Petersburg or Richmond for a fair amount of money."

"Do you have an identity on the body?"

"Actually, that was why I called you." A. G. put the bullet on the desk and picked up the military identification card, holding it up as if the lieutenant could see it over the telephone line. "The decedent appears to be, or I guess more properly appears to have been, an officer from out at the fort. A Captain Martin P. Fitzgerald. Ring any bells?"

Giles whistled again, a habit A. G. idly thought he would break quickly if the man worked for him.

"Does it ever," the young man said, excitement evident in his voice. "Captain Fitzgerald's wife called in a missing-person report to the provost marshall's office early this morning. She said he never returned home from the officers club last night."

"We may now know why," A. G. observed, more to himself than to Lieutenant Giles. "We'll need to arrange for Mrs. Fitzgerald to identify the body today if possible. And of course I'm going to want to visit with her at some length, although that can wait for a day or two if necessary."

"I'd better call Major Williams"—Fort Lee's provost marshall—"right away. He'll know how to handle this. I mean, how to notify Mrs. Fitzgerald, what to do about identifying the body, and like that. Could you wait there, at your office, and I'll call you right back?"

A. G. glanced briefly at his watch, although his stomach had already told him it was after one o'clock. He sighed. "I'll wait."

A. G. carefully locked the captain's wallet, military identification card, and the bullet in his desk drawer and stood up, yawning and stretching as he did so. Glancing out his first-floor window, he could see that the street outside was deserted, hardly surprising on a Sunday, and he knew that the asphalt would be soft and tacky in the fierce afternoon sun. While he waited he wondered idly what sort of man Captain Fitzgerald had been. Several of the ribbons on his uniform blouse indicated service in Europe during the war, so A. G. guessed he was a career soldier. The captain had worn no college or lodge ring, a fact that elevated him a degree or two in A. G.'s estimation.

The telephone rang.

"That's him."

The newly widowed Theresa Fitzgerald looked up from the stainless-steel embalming table bearing the remains of her husband. She was tall, five eight or five nine, A. G. guessed, and slender, no more than one hundred and twenty pounds. Long, blond hair had been gathered and pinned at the back of her head, a style coolly appropriate for the exceedingly hot weather, and other than an unadorned gold bracelet on her left wrist, she wore no jewelry, not even, he was somewhat surprised to note, a simple wedding band. Inasmuch as her cornflower-blue eyes were neither red nor swollen, A. G. assumed that she had not been weeping copiously since learning of the demise of her husband a mere hour earlier.

Behind them A. G. could hear the rapid breathing of Lieutenant Giles, who had accompanied Mrs. Fitzgerald to the Creech Brothers Funeral Home. Based on what sounded like hyperventilation, A. G. guessed that this was the first dead body Giles had ever seen or, at the very least, the first with a gunshot wound to the head.

"Thank you," A. G. said, carefully refolding the cotton sheet over the face of Captain Fitzgerald. He took Mrs. Fitzgerald's arm and escorted her and the lieutenant out to the olive-drab army sedan that waited under the funeral home's porte cochere.

"Have you any idea what might have happened?" she asked in a low voice as he handed her off to the sedan's driver, an obviously dull-witted but extremely polite private first-class in starched khakis that were rapidly wilting in the unrelenting late afternoon heat.

"No, ma'am, I don't, not yet." A. G. was acutely aware of the scent of her perfume as it volatilized off the flushed, slightly damp skin of her bare neck. "But I will almost certainly find out." He paused for a second as she got into the sedan. He courteously averted his eyes but not quickly enough to avoid seeing a flash of white thigh above her nylons as her dress rode up. The driver, seeing the same thing, shook his head as if unable to believe his good fortune while he carefully, albeit with obvious reluctance, closed the passenger door behind her. A. G. knelt down by the side of the sedan. "I would like to talk to you tomorrow, if I may," he said, slightly embarrassed by what he had seen. "About your husband," he added quickly, almost as if afraid that, assuming she had caught his inadvertent glance, she would misunderstand the nature of his interest in her.

"Would ten-thirty be too early?" she asked, not quite smiling.

"No, ma'am," A. G. assured her, standing up, "ten-thirty tomorrow morning would be fine."

"The lieutenant can give you directions to our, Marty's and my, quarters on the post," she said, fanning herself with a silk Japanese fan she took from her purse.

A. G. looked across the sedan at the ashen-faced young lieutenant. "You'll see that Mrs. Fitzgerald gets home safely?" he asked, rather unnecessarily.

Giles nodded, swallowing several times as if a wave of nausea was just then washing over him.

"Are you going to be okay?" A. G. suddenly realized that the sight of the captain's body had been more of a shock for the young man than he had initially guessed. Far more of a shock, as a matter of fact, than A. G. could discern on the widow's part. He quickly shrugged off the latter thought as unkind.

Giles nodded again and regained a modicum of composure. "Yes, sir, I'm fine." He wiped at his brow with an already damp handkerchief and took a last, deep breath. "Major Williams asked if you would come to his office first thing in the morning."

"Indeed I will," A. G. responded, stealing a last, covert glance at the widow Fitzgerald through the sedan's window.

Not a breath of air moved across the broad front porch of the house A. G.'s grandfather had built in the summer of 1880. A. G. had been born there, in his mother's bedroom, and, other than the four years in Charlottesville while attending the University of Virginia, had not spent five consecutive nights outside it in his entire life. The house had settled somewhat unevenly on its brick foundation, giving it a richness of character that typically comes to both people and their buildings only with age and a hint of imperfection. The main floor consisted of a living room, dining room, music room, and study. A large kitchen and pantry had been added on in 1918, when the original kitchen, contained in a small separate building to the rear of the house, was torn down. A sweeping staircase off the entry hall led to the second floor and five bedrooms.

Sprawled across a glider sofa with frayed and worn cushions, A. G. tried hard to relax himself into a good night's sleep, an effort he knew was all but futile in the relentless July heat. Although the sun had fully set over an hour earlier, the temperature remained above ninety degrees, with no significant cooling likely between dusk and dawn. His stomach rumbled loudly as he thought of the fried chicken and mashed potatoes he hadn't eaten earlier that day, and he sat up with a sigh, reaching for his cigarettes on the table beside the sofa. His evening meal had consisted instead of a far more prosaic can of tuna, a sliced tomato, and a cold glass of buttermilk, for not only had the discovery of Captain Fitzgerald's body badly upset his normally casual Sunday routine, but Dolores Anderson—the woman everyone in the county who thought about such things assumed he would marry one day, and who otherwise would have prepared the fried chicken and mashed potatoes—was in Raleigh, North Carolina, wrapping up the estate of a maiden aunt who had passed away the previous week.

"I hope she had a better supper than I did," he said somewhat peevishly as he lit his cigarette, the sudden flare of the lighter on the dark porch revealing that he was talking to himself. He shook his head, chagrined at having voiced so petty a thought, even though no one had heard it save himself. Dolores was due back on Tuesday, and he looked forward to seeing her after a week's absence. "Maybe we *should* get married," he mused, leaning back against the sofa's cushions.

As an owl hooted softly somewhere in the darkness, the sweet smell of a flowering magnolia drifted across the porch, stimulating in A. G. a sudden recollection of the scent of Theresa Fitzgerald's perfume. He closed his eyes and saw, with eidetic clarity, the astonishingly erotic image of the pale white skin of her inner thigh above her nylons, exposed when she bent down to get into the army sedan.

Chapter Two

The provost marshall's office at Fort Lee occupied a stand-alone, single-story wood-and-concrete-block building surrounded by a white gravel walk and a small but immaculately maintained lawn. A large, gaudily painted sign bearing an arcane heraldic device identified the building as the military-police headquarters, and two brightly shellacked artillery shells stood guard on either side of the entrance.

Smiling self-consciously, A. G. bent down and briefly examined one of the two artillery shells flanking the entrance, feeling precisely like a boy mightily impressed with things that go bang. He straightened up and, with a quick glance about to see if anyone had observed his momentary curiosity, opened the door and stepped into the building. Inside, the casual visitor first noticed a gleaming black-and-white linoleum floor and then immediately encountered a noncommissioned officer seated at a standard-issue metal desk. The desk, and indeed most of the room, sat protected behind a low wooden railing that defined a small public area. The large room smelled not unappealingly of paste wax and starched khaki.

"Yes, sir?" The duty NCO eyed A. G. with an obvious suspicion, tempered by the concern that, although A. G. was dressed in a civilian suit, the possibility existed that he might be more than a mere civilian. The *sir* of his interrogatory *yes, sir?* clung precariously to a finely drawn line between overt insolence and guarded respect. After a split second's hesitation—again, just enough of a one to make a point—he stood up and assumed a position of relaxed attention, clearly prepared to be more than a little annoyed if it turned out that A. G. did not warrant such a display of military decorum.

"Those artillery shells out by the door," A. G. half turned and pointed at the door through which he had just entered, "they aren't real, are they?"

His suspicions confirmed, the NCO immediately sat back down. "No, sir, they're duds."

"Duds?"

"All the powder has been removed. Can I help you with something?"

"I don't recall seeing them the last time I was out here."

The NCO leaned back in his chair and sighed deeply, obviously disappointed in the direction the conversation was taking. "No, sir," he replied peevishly, "they're new. Major Williams, the provost marshall, had them placed there when he assumed command of the military-police garrison here at Fort Lee. Now," he sat up straight and gave A. G. his best no-nonsense stare, "can I help you with something?"

"You may." A. G. smiled and leaned forward slightly, peering at the nameplate pinned to the sergeant's khaki shirt. "Sergeant Dickey, my name is A. G. Farrell, and I'm sheriff over in Hopewell." A. G., never quite able to shed the notion that it sounded rather medieval, always felt vaguely silly when he had to announce the fact that he was a sheriff. "I'm here to see Major Williams." He paused for a second to allow the sergeant to mentally absorb and process the information. "I believe he's expecting me."

"Do you have any identification?"

Amused at the sergeant's impertinence, A. G. carefully pointed out the window toward his car. "You can't see it from this angle," he said, "but it says *Sheriff* on each door of that Ford." He smiled again. "And, of course, there's a red light on top."

The two men were now at an impasse, A. G. enjoying it, the sergeant not. Before either could say anything further, Lieutenant Giles walked in.

"Sheriff Farrell," he said, obviously pleased to see A. G. "Come on, I'll take you back to Major Williams's office."

When they had shaken hands, Giles escorted A. G. past the duty NCO and into the hallway leading back to the private offices. The sergeant salvaged as much dignity as he possibly could by refusing to acknowledge A. G.'s passage with so much as a glance.

"Does the major know you're here?" Giles asked.

"I don't believe so," A. G. answered. "The sergeant and I hadn't yet gotten to that point in our negotiations."

Giles, noting the hint of amusement in A. G.'s voice, nodded his head. "Sergeant Dickey," he said, his tone of voice conveying more than mere identification. "The MP garrison NCOIC."

"NCOIC?"

Giles laughed. "Army talk for Noncommissioned Officer in Charge. In plain English, the ranking NCO in a given outfit. Dickey transferred into the unit two months ago, shortly after Major Williams assumed command. He served with the major in his last posting, at Fort Bragg, and before that he was with the correctional staff at the prison at Fort Leavenworth, Kansas." Giles lowered his voice. "He's not . . ."

"Lieutenant Giles." A voice boomed out from a doorway at the end of the corridor, interrupting the lieutenant.

"Yes, sir," Giles answered, suddenly nervous. "Major Williams," he said, sotto voce, to A. G.

The major appeared in the doorway. Although short, perhaps five feet six inches tall, and trim, no more than one hundred and twenty pounds, the major projected an air of extreme aggressiveness. His khakis were starched and pressed almost literally to a knife's edge, and a plumb bob could have been hung along the line that projected down from his chin, along his shirt's placket, past his polished brass belt buckle, extending along the edge of his trousers' fly, and terminating at the base of his crotch. His army brogans gleamed like mirrors even in the low light of the hallway. "What, exactly," he asked Giles, "were you telling Sheriff Farrell?" The major shifted his unfriendly gaze to A. G. "I presume you are Sheriff Farrell?"

"Indeed I am," A. G. said affably, attempting to deflect the major's attention from the stricken Lieutenant Giles. He held out his right hand. "We've not . . ."

"Just a minute," Williams said brusquely, turning back to Giles. "I asked you a question, Lieutenant."

"Well, sir, I was just explaining to the sheriff how Sergeant Dickey served with you at Fort Bragg."

"You are never to discuss personnel matters with anyone outside this office without my prior knowledge and consent. Do I make myself clear?" A vein bulged in Williams's neck, palpable evidence of his sudden and very real anger.

Giles swallowed hard. "Yes, sir."

"Good." He turned back to A. G. "Come into my office."

Entering the provost marshall's office was much like entering a cave, A. G. thought. Heavy drapes were pulled across the windows, plunging the large room into semidarkness. A Quartermaster-issue leather sofa and club chairs were grouped against one wall, and two metal file cabinets, both locked and secured with ostentatious steel bars, stood along another. The room was dominated by a massive wooden desk, fully eight feet long and four feet wide. A. G. guessed the wood to be black walnut and estimated that the graceless object must weigh five hundred pounds if it weighed an ounce. Carved in deep bas-relief across the front was a particularly atrocious Schwarzwald hunting scene, a terror-stricken stag brought to bay by a pack of fierce hunting dogs. A large nameplate, carved from the same wood, possibly the same tree, identified the owner as Williams, Oliver P. To either side of the name were mounted the crossed-musket emblems of the U.S. Army's military police corps.

"I acquired the desk in Germany five years ago," Williams explained, mistaking A. G.'s interest for admiration, "for little more than a pair of silk stockings and a carton of American cigarettes." He ran a proprietary hand caressingly over the top of the desk. "As soon as I saw it I knew I had to have it."

"Imagine that," A. G. murmured, idly wondering which high-ranking member of the Third Reich had owned the ap-palling piece of furniture before Williams acquired it. He sat down in one of the two plain wooden chairs fronting the desk, and Lieutenant Giles sat in the other. "One can almost hear the Valkyries keening as they bear a slain hero off to Val-halla," he said, taking care to keep his voice free of irony or sarcasm.

"What?"

"Wagner," A. G. explained, pointing at the desk. "The *Ring* cycle."

"Oh, yes," Williams replied, obviously without knowledge of either Wagnerian opera or Germanic mythology. He turned and glared briefly at Giles as if he blamed the young lieutenant for A. G.'s unexpected erudition. "Now," he said abruptly, the niceties dispensed with, "what can you tell me about the murder of Captain Fitzgerald?"

"Almost nothing," A. G. replied candidly. "In fact, as I sit here this morning I would not wish to go so far as to make a definitive statement that the captain's death was the result of murder." He smiled. "I *assume* it was, but . . ."

"What?" the major interrupted, incredulity amply conveyed in the harsh tone of his voice.

"As I explained to the lieutenant yesterday," A. G. nodded toward Giles, "the possibility of suicide, although admittedly small, can't be entirely ruled out at this point."

"I can assure you," Williams said, not quite sneering at what he perceived to be A. G.'s astonishing insolence, "that Captain Fitzgerald did not kill himself. He was an exemplary officer, a credit to both this command and the United States Army. And, I might add, happily married. No," Williams could barely conceal his annoyance at the suggestion of suicide, "I think the less time wasted considering any such notion the better."

"Let's chat about Captain Fitzgerald for a moment," A. G. suggested, ignoring both Williams's words and his intentionally offensive tone of voice. "What were his duties here at the base?"

"Captain Fitzgerald was attached to the Quartermaster School. I have assigned to Lieutenant Giles," Williams paused and looked skeptically at Giles as if reconsidering the wisdom of his choice, "the initial responsibility of compiling a list of the officers and noncommissioned officers who worked closely with the captain. We will interview them to determine whether any have information that may be pertinent to your investigation."

"Actually," A. G. said carefully, "I would prefer that, for

the time being, the lieutenant do nothing more than compile the list. I'd like to go over it with you, or him, and determine the order in which I interview everyone." Although A. G. had not emphasized *I*, he knew that Williams had understood what he was saying.

Major Williams started to say something and abruptly changed his mind. He nodded his head. "I will for the time being limit Lieutenant Giles's efforts to compiling a list of personnel to be interviewed. Where is Captain Fitzgerald's automobile?"

"I have it stored in Hopewell. The State Bureau of Investigation is lending me a fingerprint technician this afternoon to go over it for latent prints."

"Was there any physical evidence in the car or at the scene?"

A. G. shook his head. "Not much. No weapon, no . . ." he smiled sweetly at Williams, "suicide note, nothing beyond the captain's body itself to tell us what might have happened. There was sufficient blood and tissue on the pavement to support the hypothesis that the captain was shot where his body was discovered. Of course, my examination of the automobile was rather superficial—I did not want to risk disturbing any latent fingerprints. I will go over it a great deal more thoroughly later today after it has been dusted. As to any other gross physical evidence, however, there appears to be none." A. G. suddenly remembered the bullet. "No, wait, that's not exactly true. I did recover what appears to be the bullet that passed through the captain's head."

Williams sat up straighter in his wooden swivel chair. "Good. That should enable us to determine the weapon used."

"Yes and no. I believe it was a .45 caliber, but in the course of passing through the captain's head and impacting on the tree in which we found it, it has undergone severe deformation. I doubt seriously that the crime laboratory in

Richmond will be able to ascertain anything beyond the caliber."

"Was there a shell casing at the scene?"

A. G. shook his head. "No, which would support the reasonable inference that, regardless of whether the captain's death was the result of murder or suicide, the weapon used was a revolver." He smiled again. "Or, assuming, as I think we all do, that the captain was murdered and the weapon used was an automatic, we may infer that the killer was an unusually careful man, one who thought to retrieve the shell casing after it had been ejected."

"When may Lieutenant Giles examine Captain Fitzgerald's automobile?"

A. G., looking somewhat surprised, shrugged. "I hadn't considered that he would want to, but I certainly have no objection. In fact," A. G. turned to Giles, "if you would like to assist me in my examination after the car has been checked for fingerprints, you're more than welcome."

"I assume an autopsy will be performed."

A. G. nodded. "It has been scheduled for Wednesday morning."

"Not sooner?" Williams asked, annoyance creeping back into his voice.

"Unfortunately, we currently have no qualified coroner, so I have to borrow a pathologist from the state. They don't mind helping out." A. G. smiled, recalling his conversation earlier that morning with a rather harried administrator in the state crime lab in Richmond. "Well, actually," he quickly amended, "they *do* mind, but they can't . . ."

Major Williams impatiently cleared his throat, signaling his lack of interest in A. G.'s explanation.

"Yes, as I was saying," A. G. continued, "the earliest they can spare a pathologist for the autopsy is Wednesday morning."

"Lieutenant Giles tells me that you're meeting with Mrs. Fitzgerald this morning."

"I am." A. G. looked at his watch. "In about twenty minutes, as a matter of fact."

"Lieutenant Giles will sit in with you when you interview her." Williams's tone of voice left no doubt that it wasn't a request.

A. G. shook his head slowly. "To be honest, I'd rather he didn't."

"Why not?"

"Well, for one thing, Captain Fitzgerald was an officer at this base. If, for example, they were having marital difficulties, Mrs. Fitzgerald might be uncomfortable discussing it with another officer present."

Major Williams leaned forward aggressively. "Perhaps I didn't make myself entirely clear, Sheriff. I want to be, I want this office to be, intimately involved in the investigation of Captain Fitzgerald's murder."

"I understand, but the captain was murdered in Hopewell. . . ."

"You don't know that," Williams interrupted. "The body could have been moved there after the crime was committed."

"As I mentioned a minute or two ago, the physical evidence, primarily blood and tissue on the pavement outside the vehicle, clearly supports an inference that death occurred at the site where the body was discovered." A. G. paused briefly. "Major, I would very much appreciate any help your office can give me in this investigation. In fact, I don't think it would be an overstatement to say that your help will be crucial to solving the mystery of Captain Fitzgerald's death. However, as I'm sure you can understand, only one of us can be in charge, and I'm afraid that's going to have to be me."

Williams sat back in his chair, anger evident in the set of his jaw. After several seconds he reached out and flipped a switch on an intercom box. "Sergeant Dickey," he commanded in a brusque tone of voice, "get in here."

The sergeant was in the office so quickly that A. G. wondered if he had been listening outside the door. Ignoring A. G. and Lieutenant Giles, Dickey snapped to attention at the side of Williams's desk. "Yes, sir," he barked.

"Issue the sheriff a temporary automobile sticker." Dismissing the sergeant with a peremptory wave of his hand, Williams looked back at A. G. "The sticker will allow you access to the post twenty-four hours a day, without prior approval from this office." He pointed, somewhat rudely, A. G. thought, at the lieutenant. "Lieutenant Giles will be your liaison with this office. I expect you to coordinate all of your on-post activities with him. I further expect that you will advise me on a daily basis, through the lieutenant, of any and all progress you make in your investigation, particularly," Williams paused briefly to reemphasize the word *particularly,* "particularly any evidence or suspicion that points to any member of this command."

"Thank you," A. G. said, rising from his chair. He turned and smiled at Giles. "I think the lieutenant and I will make a good team." He leaned across the desk and extended his right hand to the major.

Williams said nothing, although his expression as he looked from A. G. to Giles indicated no such confidence. Without a great deal of noticeable enthusiasm, he shook A. G.'s proffered hand.

"Oh, by the way," A. G. asked, almost as if the thought had just occurred to him, "do you have any reason to believe that someone here at Fort Lee, how did you put it, a member of this command, might have had something to do with the captain's death?"

"No." Williams stared stonily at A. G. for several seconds. "Good day, Sheriff," he added by way of dismissal. "Lieutenant Giles will give you directions to Captain Fitzgerald's quarters."

Williams sat quietly at his desk until he was sure A. G. had left the outer office. Picking up the telephone, he dialed a four-digit number. "This is Major Williams," he said as soon as the phone was answered. "Yes, sir. He left a few minutes ago. . . . Yes, sir. He's on his way over to interview Mrs. Fitzgerald." Williams paused to listen. "No, sir, I'm afraid he may be something of a problem. I did not get the impression that he . . ." Interrupted by the voice on the other end, Williams listened for several seconds, nodding his head. "Yes, sir, I agree, but I think before we do anything we need a much better idea of just who it is we're dealing with. . . . Yes, sir, I have someone in mind. Yes, sir." Williams hung up the telephone and flipped the switch on his intercom. "Sergeant Dickey, get back in here."

On-post housing for married company-grade officers such as Captain Fitzgerald consisted of pre–World War II wooden barracks that had been remodeled and subdivided into two-bedroom triplexes. The clapboard siding was painted a cream color with olive-drab trim around the windows and doors, and much of the area around and between the converted barracks was paved over with gray concrete. The entire complex, consisting of thirty barracks converted into ninety units, was named, with no irony intended, Martinelli Gardens, after an obscure quartermaster colonel killed in an automobile accident in London during the Second World War. As A. G. walked up to the corner unit of Building 14, he saw two women watching him closely over the laundry they were hanging out to dry. When he smiled and tipped his white straw hat, they both immediately looked away without acknowledging his friendly greeting. A wooden plaque next to the door of the corner unit identified it as Quarters No. 14-A, and beneath that, in block letters, Fitzgerald, Martin P., Captain, Quartermaster Corps. A. G. stood for a second in front of the screen door of the late Captain Fitzgerald's apartment. From the relative darkness inside he could hear Peggy Lee singing about a small hotel, accompanied by a surprisingly good, at least to A. G.'s ear, live soprano.

"Hello?" A. G. tapped on the door frame and put his nose to the screen door, trying rather unsuccessfully to pierce the darkness within. "Mrs. Fitzgerald?"

A woman's body materialized in the doorway, inches from A. G.'s face. Startled, he pulled back.

"I'm sorry," he said, quickly removing his hat with his left hand. "I wasn't sure . . ."

"Come in, Sheriff," Theresa Fitzgerald interrupted, pushing the screen door open. "Hurry up, or you'll let all the cold air out." Seeing his puzzled face, she smiled, and A. G. noticed for the first time that she had the merest hint of an overbite, a feature he found immediately attractive. "Marty and I used to say that to each other. To joke," she added, seeing that A. G. still didn't get it, "about the fact that these dumps," she waved an arm to include all of Martinelli Gardens, "aren't air-conditioned."

A. G. smiled. "I like it," he said, pulling the screen door behind him. "The joke, I mean," he added quickly. To his immediate left a doorway opened into a ridiculously small, galley-style kitchen, and he realized that she must have just stepped from there when he knocked.

She saw him eyeing the kitchen and laughed. "A simpleton designed these units," she said, leading A. G. down a narrow hallway to the living room. "Or someone from the post engineer's office, which is to say the same thing. Guess where they put the single bathroom?"

"I haven't the faintest," A. G. responded tentatively, thinking that perhaps she was pulling his leg. It was obvious as he followed her that Mrs. Fitzgerald was wearing no foundation garments, and he was relieved that the ambient light level was low. The blond hair that had been gathered up and pinned at the back of her head the day before was now tied back in a ponytail that bounced as she preceded him down the hallway.

"Right off the dining room. And, as you might imagine," she stopped and thumped on one of the walls with a knuckle, "these walls are little more than paper thin." She shook her head and continued back to the living room. "Believe me, it makes for interesting dinner parties, particularly after everyone's had a few drinks." In the living room she indicated a cloth-covered sofa with a sweep of her hand. "Make yourself comfortable, Sheriff—you paid for it."

"I beg your pardon?"

She laughed again. "Almost everything you see is standard-issue Quartermaster furniture—sofa, chairs, tables, beds—you name it, the taxpayers own it."

A. G. smiled. Her laughter was infectious—appealing, genuine, and somehow, at the same time, extremely feminine. "I had no idea the army was so generous with the taxpayers' money," he teased.

"Well, to be honest, the pay's not grand, but the benefits, as you can clearly see for yourself," she smiled sardonically, "are nonpareil." She nodded in the direction of the tiny kitchen. "I just put some coffee on. Would you like a cup?"

"That would be nice, thank you," A. G. replied, thinking he had never before heard anyone use the expression *nonpareil* in everyday conversation. As to her offer of coffee, in fact he seldom drank it but felt that to refuse would be impolite. Left temporarily alone while she went back to the kitchen, he stood up and looked around. Heavy curtains, intended to keep the sun out of the interior of the apartment, were drawn across the windows, throwing the room into deep shadows and creating a false, though by no means unpleasant, atmosphere of late evening. Even as his eye was attracted by what appeared to be two framed prints hanging side by side on the opposite wall, he noticed that beyond the pleasant smell of brewing coffee and a subtle hint of the same perfume he had smelled when he first met her the day before, there were no cooking odors, or any of the other everyday smells that identify a house or apartment as occupied. He walked over to look at the two prints.

"How do you take your coffee, Sheriff?"

"Cream and sugar?" A. G. called over his shoulder as he bent from the waist to more closely examine the two prints.

"That's a very southern way of answering," Theresa said from the kitchen.

"How do you mean?"

"Inflecting your voice, raising the pitch ever so slightly at the end of your sentence, making your answer sound like a question."

"Actually, in this case it *was* sort a question—to myself," A. G. responded. "To be honest, I seldom drink coffee and I had to think for a second how I take it when I do. Oh, and please," he added, "call me A. G."

"And you may call me Theresa."

A. G. straightened up and turned around. Theresa stood behind him, holding a silver serving tray with two china cups and saucers and a silver coffeepot.

"I know you said cream and sugar," she said, "but you really should try this particular coffee black. It's a special blend, roasted in very small quantities by an importer in Washington. He's an absolute wizard at roasting the beans and supplies most of the embassies in Georgetown as well as the White House, I'm told." She placed the tray on the coffee table behind them and sat down, indicating with her hand that

A. G. should join her on the sofa. "Do you like the prints?" she asked.

A. G. nodded. "The Dürer particularly," he said, watching as she poured the coffee.

"You have a good eye," she said. "Do you know the other one?"

"No, not exactly." A. G. took a sip of coffee. It was hot and, to his taste, very bitter. "I'd venture to say that it's from the Dutch school, and I'd wager that it's not by Vermeer, but beyond that I'd hesitate to say more."

"You have a very good eye," Theresa amended. "The etching on the left is indeed an Albrecht Dürer, and the other is a Rembrandt." She smiled. "Reproductions, of course."

"Of course."

Theresa took a sip of her coffee and eyed A. G. contemplatively. "I must say that it comes as something of a surprise to meet a rural southern sheriff with an appreciation for seventeenth-century art."

"The same could be said for a career army officer and his wife," A. G. pointed out. "My appreciation, such as it is, is the result of an all too brief exposure during an art history course as an undergraduate at Charlottesville."

"You mentioned Vermeer. Have you seen much of his work?"

"Only reproductions, I'm sorry to say. Rural southern sheriffs don't generally get paid enough to finance art tours of Europe." He smiled. "Or even New York, for that matter."

"More's the pity. Whatever the cost, you should make the effort. Vermeer's paintings, in fact the paintings of all the Dutch masters, are extraordinary beyond description in their rendering of light. So striking is the effect that they appear to be lit from behind, to glow with an almost radioactive energy." She nodded toward his coffee cup. "How do you like the coffee?"

"If it's good enough for President Eisenhower," A. G. smiled, not quite answering the question, "I'd have to say that it's good enough for me." He took a sip and placed the cup carefully back on the table. "Tell me, was your husband an aficionado of fine art?" The word *aficionado* pleased him, for while it didn't quite trump *nonpareil,* it came reasonably close.

"No," Theresa answered, rather abruptly, A. G. thought. "Marty's taste in art was . . ." she paused, searching for the correct adjective, "was rudimentary at best. He, like most of his fellow army officers, was a connoisseur of little more than the newspaper funny pages." She took another sip of her coffee. "Not a very wifely thing to say, was it?"

"How long have you been married?" A. G. asked, ignoring what he assumed was a rhetorical question.

"You mean 'How long *were* you married?' don't you?"

A. G. inclined his head but did not repeat the question.

Theresa shrugged. "Five years. We met in 1949, in Washington. I was working at a gallery in Georgetown, and Marty was a first lieutenant stationed at Fort Myer, across the Potomac." She reached for a small silver box on the coffee table and took out a cigarette. She offered the box and a matching silver lighter to A. G. "Would you like one?"

"Thank you." He lit her cigarette first and then his. "You worked in an art gallery?"

She nodded, delicately picking a fleck of tobacco off her tongue. "Marty and I met at a cocktail party at Fort Myer. I had been invited to the party because I sold an absolutely wretched painting to the wife of his commanding officer, a woman stupid, as I recall her, almost beyond belief."

"Where was he from? Originally."

"Niles, Ohio." Her voice carried a subtle undertone of disbelief, as if after five years she still couldn't imagine anyone actually being from such a place.

"And you?"

"California, and later, New York." She sighed. "Marty was a good man, Sheriff. . . ." She paused and smiled. "I mean, A. G. By the way, what does A. G. stand for?"

"Augustus George," A. G. replied easily, as if to imply that *Augustus* was no more uncommon a name in the state of Virginia than *John* or *Michael*. "You were saying that your husband was a good man?"

"Marty was a good man," Theresa continued, "but to be honest with you, I still can't believe I married him. He was strong and handsome and," she shrugged again, "simple. Not stupid," she hastened to reassure A. G., "but, God knows, not too bright either. No, when I say simple I guess I mean uncomplicated. Most things to Marty were either black or white. He saw no shades of gray, no subtlety or nuance. And although he didn't exactly sweep me off my feet, that simplicity, after several years of selling art to the diplomatic community in Georgetown, seemed like a desirable quality." She toyed with her cigarette and smiled ruefully. "I must say that it became decidedly less so rather quickly."

"Had he attended college? West Point?"

"No. He graduated from high school in 1943 and immediately joined the army. He managed to obtain a battlefield commission and, after the war, a transfer from the infantry to the Quartermaster Corps." She paused while stubbing out her cigarette. "You now know as much about Marty's early military career as I do. Anyway, four years after the war ended we met in Washington and shortly thereafter got married."

"I wouldn't have thought it would have been easy to pull off such a transfer," A. G. mused. "Particularly with all the combat experience he must have had during the war."

"As I said," Theresa reminded him pointedly, "I know next to nothing about Marty's military affairs. Presumably his commanding officer at the Quartermaster School can fill you in on any details that may be of interest to you or pertinent to your investigation. Frankly, I found the army so boring that we had an agreement: He never discussed his career with me, and I never discussed mine with him."

"Your career?"

"I don't want to seem rude, A. G., but don't you want to ask me if I know anything that might assist you in identifying and apprehending Marty's killer?"

A. G. smiled. "I'm sorry, I didn't mean to sound as if I was prying. It's just that . . ."

"I understand," Theresa interrupted. "I hardly fit anyone's description of either an army wife or a grieving widow, and you're naturally curious, as is, I'm sure," her voice took on a sarcastic edge, "all of Fort Lee." She sat forward on the edge of the sofa and held A. G.'s eyes with her own. "The fact is that Marty and I were fond of each other. Fond," she shook her head emphatically, "but not in love. We had discussed the possibility, actually the probability, of divorce, but I never pushed it because I didn't want to do anything that might have interfered with his promotion to major. However, as soon as that milestone was accomplished, Marty knew that I intended to return to Washington. Without him." She paused for a second. "Don't get me wrong—I will grieve for Marty, but as I see fit, and most definitely in private."

A. G. nodded. "Do you know of anyone who might have wanted to kill him?"

"No." She again shook her head emphatically. "Marty was, as far as I could tell, a very popular and respected officer." She smiled. "His very simplicity made him so. Everyone, both his superiors and his subordinates, knew exactly what to expect from him at all times." Her smile faded. "And believe me, in the intellectually barren world of the military, predictability, particularly in a company-grade officer such as Marty, is by far a more generally esteemed trait than either creativity or originality."

"Lieutenant Giles told me that you had called the military police to report that your husband had not returned from the officers club here at Fort Lee Saturday night, the night before we found the, um . . ." A. G. stumbled for a second. "Before we found . . ."

"Marty's body," Theresa interrupted. "And, yes, I did call the MPs about his failure to return home Saturday night."

"Did he frequent the club regularly?"

Theresa laughed. "You obviously don't know a great deal about the military. Saturday night at the officers club is de rigueur for career advancement."

Somehow, A. G. thought, her use of such expressions as *nonpareil* and *de rigueur* didn't seem as pretentious as he might otherwise have expected. "You weren't with him?"

"I was indisposed."

She took another cigarette from the box on the coffee table and leaned toward him for a light. As he touched the lighter's flame to the tip of the cigarette, his eyes strayed down to the white silk blouse she was wearing, and the distinct impressions her nipples made in the opaque fabric. He looked quickly back at her face to see her eyes locked on his own. He did not need to feel the sudden warmth in his cheeks to know he was blushing. "Pardon me," he murmured, angry with himself. He assumed she had dressed provocatively on purpose, and he was tempted to ask her why but decided against it. "Were your husband's financial affairs in order?" he asked, putting the lighter back on the table.

"So far as I know." She smiled at A. G.'s sudden expression of skepticism at her answer. "You aren't married, are you?" she observed, her tone of voice making her words more a statement of fact than a question.

"No."

"I thought not. In our marriage, mine and Marty's, as in most that I'm aware of, Marty's control of our joint assets was very much a part of his blue-collar sense of masculinity and propriety. Consequently, we never talked about money." She waved an arm to encompass the room and its furnishings. "And, in any event, as you can see here, it takes relatively little financial acumen to sustain an army lifestyle."

"I understand," A. G. said quietly. He finished the last of the coffee in his cup, now tepid and seemingly even more bitter, and stood up. "Thank you for taking the time to talk to me this morning."

If Theresa was surprised at the abrupt end to A. G.'s visit, she did not show it. She quickly stubbed out her cigarette and rose from the sofa. "It was either you or the post chaplain," she said with a smile, "a lieutenant colonel of dubious piety and a love of distilled spirits, so I'm told. He called yesterday evening to offer me the benefit of a pastoral visit this morning. I think he was rather relieved when I told him that your investigation would have to take precedence over the Lord's work."

A. G. returned her smile. " 'Render unto Caesar . . .' "

" ' . . . that which is Caesar's, and unto the Lord . . .' " Theresa interjected.

" ' . . . that which is the Lord's,' " A. G. finished. He handed her a piece of paper. "I've written out my telephone number, both office and home, in the event you think of anything that may be of use to me."

She took the paper from his hand, her fingers brushing his casually. They seemed to linger, but for so short a time A. G. couldn't be certain that it was intentional.

"Thank you," she said, walking him the short distance to

the door. "Will you keep me apprised of the progress of your investigation?"

A. G. nodded. "I will," he assured her, his hand still tingling from the lightness and warmth of her touch. "Indeed I will."

Chapter Three

"Morning, Sheriff." Mildred Tatum, county clerk, county tag agent, and, when she had the time and was so inclined, secretary to A. G., sat at her desk pounding vigorously on one of Hopewell's three Underwood manual typewriters. A small, feisty woman, scarcely five one in height and not an ounce over ninety pounds, she had red hair shot with gray and a swath of faded freckles across the bridge of her nose. Her fingers were smudged with carbon paper ink and an unlit Pall Mall hung from the corner of her mouth. "I understand young Warren Elam made quite an impression at Calvary Baptist yesterday." She had worked for the city for some thirty-five years and little that transpired within its borders escaped her notice.

"Good morning, Mildred," A. G. replied, stopping to light her cigarette. He wasn't surprised that Mildred had heard about Warren interrupting the service yesterday. In fact, he doubted that a soul could easily be found anywhere in Hopewell and the surrounding vicinity who didn't know almost as much about the discovery of Captain Fitzgerald's body as he did. Or at least thought they did. "I expect anyone who hasn't heard about it from a member of the congregation has gotten it from Warren himself by now."

"I wouldn't doubt it," Mildred snorted, squinting her pale green eyes against the rising smoke from her cigarette. She looked up from the Underwood and took the Pall Mall out of her mouth. "You been out to the fort this morning?"

A. G. nodded as he picked up the mail from the corner of her desk and thumbed through it. "Met the new provost marshall and then visited with the captain's widow." He tossed the mail back onto her desk. "Nothing here I need to see. You can file what needs filing and toss the rest." He ran a hand through his sandy-blond hair. "Lord, it must be close to ninety degrees in here already," he said, more to himself than to Mildred. He glanced toward the ceiling as if to assure himself that the ceiling fan was indeed turned on.

"And fixin' to get hotter," Mildred added cryptically. She knocked the ash off her cigarette. "Julie Brown, Leona and Sam Brown's daughter, died last night."

"What?" A. G.'s shock was reflected in his disbelieving tone of voice. "Was it an accident?"

"I didn't get many details, but what I heard was, it was some sort of an infection."

"Good Lord—she was just a kid, wasn't she?"

Mildred shrugged. "Fifteen, maybe sixteen. If I recall, she was born in 1939, about the time Sam went into the army."

"I didn't even know she'd been sick lately."

"Nobody did." Mildred shook her head in obvious disapproval. "You know how Sam is, living out there in the woods like some sort of hermit—he must have waited too long to get old Doc Maple out there to take a look at her." She snorted derisively. "Not that Doc Maple could have done her much good anyway."

Not many people in the county got along with or much liked Sam Brown. The illegitimate son of alcoholic parents, both of whom were dead before he turned twelve, Sam had been in and out of increasingly serious trouble as a teenager until, at the age of nineteen in 1941, when a municipal judge in Richmond, about to sentence him to five years in the state penitentiary for the transportation of illegal whiskey, offered him the choice of enlisting in the armed forces. Sam and Leona, his common-law wife, had three children by then, and Leona and the babies barely survived for almost four years on Sam's minuscule military-pay allotment and charity, mostly in the form of groceries, from her neighbors. Sam returned to the county in 1945, minus one leg lost in the Pacific campaign, and took up precisely where he had left off, in both the manufacture and sale of illegal whiskey and the making of babies. The latter activity ceased only when a sympathetic obstetrician in Petersburg, unbeknownst to Sam, tied Leona's tubes in 1952, after the particularly difficult birth of their seventh child.

"I'll pick up a smoked ham or something and drop it off later today or tomorrow," A. G. said, more to himself than to Mildred. "Sam's been nothing but a pain in the neck to a lot of people over the years, but nobody likes to see a child die."

"The funeral's set for tomorrow at noon," Mildred said. "Out at the Rose of Sharon Freewill Baptist Church."

A. G. nodded. "I suppose I should go," he said quietly. "I can drop the ham off then."

"Dolores still due back from Raleigh today?" Mildred asked, changing the subject.

"At five-thirty," A. G. confirmed. "I've got to pick her up at the train station in Richmond." He turned to walk back to his office.

"By the way, you got a call from Bud Taylor this morning."

"Did he say what he wanted?"

"Not exactly." Mildred looked up from the typewriter again and didn't quite smile. "I'm guessing he wants to know when you plan to get the dead man's car out of his warehouse."

In his office A. G. opened the window and was rewarded with little more than a wan puff of warm air. He switched on the ceiling fan to high and sat down at his desk. Picking up the telephone, he dialed a number and then swiveled around and put his feet up on the window ledge. "Lieutenant Giles, please. This is A. G. Farrell calling."

While waiting for the lieutenant, A. G. watched Dorcas Craige go into Troutman's Drugstore across the street. Dorcas had lost both of her sons in the war and her husband a year after when he rolled a tractor over onto himself while mowing a field for Bud Taylor. She had since become addicted to paregoric and codeine, both of which she obtained from Doug Troutman, Hopewell's sole pharmacist. The not terribly bright son of an influential surgeon in Richmond, Doug had graduated from pharmacy school and gotten licensed by the state pharmacy board only by virtue of his father's position as head of the state medical society and major contributor to the Democratic Party. His father had purchased the drugstore some five years earlier, and Doug and his wife had rather reluctantly moved to Hopewell from Richmond.

"Yes, Lieutenant." A. G. sat up straight when young Giles finally came on the line. "Listen, I called for two reasons. First, I need to start getting a better idea of just what Captain

Fitzgerald was doing Saturday night. That's right, leading up to the time of his presumed murder. Mrs. Fitzgerald believes that he spent the evening at the officers club." A. G. paused as Giles asked a question. "I wondered the same thing. She said she was indisposed, whatever that means. In any event, we need to determine when, what time, he arrived at the club, and then identify everyone who saw him there, had a drink with him, spoke to him, that sort of thing. I would particularly like to know what time he left and, of course, whether or not anyone left with him. Can you start on that for me?" He paused and automatically nodded his head as Giles answered affirmatively. "Good. The other reason I called was to give you directions out to Bud Taylor's warehouse. The fingerprint technician from Richmond is meeting us there at one o'clock, assuming you're still planning to join us." A. G. gave the necessary directions and hung up in time to watch Dorcas Craige leave the drugstore.

"Clean as a whistle." The fingerprint technician, a tall, thin redheaded man with a coastal Virginia accent and a prominent Adam's apple, didn't appear to be much of a talker. "Only a couple of prints on the door here"—he pointed at the driver's-side door, near the handle—"and I expect they'll probably match your decedent."

"I don't doubt it," A. G. agreed affably, "but I appreciate your taking the time to drive over and help us out."

"Didn't have no choice," the man pointed out rather gracelessly as he carefully packed his powder, brushes, and tape in a small leather satchel. " 'Course, that don't mean I minded none," he added quickly, not so much for A. G.'s sake as for Lieutenant Giles, whose uniformed presence troubled him in a way he could not have defined, much as a free-ranging cow might be troubled by the sight of a man on horseback. "Always happy to help out the army any way I can," he said, smiling obsequiously at Giles.

"Sort of a weasel, wasn't he?" Giles mentioned after the technician left. " 'Always happy to help out the army . . . ' " he mimicked, catching the man's high, scratchy voice perfectly.

A. G. smiled and opened the driver's-side door of the DeSoto. "Let's pull these seats out," he said, motioning for Giles to walk around to the passenger side. "I looked it over yesterday pretty carefully without touching anything, but we'd better see if something interesting might not have slipped down under the seats."

The front seat yielded only a few coins, but their discovery caused A. G. to smile, for they reminded him that when he was a boy his mother had always let him keep the change she occasionally found behind the sofa cushions. Found money, she had called it, and he could still hear the wonderful sound the coins made as he slowly dropped them, one after another, into his piggy bank. The rear seat, however, concealed a much more provocative item.

Giles whistled as he held up an unused condom for A. G.'s inspection.

"Interesting," A. G. murmured. "From the looks of the foil wrapper I'd say that it hasn't been there for very long." The condom bothered him, and, more troubling, somehow called to mind the disturbingly erotic image of Theresa Fitzgerald sitting next to him on the sofa that morning. He shook his head, trying, somewhat unsuccessfully, to turn his mind back to the business at hand. "Let's finish this up," he said to Giles, "and I'll buy you a cup of coffee."

Half an hour later the two men were sitting in A. G.'s office, paper cups of coffee on the desk between them.

"Funny thing," A. G. said contemplatively, more to himself than to Giles, as he took a careful sip, "I almost never drink coffee, and this is my second cup today." He took another sip, struck by how weak it tasted compared with what he had had that morning. "How soon do you think we'll be able to interview anyone who might have seen or talked to Captain Fitzgerald at the officers club Saturday night?"

"Very soon," Giles answered. "Colonel Peterson, the post commander, is having an officers call this afternoon at 1730 hours."

"An officers call?"

Giles nodded. "A meeting of all the officers on the post. Colonel Peterson calls them periodically, mostly to chew everyone out about one thing or another. The last one was called because the colonel had observed a number of enlisted men going about their duties on the post with their collars unbuttoned." He shook his head, remembering the colonel's very real anger at that meeting over what he, Giles, considered to be, at worst, an exceedingly minor infraction of the military dress code. "Anyway, he and Major Williams decided that an officers call would be a good way to deal with Captain Fitzgerald's murder. Major Williams is going to ask everyone who was at the club Saturday night to call and schedule an interview with me as soon as possible. I would think that within a day or two I should have a pretty clear picture of who the captain was with and what they might have said that night. And," Giles added quickly, "when, exactly, he left."

"Good." A. G. sat back in his chair and steepled his hands in front of his face. "I want to start getting as many snapshots of Captain Fitzgerald as I can."

"Snapshots?"

A. G. smiled. "In a manner of speaking. I've come to believe that investigating a crime, almost any crime you can think of, involves little more than taking a series of mental snapshots and then comparing the resulting images. Typically, the various images that we 'develop' will provide us with a certain degree of dissonance."

Giles shook his head, confused. "I'm not sure what you mean by *dissonance*," he admitted.

"A good word, isn't it? In music it stands for a mingling of discordant sounds. Outside of music, though, I like to think of it as a term of inconsistency, a matter not fully resolved. In Captain Fitzgerald's case, we have an 'official' snapshot of the man—your boss Major Williams gave it to me this morning in his office. Fitzgerald was, how did he put it, an exemplary officer, a credit to both the Quartermaster School at Fort Lee and the army. I got another snapshot from his wife this morning, or at least the beginnings of one. From others, principally his coworkers, both officers and enlisted men, we'll try to get a series of nonofficial snapshots. We'll compare all of them—mine, yours, the ones we gather in interviews—with the 'official' one that Major Williams gave us, and look for dissonance." A. G. unsteepled his fingers and leaned forward. "My guess is that we'll find something."

"Do you have anything in mind?"

A. G. shook his head. "No, I don't. I do know, however, that people are seldom killed for doing nothing whatever. It's possible that this was a crime of passion, a murder committed by a jealous husband." A. G. saw Giles's eyes drop to the unused condom wrapped in silvery foil sitting on his desk, the one they found under the backseat in Fitzgerald's car. "Exactly," he said, pointing at the condom for emphasis. "This can be fairly said to be dissonant with the 'official' snapshot of the captain we got from your boss this morning. Why would a happily married man have a condom in his automobile? In his bedroom at home, yes, but his automobile?" A. G. shrugged. "Or, Fitzgerald could have been involved in some sort of criminal activity that led to his murder. Whatever the motive, I think it's extremely likely that someone at Fort

Lee knows, if not precisely *who* killed the captain, at least *why* he was killed."

Impressed, Giles whistled, a long, low note.

"Indeed," A. G. said, repressing a smile. "We, you and I, are going to have to take a great many 'snapshots' out at the fort to compare with the 'official' version."

Giles took a sip of his coffee. "What did you learn from Mrs. Fitzgerald?"

"Not a great deal," A. G. said carefully, knowing the lieutenant was under orders to report everything he learned to Williams. "Perhaps when she's had a chance to get over the immediate shock of her husband's murder she'll be of more assistance." He took his pack of Chesterfields out of his desk and offered one to Giles. After lighting both cigarettes he sat back again. "You're not married, are you?"

"No." Giles shook his head. "No, I'm not. Why do you ask?"

"Since we're speaking of gathering snapshots, I'd like to know more about how Mrs. Fitzgerald is viewed within the officers' wives community, and I doubt seriously that anyone but a wife could provide us with such information. Unfortunately," A. G. smiled, remembering the two women at Martinelli Gardens that morning who had turned away from his greeting, "I have my doubts that any self-respecting army wife on the post would be likely to be candid with me, a civilian, or even, for that matter, with an officer, a single officer, from the provost marshall's office about such a delicate and potentially embarrassing matter."

"I have a friend on the post," Giles said, "a good friend actually, who *is* married and lives in the Martinelli Gardens housing where the Fitzgeralds live. Or lived. My guess is that his wife knows Mrs. Fitzgerald or, if not, would have certainly heard about her from the other wives." He nodded, more to himself than to A. G. "I think if I approach both of them, my friend and his wife, discreetly, I can persuade her to tell me what she knows or might have heard."

"I think that's a good idea, but I'd like you to go just a little further. I'd like you to ask her to ask around a little herself—discreetly, as you put it. In addition to anything about Mrs. Fitzgerald, I would particularly like to know of any gossip concerning Captain Fitzgerald himself." A. G. paused for a second to make sure the young lieutenant was following him. "I'm thinking of things like, was he a heavy drinker, or was he known for getting mean when he drank."

"You think he might have beat her up?"

A. G. shrugged. "That's one of the things we hope to find out. Another one is, did he have a reputation as a ladies' man, and if so, might he have been having an affair with another officer's wife?" A. G. stood up. "I'm afraid you're going to be rather busy for a while."

Giles smiled enthusiastically. "Believe me, this investigation will be a lot more interesting than chasing down the occasional AWOL in Richmond or traffic-control duty on the post."

"I don't doubt it." A. G. put a hand on the younger man's shoulder. "Talk to your friends over in married housing tonight. And schedule those interviews with anyone who saw Fitzgerald at the club Saturday night right away—tomorrow if possible." He walked Giles out past Mildred Tatum's desk. "Call me first thing in the morning."

"Did you talk to Bud Taylor?" Mildred asked as soon as Giles left.

"Before the lieutenant and I left the warehouse," A. G. responded, looking at his watch. It was a little after three o'clock. The sun was still so high he had lost track of the time. "I told him I'd have the car out of there tomorrow morning." He sat on the edge of her desk. "How're the Senators doing?"

Mildred shook her head morosely. "Twenty-one games out of first and heading rapidly for the cellar." An avid baseball fan, she knew that A. G., although he cared almost nothing for the national pastime, relied on her almost encyclopedic knowledge of the game for enough information to at least keep himself up-to-date on the standings in each league. "They'll be lucky to finish the season ahead of either Philadelphia or Boston." Like many Virginians, she considered the Washington Senators her home team.

"Isn't the All-Star game coming up soon?" he asked, mildly curious.

"Next week, in Cleveland. Casey Stengel is managing the American League team, and Walt Alston the National."

Someone passing on the sidewalk outside the window caught A. G.'s eye, and he suddenly remembered something he wanted to do. "I believe I'll walk across the street to Troutman's and get a fountain Coke. Want me to bring you one back?"

Mildred shook her head and turned her attention back to the Underwood. "Thanks anyway."

A. G. got to the door and turned back toward Mildred "Say," he said casually, "have you seen Angie Troutman," Doug's wife, "the past week or so?"

Mildred looked up, sudden interest in her eyes. "I understand she's staying with her sister over in Norfolk for a while. Took off right after Doug bought her that new Buick." She put a Pall Mall between her lips and lit it, squinting at A. G. through the smoke. "Why do you ask?"

A. G. shook his head and suppressed a smile. Angie Troutman, seven years younger than her husband and attractive in a gaudy sort of way, was a fertile source of gossip in the county. "No reason," he said over his shoulder, turning to leave. "Oh, after I visit with Doug for a few minutes I think I'll stop by Doc Maple's office," he added, almost out the door. "I want to ask him a couple of questions about Julie Brown's death."

The interior of Troutman's wasn't a great deal cooler than the temperature outside, and as A. G. sat down on one of the stools at the marble fountain counter, he wondered why Doug had not yet installed air-conditioning. The drugstore was empty, and Doug stood behind the large brass cash register near the door, shifting his weight uneasily from foot to foot. He was sweating copiously and looked as if his belt was cinched too tightly. He walked over behind the counter and tied an apron around his waist.

"What can I do you for, A. G.?" he asked, sounding more relaxed than he looked. His eyes were set too closely together, giving his face an unpleasantly narrow appearance, a look he unwittingly accentuated by slicking what was left of his rapidly thinning hair back with a heavy-handed use of Vitalis hair oil. "Say, that was some bad business with that murdered officer from out at the fort, huh?"

A. G. nodded and took a straw from the glass container on the marble counter. "It was indeed. Let me have a cherry Coke, Doug," he said, sighting through the straw. "Plenty of ice." He swiveled around 360 degrees like a playful kid. "Must be too hot for folks to be out shopping."

"Tell me about it." Troutman filled a glass with shaved ice, put in a splash of cherry extract, triggered the glass full of Coca-Cola from the fountain, and put it in front of A. G. "I'm not even getting any counter trade to speak of at lunch." He took off the apron and leaned against the back counter. "I had to tell Claire," his only employee, "to take the week off." He placed a toothpick in the corner of his mouth. "You got any leads on the killing?"

A. G. shook his head and took a sip of Coke. "Nothing yet. How's that new Buick of yours running?"

Doug grunted sourly. "Just fine. Angie's got it over at her

sister's in Norfolk." He rather indelicately scratched at his stomach. "I like to let her go over there for a few weeks in the summer, visit family, relax a little, that sort of thing."

A. G. smiled and stirred the ice in his glass with the straw. "Hot as it is these days, I know she appreciates that air conditioner." An air-conditioned automobile was still something of a rarity, and more than a few of Hopewell's citizens ground their teeth with envy whenever they saw Angie Troutman driving the new Buick Roadmaster with the windows rolled up. "Say, I saw Dorcas Craige coming in here a little while ago," he said casually, as if out of the blue. "How she doing these days?"

Suddenly nervous, Doug, apparently unaware that he had just taken it off, retied the apron around his waist. "Said she was having trouble with some sort of rash. Wanted me to mix her up a calamine lotion."

A. G. shook his head sympathetically. "Not much worse than a rash in July," he confirmed. "Doc Maple still prescribing codeine pills for her nerves?"

Doug shook his head and, for the second time in less than a minute, untied the apron again. "You'll have to ask Doc about that, A. G." His voice took on a whiny quality, and his close-set eyes would not meet A. G.'s. "You know I can't . . ."

A. G. held up a hand, interrupting him. "You're right, Doug, forget I asked." He finished the Coke and put a nickel on the counter. "I just worry a little about Miz Craige from time to time, you know what I mean?" He paused for a second. "Say, did you know that her grandfather was born a slave?" He nodded, as if confirming the veracity of his own statement. "Hard to believe in 1954, isn't it, a man being born into slavery. Her daddy used to work for my mother's family over near Williamsburg, so I've been knowing Miz Craige and her people all my life." He smiled and got up from the stool. "Folks around here are right fond of her, always have been, what with losing her boys in the war and then her husband, Percy, getting killed and all."

"Julie Brown died of heart failure, secondary to septicemia."

"Blood poisoning?" A. G. asked.

Henry Maple nodded, his sad, rheumy eyes blinking several times, as if he was not quite sure why this conversation was taking place. At the age of seventy-six, many in the county thought he should have retired from the practice of medicine years ago. Much of his practice had died off, literally, as lifelong patients passed away and younger generations consulted better-trained, more competent physicians in Petersburg. About the only remaining people who sought his expertise, such as it was, were the county's poorest citizens, those unable to pay except in installments, often in the form of homegrown vegetables and home-dressed meats.

"What was the cause of the infection?" A. G. leaned forward in his chair in Maple's office. "I mean, what kind of infection was it?"

Maple shrugged. "I have no idea. Her mother told me that she had been complaining of abdominal pain, so perhaps it was a burst appendix or an ovarian cyst of some sort." He shook his head. "It could have been almost anything. If we had gotten her into the hospital, I would have ordered some blood work to narrow it down, but by the time I first saw her it almost certainly wouldn't have made any difference."

"Well, how long had she been sick?"

"I would guess probably the better part of a week, at least the acute phase of the infection, although neither Sam nor Leona could say exactly when she started feeling poorly. When I got out there, yesterday evening, it was already too late to do anything. I could see right away she was near death, but nevertheless I told them we needed to get her admitted to the county hospital as soon as possible." He shook his head again. "She died before we could even get around to moving her."

"Are you planning to do an autopsy?"

Maple looked at A. G. as if he thought him simpleminded. "Who in the world would pay for such a thing? Believe me, I'll be lucky to collect a fee for my house call last night, much less ask Sam and Leona to pay for an autopsy. Besides, you know folks around here are squeamish about things like that." He leaned back in his chair and clasped his hands across his ample stomach. "No, I doubt seriously they'd agree to an autopsy even if it wasn't going to cost them anything."

"You don't think they'd like to know what caused the death of their daughter?"

"What's to know? She's dead. Listen, Sheriff, for all this fancy talk in the newspapers about penicillin and the new antibiotics that have been developed after the war, people still die from the same kinds of infections they always died of. What difference does it make what caused the infection, as long as it wasn't a gunshot or a knife wound? Will it make them feel any better to know she *might* still be alive if they'd brought her to the hospital three days ago? Folks around here don't go running to a doctor the minute they or one of their kids starts feeling bad—you know that as well as I do. Are you going to put them in jail because they didn't call me sooner? She's dead, and that's all there is to it. No, Sheriff," Maple shook his head with finality, "the whys and the wherefores are between them and the good Lord now."

A. G. sat quietly in the dark, watching lightning bugs dancing outside the screened-in porch of Dolores Anderson's ridiculously small one-bedroom house. He heard the toilet flush inside the house and thought immediately of Theresa Fitzgerald's amusing, if caustic, remarks about the inadequacies of the married-officers' housing at Fort Lee. Dolores received her house, not entirely unlike the Fitzgeralds' and other military personnel's, rent free as a large part of her compensation as organist and choir director of the Calvary Baptist Church. Inasmuch as the cash portion of her salary was little more than an honorarium, she was expected to, and did, supplement it by giving private music lessons—organ, piano, and violin—in her home.

"Would you like a glass of tea?" Dolores called from the kitchen. "I'm going to have one, so it would be no trouble."

"No, thanks."

They had stopped in Richmond for supper and, oddly enough, A. G. had had a cup of coffee with his dessert.

"Why, A. G., I don't believe I've ever seen you drink a cup of coffee before," a rather surprised Dolores had remarked.

Over dinner he told her about the discovery of Captain Fitzgerald's body, and about meeting both the provost marshall, Major Williams, and the widow Fitzgerald, at Fort Lee.

"It must have been terrible," Dolores said, swirling the tea and ice in her glass as she joined A. G. on the back porch. "I mean, having to talk to the poor woman about her husband and all, right after he was murdered." She sat down next to A. G. and took his right hand in hers, unable to imagine such an ordeal. "It must have been awful," she repeated.

Not *really,* A. G. thought but did not say. Dolores's touch reminded him of how Theresa's fingers had lingered on his that very morning, warm and, improbable as it may have seemed, somehow inviting. He shook his head reflexively and reached for a cigarette, closing his eyes momentarily against the sudden flare of his lighter. *Inviting.* That was the word he had been thinking about all day, whenever the memory of her touch had tickled his consciousness—warm and inviting. Unfortunately, one memory inevitably led to another, and he could not help but recall, all too vividly, the erotic image of her erect nipples pressing against the white silk blouse she wore, and, in turn, the whiteness of her blouse evoked his fleeting glimpse of the inside of her thigh as she had gotten into the army sedan the day before. A. G. realized with a start that he was becoming physically aroused, and he blessed the darkness that had settled in around them.

"I should take off," he said, standing abruptly and turning slightly away lest Dolores notice, despite the darkness, the sudden tightness of his trousers. "You've been traveling all day and must be exhausted."

"I *do* need to unpack," Dolores agreed as she, too, stood up, thinking that he was still upset by his meetings at Fort Lee that morning. Understandably. "We both should get to bed early tonight." She leaned in rather awkwardly and kissed him, brushing her lips quickly across his. "Sweet dreams."

Chapter Four

A. G. woke, as he normally did, half an hour before sunrise. He lay quietly for ten minutes listening to the beating of his heart and thinking about Theresa Fitzgerald. A warm breeze through the open bedroom window ruffled the mosquito netting over his bed and brought with it the sweet fragrance of magnolia blossoms. He closed his eyes and, without conscious thought, began to caress himself, his right hand slipping easily inside the waistband of his pajama bottoms. As his hand began to move with some urgency he suddenly realized what he was doing and the exceedingly pleasurable fantasy came to an abrupt end. "Damn," he murmured guiltily, withdrawing the offending hand from his pajamas and looking at it as if it were some sort of independent, and highly irresponsible, appendage. He shifted his body, trying, remarkably unsuccessfully, to replace Theresa Fitzgerald's image in his mind with that of Dolores Anderson. "This is childish," he admonished himself, knowing his thoughts to be anything but childlike, even as he articulated the words in the darkened bedroom.

In the middle distance he heard the lowing of a cow and, in the hallway outside his room, the soft, arthritic footsteps of Pearl, his late mother's calico cat. Pearl had never accepted the fact of his mother's death three years earlier and still slept each night on the rug next to her bed, convinced, A. G. supposed, that one morning she would awaken to find once again the old woman who had loved her since she was a kitten. He dangled a hand over the side of the bed as he had done every morning for three years to reassure the elderly cat that he had not, as his mother had done, gone away during the long night.

He sat up with a sigh, brushing the mosquito netting aside, and swung his feet over the edge of the bed. Although still dark, a number of larger objects in the room began slowly to resolve out of the greater gloom: an armoire against one wall, a table at the foot of the bed, a small secretary and chair opposite the armoire. All were antiques—the armoire constructed of heart pine and cedar; the table, black walnut; the secretary, bird's-eye maple.

"Come on, Miss Pearl," A. G. said quietly, standing up and stretching, "let's go downstairs and see about some breakfast."

The sun hadn't been up an hour when A. G. opened the screen door of Casey Bartlett's Easy Street Cafe and walked in. The air was redolent with the smell of fresh coffee and frying bacon. He walked across the small room, waving or nodding at each of the ten or twelve customers, and slid into one of the small booths along the back wall.

"Morning, A. G." Jimmy Morton had mixed his scrambled eggs, sausage patty, and grits into a single conglomeration and was busily consuming it when A. G. sat down. "It's going to be another hot one," he predicted cheerfully. "I got up this morning feeling like I was coated with thirty-weight motor oil."

Jenny Bartlett, Casey's wife, stopped at the booth, a pot of coffee in one hand and a breakfast order in the other. She had flame-red hair and was six months gone with their fourth child. "Breakfast?" she asked, blowing an errant strand of hair from in front of one of her eyes.

"Not this morning," A. G. said. "I just came in to visit for a minute with Bud." He pointed at Bud Taylor, the booth's other occupant. "I left the extra key to your warehouse with Lieutenant Giles," he told Bud after Jenny left. "He's arranging for a couple of soldiers to pick up the captain's DeSoto this morning. I'll get the key back from him in the next day or two."

Bud grunted in reply and watched in some distaste as his nephew, the Reverend Morton, wiped his plate clean with a piece of toast. Bud's breakfast had been limited, as it frequently was, to a headache powder and a cup of coffee.

"Sit down," Jimmy said, chewing vigorously all the while. "How's your investigation into the murder coming along?"

A. G. shook his head. "I can't stay but a minute. As to the investigation, it's just getting started." Leaning down, he reached across the table and took Jimmy's last piece of toast. "No telling how long it's going to take." He turned to Bud. "I'm thinking I might drive over to Richmond later this morning. Anything I can do for you while I'm over there?"

Bud thought for a second and shook his head. "No, but I appreciate you asking. You heard about the Brown girl dying Sunday evening?"

A. G. nodded. "I talked to Doc Maple about it yesterday afternoon."

"What'd he say?" Bud asked, curious.

"Not much, just that she died of heart failure due to blood poisoning." A. G. shrugged. "He thought it could have been due to a ruptured appendix or a cyst of some sort." He did not mention the discussion they had had about an autopsy.

"It's a damned shame to see a young girl dying like that. Still"—Bud shook his head—"life goes on."

"Amen," Jimmy agreed, his voice taking on the typically mournful quality of his chosen profession. He suddenly thought of something and brightened considerably. "And speaking of life, I saw in the paper yesterday that that radio preacher from North Carolina, Billy Graham, had a hard time of it on his so-called crusade to England and Europe."

"Is that right?" A. G. knew that a lot of Baptists in the South were discomfited by the extensive news coverage devoted to the peripatetic young evangelist. And jealous.

"The paper said he just got back last week and that he had lost twenty pounds and had had five kidney-stone attacks while he was over there." Jimmy didn't even try to hide the glee in his voice. He himself, having been rated 4-F by the local draft board due to flat feet and a heart murmur, had never been out of the state of Virginia. "Must've been the foreign food."

"Sounds like doing the Lord's work is turning out to be a little more strenuous than he anticipated," A. G. said dryly, turning to leave.

A. G. hadn't been in his office ten minutes when the telephone rang.

"Sheriff, this is Lieutenant Giles."

"Yes, sir," A. G. answered. "What do you know this morning?"

"Not much more than I knew yesterday afternoon," Giles

admitted. "The officers call went pretty well, I guess. Only three or four officers remembered seeing Captain Fitzgerald at the club Saturday night, and they had no specific knowledge of anything out of the ordinary. To the best of everyone's recollection, he was in the bar for an hour or so, talked to a couple of people about nothing in particular, and then left. No one seems to remember the exact time, although everyone I spoke to believes it was well before nine o'clock, perhaps as early as eight."

"Say, I wonder if the bartender might remember something?" A. G. mused.

"I wondered the same thing," Giles said, sounding inordinately pleased with himself. "So I went over to the club last night after the officers call. The bartender is an enlisted man, a PFC who moonlights at the club after duty hours. He remembered Captain Fitzgerald's being there, remembers that he had two draft beers, and, get this, remembered that he used the telephone at the bar to make a single call."

"Bingo," A. G. said, snapping a finger. "Does he remember the time?"

"He thought it was right around eight o'clock."

"Good. The telephone company usually requires a court order before they open up their records, but that'll take a day or two." A. G. thought for a second. "I've got a friend in the district attorney's office in Richmond," he said, more to himself than to Giles, "who should be able to help us speed things up."

"Not necessary," Giles said, a broad smile evident in his tone of voice. "I've already spoken to the phone company this morning, and they should have the information for us by early afternoon."

"My, my," A. G. said, resisting a sudden urge to whistle. "A friend in the phone company?"

"Even better—a World War II veteran. I explained the

situation, and he was more than happy to help us out infor-
mally while you get the wheels turning on obtaining a court
order."

"I'm impressed with your initiative. Did you get a chance
to talk to your friend and his wife about Mrs. Fitzgerald?"

"I did. Unfortunately, my friend's wife didn't know a
great deal about her. She's met her, of course, but knows almost nothing about her. Worse, she said she doubted that any
of the other wives would be of much more use. Interestingly
enough, I had the distinct feeling that my friend's wife, in fact
most of the wives, admired her. She kept talking about the
fact that Mrs. Fitzgerald was a little older than the rest of the
lieutenants' and captains' wives, a college graduate, a career
woman in her own right, that sort of thing." Giles shrugged
and shifted the telephone from his right ear to his left. "Anyway, I told her to think about it, talk to some of the other
wives, and that I'd get back to her."

"Any gossip having to do with the captain himself? Being
a ladies' man, that sort of thing?"

"Nothing."

A. G. shook his head, disappointed. "Well, give your
friend's wife a couple of days, and then talk to her again.
Something may yet turn up."

"Something may, but . . ."

"But?"

"I don't think anything will," Giles said. "Not from the
wives, anyway. Oh, while I'm thinking about it, I've started
putting together the list of Captain Fitzgerald's immediate superiors and subordinates over at the Quartermaster School.
Perhaps you might drop by the provost marshall's office sometime today and we could start scheduling interviews with
them."

"That's fine. I'm going over to Richmond later this morning but should be back by early afternoon. I'll call you. And listen, Lieutenant, you're doing a good job, a fine job."

A. G. hung up the telephone and sat back in his chair. "Interesting," he murmured to himself, "an interesting woman." Realizing what he had just said, he corrected himself. "Couple," he said quickly, a little louder, as if somehow to cancel out his earlier use of the singular *woman.* "An interesting *couple.*" He took a cigarette out of his desk and started to light it, holding off the flame from his lighter at the last second and putting the cigarette back into his drawer. Suddenly restless, he leaned over and opened the office window, looking down the sidewalk and the street in both directions. He heard the outer office door open and someone enter.

"Good morning, Sheriff." Mildred put her head into A. G.'s office. "You're in here bright and early," she added, her tone of voice clearly implying *for a change.*

"Good morning, Mildred," A. G. answered brightly, pleased, for a reason he could not quite put his finger on, to have someone to talk to just then. He walked out to greet her. "That coffee smells good," he said, nodding toward the paper cup on her desk.

Somewhat surprised, Mildred looked up at A. G. "Since when did you start drinking coffee?"

A. G. shrugged. "To tell you the truth, I don't know that I have," he answered. "When you have a minute, would you mind getting Spencer Lee on the telephone for me?"

Back in his office A. G. lit the cigarette he had put back into his drawer minutes earlier and listened as Mildred placed the call to Richmond. Several seconds passed as she worked her way through first the telephone operator, then the switchboard operator in the district attorney's office, and then, finally, Spencer's secretary.

"Spencer Lee is on the line," Mildred called out.

A. G. had the phone in his hand before Mildred could finish the sentence. "Spencer, A. G. here. How about buying me lunch today?"

Spencer Lee was the number-two attorney in the Richmond district attorney's office and a rising star in the state Democratic Party apparatus. Fraternity brothers at the University of Virginia, Spencer and A. G. had maintained a close friendship ever since.

"Wait a minute, wait a minute," Spencer answered. "I thought the person doing the inviting does the buying."

"I'm driving all the way over there, so it seems to me that the least you could do is buy."

"You're driving over here because you want something," Spencer pointed out good-naturedly. "Besides lunch."

"You win," A. G. conceded. He looked at his watch. "I've got a funeral to go to at two o'clock, so let's make it on the early side. How about I meet you at eleven-thirty at the Capital Grill?"

He hung up and sat back in his chair, swiveling around to look out the open window. The telephone rang.

"Sheriff Farrell."

"Sheriff, this is Theresa Fitzgerald. I hope I'm not catching you at a bad moment."

A. G. sat up. "Not at all, Mrs. Fitzgerald. How may I help you?"

"I wonder if it might be possible for us to get together again. There are a number of things we did not discuss yesterday that may be of some assistance to you in your investigation."

"Of course we can get together. I'm driving over to Richmond a little later this morning and then I've got a . . ." He paused suddenly, realizing that it might be somewhat indelicate to mention attending a funeral to a woman whose husband has just been murdered. "I've got some business here in Hopewell when I get back from Richmond, but I should be free after, say, three-thirty. Would that be a convenient time?"

"Yes, that's fine." She hesitated for a second. "Would it be possible for you to meet me in Petersburg instead of here at Fort Lee?"

"Certainly," A. G. replied, suddenly even more curious. "Where in Petersburg would you like to meet?"

"Do you know Watts Avenue? Down by the river?"

"I believe I do. It's mostly warehouses down there, isn't it?"

"Yes. I have a . . ." she hesitated again, "a friend who owns an art studio in that neighborhood, at 441 Watts Avenue. I'll see you there at three-thirty."

The Capital Grill was housed in a small one-story brick building two blocks from the state capital. Built the year after much of Richmond had been razed by a vindictive Union army, it had a long marble counter with fifteen stools, twelve tables with four chairs each, and five booths lining the back wall. The floor was ceramic tile set in a black-and-white checkerboard pattern, and the ceiling featured a clerestory of the style normally seen only in industrial buildings. Putatively air-conditioned since 1951, the place had three ceiling fans, which struggled to circulate what was in fact mostly warm air. A. G. was sitting in one of the booths at the rear of the restaurant when Spencer Lee walked in. Spencer was wearing a seersucker suit with a blue silk tie and tan-and-white spectator shoes. He seemed to know or be known by everyone in the restaurant and stopped briefly at several tables to share a word or a joke. A. G. was smiling and shaking his head when Spencer finally reached him.

"Lord, boy, anybody didn't know better would say you were running for governor."

"I am," Spencer replied with a wink, meaning it. Able to trace his family's ongoing involvement in Virginia politics back to the colonial era, he had decided as early as his junior year in high school that he would one day be governor of the state of Virginia and had never been shy about sharing his ambition with A. G. He sat down across from his old friend. "And the first thing I'm going to do when I get myself elected is find you a *real* job." As with his electoral ambitions, Spencer never hid his belief that A. G. was wasting his time in rural law enforcement.

A. G. smiled and waved a hand. "Listen, Spencer, the reason I wanted to get together . . ."

Spencer groaned and interrupted A. G. "Let me at least enjoy my lunch before you tell me what it's going to cost, okay?"

The two men talked casually during lunch, primarily A. G. catching up on the political scene in Richmond and on the Virginia congressional delegation in Washington.

"Everyone in Washington is worried about the French losing Indochina to the Communists," Spencer said as the conversation turned to current events.

"Is the war really going that badly for them?" A. G. had, of course, been seeing the gloomy headlines, but frankly hadn't been paying that much attention. "And anyway, why do the French need a colonial presence in Asia?" He shook his head dismissively. "Seems to me they've got enough problems in their own backyard without looking for more halfway around the world."

Spencer shook his head in mock sorrow. "Haven't you heard about the Communist world conspiracy?" he said, only half jokingly. "Anyway, from what I hear from a friend at the Pentagon, it's only a matter of time before the French are kicked out, even with all the help we've been giving them." He took a sip of tea and finished his cigarette. "Eisenhower and Dulles are madder than hell about it—that's one reason why Ike and John Foster are so determined to keep Red China out of the UN."

"What about you?" A. G. asked, eager to move the conversation closer to home and the reason he had wanted to have lunch with Spencer in the first place. "What's going on in the DA's office these days?"

"Well," Spencer said, as their dishes were cleared away, "assuming Bill Campbell," the district attorney, "retires next year like he's supposed to, I've been led to believe that the right people intend to support my candidacy. And from there . . ." Spencer smiled and shrugged. "Enough about who's doing what to whom in Washington and Richmond. What's on your mind?"

Finally, A. G. thought, finishing the last of his iced tea. "You heard about the murder in Hopewell?"

"I did. Bill Campbell told me yesterday. He got wind of it from the state coroner's office. I believe he said a soldier stationed at Fort Lee was killed."

A. G. nodded. "A Quartermaster captain from Fort Lee by the name of Martin Fitzgerald. Shot once in the head by a large-caliber weapon, probably a .45. No shell casing, so it was either a revolver or a careful killer."

"Where did it happen?"

"In front of Bud Taylor's feed warehouse."

Spencer chuckled. "I'll bet that pleased him to no end."

"And to add insult to injury, Bud's the acting county coroner right now," A. G. pointed out with a smile on his face. "That's why the state coroner's office is involved—we're having to borrow a pathologist from their office to do the autopsy. Anyway, according to the provost marshall out at the fort, Fitzgerald was an exemplary officer."

"Somebody didn't think so," Spencer interjected.

"Exactly. And it wasn't a robbery, because nothing was

taken. He still had his watch and billfold when he was found."
A. G. leaned across the table to emphasize his point. "Somebody wanted him dead."

"Jealous husband maybe? Unhappy wife? Alcohol? Most
of the murders we see at the DA's office involve at least one
of the three, frequently two, and sometimes," he chuckled sardonically, "all three."

A. G. shook his head. "Could be, but I don't think so. My
intuition tells me that Fitzgerald was involved in something
criminal. I'd like you to check with your friends in the Richmond police department and see if anyone has heard anything
about him. Have them ask around on the street, that sort of
thing."

"If that's all you want, consider it done."

"That's not all," A. G. said. "I want you to check with the
state attorney general's office, too. See if anyone over there
has ever heard of him."

"You could do that yourself," Spencer pointed out.

"I could," A. G. agreed, "but you'll get a hell of a lot
more attention than I would. And while you're doing that I
can concentrate my efforts, at least for the time being, on the
military side of things."

"I assume you've met Major Williams, the provost marshall."

"You know him?" A. G. asked, surprised.

Spencer nodded. "Two, maybe three, months ago, not long
after Williams arrived at Fort Lee, one of his soldiers got into
a fight with a couple of drunks in a pool hall here in Richmond. In my dealings with him I found him, Major Williams,
to be rather . . ." Spencer hesitated for a second, searching for
the right word, "to be rather *doctrinaire,* if you know what I
mean."

"I think I do. He wasn't terribly happy when I insisted on
maintaining control of the investigation into Fitzgerald's kill-

ing, but there wasn't much he could do about it. Fortunately, the young lieutenant he assigned to watch over me is turning out to be more helpful than I suspect the major would have liked." A. G. smiled. "Perhaps that's unkind. In any event, I'll be concentrating on Fitzgerald's military associates for the time being."

"What about his wife?"

"An interesting woman," A. G. said carefully. "I talked to her yesterday, and I'm meeting with her again this afternoon."

Spencer looked at his watch and stood up. "Back to the salt mine. I'll check with both the police and the attorney general's office and let you know what I hear. Keep in mind that it might take them a day or two to get back to me."

"Sooner would be better than later."

Spencer started to say something and stopped. He smiled. "Your confidence in my modest ability touches me. By the way, who died?"

"What?"

Spencer smiled at his friend's sudden confusion. "When you called this morning you said you were going to a funeral after lunch. Who died?"

"Sam and Leona Brown's daughter Julie."

"Sam Brown the bootlegger?"

A. G. nodded and told Spencer about his conversation with Doc Maple, including his, A. G.'s, thought that an autopsy might be advisable.

"I don't know, A. G., I might have to go with the doctor on this one," Spencer said, sitting back down for a second. "You know as well as I do that an autopsy isn't required in the absence of a crime, or at least suspicious circumstances. If Maple's professional opinion is that the girl died of an infection of undetermined but nonsuspicious origin"—he shrugged—"I'd say that's that. Besides, he's right about lots of people being exceedingly squeamish about having a loved one cut up and examined after death. My guess is that Sam and his wife would never agree to it. Hell, I'm not sure I would myself." He stood up again. "Thanks for lunch. Oh, and by the way, Carole is having a big to-do for the lieutenant governor and his wife in three weeks and wants you and Dolores to come. Now, listen," he added before A. G. could decline the invitation, "this is a chance for you to meet some important people."

A. G. laughed and shook his head. "Dolores and I would stand out like a couple of country cousins at a fancy affair like that," he said. "And as for important people . . ." He waved his hand dismissively, the gesture effectively finishing the sentence for him.

Spencer pointed at A. G. to lend emphasis to his words. "You need to get off your backside and make some decisions about the future," he said. "I mean it—it's time you stopped moving sideways. You know as well as I do that you're just wasting your time in Hopewell." He shook his head irritably. "Listen to what I'm telling you, A. G.—you need to be settling down, you and Dolores both, and thinking about where you're going to be and what you're going to be doing a year from now."

Julie Brown was laid out in a plain pine coffin in front of the unadorned altar of the Rose of Sharon Freewill Baptist Church. Somebody, to the intense displeasure of the self-ordained pastor, B. Denny Cole, had put a dab of rouge on her cheeks, and the color stood out against the pallor of her face. Her hair had been neatly combed, and she was dressed in her nicest Sunday outfit, a dress of robin's-egg blue with ruffled sleeves. A hand-lettered sign posted prominently on one wall of the sanctuary assured the reader that the road to hell was paved with, among other things, lipstick, dancing, impure thoughts, and the consumption of carbonated and/or alcoholic beverages. A. G. found the prohibition relating to the consumption of alcoholic beverages particularly ironic given Sam Brown's lifelong occupation as a distiller of illegal whiskey. The small chapel had an uninsulated tin roof that seemed to gather and focus the heat like a Dutch oven, leading A. G. to conclude that if B. Denny didn't preach an expeditious funeral service Julie Brown would be joined shortly in the hereafter by a number of the congregants, himself included.

Upon entering the rustic sanctuary, he saw Julie's parents, Sam and Leona, gathered around the coffin with five of their remaining six children, and A. G. remembered that the oldest boy, Tommy, was serving a twenty-year sentence in South Carolina for manslaughter. He slipped into one of the rough-sawn pews at the rear of the sanctuary and noted with some interest that the linoleum flooring in the center aisle leading up to the altar was worn through to the wood underlayment in many places. *When B. Denny says, "Come to Jesus," they must take him literally,* A. G. thought with some amusement. Shortly after he sat down, Sam Brown, assisted by two of his sons, put the top on the coffin and nailed it in place. The Brown family then seated themselves in the front row, and B. Denny Cole began the service. He started with a prayer that left little doubt that anyone not a tithing member of a charismatic, Pentecostal flock such as his own had little chance at salvation, and moved quickly into a funeral service that consisted primarily, if confusingly, of retelling the story of Noah and the Great Flood. No music was played, no hymns were sung, and B. Denny Cole, to the heartfelt appreciation of A. G., wrapped matters up in no more than twelve to fifteen minutes from the time he started. An interment service, he announced after a final, lengthy prayer, would be held privately at graveside.

"Sam, Leona," A. G. said quietly to the grieving parents, outside the chapel, "I can't tell you how bad I feel about Julie's passing."

Leona broke into fresh tears, and Sam, leaning on his ever-present crutch, nodded but did not speak, his gaze cold and unyielding, his jaw clenched so tightly that the corded muscles stood out from his neck.

Watts Avenue, an urban interface between light industrial use and out-at-elbow residential housing, ran roughly parallel to the Appomattox River as it meandered around Petersburg. The road was poorly maintained, forcing traffic to deal as best it could with numerous potholes, where the original brick and cobblestone roadbed lay exposed. A. G. had no trouble finding the address—a narrow, two-story brick commercial building. He drove slowly past it to the end of the block before turning around and coming back to park directly in front.

"Hello."

Her voice came from above him as he got out of the car.

"Up here," she repeated, smiling and waving an arm through an open window on the second floor at the rear of the building. "Just a minute—I'll be right down."

A. G. realized he was smiling as he walked up to the building and reminded himself, not for the first time since leaving Julie Brown's funeral twenty minutes earlier, that this was an official visit, a continuing interview in an ongoing homicide investigation.

"Thank you for meeting me here," Theresa said, taking A. G.'s right hand in her own. Her hand lingered the merest fraction of a second longer than what most people would have deemed appropriate for a formal greeting. "Please come in."

A. G. was surprised to see that two thirds of the second floor of the building had been completely removed, leaving only what appeared to be a two-story enclosed office space at the rear. The result was an open floor plan with airspace that soared almost twenty-five feet to the peak of the steeply pitched roof. The exposed roof joists were supported by five massive twelve-by-twelve white-oak structural posts, and the roof itself was lined on both sides with a series of small, rectangular windows that flooded the interior with light. The flooring consisted of six-inch unfinished pine planks laid in a striking herringbone pattern. Motes of dust hanging in the still air refracted the shafts of sunlight streaming through the sky-light windows, giving the interior a smoky, surreal atmosphere.

"Back this way," Theresa said over her shoulder as she walked to the rear of the building. She wore a sleeveless white silk blouse and a knee-length cotton skirt. "Unlike the family housing at Martinelli Gardens, the living quarters here really are air-conditioned."

Living quarters? A. G. wondered. He followed silently, his attention drawn to the interior construction details. Clearly someone had spent a considerable amount of money turning what must have been a run-down warehouse into what Theresa had described during their brief telephone conversation that morning as an art studio.

"I believe you said this was an art studio?" he asked, walking quickly to catch up to her, a sense of not-quite disbelief evident in his voice.

"Yes, that's correct." She led A. G. through a door into a small apartment—living room, small galley kitchen, and bedroom—built into the back third of the warehouse. She closed the door behind them with a smile. "And again, unlike at Martinelli Gardens this door really would let all the cool air out." She nodded at a small leather sofa. "Sit down, and I'll make us some coffee. Unless you'd like something stronger? I have beer chilled as well as a bottle of white wine."

A. G. shook his head. "Coffee will be fine." He looked around with open curiosity. "I would never have thought of living in a warehouse," he said.

The apartment, featuring finish carpentry much as one would have expected to find in a well-built home, had ten-foot ceilings and the same pine floors as the rest of the warehouse. Although the ceiling cut off the natural light from the warehouse's skylight windows, several conventional windows, all with wired industrial safety glass and external security bars, had been cut into the building's exterior walls.

"It's not at all uncommon in Europe," Theresa said from the kitchen. "Particularly among artisans. Buildings like this provide both the open work space so critical to many artistic disciplines and, at the same time, affordable living space." She came out of the kitchen carrying a small coffee mill. "Would you mind?"

A. G. took the grinder, placed it between his knees, and began turning the crank handle. "I haven't done this in more years than I can remember," he said, grinding with obvious pleasure. "I had an aunt in Richmond, my mother's sister, who ground her own beans at home, but you don't see it done too much these days. Whenever I'd visit her she'd put me to work doing the grinding." He inhaled deeply. "I love the smell of the freshly ground beans." He shook his head, pleased at the almost eidetic recall of his aunt's image that the act of grinding the beans summoned forth. "I guess it's too easy these days to buy the beans already ground."

Theresa retrieved the mill. "The only way to brew good coffee is to start with freshly ground beans. Did your aunt reward you with a cup every now and then?"

A. G. laughed. "Lord, no. She used to say that coffee would turn me brown and stunt my growth if I drank it before I was a grown-up. Oh, I'd sneak a taste once in a while, but it was far too bitter to tempt me often. In fact, I used to wonder how something that smelled so good could taste so bad, and why she loved it so, particularly since no one else in the family drank it."

"Did she travel?"

"As a matter of fact, she did. She married into a great deal of money and traveled extensively. Why do you ask?"

"In much of the world coffee is an essential social lubricant. The French, for example, would be horrified at the thought of starting the day without coffee. I suspect your aunt learned to appreciate its subtleties while abroad."

"Did you?"

"In a manner of speaking. My father was a physician who had trained for a time in France and developed a love of coffee in Paris. He converted my mother and, in time, me." She smiled. "Fortunately, he did not subscribe to your aunt's physiological theories regarding the effect of caffeine on adolescents, because I began drinking coffee at home when I was fifteen."

With no noticeable deleterious effects, A. G. thought but did not say. "Does your father still practice medicine?"

Theresa came out of the tiny kitchen carrying two cups. "No," she replied, handing one of the cups to A. G., "both he and my mother are dead."

A. G. took a cautious sip of coffee.

Sitting down next to him, Theresa laughed delightedly. "You didn't make quite as bad a face this time as you did the last," she said.

"I'm beginning to think I might actually learn to like it," he allowed, acutely aware of her nearness on the sofa, the now familiar smell of her perfume. "I might indeed."

As if sensing his sudden discomfort, Theresa put her cup down on the small table in front of the sofa. "Again, I appreciate that you agreed to meet me here rather than back at Fort Lee. I'm sure it was an inconvenience for you."

"Not at all, although I must admit that I am curious why you wanted to meet off the base."

"I'm embarrassed to say that it was nothing more than a vague sense of discomfort at the prospect of talking to you about . . ." she hesitated for a second and shrugged, ". . . about Marty." She paused and took a sip of coffee. "As you will recall from our previous conversation, our marriage, Marty's and mine, was, for all intents and purposes, *finis.* We were merely waiting for the best time, career-wise for Marty, to separate and get a divorce. One of the problems, one of the big problems, I had with army life, right from the beginning, was the oppressive lack of privacy on the post. It could not have been worse living in Puritan New England from the point of view of an externally imposed standard of behavior, coupled with almost obsessively curious neighbors." She smiled ruefully at A. G. "Furthermore, as I've already told you, although I'm sure you would have surmised it on your own, I did not exactly fit the regular army image of an officer's wife. Not only did I have a university education, I had actually had a career, a successful career, on my own before Marty and I got married." She shook her head angrily. "Believe me when I tell you that an educated woman has never been considered an asset so far as an army officer's career is concerned. Quite the contrary. And even more threatening to the military status quo was the fact that I made no secret of my intention to return to the art business." She rose from the sofa and walked into the kitchen, returning with a pack of Lucky Strikes and an ashtray. "Cigarette?" After A. G. lit both of their cigarettes she settled back on the sofa with a sigh. "I'm sorry for the soap-box speech, but it was all so irrational and unfair."

"I'm sure it was," A. G. agreed, meaning it. A beam of late afternoon light coming through the window was striking Theresa on her right side, effectively backlighting her. When she turned toward A. G. the silk blouse she was wearing, theretofore completely opaque, was now only partially so, and he could see quite clearly the outline of her breasts. He quickly looked away, profoundly disturbed by the power of his body's immediate reaction to the sight.

"In any event," Theresa continued, seemingly unaware of both the suddenly revealing combination of light and posture and its consequent effect on A. G., "when we talked on Monday you asked if I knew anyone who might have wanted to kill Marty and I told you that I did not."

A. G. nodded, but unsure of his ability at that instant to speak as if nothing untoward were going on in his mind, he remained silent. He tried not to look, tried not to imagine his hands exploring her body, but failed, and his eyes dropped repeatedly to her blouse.

"Marty was an almost compulsive gambler, a poker player to be precise." Theresa paused and looked toward the window. "In thinking about it, I wondered if perhaps his death might somehow be related to the gambling."

"It could have been," A. G. allowed, trying desperately to focus his thoughts. "Do you know where and with whom he played? Was it on the base?"

Theresa shook her head, her eyes still focused on the window. "No, he told me once that he never gambled with fellow officers—it would have been too risky for his career. I do know that he played in Richmond one evening a week, and I'm sure there was a regular game close to Fort Lee—perhaps here in Petersburg, although exactly where I can't say."

"Did he ever mention owing anyone money from these games?"

"No." Theresa suddenly looked back at A. G., a sad smile on her face. "You must think me a poor wife," she said quietly, "knowing as little as I do about my husband and his activities."

A. G., certain that she had noticed him staring at her

breasts, felt a rush of heat to his face and he realized, mortified, that he must be blushing. "I'm sorry," he blurted out after what seemed an eternity, standing suddenly. "I'm sorry, but . . ."

"Are you all right?" Theresa asked, a look of ostensible concern on her face. "Is something the matter?"

"No," A. G. said, shaking his head, "I just need . . ." He paused, suddenly aware he had no idea what he was saying. "I'll call you tomorrow. This," he paused again, searching for words, desperately trying to sound professional and detached, "this conversation has been helpful."

She stood up and put a hand on A. G.'s arm. "I'm frightened," she said, looking into his eyes in a startlingly intimate manner. "I'm frightened, and I need a friend right now more than I ever have in my life. May I call you from . . ." her voice dropped to little more than a whisper, "from time to time?"

Leaning against the kitchen counter, A. G. smoked a Chesterfield and watched Pearl eat the last of the fried chicken breast and country gravy he and Dolores had had for supper earlier that evening. Although Pearl had been an extremely picky eater while his mother lived, A. G.'s laissez-faire approach to dining, both his own and Pearl's, had greatly expanded her universe of acceptable alternatives. Nevertheless, he knew better than to offer her any of the stewed tomatoes and okra Mildred had brought to the office in a mason jar the day before. When she was done they both walked out to the porch, A. G. to finish his cigarette and enjoy the last colors of the late evening, Pearl to groom her whiskers and dream of slow-moving mice. As if hurrying the no-longer-visible sun along, a three-quarter moon was rising like an apparition in the now darkened east, its cold paleness bearing tidings of an autumn yet months away. The sky, caught between day and night, reflected the contrasting colors of the dying sun and birthing moon like a painting turned at a sharp angle away from the viewer, the intensity washed out, replaced by a none-theless compelling rose-colored translucence.

Dolores and A. G. usually ate supper together two or three times a week. How they had fallen into such a pattern of careless domesticity he could not precisely say—he only knew that it had developed over a period of two or three years and seemed to please both of them.

"I was shocked," Dolores had said, as she sat down at the table with A. G. that evening, adding, as she served him chicken and mashed potatoes, "although, Lord knows, I guess I shouldn't have been. Aunt Alice had made it clear, after Momma and Daddy died, that she was planning to leave everything to me."

"How much do you suppose the house is worth?" A. G. asked, his participation in their conversation halfhearted at best.

Dolores shook her head. "Not a great deal. It's small, not much larger than this one," she looked about somewhat rue-fully, "although it has a beautiful rose garden in the backyard, and it's in a very nice neighborhood near downtown Raleigh. The probate lawyer said that if I didn't need the money right away he could easily rent it out for me while I decided what to do in the long run."

A slight inflection at the end of her sentence invited a specific kind of response from A. G., an invitation he did not wish to accept, at least not right then.

"That's probably a good idea," he said slowly, knowing that she wanted reassurance from him, words confirming that she would have no need for a house in Raleigh, not now, not in the long run. Reassurance he found himself unable to give her that evening, for reasons he preferred not to think about.

"No need to hurry a big decision like that," he added, his words sounding hollow and insincere in his own ears.

He left shortly after they had finished eating, telling her that he was tired and had a mild headache.

"It's going to be hot again tomorrow," A. G. informed Pearl, smiling as the old cat yawned in return. "Hot and humid." He leaned back into the cushions of the glider sofa, gently moving back and forth. "I don't know what to think about that woman," he said quietly to himself, meaning of course Theresa Fitzgerald, his soft words soothing to Pearl's ears as she prepared to relax herself into a good night's sleep. How indeed, he wondered, does one think about a woman unlike any other? In a rational way? Who, if not the cat, does one talk to about feelings such as were crowding into his consciousness? Other than Spencer Lee, A. G. had no close friends, none whatever, and he could no more see himself confiding to Spencer that his thoughts were filled with the erotic image of the newly widowed Theresa Fitzgerald than he could imagine himself reaching out and touching the moon rising over the cultivated fields of Prince George County. And not just her image. Sitting there on the porch with Pearl he could smell the spicy sweetness of Theresa's perfume as clearly as if she sat there with him, could hear the pure contralto of her voice.

I'm frightened. Her words came back as clearly as if she were sitting there next to him. *I'm frightened, and I need a friend.*

The countryside was awash in moonlight when A. G. rose from the glider and, with Pearl, went into the house. He watched as the cat slowly climbed the curved staircase to take up her lonely vigil at his mother's vacant bedside. Then, turning out the kitchen light, he climbed the stairs himself.

Chapter Five

Jubal Bishop's roadhouse sat a quarter of a mile off the narrow two-lane road that ran between Petersburg and Hopewell. It had a ludicrously faux log-cabin facade and a small neon sign that proclaimed it to be the Club St. Louis. A country-and-western band played six nights a week, and in the back, through the kitchen, Jubal offered the sportsmen of Prince George and surrounding counties both poker and craps tables. The main room, which had a large dance floor and seated at least a hundred people, smelled as if it had never seen the light of day. Numerous aromatic molecules mingled and competed for olfactory notice: malt and hops from the beer, vinegar and brine from the pickled eggs and pigs' feet, cooking grease that had drifted out from the busy kitchen, where almost everything was heavily breaded and fried, either in bubbling deep-fat fryers or cast-iron skillets, and, not least, pine sap from the fresh sawdust Jubal kept sprinkled on the rough-sawn plank floor.

"Morning, Jubal," A. G. said cheerfully as he walked in at nine o'clock in the morning, politely reaching back with his left hand to catch the screen door so it wouldn't slam behind him.

Jubal Bishop, tall and heavyset, was counting money at one of the tables near the long bar. Two of his five sons sat with him, and a third was working behind the bar, mopping the floor desultorily. His oldest boy, Jubal Jr., was in the army, stationed in Japan, and his youngest, Earl, was in the state prison in Richmond doing a year and a day for auto theft

"Sheriff Farrell," Jubal exclaimed, looking up in surprise. He pushed back his chair and stood up, positioning himself between A. G. and the money on the table. "You're a little bit outside your jurisdiction here, aren't you?" He smiled crookedly, much like a man whose wife has caught him with a telephone number he shouldn't have. "Unless, of course, you're just stopping by for a beer," his smile broadened, "in which case we're not open yet." Jubal paid a good deal of money every month to various law-enforcement agents and officials at the county and state level, as well as to the county and state Democratic Party organizations, in order to avoid scrutiny of his various entertainment enterprises.

"Jurisdiction," A. G. said contemplatively, as much to himself as in response to Jubal's query. "Jurisdiction," he said again, this time pronouncing the word slowly, almost lovingly. "I've always liked the way that word rolls off the tongue, the syllables following one after the other just about as seamlessly as a fellow could hope for." He looked at Jubal and smiled. "Some words are like that, aren't they? Unfortunately," he continued, shaking his head regretfully, "its euphonious nature notwithstanding, *jurisdiction* also happens to be one of the most frequently misunderstood of statutory conceptions, particularly among those individuals and businesses that operate on the, shall we say, *fringes* of legal behavior. And, no," he shook his head again, "this isn't exactly what you'd call a social visit, although your boy there doesn't need to worry about trying to hide all that cash." A. G. nodded at Jubal's son, who was indeed in the process of hurriedly stuffing the cash that had been piled on the table into a greasy paper bag. "Hey, Mason, how're you doing? You getting that money together for the IRS?"

"Fine, Sheriff," the young man mumbled, avoiding A. G.'s gaze as he tucked the last of the bills into the bag and stood up. "I'm doing fine." Heavyset like his father, and unshaven, he turned and walked quickly behind the bar and into the kitchen, the bag clutched tightly in his beefy hands.

"What can I do for you, A. G.?" Jubal asked carefully, motioning for A. G. to join him at the table. It troubled him that A. G. had never taken a dime from him, either directly or indirectly. "You want a cup of coffee?" Without waiting for an answer he looked at the son, Aaron, standing behind the bar and jerked a thumb in the direction of the kitchen.

"I believe a cup would be just fine," A. G. answered, sitting down. "Black," he added, thinking of Theresa's coffee. "I take my coffee black these days. And as to what you might be able to do for me, I'm going to go out on a limb here and guess that you already have a good idea." A. G. laid the black-and-white photograph of the late Captain Martin Fitzgerald he had gotten from Lieutenant Giles on the table.

"The soldier that was killed over by Bud Taylor's warehouse," Jubal said, glancing briefly at the photograph and then back at A. G. "Fitzgerald's his name."

A. G. looked up as Aaron Bishop brought two steaming mugs of coffee to the table. He smiled a thank-you and picked up one of the mugs, automatically blowing across the lip. The coffee was weak, almost tealike. "I'm wondering," he said to

Jubal, "since you obviously knew him, why you didn't call me when you heard he had been murdered."

Jubal, too, blew on his coffee and shrugged. "It didn't mean nothing to me," he asserted aggressively. "I mind my own business and expect others to mind theirs."

A. G. nodded politely, but the smile left his face. "I'm afraid you're laboring under something of a misconception here, Jubal. I think you believe that the reason nobody bothers you out here is the money you spread around amongst various law-enforcement officials and politicians." A. G. took a careful sip of coffee and shook his head. "That's not it at all. For example, you've been reading in the paper these past few weeks about that mess down in Phenix City, Alabama, haven't you? Well," A. G. continued without waiting for a response, "those folks down there thought that all they had to do was spread a little of that gambling money around to the local politicians, didn't they? Then, as you know, things got so completely out of hand, what with the state attorney general being murdered and all, that the governor finally had to declare martial law and send in the National Guard." A. G. shook his head, appalled, as much of the country had been, by how badly things had gotten out of control before the governor stepped in. "That's hard to believe, isn't it, National Guard troops having to move in to take over a town in this day and age." He paused for another sip of coffee, feeling the tension build between himself and Jubal. "I'm not saying such a thing could happen here, in a civilized state like Virginia, but it takes constant vigilance, doesn't it, to make sure nobody gets to feeling they're above the law. Now, don't get me wrong," A. G. held up a hand, "I don't doubt, I'm sorry to say, that the money's important, but I thought it might be helpful to our conversation this morning to point out that it's not, in and of itself, what keeps your doors open."

"The money's not important to *you*," Jubal pointed out.

"The city of Hopewell already takes adequate care of my modest financial needs," A. G. pointed out dryly. He put both hands on the table, palms down. "I'll be honest with you, Jubal—I don't like what you do out here. That is to say, I don't like your business. I'd like it a whole lot better if folks didn't want to drink and gamble and whatnot, but they do, and that's a plain and simple fact. Of course, if they didn't," the hint of a smile flickered across his face, come and gone so fast that Jubal didn't even notice it, "there wouldn't be much work on Sundays for the likes of the Reverend Morton and his brethren, but that's neither here nor there, is it?" He paused for a second, collecting his thoughts. "Anyway, like I was saying, your money may be important to some people, but in the final analysis the only reason nobody bothers you out here, including me, is that you have a reputation for running a clean operation. Everybody from here to Richmond knows you sell bootleg whiskey, and they know about the poker room and the craps table, too, but they also know that you're not running a whorehouse out here, and they know that the poker and craps are honest—no loaded dice and no marked cards. Nobody gets cheated, nobody gets beat up, and nobody gets poisoned drinking rubbing alcohol flavored with mint leaves, or whatever." A. G. took another sip of coffee. "Do you get my point?"

"I don't know why he was killed," Jubal said defensively, "and I doubt that anyone he played with out here done it."

"He was a regular?"

Jubal nodded. "Thursday nights. He always played at the big table, mostly with the same people."

"A big loser?"

Jubal laughed, a short one-bark note devoid of humor. "Not here he wasn't." He leaned forward and tapped on the table with his index finger to emphasize his point. "That man could flat play poker. Roger"—Jubal's poker manager, who always ran the Thursday-night game—"told me he doubted that Fitzgerald lost at more than one sitting in five."

"High stakes?"

Jubal shook his head. "You've got to go over to Richmond for the high-stakes action. Here, a man can win or lose a couple hundred a night, not much more. The action's good, and, don't get me wrong, the stakes aren't exactly penny ante, but," he shrugged, "not big enough to kill someone over. Leastwise, I wouldn't think so."

"Could he have been holding anyone's markers?"

Again, Jubal shook his head. "Maybe a few, but not for more than a hundred or two. Like I said, anyone wants big action, they go to Richmond, or Washington. Up there you can dig a grave as deep as you want."

"What do, did, you know about him?"

"I knew he was in the army."

"Nothing more?" A. G.'s tone of voice expressed skepticism. "You saw him every week and knew nothing more than that about him?"

Jubal smiled sardonically. "Serious poker players generally don't spend much time talking about anything, particularly themselves."

"Was he a drinker?"

"Not a drop, leastways not while he was playing. All he ever had was coffee, and he didn't like it much either. Claimed it was too weak." Jubal chuckled. "Told me once he had a mind to bring his own in a thermos. Said his wife made the best coffee he'd ever had. I said he was welcome to, but that I'd have to charge him corkage."

"Sounds like you liked him."

Jubal shrugged. "I get a whole lot worse than him in here, I can tell you that."

A. G. took a final sip of his coffee and stood up. "I want you to do me a favor, Jubal. I want you to ask around, discreetly, and find out if anyone Fitzgerald played with, and it may have been someone who sat in on just one game, lost enough to want him dead."

"Nobody's going to say nothing." Jubal remained seated and looked up at A. G. "I'll do it because you're asking, but you got to remember, this here's a roadhouse, not some church social club. Folks come here to drink and dance, they come to raise a little hell. Most men come without their wives, and they'll shy away from talking about it, especially the ones who like to play a little poker or shoot craps. Believe me, there ain't nobody looking to have you stop by their house or job to ask questions about what they might have seen or heard out at Jubal Bishop's place." He shook his head to emphasize the point. "Not nobody."

"I don't doubt you're right, but asking won't hurt. You never know what you might turn up."

Jubal nodded and pursed his lips. "I guess you heard about Sam Brown's daughter dying suddenlike," he said, rather too casually.

A. G., about to leave, sat back down. "I did." He was aware that Jubal occasionally bought corn whiskey from Sam Brown. "What do you know about it?"

"Nothing much. I was just wondering if you'd heard about it."

A. G. sat quietly, looking at Jubal and letting the tension build while waiting for him to say more.

" 'Course, I don't know for a fact," Jubal finally said after several uncomfortable seconds, "and I probably shouldn't be saying this, but word is, I mean, I heard she was, um, expecting when she died."

"Pregnant?" A. G.'s voice rose in disbelief. "She was only fifteen years old, Jubal, how could she have been pregnant?" As soon as he said it, he realized how foolish he must have sounded. "I mean," he added quickly, waving a hand as if trying to erase his earlier words, "I know how she could have gotten pregnant, but are you sure?"

Jubal shifted in his chair, clearly uncomfortable with the subject he had brought up. "She was a big girl for her age, if you get my point." He cupped both hands in front of his chest. "Big. And wild, too. She showed up here a couple of months ago with some soldier from out at the fort. No," he quickly added when he saw A. G.'s reaction, "not Fitzgerald. Some kid that looked to be not much older than she was, probably just out of basic training. They were both half drunk when they got here. Of course, I threw them out as soon as I saw her—her daddy would have shot me on sight if he thought I was serving whiskey to her." He shook his head. "Believe me when I tell you that that girl was the light of Sam Brown's life. He thought the world of her. Her death's going to be hard on him, real hard."

"Did Sam tell you she was pregnant?"

"Lord, no." Jubal looked shocked. "And for Christ's sake, Sheriff, don't you be telling him I told you so, you hear what I'm saying?" He paused to mop his brow with a paper napkin. "God alone knows what Sam would do if he found out I was telling you this about his daughter."

"Don't worry, Jubal, I won't. Where did you hear about it?"

"One of my boys told me. He got it from a friend who heard someone else talking about it, that sort of thing. Listen, it's probably not even true. You know how folks like to talk, particularly with Sam not the most popular man in the county, if you know what I mean. But even if it was true, I doubt it had anything to do with her dying and all."

"Why'd you mention it to me?"

"Well, I don't want you mad at me about the Fitzgerald thing, not calling you when I found out that he'd been murdered. And something else." Jubal leaned across the table to make his point. "You bringing up that thing in Alabama with the governor and the National Guard, well, I got your point and it troubles me—a lot. I don't want you or anyone else thinking that maybe I'm getting to be like those crazy folks down there. So, I heard about this thing with Sam's daughter and thought I'd pass it along for whatever it might be worth, that's all."

A. G. stood up again and looked down at Jubal. "I appreciate it, Jubal. And don't worry—no one'll find out I heard about it from you."

Mildred Tatum, her usual unlit Pall Mall dangling precariously from the corner of her mouth, looked up from her Underwood when A. G. walked into the office. "Did you and Dolores eat those okra and tomatoes I put up for you?" she asked in lieu of saying good morning.

"I tried to give them to sweet Miss Pearl," A. G. answered, deadpan, "but she wouldn't have anything to do with them." He picked up a book of matches from her desk and lit her cigarette. "So we had to eat them instead."

"Your momma's old cat's got more sense than you do," Mildred responded tartly, without taking the cigarette from her lips. "And better manners."

A. G. smiled and leaned against one of the two metal filing cabinets across from Mildred's desk. "What do you hear around Hopewell these days?"

"Angie Troutman hasn't returned from visiting her sister in Norfolk. She was due to come back a day or two ago, but I guess she's liking it at the beach. Word is that Doug drove over to Richmond yesterday and bought her one of those television sets. I guess he's planning to surprise her with it when she gets back."

"I imagine that cost him a pretty penny," A. G. mused.

"Sounds like keeping Angie happy is getting to be an expensive proposition. Plus," A. G. chuckled, "you can bet that more than one or two other husbands around here will have to follow suit now that Doug has fouled the well, so to speak."

"I wouldn't doubt it," Mildred agreed, shaking her head. "Not with all the fools that populate this county. Did you make it over to Julie Brown's funeral yesterday?"

A. G. nodded. "Yes, and I thought I was going to die—the chapel was like an oven. I think Sam and Leona were pleased I was there, but other than me passing along a word or two of sympathy, we didn't speak." He casually tamped a Chesterfield against his watch crystal. "What do you know about Julie Brown? I mean, who she ran around with, her reputation, that sort of thing."

"Not much. Why do you ask?"

"Just curious. Do me a favor and ask around, would you?" A. G. lit his cigarette and watched the smoke drift up to the ceiling. "On the QT." He turned and started for his office.

"Before I forget it, that lieutenant from out at the fort's been trying to reach you this morning." Unspoken but implied was *Where have you been?*

"See if you can get him on the line for me, would you?" A. G. walked into his office, having decided on the drive back from Jubal Bishop's roadhouse not to inform Mildred of the visit.

"Oh, and Spencer Lee called from Richmond," Mildred added before A. G. could sit down.

"See if you can get him on the line first," A. G. said, raising his voice slightly to carry out to Mildred's desk and over the renewed clacking sound of the Underwood. "I'll talk to Lieutenant Giles after I've spoken with Spencer." He sat down and leaned back, glancing out the window. Doug Troutman was on the sidewalk, unrolling the green canvas awnings above the drugstore windows. Watching him reminded A. G.

of Dorcas Craige, and he decided to visit with her sometime in the next day or two.

"Spencer Lee's on the line," Mildred called out.

"Spencer," A. G. said as he picked up the telephone. "Talk to me."

"Your dead captain has raised an eyebrow or two over here in Richmond," Spencer announced without preamble.

"Let me guess," A. G. said happily, leaning back in his chair and closing his eyes. "He was a regular player in some sort of high-stakes poker game."

The telephone sat silently in A. G.'s hand for several seconds before Spencer again spoke.

"Goddamn it, A. G., if you already knew, why did you ask for my help?"

"Calm down, Spencer, I only put two and two together this morning."

"The widow tell you?"

"Not in so many words," A. G. said, being intentionally vague, "but like I said, it wasn't too difficult putting two and two together. I had a little chat with Jubal Bishop out at his place this morning . . ."

"Ah, the infamous Club St. Louis," Spencer interjected.

". . . and it seems that Captain Fitzgerald was a regular out there as well," A. G. continued. "And get this, if playing poker had anything to do with his death, at least as far as Jubal seems to think, it wasn't because he owed someone a lot of money. If anything, it was the opposite."

"So he won more than he lost."

"A lot more, although Jubal assured me that the games at his place aren't exactly high-stakes poker."

"That apparently was not the case in Richmond. My informant indicated that the games Fitzgerald played in were big table-stakes affairs, with comparably big players. He seemed to think that they occasionally attracted high rollers from as far away as Washington and New York." Spencer paused for a second before continuing. "A man could make serious enemies in a game like that."

"Indeed he could," A. G. mused. "Winning *or* losing."

"By the way, how did the autopsy go?"

A. G. looked at his watch. "It should be starting just about now."

"You're not going to sit in?" Spencer teased.

"I doubt I could add anything useful to the proceedings," A. G. said dryly.

"Where is he going to be buried?"

"I don't know. I believe the widow's having the body picked up as soon as the pathologist is finished with it. Probably tomorrow. Listen, Spencer, back to Fitzgerald's poker habits—I'm going to need to know who he played with."

"I guessed as much," Spencer replied. "I've already asked my man to find out as much as he could about the who, when, what, and where, but . . ."

"I know, I know," A. G. interrupted. "Nobody likes to talk about who they play poker with, particularly when the stakes are large and a body crops up. Nonetheless . . ."

"I'll do what I can," Spencer interrupted in turn, "keeping in mind the fact that Bill Campbell," the district attorney, "not unreasonably expects me to devote approximately one hundred percent of my time to *his* business."

A. G. smiled as he hung up, knowing that Spencer, despite his protestations, would enjoy digging up information about Fitzgerald's gambling activity in Richmond. He took a Chesterfield out of his desk, but before he could light it, Mildred's voice came through the open door of his office.

"Lieutenant Giles is on the line."

"Thanks, Mildred." A. G. put down the cigarette and picked up the telephone. "Good morning, Lieutenant."

"Good morning, Sheriff. Sorry to bother you, but Major Williams wanted to know if Captain Fitzgerald's autopsy had been completed yet."

"No bother, Lieutenant, and, no, I haven't heard from the pathologist yet. I expect he's about done, though. I'll call you as soon as I hear something." A. G. paused for a second. "Anything new to report on your end?"

"I'm afraid not. I'm still putting together the list of officers and enlisted men who worked closely with Captain Fitzgerald. As soon as it's done we can sit down and schedule interviews with them. How about you?"

A. G. shook his head as if the lieutenant could see him over the telephone line. "Not really." He didn't know enough yet to feel comfortable discussing Fitzgerald's gambling habits, particularly during a rather casual telephone conversation that Giles would most likely feel obligated to report to his boss, the provost marshall. "By the way, do you happen to know where the captain is going to be buried?"

"As a matter of fact I do, and that's the reason Major Williams is so interested in knowing about the autopsy. Colonel Peterson, the post commander, called and told him that the burial is going to take place at Arlington National Cemetery. Assuming you and the pathologist release the body, it's scheduled to be transported to the army mortuary at Fort Myer this afternoon."

"When is the funeral?"

"There's going to be a public service at the chapel here at Fort Lee tomorrow afternoon, and interment at Arlington on Friday." Giles paused for a second. "Are you planning to attend the service?"

"I doubt it," A. G. said, an unlikely image of Theresa Fitzgerald dressed in widow's weeds coming to mind. "I'll call as soon as I hear from the pathologist." He hung up and walked out to Mildred's desk. "I'm going to drive over and see if the autopsy on Captain Fitzgerald is finished," he told her.

"Why don't you just call?"

A. G. smiled. "I'm also going to run out and check on Miz Craige. I haven't talked to her for some time, and I'm a little worried about her."

Mildred shook her head. "She and a lot of other people in this county, colored *and* white, would be a lot better off if Doug Troutman would quit dispensing paregoric like it was soda pop." She looked up from the Underwood. "You taking her out some groceries?"

A. G. nodded.

Mildred smiled briefly. "I didn't mean it when I said your momma's old cat has better manners than you." The smile disappeared. "But she does have more sense."

Although he knew it would annoy Bob Creech, A. G. parked his car in the shade of the funeral home's porte co-chere, the already fierce midmorning sun all the incentive he needed. Creech's oldest daughter, Elizabeth, greeted him in the reception parlor, a dark, gloomy room with permanently drawn drapes and massive, overstuffed furniture.

"You know Daddy doesn't like people parking there," she pointed out rather peevishly. "It's supposed to be reserved for loading and unloading."

"That's why I did it," A. G. teased, handing her his straw hat and winking. He took no offense from the tone of her voice, guessing, based entirely on her appearance, that she was exceedingly uncomfortable. "When's the baby due?"

She rolled her eyes dramatically. "In four weeks, and I wish it was yesterday. Leroy," her husband, a private stationed at Fort Riley, Kansas, "says his company commander won't give him an emergency leave to be here." She looked closely at A. G. as a thought suddenly occurred to her. "Say, do you know any generals at Fort Lee? I mean, what with this business with the dead captain and all, maybe you could talk to someone and . . ."

"Sheriff Farrell." Bob Creech's voice interrupted Elizabeth. He came into the parlor with a large, heavyset man in tow. "I was just going to call you. This is Dr. Ira Singer, the pathologist from Richmond. He's finished the autopsy on Captain Fitzgerald."

"Sheriff," Singer mumbled, reluctantly extending his right hand and abruptly snatching it back almost before A. G. could shake it.

"I appreciate your driving over from Richmond to help us out like this," A. G. said politely. "Did the autopsy turn up anything of interest?"

"No," Singer replied shortly. "The man died from a gunshot wound to the head. A gross examination of the organs revealed absolutely nothing out of the ordinary."

"May we release the body to the next of kin for burial?"

"You may as far as I'm concerned," Singer grunted. "The lab tests won't be back for several weeks, but don't expect them to tell you anything you don't already know." He sighed despondently, as if the effort of talking to A. G. was costing him a good deal more than he wished to pay.

"I just now called the lieutenant out at Fort Lee," Creech interjected. "Giles," he added, looking at a piece of notepaper. "Not two minutes before you got here. They're going to pick up the remains in about an hour and . . ." He paused, startled at the sudden and unexpected departure of Dr. Singer. "Just a minute, Doctor," he called out, ignoring A. G. and turning to hurry after the rude pathologist, "I'll show you out."

A. G. turned back to Elizabeth and retrieved his hat. "Unfortunately, I don't know a soul at Fort Lee who could do anything about getting your husband back here from Fort Riley, Kansas," he told her, one hand on the front door. "You'd be better advised to get your daddy to call Maynard Phillips's office." Phillips was the congressman whose district included Hopewell. "My experience has been that he's not generally worth a great deal to his constituents, but he may be inclined to do your daddy a favor." *Depending entirely,* A. G. thought cynically but did not say, *on whether he contributed anything to Phillips's last campaign.*

Dorcas Craige lived five miles east of Hopewell, on an aimlessly meandering dirt road that led nowhere in particular. She and her husband, Percy, had built the small house in 1921, the year they got married, on six acres of bottomland he had purchased from Bud Taylor's wife's father. They lived in a small canvas tent most of that summer while they worked on the house evenings and Sundays, building it with green wood from trees felled and milled on the site. Their two sons had been born in the house, both births attended by Percy's great-aunt, an old woman skilled in the arcane ways of midwifery. Twenty-one years later, first one, then the second of the two boys, had come home in metal coffins, returned by a War Department that expressed its and the country's appreciation for their sacrifice in a letter neither Dorcas nor Percy could read.

"Hey, Miz Craige, you home?" A. G., carrying a grocery bag in the crook of one arm, stooped and peered through the screen door. "It's A. G. Farrell." Able to see nothing, and hearing no response to his greeting, he stepped back off the tiny front porch and walked around to the rear of the house, noting with some sadness its out-at-elbow, ramshackle appearance. Before the war, while the boys were still alive, and even to a slightly lesser degree after, before Percy's fatal accident, the house and yard had shone with the pride of ownership, gaily painted and surrounded with sunflowers, pansies, and flowering crepe myrtle. The screen door in the back stood open, its spring hanging limply where it had become detached from the door frame. A frumpy, worn-out–looking cat, ill used by the heat and exhausted by an obviously late-term pregnancy, lay sprawled in shade at the corner of the house, watching A. G. with the hope that he wasn't going to do anything that would further complicate her life. A. G. smiled at her and, putting his head into the door opening, called out, "Miz Craige, it's me, A. G. Farrell, come to visit." He waited a second and then stepped carefully into the house, pausing briefly once inside to let his pupils dilate and adjust to the dark interior. The house looked and smelled of neglect, stale cooking odors mixed with the unmistakable scent of unwashed bodies and dirty clothes. Shaking his head, A. G. moved through the kitchen to the front of the house, glancing into the two bedrooms as he passed them. In the front room, sitting on a sofa with several holes in it, was Dorcas, her eyes closed, her upper body rocking gently to an unnamed melody only she could hear. "Miz Craige," A. G. knelt down on one knee in front of her, "Miz Craige, it's me, A. G. Farrell."

Her eyelids opened as if in slow motion and took what seemed like several minutes to focus on the white man kneeling in front of her. "Who is it?" she asked, her words slurring softly past her tongue and palate. "Who's there?" Before A. G. could answer, almost as soon as the words were out of her mouth, she recognized him and smiled, lifting a hand to pat the sofa cushion next to her. "Sit down, sit down." Her hand went to her matted, unkempt hair and fluttered about her dress and lap. "Lord," she added, her eyes wandering from A. G. to the cluttered room and back, "this old house ain't hardly fit for no company, is it?"

A. G. got up and sat on the sofa next to her. "Have you

eaten today, Miz Craige?" he asked, greatly concerned about
her lackluster appearance. Although he knew her to be in her
middle fifties at most, she looked and moved more like someone approaching seventy.

"You know I don't hardly eat like no bird," she answered,
a smile playing across her lips.

"Well, look here, I brought you a chicken-salad sandwich
and some slaw. Why don't you come over to the table and eat
a little something for me." He helped her rise from the sofa
and walked with her to the small table in the kitchen. From
the larger grocery bag he took a smaller bag and unwrapped
the sandwich and a small, cardboard container of slaw. "I even
brought you some iced tea."

While she ate he unpacked the groceries he had brought,
lining everything up on the counter next to the sink. "You can
put these away after you finish eating," he said, sitting down
at the table with her.

When she had eaten half the sandwich and a portion of
the slaw, Dorcas indicated that she was through. "I couldn't
eat another mouthful," she said, wrapping the remaining half
sandwich back up in the waxed paper it had come in. "I'll
finish it later this afternoon."

"That's fine," A. G. assured her, pleased that she had eaten
as much as she had. He took out his Chesterfields. "Would
you like a cigarette while you finish your tea?" He lit two,
handed one to her, and leaned back in his chair. "What do
you hear around the county?" he asked.

Dorcas sat quietly, obviously enjoying her cigarette. Finally, just as A. G. was deciding that she hadn't heard his
question, she spoke.

"I heard about that young girl, the whiskey man's daughter, passing."

Surprised, A. G. sat up straight. "Bad news travels fast,"

he murmured, more to himself than to Dorcas. "How did you hear about it?" he asked.

"Sarah Martin stopped by yesterday. She told me. Her cousin works for the girl's daddy from time to time. He told her about it." Dorcas shook her head. "It's a mighty shame a child that young passing, but she's not the first to die that way. Not around here."

"What way?" A. G. asked, not sure he had understood her correctly. "And what do you mean 'she's not the first'?"

Dorcas finished her tea and pinched the glowing ember off the end of her cigarette, intending to save what remained for later. "They's been several young girls died the past four or five years," she said, her voice slowing down noticeably. "All colored girls 'til this one." She stood up and started walking slowly back to the living room. "I got to go lay down now, Sheriff. You can come back later."

"How was Dorcas Craige doing?" Mildred asked when A. G. walked into the office.

"No better than middlin', I'd say, if that well." A. G. paused to hang his hat on the rack by the door. "She ate half a sandwich and some slaw, though. I'd ask Doc Maple to stop by and see her but," A. G. shook his head cynically, "I doubt he'd know what to do in any event."

"All he knows how to do is prescribe codeine and paregoric," Mildred opined tartly. "That old fool wasn't much of a doctor when he was young, much less now, fifty years later."

"Do me a favor, will you?" A. G. asked, changing the subject. "When you get a chance, sometime today or tomorrow, go down to the file room in the basement and pull out all of the county death certificates for the past five years."

"What are you looking for?" Mildred asked, surprised by the unusual, to say the least, request.

"I'm not sure—for now I guess I just want to look back and see who all's died recently." A. G. turned and headed toward his office. "And of what," he added, too quietly for Mildred to hear.

Before Mildred could respond with another question the telephone rang. "It's for you," she said with obvious annoyance after she answered it, holding one hand over the receiver. "Mrs. Theresa Fitzgerald."

It was just past four o'clock when A. G. pulled up to the converted warehouse on Watts Avenue in Petersburg. The sun seemed hardly to have moved past its noon prominence, and the street, like a sponge too saturated to hold any more water, radiated heat that rose up and assaulted the casual passerby like a slap in the face.

"A. G." Theresa took his right arm and led him in.

"Theresa." Even as he said her name A. G. marveled at how effortlessly it had come to his lips. *Theresa.* No longer was he able to think of her as Mrs. Fitzgerald, much less the widow of Captain Martin Fitzgerald. He knew something had changed as soon as he heard her voice earlier that afternoon, on the telephone.

"I hope you don't think me too forward for calling you like this," she had said, "but frankly, I was worried. You left so abruptly yesterday I thought that perhaps you were ill."

"I'm afraid I wasn't very articulate," A. G. had responded, wishing he had closed his office door. "As a matter of fact, I was feeling slightly light-headed," he had added truthfully.

"Thank you for meeting with me again," she said as they walked slowly, his arm still in her hands, to the small apartment at the rear of the warehouse. "As I mentioned on the telephone, I'm going away for several days . . ."

"To Arlington," A. G. interrupted. *To bury your husband,* he thought but did not say.

She nodded. "I wanted to see you, to *talk* to you," she quickly amended, "before I left. To be sure we had covered everything that might help you in the investigation."

She wore a simple white cotton shift, and her hair, which she had always before worn tied back, was combed out and fell to the top of her shoulders in a single, shimmering wave. A subtle hint of sweet spice swirled in her wake, and A. G. could see that her body was unencumbered by undergarments. He heard her voice, knew she was talking to him—"*as I mentioned on the telephone, I'm going away for several days and*"—but could not for the life of him understand what she was saying. With an almost insane lucidity he was able to identify and catalog an extraordinary range of sensory perceptions: the rapid beating of his heart, the springiness of the rough pine flooring beneath his feet, the infinite gradations of light and dark from the skylight windows to the floor, front to back, in the warehouse proper. Most startling was the sensation that the body walking along with Theresa was not his, that it was a doppelgänger, an exact replica of himself that somehow he was able to both observe from a distance and physically experience at precisely the same time. He could feel his tongue on his lips, the dampness of perspiration on his palms, the surge of blood and heat to his private parts, and yet simultaneously feel that he was witnessing a developing tableau, as if peering voyeuristically through an unshuttered window. Entering the apartment, Theresa turned, closing the door behind them. Then, as if it were the most natural thing in the world, she came into his arms, her mouth eagerly seeking his.

Chapter Six

Dawn was no more than a faint promise on the eastern horizon when A. G.'s Ford pulled slowly around the circular drive, its tires crunching quietly on the gravel. He turned off the engine and got out, pausing to stretch and yawn before walking up the steps to the porch. A gentle breeze, heavy with moisture, rustled through the leaves of the magnolia tree in the front yard, stirring a small owl that hooted softly to express what A. G. assumed was its disapproval at his unexpectedly late arrival. He opened the screen door and stepped across the threshold, automatically reaching for the foyer light switch as he did so. The sudden light caught Pearl, making her way carefully down the sweeping staircase, utterly by surprise. Clearly annoyed, first for being left alone all night and then for the unexpected bright light, she sat blinking for several seconds. She recommenced her journey down the stairs, taking each step with great deliberation, first her forepaws descending and then her hindquarters, the process repeating itself with almost comic slowness until finally she joined A. G. in the foyer.

"Sweet Miss Pearl," A. G. murmured, stooping to rub the old cat between the ears. "You wouldn't believe it if I told you where I've been and what I've done." He straightened up with a sigh and ran a hand across his day-old beard. "I doubt I'd believe it myself if someone told me," he added, more to himself than to the cat.

In the kitchen he took some boiled chicken out of the refrigerator and diced it for Pearl, putting it on the floor with a small bowl of buttermilk, a rare treat to partially salve his guilty conscience. He thought about slicing bread and bacon and scrambling eggs but decided to wait, opting instead for a glass of the same buttermilk Pearl was loudly enjoying. Taking his glass in hand, he walked back out to the porch and sat on the glider, lighting a Chesterfield and listening to a freshening breeze kick up in the stand of hardwoods off to one side of the house. He could sense a field of static electricity skittering through the air and knew that the storm it was heralding wouldn't be long in coming.

"It's fixin' to rain this morning," he informed Pearl when she joined him a few minutes later. "If you were planning a stroll around the yard, I would advise you to do it sooner rather than later."

Unimpressed, the cat yawned and began to groom her face, licking one paw and drawing it slowly across her muzzle. The words were scarcely out of A. G.'s mouth when lightning lit the southern sky several miles away and the first fat, heavy drops of rain began to dance across the front yard and up to the steps of the house. Although he sat ostensibly watching the storm, A. G. heard only Theresa's voice, soft and teasing, urgent and demanding, as they coupled in the small apartment hidden away at the rear of the warehouse on Watts Street. She did not at first believe that he had never before been with a woman, and when she finally accepted the truth of his words, she cried. "Dearest A. G.," she had whispered repeatedly, her tears of wonder and joy so moving him that he, too, cried, holding her as tightly as he dared until, rearoused, they made love yet again.

"Lieutenant Giles," A. G. said, trying and failing to stifle a yawn, "come in, come in."

Giles smiled as he strolled into A. G.'s office. "Late night?" he asked teasingly.

"Couldn't get to sleep for the life of me," A. G. answered lightly, more truthfully than the young lieutenant could have known. "Say," he continued, deftly changing the subject, "that was some storm this morning, wasn't it?"

"Was it ever," Giles agreed, punctuating his words with a short whistle. "The lightning almost knocked me out of my bed at the BOQ, although it sure passed through fast enough." He pointed out A. G.'s office window. "Looking out there now you wouldn't even know it had rained a couple of hours ago."

He was right. At a little past ten A.M. the sky had cleared to an almost painfully brilliant cerulean blue, and the scalding sun had long since evaporated any evidence of the predawn cloudburst.

A. G. nodded as Giles sat down. "You said you had something you wanted to talk about. And by the way, I appreciate your coming to Hopewell and saving me a trip out to the fort." He took the pack of Chesterfields out of his desk drawer and held it across the top of his desk. "Cigarette?"

"Thanks." Giles took one and lit both his and A. G.'s with his lighter. "I tried to catch you late yesterday afternoon, but your secretary said you'd already left. Anyway," he shifted in

the wooden office chair and discreetly adjusted his privates to
a more comfortable position inside his khaki uniform trousers,
"you'll recall my telling you that the bartender at the officers
club remembered Captain Fitzgerald making a telephone call,
and that a veteran at the phone company was going to get the
number for us?"

A. G., suddenly interested, sat forward in his chair.

"Well," Giles continued, "you're going to love this. The
number he called belongs to a young woman, a civilian employee at the Quartermaster School at Fort Lee."

"Single?"

"Married." Giles shook his head, clearly disturbed. "To
an enlisted man, a PFC, stationed at the fort."

"Is the husband at the Quartermaster School as well?"

"No, he's a mechanic at the post motor pool. But get this:
the wife hasn't been at work since Fitzgerald's body was discovered."

A. G. put his lips together and started to whistle, catching
himself only at the last second. Suppressing a smile, he nodded at Giles. "Good work. I suspect you've discovered the
reason for the condom in the captain's car." He thought for a
second. "Do they live on the base?"

Giles shook his head. "No. As a PFC the husband doesn't
have enough rank to qualify for on-base married housing—
they live in Petersburg."

"Have you . . ." A. G. paused for a second, "have you told
Major Williams about this?"

"No, not yet." A look of concern passed quickly across
Giles's face. "Strictly between you and me, Sheriff, the major
can be something of a bull in a china shop, if you know what
I mean. It occurred to me that Captain Fitzgerald's call could
have been quite innocent, and, if so, even the hint of a scan-
dal . . ." Giles paused and shrugged, "would be highly embarrassing for the private and his wife, not to mention Mrs.

Fitzgerald. Anyway, I thought it might be best to discuss it with you first."

"Good. I think we, you and I, should handle this—at least initially—with, if anything, an excess of discretion." A. G. leaned back in his chair and put his hands behind his head. "There are several possibilities here we need to think through. First, as you said, there could be a completely innocent explanation for the captain's after–business-hours telephone call—and by the way, let's find out if the woman's husband was on duty at the motor pool and away from home at the time the call was made."

"I checked and he was."

A broad smile spread across A. G.'s face. "I declare, Lieutenant, I doubt Major Williams has any idea what a first-rate detective he's got working for him."

Giles blushed with pleasure. "Private First Class Carbone—that's his name by the way, Joseph Carbone."

"What's the wife's name?"

"Wanda. Anyway, Private Carbone was CQ that night."

"CQ?"

"It stands for Charge of Quarters and means that Private Carbone had to spend the night at the motor-pool barracks with the duty sergeant."

"So he was on the base all night?"

"Theoretically."

"Theoretically?" A. G. smiled. "A fellow could hide a multitude of sins behind a word like *theoretically,* couldn't he?"

"I suppose so," Giles admitted ruefully. "Army regulations require that both the duty sergeant and the CQ remain awake at all times, but the fact is that if the duty sergeant decided to take a little nap sometime during the night, a not-infrequent practice among those with overnight duty, Private Carbone could easily have slipped off the base for an hour or two, and no one would have been the wiser. Particularly," he added after a second's pause, "since the duty sergeant would never voluntarily admit that he had fallen asleep while on duty."

"What would happen to him if he did?"

"Depends on his commander. Anything from administrative punishment such as a letter of reprimand, which would kill his chances for promotion, to an actual court-martial, where he could be reduced in rank, fined, or even sent to the stockade."

"So assuming for the sake of argument that Wanda and the captain were having an affair, the possibility exists that the private, her husband, found out about it, decided to kill Fitzgerald, waited until he, Carbone, had overnight duty, waited until the duty sergeant fell asleep, left his post to commit the murder, and then slipped back to his post without anyone having noticed his absence."

"Theoretically."

"That wonderful word again. Of course other possibilities exist, but this particular one that we've just run through interests me for the moment." A. G. stubbed out his cigarette and looked at his watch. "Is Private Carbone at work at the motor pool this morning?"

Giles nodded. "He is."

A. G. stood up. "I think we, you and I, should pay a surprise visit on Wanda before her husband gets home for lunch, or whatever."

Mildred was just coming into the office as A. G. and Giles were leaving.

"I'm going to be out for a couple of hours," A. G. told her. "The lieutenant and I are going over to Petersburg." He looked at his watch. "I doubt I'll get back before lunch."

Unimpressed, Mildred nodded an acknowledgment. "I've been down in the records office," she explained, holding up a large manila envelope. "I pulled the records you were interested in."

"I appreciate it. I hope it wasn't too much trouble."

Mildred looked at him as if to say *so what if it was?* "I'll keep them in my desk until you get back," she said.

The Carbones lived in a mean and depressing part of Petersburg, a neighborhood of mostly low-slung, wood-framed shotgun houses that looked about as down on their luck as the unfortunate souls who occupied them. Garbage was strewn about the street, and more than a few of the automobiles parked at the curb looked like losers in a recent demolition derby. Joseph and Wanda lived in a small development of four scabrous-looking triplexes arranged in a square, reminding A. G. of a low-security prison complex. Although the place looked deserted, he could feel numerous eyes staring balefully at him from behind blinds and partially closed doors as he and Giles walked up the sidewalk from the street to the complex.

"I almost wish I wasn't wearing this uniform," Giles said nervously, feeling the tension all around them.

"You and I would stand out in this neighborhood like sore thumbs no matter *what* we were wearing," A. G. assured him as they walked up onto the low stoop of the Carbones' apartment.

"Yes?" A young woman looked suspiciously through the screen door. Although it was hard to see her face clearly through the dark screen, A. G. estimated that she couldn't have been more than nineteen or twenty years old. Her suspicion turned to concern when she saw Lieutenant Giles standing behind A. G. on the front stoop. "Is something wrong?"

"No, ma'am," A. G. said hurriedly, "absolutely nothing is

wrong. I'm Sheriff A. G. Farrell of Hopewell, and this is Lieutenant Giles from Fort Lee. Are you Wanda Carbone?"

Wanda nodded silently, her concern obviously not the least ameliorated by A. G.'s words.

"The lieutenant and I would like to chat with you for a few minutes. May we come in?" Without waiting for a reply, A. G. pulled the screen door open and started to step across the threshold. He stopped abruptly, causing Giles to almost walk into his back. "Ma'am, are you all right?"

Wanda instinctively put a hand to her face, trying unsuccessfully to hide her blackened right eye and badly bruised cheekbone. "Come in," she mumbled, turning her back on A. G. and Giles and retreating to the gloomy interior of the apartment. "Have a seat," she invited unenthusiastically, waving at a threadbare sofa propped up on one end by a cinder block.

The small apartment was hot and dank, the febrile air compounding the sense of hopelessness and despair one normally associates with the tropics. In spite of the heat, A. G. shivered involuntarily, a sense of foreboding causing the short hairs on the back of his neck to prickle and stand up. The only furniture in the room other than the sadly dilapidated sofa was a battered coffee table scarred with numerous blackened cigarette burns and a fabric-covered, overstuffed easy chair with a rip in one armrest. From the adjoining apartment a radio could be heard playing through the paper-thin walls. *Peggy Lee,* A. G. guessed. *Or Rosemary Clooney.*

Instead of sitting in the easy chair, Wanda dragged a metal folding chair from the kitchen. "I guess you already know about me and Marty," she said simply as she sat down, assuming that A. G. and Giles were there for little more than confirmation. Pretty in an unformed, juvenile sort of way, Wanda sported a peroxide-blond hairdo cut in a pageboy fashion currently featured in all the Hollywood fan magazines. "I guess that's why you're here."

"We do, Wanda, but why don't you go ahead and tell us everything anyway," A. G. replied gently, putting a finger to his lips when she turned her head for a second, signaling Giles not to interrupt or say anything. Wanda put her battered face into her hands and began to weep quietly. A. G. reached out from the sofa and patted her arm. "We'd like to help you if you'll let us," he assured her. "Sometimes the best way to start is to just talk things out." He paused for a second. "When did you and Captain Fitzgerald begin having an, um, affair?"

"A couple of months ago." Wanda looked up from her hands, her cheeks wet and glistening in the low light. "We loved each other. He promised to take me away from . . ." She began crying again, unable to finish the sentence.

"Away from your husband?" A. G. prompted.

Wanda nodded but did not speak.

"You knew that Captain Fitzgerald was married?"

"He didn't love her," Wanda hissed, looking angrily from A. G. to Giles. "He was going to leave her." Wanda's anger dissolved once more into tears. "For me," she added, more to reassure herself than her visitors.

"Did Mrs. Fitzgerald know about you and her husband?"

"No," Wanda said, shaking her head emphatically. "Marty said she never had no idea about us."

"Did your husband know about you and Captain Fitzgerald?" A. G. offered her his handkerchief. "Is that why he beat you?"

Wanda started to shake her head. "No," she said, taking his handkerchief with a hesitant smile. "I mean, yes, but not until . . ." She started crying again.

"He found out after the captain was killed?"

"Someone at the motor pool told him." Wanda looked up

at A. G. "The night Marty was killed. Joey had the duty that night, but when he came home Sunday morning, he said someone had told him. Then he . . ." Wanda shrugged.

"Then he beat you up," A. G. said softly.

Wanda nodded. "I couldn't go back to work looking like this," she said, waving a hand at her face, "so I called in sick." She looked from A. G. to Lieutenant Giles, sadness apparently all but overwhelming her. "I guess on top of everything else they'll fire me out at the fort now, huh? I mean," she hiccuped suddenly, obviously close to becoming hysterical, "why wouldn't they?"

"No," A. G. assured her soothingly, patting her hand, "you're not going to be fired. As soon as you feel like going back to work, your job will be waiting for you. The lieutenant here," he nodded toward Giles, "will see to that. Now, Wanda, did Joey say who told him about you and Captain Fitzgerald?"

"No, just that someone told him. I guess somebody at the motor pool must have seen us in Marty's car or something."

"Wanda," A. G. leaned forward and patted her reassuringly on the arm once again, "I'm going to have to ask you a difficult question: Do you think it's possible that your husband, Joey, might have killed Captain Fitzgerald?"

"What the hell's going on here?"

Before Wanda could respond to A. G.'s question, the screen door slammed open and a large, beefy man in army fatigues burst into the room. The white name tag sewn over the right breast pocket of his fatigue shirt read CARBONE. Wanda closed her eyes and shrank in fear, turtling her head between her narrow shoulders, and for the first time in longer than he could remember, A. G. thought about the pistol he never carried. Joey Carbone took a quick step toward them and grabbed Wanda's arm in a rough grasp.

"I asked you a question, goddamn it," he snarled, jerking her to her feet. "Who the hell are these men?"

"At ease, soldier," Lieutenant Giles said, rising to his feet from the rickety sofa. He nodded toward Wanda, cowering in what was obviously a painful grip. "Let go of her."

"I'm damned if I will," Carbone said, his voice grating and his face flushed bright red. "This is my wife and my home," he took a threatening step toward Giles, "and just who the fuck are you?"

"Wait now," A. G. rose and held both hands open in front of himself in an obviously pacifistic gesture of goodwill, "wait now. This is Lieutenant Giles, a military policeman from Fort Lee, and . . ."

Carbone turned to A. G., malevolence twisting his face. "Who are you?"

A. G. smiled and forced himself to speak slowly and calmly. "I'm A. G. Farrell, sheriff over in Hopewell. I take it you're Private Carbone? Joseph Carbone?" When the man didn't immediately answer, A. G. continued speaking in a placating tone of voice. "The lieutenant and I were just having a little chat with your wife about the recent death of Captain Fitzgerald."

Carbone laughed, a short bark more in anger than humor. "I hope that bastard is rotting in hell," he informed them derisively, "and this lying bitch," he rattled Wanda back and forth in his huge hand, "is just lucky I didn't send her to join him."

"Private Carbone, I know why you're upset," A. G. edged closer to Joey and Wanda, "believe me, I do, but hurting her," he nodded at Wanda, "will only make matters worse. A lot worse. Now, please," A. G. put both hands up again, palms turned toward Carbone, "let her go."

Carbone looked at A. G. for several seconds, obviously considering his words, and finally, with a grunt of frustration, flung her toward the sofa. He stood silently for several more seconds, breathing heavily and staring at the floor, and then looked at A. G. "I'm not going to hurt her," he said almost quietly. "Now, get out of here," he jerked a thumb toward the front door, "both of you, and leave us alone."

A. G. grabbed Giles's arm and steered him quickly through the screen door and out to the street.

"Aren't you going to arrest him?" Giles asked as soon as they were in A. G.'s car.

"For what, murdering Captain Fitzgerald?"

"Don't you think he did it?"

A. G. shrugged, his mind busy cataloging all he had heard and seen. "I don't know yet."

"How about for beating up his wife?"

A. G. shook his head. "In the first place, this is Petersburg, not Hopewell. I'm frankly not so sure that Tug Benson, the chief of police here in Petersburg, would be any too happy to hear that I was running around arresting folks in his city. Furthermore, I doubt seriously that Jim Malone, the local district attorney, would even consider indicting Carbone for assault and battery based on the facts as we presently know them."

"What facts are you talking about?"

"Primarily the fact that Carbone caught his wife almost, I believe the proper Latin expression is, in flagrante delicto. Most law-enforcement folks wouldn't consider what Carbone did to be an actionable matter. I know, I know," A. G. raised a hand to forestall Giles's protest, "I didn't say it was right, or that I agreed with it, but that's the way things are." A. G. looked over at Giles. "In any event, I don't think he's going to hurt her any more."

"Why not?"

"My initial impression is that, believe it or not, he still loves her."

"He's got a hell of way of showing it," Giles muttered.

"I could be wrong," A. G. admitted, perfectly willing to

assume that he knew less about love than most men, "but, in any event, by us getting out of there as quickly as we did, we give him a chance to calm down and get over the shock of walking in and finding us talking to her."

"What do you think we should do?"

"I'm afraid it's time to get Major Williams involved. We need to sweat Private Carbone a little bit, find out exactly how he heard about Fitzgerald and his wife, when he heard it, things like that. Things he's not likely to tell us voluntarily, at least not right away." A. G. paused for a second before continuing. "Carbone's an imposing and difficult man in his own castle, if you get my point, but I'm thinking that perhaps with your Sergeant Dickey looking on while Major Williams asks questions, well, we may see a more cooperative side of him. Oh, and while I'm thinking about it, we'll want to get that duty sergeant in for questioning, find out whether or not he took himself a little nap when he was supposed to be minding the store." He smiled and again looked over at Lieutenant Giles. "Carbone strikes me as a hot-blooded young man. If he killed Fitzgerald, I doubt he'll be able to keep it to himself for very long."

If Major Williams was pleased at the initiative shown by Lieutenant Giles in tracing Captain Fitzgerald's last telephone call and thereby bringing to light the illicit relationship with Wanda Carbone, he managed quite handily to conceal it. After hearing of the interrupted visit to Petersburg, he immediately sent Sergeant Dickey and two military policemen to the motor pool to bring Carbone in for questioning.

"If he hasn't returned yet, wait there until he does," Williams ordered.

"I would exercise caution in approaching Private Carbone," A. G. advised Dickey. "He was extremely agitated when we left him a short time ago." A. G. looked from Dickey to Major Williams. "I also would make it clear to him that he's not being arrested, just brought in for questioning."

Unimpressed with A. G.'s counsel, neither Williams nor Dickey bothered to respond.

"Unfortunately, we've completely lost the critical element of surprise in our interrogation of Private Carbone," Williams complained in a lecturing tone after Dickey left. He pointed at Giles. "Because of your failure to advise me of . . ."

"Actually, Major, it's my fault that the lieutenant and I went out to interview Mrs. Carbone without telling you," A. G. interrupted, trying to deflect Williams's anger from Giles to himself. "Keep in mind that, although we might have suspected it, we did not know for a fact that she and Captain Fitzgerald had been having an affair. I felt it important to question her as soon as possible and to do so in such a way as to preclude arousing any suspicion on the part of her husband. Obviously we had no way of knowing ahead of time that, first, she would confess to the affair almost before we were in the door and, second, her husband would show up when he did."

"Had I known," Williams continued, looking at Giles as if A. G. had said nothing, "we could have, no, strike that, we *would* have coordinated the interrogations—while the sheriff here called on Carbone's wife in Petersburg, we would have brought Private Carbone in here for questioning and caught him completely off guard."

"And what would you have done had it turned out that Captain Fitzgerald's telephone call had been completely innocent, that he and Mrs. Carbone in fact had not been lovers?" A. G.'s rising tone of voice reflected his growing annoyance at Williams's bullying manner.

"What do you mean?"

"I mean that you would have gained nothing and, worse,

would have planted an unfounded suspicion in Private Carbone's mind regarding his wife and Captain Fitzgerald. Additionally, I was greatly influenced by my concern for Captain Fitzgerald's widow. If I had questioned Mrs. Carbone 'officially,' either at my office in Hopewell or here at Fort Lee, rumors would have inevitably spread regarding her and the captain, rumors that, if unfounded, would have needlessly hurt Mrs. Fitzgerald. Not to mention," A. G. added, almost as an afterthought, "the captain's posthumous reputation."

Williams slammed a fist down on his massive desk in frustration, causing Giles to flinch involuntarily. "I am more concerned about finding Captain Fitzgerald's murderer than I am with the hurt feelings of a private in the motor pool. In fact, Carbone's wife was having an affair with Fitzgerald and Carbone himself admitted to his wife that someone here on Fort Lee had wised him up about it. We now have a situation where Carbone knows he's a suspect, and he's had more than ample time not only to prepare himself mentally for questioning but also to take care of any incriminating evidence he may not have disposed of heretofore. And Captain Fitzgerald's reputation, obviously already a casualty of his own infidelity," Williams waved a hand in dismissal and leaned back in his chair, "is therefore no longer my concern."

A. G. started to respond but managed, knowing there would be little to be gained in losing his temper, to restrain himself. "If Private Carbone killed Captain Fitzgerald, I don't think we'll have all that much difficulty putting a case together," he said. "I doubt he has a great deal of experience in such matters, certainly not as much," A. G. smiled without humor, "as you and I."

Sergeant Dickey reported back with a split lip and an eye already turning black and purple.

"Good God, Sergeant," Williams exclaimed. "What happened to you?"

"Sir, the prisoner resisted arrest," he said tightly, one hand twitching slightly as he stood at attention in Williams's office.

"Prisoner?" A. G. asked. "I thought we agreed that Private Carbone was only being brought in for questioning at this time."

Dickey ignored A. G.'s comment. "Sir," he continued stiffly, directing both his report and gaze at Major Williams, "when I arrived at the motor pool Private Carbone appeared to be cleaning out his locker in preparation for going absent without leave."

"What?" A. G.'s tone of voice conveyed his incredulity. "That makes no sense at all. Why would Carbone return to the motor pool if he were planning to flee?"

"Because of this," Dickey snarled, finally looking at A. G. He laid an object wrapped in a greasy rag on Williams's desk. Even through the folds of the rag the object's shape was distinctively obvious: an army .45-caliber automatic pistol.

Chapter Seven

"Where did you recover this weapon?" Major Williams asked, flipping the corners of the rag away from the pistol in an incongruously delicate, almost feminine manner.

"From Private Carbone's locker," Dickey replied with obvious satisfaction. "After placing him under arrest for assaulting a non-commissioned officer, I searched his locker at the motor pool." He cut his eyes toward A. G. and curled his lip. "Carbone had obviously returned to the motor pool to dispose of it." He looked back at Williams. "I already checked the serial number, and it's the one stolen from the small-arms firing range a month ago."

Williams nodded grimly. "Completely aside from the murder of Captain Fitzgerald, which is, of course," he smiled coldly at A. G., "a civilian matter, between assaulting Sergeant Dickey and the theft of government property," he nodded at the pistol on his desk, "Private Carbone has pretty much assured himself of ten years' hard labor at the Disciplinary Barracks at Fort Leavenworth, Kansas, and a dishonorable discharge." He swung his gaze to Dickey and abruptly stood up. "Where is Private Carbone now?"

"In the interrogation room."

Carbone sat manacled to a wooden chair, his head and shoulders slumped toward his knees. Blood dripped slowly to the floor from an ugly gash on his forehead, just above his right eyebrow.

"This man needs to see a doctor," A. G. said angrily, gesturing toward Carbone.

Carbone looked up, his eyes sweeping from Williams to Giles to A. G. "I'm okay," he said, surprising everyone with the strength of his voice.

"No, you're not," Williams responded crisply. "You've assaulted a noncommissioned officer, stolen government property, and, based on the evidence I've seen so far, in all likelihood you murdered Captain Fitzgerald." He pulled up a wooden chair and sat in front of Carbone. "In fact, I'd say you're as not okay as any soldier I've ever seen." He paused for a second and gestured toward A. G. and Giles. "You've already met Sheriff Farrell and Lieutenant Giles. I'm Major Williams, the provost marshall here at Fort Lee. We would like . . ."

"I didn't steal the .45, and I didn't kill Captain Fitzgerald," Carbone interrupted. "As far as your sergeant is concerned," he shrugged as best he could given the manacles that shackled him to the chair, "it was as much self-defense as anything else."

"If you didn't steal the pistol, how did it come to be in

your locker at the motor pool?" Williams asked.

"Somebody put it there."

" 'Somebody put it there, *sir,*' " Williams said sharply.

"Somebody put it there, sir," Carbone repeated in a careful monotone.

"Who?"

"I don't know. I discovered it the Monday morning after Captain Fitzgerald was killed. Just sitting on the top shelf of my locker."

"And yet you told no one." Williams snorted in disbelief. "I think we can safely assume your fingerprints are all over the weapon."

"Yes, sir, they probably are," Carbone replied heatedly, "but that don't mean I used it to shoot anyone."

"Why don't you drop this foolish charade and tell us the truth," Williams said, his voice rising. "How did you lure Captain Fitzgerald out to Hopewell?"

"Private Carbone," A. G. interjected in a calm voice before Carbone could respond in kind to Williams's angry tone, "your wife told us that someone at the motor pool told you about her affair with Captain Fitzgerald. Who was it?"

Carbone shook his head. "I don't know. I got a telephone call at the motor pool the Saturday afternoon the captain was killed. I was CQ all day, 'til Sunday morning. The guy who called never said who he was."

"What *did* he say?"

Carbone laughed, a sound completely devoid of humor, and looked down at the floor. "Said Captain Fitzgerald was fucking my old lady," he murmured, the words coming slowly and with obvious effort. He looked back up at A. G. "Said I could catch them together that very night."

"Did you?" A. G. asked gently.

"I already told you—I was CQ until Sunday morning. I

couldn't have went anywhere if I wanted to. Sergeant Mc-Bride, the weekend duty sergeant, was with me the whole time."

"What were you going to do with the pistol in your locker?" A. G. continued, intentionally maintaining a calm, quiet voice.

"After I came home and found you and the lieutenant talking to Wanda, I thought I'd better get rid of it PDQ. I knew it must have been stolen, and by then I'd guessed that maybe it was the one killed the captain. Even with Sergeant McBride to alibi me, I figured if I got caught with the gun, it would look pretty bad, what with the phone call and Wanda and all." Carbone looked from A. G. to Williams and then back to A. G. "I might have wanted Captain Fitzgerald hurt bad for . . ." he paused momentarily, his gaze returning to a spot on the floor, ". . . for being with Wanda, and maybe even I wanted him dead, but," he looked back up, "I didn't do it."

"Sounds like an open-and-shut case," Mildred opined, handing A. G. a Pall Mall and a box of matches. "Jealous husband, cheating wife, murder weapon found in husband's possession—just like the movies." She leaned forward to allow A. G. to light her cigarette. "But you don't think so."

A. G. slowly shook his head. "Not even a little bit," he said, perhaps somewhat more emphatically than he meant to. "Oh, I guess it's possible, but it just doesn't feel right to me. Unfortunately, the volatile young Private Carbone has so turned Major Williams's head that the major's taken the bait hook, line, and sinker."

"The bait?"

A. G. nodded. "It looks to me as if someone has dangled Private Carbone in front of our eyes like a fat worm in front of a hungry catfish. If that's the case, then the real question isn't whether Carbone killed Fitzgerald but who wants us to think so."

"I take it then you're not planning to arrest Carbone in the immediate future."

A. G. shook his head. "Fortunately, I don't have to. Major Williams has him incarcerated in the post stockade for the time being on the assault and stolen-weapon charges. That should give me all the time I need to dig a little deeper into this mess."

"You'll recall that you asked about Julie Brown's reputation," Mildred said, deftly changing the subject while crossing her arms and leaning back in her chair.

A. G. nodded and sat on the corner of her desk without saying anything.

"Apparently she was developing quite a reputation for someone so young. Word is that she was running around with a couple of soldiers from out at the fort, drinking, carousing, that sort of thing. Folks were starting to talk."

"Interesting," A. G. murmured, recalling Jubal Bishop's story of how she had showed up at his roadhouse with a soldier, both of them drunk. Jubal had gone further, though, passing along the rumor that she had been pregnant when she died, a rumor Mildred had obviously not yet heard.

"Now," she uncrossed her arms and leaned forward, "*why* were you asking?"

"To tell you the truth, I'm not exactly sure. I had heard something similar from someone else, and I guess I just wanted to know whether it was true."

"I'd say it probably was." She opened a desk drawer and took out the manila envelope she had shown A. G. that morning. "You going to look at these now?"

A. G. looked at his watch and was somewhat surprised to see that it was already a quarter past two. "No, hold onto them a little longer. I think I might get a bite of lunch first."

"You want me to get you a sandwich across the street?"

"Thanks, but I'll get something myself in a minute. I want to make a quick phone call first."

A. G. walked into his office and turned on the overhead fan. He sat at his desk, running Carbone's description of the telephone call he had received at the motor pool back through his mind. *"Said Captain Fitzgerald was fucking my old lady." Harsh and unhappy words for any man to have to hear,* A. G. thought, wondering if he had been too hasty in dismissing Carbone as a suspect. He picked up the telephone and dialed Lieutenant Giles's number. "Yes, Lieutenant, this is A. G. Farrell," he said when Giles answered. "Listen, I wondered if you and Major Williams have had a chance yet to talk to that motor-pool sergeant, the one Private Carbone thinks will provide him with an alibi?"

"We have and he didn't," Giles responded.

"He didn't alibi Carbone for all of Saturday night?" A. G. asked, surprise evident in his voice.

"At first he did, but under close questioning by Major Williams he admitted that he had slept a good deal of the time he was supposed to be awake and on duty."

"I don't understand," A. G. said. "If he can be court-martialed for sleeping on duty, and no one actually caught him doing it, why would he admit such a thing to Major Williams?"

"I think," Giles responded, his voice lowered, "we should discuss this at another time."

"You're right," A. G. said immediately, understanding Giles's reluctance to speak when someone, whether Major Williams or Sergeant Dickey, might be listening. He thought for a second. "You know, we've been so busy today, first driving over to Petersburg to talk to Wanda and then with Private Carbone's interrogation, I haven't had any lunch yet." He paused a beat. "Have you?" When Giles responded in the negative, A. G. nodded his head as if the young man were sitting just across the desk from him. "Tell you what, why don't you drive over here? We'll get a quick bite to eat and chat a little bit in private."

A. G. hung up the telephone and sat quietly for several seconds, tapping his right index finger against one of his front teeth. "Mildred," he called out, standing suddenly, "do me a favor?" He walked out to her desk. "Find out where Doug Troutman bought that new television, the one he got to lure Angie back from Norfolk, would you?"

Mildred looked up suspiciously. "What do you want to know for?"

"I'm thinking about buying one for myself," A. G. replied casually. "But, look here, don't be telling anyone, especially Doug, that it was me asking."

"If you're thinking about buying one, why don't you want anyone to know?" Before A. G. could respond, Mildred sniffed and said, "I already know where he bought it: Spellman's Furniture and Appliance, in Richmond."

"Thank you," A. G. said, smiling sweetly. He walked back to his office and, after carefully closing his door, picked up the telephone and dialed a number. "Spencer, it's me, A. G. Listen, I need another favor, a small one this time." He listened, again nodding politely, as if they were in the same room, as Spencer explained that he could not possibly spare the time to do his friend any more favors. "I know, I know, but this won't take a minute. I want you to have one of your investigators go by Spellman's Furniture there in Richmond. Doug Troutman, yeah, you know him, the pharmacist here in Hopewell, just bought one of those new televisions there, and I want to know if he paid in cash, or financed it, or what." A. G. listened for several seconds. "Yes, I know how busy you are, but it couldn't possibly take more than a minute or two. Someone from your office probably goes by there at least two or three times a day. Whoever you send could do it on the way to lunch. All he has to do is go in, ask for the manager, show his badge, and boom," A. G. snapped his fingers, "it's done. The manager at Spellman's doesn't have to know why or anything like that. Just one simple question: How did Troutman pay for the television? Thanks, Spencer," A. G. cut the conversation short before his friend could object further, "I appreciate it. Oh, and listen, let's have lunch tomorrow— I want to discuss a new development in the Fitzgerald murder with you."

"Now tell me why this motor-pool sergeant . . ."

"Sergeant McBride," Giles interrupted.

". . . why he would have put his neck in a noose by admitting to sleeping on duty when nobody caught him at it?" A. G. took a sip of iced tea. He and Giles were seated in a booth at the Little Acorn café, behind Hopewell's city hall. "I mean, does that sound like a reasonable thing for a man to do? Voluntarily?"

"Believe me, McBride's so-called confession wasn't voluntary, at least not in the sense one normally attaches to that word." Giles shook his head, his facial expression an unlikely blend of both disapproval and grudging admiration. "Having seen him in action, I have to say that I have no doubt Major Williams could get a confession out of a stone. First, he had McBride brought in, without telling him what for, and then left him to stew on his own for over an hour in the interrogation room before we interviewed him. Then he started things off by telling McBride, who was sweating bullets by then, that Captain Fitzgerald's murder was a direct result of his, Sergeant McBride's, dereliction of duty. Of course, Sergeant McBride had no idea what Williams was talking about and very timidly said so. Williams started yelling at McBride, almost screaming at him, telling him that Private Carbone had all but confessed to having murdered Captain Fitzgerald and that McBride was looking at twenty years' hard labor at Leavenworth and a dishonorable discharge." Giles paused and, smiling sardonically, shook his head again. "For the life of him, poor Sergeant McBride simply could not understand why he was going to go to jail for a murder to which someone else had already confessed."

"I'm beginning to get the picture," A. G. said. "He scared the bejesus out of this sergeant and then told him that if he didn't admit to being asleep for long enough to allow Carbone to slip off the base, commit the murder, and return, he, the sergeant, would be charged as some sort of accomplice. Is that about right?"

"Exactly. The carrot at the end of the stick was that if he did admit to sleeping on duty, he would be reprimanded but not court-martialed. McBride's been in the army for fourteen years, is married, and has, believe it or not, six children under the age of ten. And an IQ, I would estimate, little above that of a moron. It wasn't much of a contest." Giles played with his fork for a second. "Nonetheless, I don't doubt that McBride was sleeping at least part of the time he was supposed to be awake and on duty."

"I don't doubt it either," A. G. agreed. "I'm more than willing to believe Carbone had a perfect opportunity to leave the base, commit the murder, and return with his absence unnoticed. The problem I'm having is far more basic than that."

"Which is?"

"Which is," A. G. leaned back in his chair again, "I don't believe Private Carbone did it. He may have had the *opportunity* to do it, and he certainly had a *motive,* but," A. G. shrugged, "I don't believe he did it."

"What about the gun?"

"The gun looks bad, no question about it. And, as with

the issues of opportunity and motive, I'm perfectly willing to believe, at least for the time being, that the pistol found in his locker at the motor pool is in fact the murder weapon."

"You think it was planted?" Giles's tone of voice conveyed a definite sense of skepticism.

A. G. nodded. "I do. And whoever planted it couldn't have picked a better target, because Carbone had enough sense to put two and two together and conclude that someone was trying to frame him, but at the same time was too stupid to realize that he was playing right into their hands by continuing to hide the gun while he tried to figure out what to do with it." He smiled and inhaled dramatically. "That was quite a sentence, wasn't it?"

Before either of them could say anything else, their waitress arrived at the booth, her arms full of plates. She had emerald green eyes, strawberry blond hair tied back in a ponytail, and a sunny disposition.

A. G., noticing that she kept looking at Giles out of the corner of her eye as she put their food on the table, smiled. "Mary Frances," he said, "I'd like you to meet Lieutenant Barry Giles. Lieutenant Giles, this is Mary Frances O'Brien. Lorraine O'Brien, Mary Frances's mother," he continued, looking at Giles, "owns this fine establishment and cooked that fried chicken," he pointed at Giles's plate, "you're getting ready to eat."

"Hello," Giles stammered, obviously smitten by the young woman.

She nodded and smiled shyly. "Don't eat these," she said to Giles, picking up the small plate of biscuits she had just put down on the table. "I'll bring you some fresh ones out in a second. A new batch is just about to come out of the oven." She seemed to have forgotten that A. G. was sitting at the table. "Can I bring you anything else?" She brushed her bangs out of her eyes and pointed at Giles's coffee cup. "Some more coffee?"

"I'd like some more iced tea," A. G. teased, holding up his almost empty glass. "After you're done taking care of the lieutenant, that is."

Mary Frances barely looked at him. "I'll be back in just a minute," she assured Giles.

"I believe," A. G. said after she had disappeared into the kitchen, "that that young woman is attracted to you."

Giles whistled a single, low note and then blushed deeply, staring intently at his fried chicken as if afraid it might start clucking and walk off the plate.

"Her daddy survived the war in Europe only to get himself killed six or seven years later in Korea," A. G. continued. "She's hardworking and smart as a whip. If she and her momma'd had any money to speak of, she'd have gone to college and be living in Washington or New York this very minute."

"I'm surprised she's not married," Giles said, trying, and failing, to affect a casual attitude.

A. G. shook his head. "Young men with any sense leave this county as quickly as ever they can, one or two to college, the rest to the service, and they almost never come back. The only ones left are too dull-witted to attract an intelligent and," he smiled, "good-looking young woman like Mary Frances."

"Present company excluded," Giles said, a sudden smile on his face.

"I'm not so sure about that," A. G. responded lightly, pleased with Giles's quick wit. *Not so sure at all,* he thought but did not add. *Why* have *I stayed here when so many others have left?* "Although I *can* tell you with some conviction that were I ten or so years younger I'd be camping on Mary Frances's doorstep." He pointed his fork at Giles. "Unless you are otherwise not available, I would advise you to consider doing the same."

Giles, embarrassed, concentrated on his fried chicken and mashed potatoes for several minutes. "Sometimes," he said, carefully changing the subject back to the unsolved murder of Captain Fitzgerald, "things are no more than they seem to be. It could be that everything, all the evidence, points to Private Carbone because in fact he *is* guilty."

"I wouldn't necessarily dismiss such thinking out of hand," A. G. assured the younger man, "at least not yet I wouldn't. But I *do* believe we should, at least for the time being, continue our investigation, if for no other reason than to rule out any other possibility."

"What more would you like to do?"

"Well, for starters, I still want to question everyone Captain Fitzgerald worked with at the Quartermaster School, especially now that we know he was having an affair with Carbone's wife. I'd like to know who else knew about the affair and how they found out. Did the captain like to brag about his exploits? Had he had other such affairs with married women? Who, exactly, called Carbone that afternoon at the motor pool? Just an anonymous friend?" A. G. shook his head. "I doubt it. And why that particular afternoon, when the caller obviously knew Carbone was on duty?" He tapped his fork on the table several times, collecting his thoughts. "Were you aware of the fact that Captain Fitzgerald was a big-time poker player, that he played in a weekly high-stakes game over in Richmond, and apparently won more than he lost?"

Giles, impressed, whistled again and shook his head. "I had no idea." He looked at A. G. with admiration. "That could mean a whole new theory of motive."

"Indeed it could," A. G. agreed, suppressing a smile at Giles's sudden enthusiasm. "So you see, even with all the evidence currently pointing to Private Carbone, we still have a little work yet to do before we deliver this case to the district attorney for prosecution."

"I wonder . . ."

"Let me interrupt you briefly before I forget this," A. G. interjected suddenly. "Now that her husband is in the stockade, I want to be sure we complete our interview with Wanda Carbone as soon as possible. In addition to asking her when exactly the affair started, and how, I want to know from her perspective who at Fort Lee might have known about the affair. Now," he smiled at Giles, "you were saying?"

"Well, with all this speculation about who knew what and when, I was just wondering if Mrs. Fitzgerald knew about her husband's affair with Carbone's wife? If she did," he paused for a second, looking at A. G., "it would mean that she, too, may have had a motive for killing him."

"Based on my limited observation of married friends and acquaintances, I would say that spouses seldom need a specific motive to consider murdering one another," A. G. teased. "Still, you're quite right in raising the point. Frankly, I'd be surprised if . . ." he almost said *Theresa*, ". . . if Mrs. Fitzgerald did know about the affair, but I intend to ask her when she returns from Arlington."

"I didn't even know she was gone." Giles shook his head ruefully. "Nobody ever tells me anything. When is she due back?"

"Tomorrow or the day after, as far as I know. The captain's body was sent up yesterday, and I believe she was planning on having him buried as quickly as possible."

"That doesn't give much time for the family to gather, does it?"

"From what I understand, Fitzgerald had no immediate family left, so Mrs. Fitzgerald was hoping to work the funeral into Arlington's burial schedule without delay."

Giles whistled. "Gives new meaning to the expression

here today, gone tomorrow," he said, mild disapproval evident in his tone of voice. "Has she said what she intends to do after everything is settled?"

That's something we haven't talked about yet, A. G. thought. "No," he replied, shaking his head, "I have no idea what her plans are, either right away or in the long run. Which reminds me, I was wondering, just idle curiosity, how long can she continue to stay in their quarters on the base?"

"Probably as long as she wants to, within reason." Giles shrugged. "I doubt there are any provisions in the army family-housing regulations dealing with the murder of a spouse. Certainly I don't see a problem with her staying there another month or two, until she gets the government-insurance money, settles her husband's estate, and like that."

"Did you save room for dessert?" Mary Frances asked, stopping at the booth to clear away dishes. "We've got fresh banana pudding and coconut cream pie." She looked at Giles and then, blushing, glanced down at the table. "I made the pie this morning."

Back at the office A. G. closed his door and began to sift through the death certificates Mildred had culled out of the county records. After first ensuring that they were in chronological order by year of death, beginning in January 1949, he started reviewing each in turn. Twenty minutes later he had a list consisting of only three names:

Susan Anderson
Born: March 6, 1932—died: April 23, 1950
Race: Negro
Cause of death: Septicemia

Cissie Jackson
Born: August 5, 1934—died: January 29, 1952

Race: Negro
Cause of death: Septicemia

Julie Brown
Born: May 5, 1939—died: July 15, 1954
Race: Caucasian
Cause of death: Heart failure, secondary to septicemia

He leaned back in his chair and lit a Chesterfield. *Have we missed something here?* he wondered. *Do these septicemia deaths fall within some sort of statistically acceptable range, medically speaking?* He quickly ran through all the death certificates a second time. Of all the deaths in the county in the five-year period from 1949 to 1954, and there weren't that many to begin with, only three were listed as due to septicemia. *And why are all three of them teenaged girls?* A knock on his office door startled him out of his reverie. He turned over the piece of notepaper on which he had written the three names.

"Yes?"

Mildred opened the door and put her head into the office. "I'm getting ready to take off for the day. You need anything before I leave?"

A. G. shook his head. "No, thanks." He looked at his watch. "I'm almost ready to leave myself." As soon as she left he picked up the telephone and dialed a number in Petersburg.

Dr. Paul Graham had soft, brown eyes and a boyish thatch of unruly hair hanging over his forehead. He, A. G., and Spencer Lee had been fraternity brothers and roommates as undergraduates at the University of Virginia. An internist with a growing reputation, he split his practice between offices in

Petersburg and Richmond, and served as an adjunct professor at the Medical College of Virginia.

"Good Lord," A. G. teased as he walked into Paul's Petersburg office, "I can't believe I got in to see you on such short notice."

Paul grinned sheepishly. "You almost didn't. And, as I mentioned to you over the telephone, I'm going to have to leave for a consultation in Richmond in," he paused for a second to look at his watch, "ten minutes. Until then, however," he spread his arms, "I'm all yours."

"I'll get right to the point then and save the social pleasantries until Spencer and I can kidnap you one evening for dinner." He put the death certificates of Susan Anderson, Cissie Jackson, and Julie Brown on Paul's desk. "Tell me what you think."

Paul looked at each for several seconds and then back at his friend. "A little odd I suppose, three teenaged girls all dying from what amounts to blood poisoning. Still," he looked back at the death certificates, "deaths are spread over, what, four years, so," he shrugged, "who knows? What are you looking for?"

"I don't know," A. G. said honestly. "For one thing, I hadn't realized that people, particularly young people, still died from septicemia."

"All the time. Unfortunately, a lot of people, thanks mainly to inaccurate newspaper articles, have come to think that the newer antibiotics just now coming on the market are capable of curing anything, but that's not the case. People have always died of septicemia and will continue to do so, as far as I can predict, well into the indefinite future."

"What could cause it, particularly in teenaged girls?"

"Lots of things," Paul said, shrugging again. He looked carefully at A. G. for several seconds, not speaking. "Are you thinking what I think you're thinking?"

148

A. G. nodded but said nothing.

Paul sucked in his breath and shook his head. "You think you've got an amateur abortionist at work in Hopewell?"

A. G. pointed at Julie Brown's certificate. "I was told, on the QT, that this girl, fifteen years old, was pregnant at the time of her death."

"Her parents told you that?"

"No, a business associate of her daddy's. He wasn't sure that either parent knew about it."

"How would he have known?"

"It's a small county, Paul, you know that. I also learned that she was running around with soldiers out at the fort, drinking, that sort of thing. It's an easy enough rumor to believe."

"I take it she's been buried?"

A. G. nodded. "I went to the funeral. Would an autopsy show whether or not she had had an abortion, and, if so, whether it was the cause of the septicemia that killed her?"

"Probably, but you'd have to do it right away. In this heat, even underground, the body is going to decompose rather quickly." He paused for a second. "Are the parents going to consent to disinterment and an autopsy?"

"I doubt it. My guess is that I'll have to get a court order, and to do that I'm going to have to convince a judge that I'm not just chasing a will-o'-the-wisp. The main reason I wanted to come over here and talk to you this afternoon was to see if you thought these three death certificates, by themselves, form a solid-enough basis for me to proceed."

"That's a tough call, A. G. Epidemiologically speaking, these," he held up the three death certificates, "probably aren't going to be good enough just by themselves. What does Dr. Maple say? He signed all three certificates."

A. G. grimaced. "He essentially told me that he saw nothing suspicious about Julie Brown's death, even though without an autopsy he admitted he had no way of knowing what caused the septicemia. I haven't asked him about the other two girls yet, but I doubt he'll even remember them." A. G. leaned forward in his chair to emphasize his point. "Paul, you know as well as I do that old Doc Maple is incompetent."

"I wouldn't argue with that, but it seems to me nonetheless that you've got an almost insurmountable handicap if he testifies that he sees absolutely no reason to do an autopsy on the Brown girl." Paul thought for a second. "Will you have any credible testimony, anything at all, about the alleged pregnancy?"

"No."

Paul shook his head. "With the combination of Dr. Maple's presumed testimony and the opposition of the parents, and with only the rumor of a pregnancy on your side, I doubt any judge in the state would order an autopsy." He pushed the certificates back across the desk toward A. G. "Sorry."

"Pretty colors this evening," A. G. murmured, sitting alone on Dolores's small, screened-in back porch, his stocking feet stretched out in front of him. He lit a Chesterfield, savoring the bite of the tobacco on his tongue as he watched the smoke drift lazily up from the tip of the cigarette. The morning's storm had long since passed through, leaving the air clean and, despite the lingering humidity, feeling fresher than it had for some time. The rain had washed the accumulated dust of several weeks off the magnolia and rhododendron bushes around town and had even managed to make the gravel roads seem a little brighter. A. G. rocked quietly and smoked his cigarette, watching the shadows lengthen until they seemed to blend earth and sky into a seamless continuum. Dusk was his favorite time of day, summer evenings in particular, when the fading light lingered with an almost feminine sadness.

"A penny for your thoughts," Dolores said as she stepped out onto the porch, a dishtowel thrown over one shoulder. She handed him a fresh glass of iced tea.

"They're hardly worth even a penny," A. G. joked, taking a sip of the tea. "I was just enjoying the colors of the setting sun."

Dolores sat on the small wicker sofa that had, as was the case with just about all of her furniture, belonged to her parents. "Did you get enough to eat?"

"Lord, yes," A. G. assured her, patting his stomach for emphasis. "I couldn't eat another mouthful if I wanted to."

An awkward silence ensued, one A. G. felt disinclined to break. He knew she had something on her mind, had known it all through supper, but he also knew intuitively that what she had on her mind was their relationship, a subject he intensely wished not to talk about.

"Come join me," she finally said, patting the sofa cushion next to her.

He put out his cigarette and stood up, adjusting and straightening his trousers before stepping across the small porch to where Dolores sat. "It doesn't sound like this old sofa wants to hold both of us," he teased as the wicker creaked and groaned when he sat down. "We might end up on the floor."

"I missed you last night," Dolores said softly after he had settled down. "I called you around nine o'clock, and you weren't in."

"I was with Lieutenant Giles over in Petersburg," A. G. said, the lie tumbling easily from his mouth, shaming him all the more for the casual glibness with which it was said even as he spoke the words. "Until late. We were following up on the Fitzgerald investigation." In a rush he told her about Wanda Carbone and the interrogation of her husband, Joseph, implying that they, he and Giles, had initially confronted the Carbones at their apartment late the night before.

"It must have been frightening," Dolores said, her voice rising barely above a whisper, "having to deal with people like that. And I can't imagine what Mrs. Fitzgerald must have thought when she learned that her husband may have been murdered as a result of an affair he had been having."

"She doesn't know anything about it yet," A. G. said, shaking his head. "She's out of town, attending to the captain's funeral at Arlington National Cemetery."

"When did she go out of town?"

The question, innocent enough on its face, hung for a brief instant like an accusation in the humid evening air.

"I believe Giles told me she left yesterday," A. G. said, thankful that the growing darkness on the porch effectively hid his face. He took his handkerchief out of his pocket and wiped it across his brow, aware that his sudden perspiration had more to do with the lies he was telling than the summer heat. *Why can't I just tell her the truth?* he wondered. *Is what Theresa and I have done so wrong?* "I'm not sure when she's coming back."

Again they sat quietly for a time, each acutely aware of the other. Finally Dolores reached out and brought one of A. G.'s hands to her face, holding it briefly against one cheek.

"You haven't kissed me since I got back from Raleigh," she said, trying for and not quite achieving a lighthearted tone of voice.

"I did too," A. G. said with mock indignation. "I distinctly remember kissing you good night the other evening," he added, trying to make a joke of it and succeeding no better than she had.

She leaned toward him, guided in the dark by his sweet

breath, until their lips were barely touching. Holding her breath and shocked at her own boldness, she steadied herself by putting one hand on his thigh, the other on his left biceps. A. G. felt her lips open and, surprisingly, the tip of her tongue searching tentatively for his. Despite his misgivings he responded and felt a sudden heat rising between them. Unconsciously his hand reached out and caressed one of her breasts, causing a powerful shudder to move through her body like a wave. Startled, he quickly pulled back.

"Dolores," he said huskily, "I . . ."

"No," she interrupted, "don't talk, don't say anything." She took his hand and guided it back to her breast, her breath ragged and hot on his face.

They kissed passionately for several long minutes, his hand alternately caressing and gently squeezing first one of her breasts, then the other, her nipples growing hard through her thin cotton shift. He unbuttoned the top three buttons of her blouse and clumsily unfastened her brassiere, freeing her breasts.

"If we go any further," Dolores whispered, her lips still brushing his, tears suddenly wetting her cheeks, "I won't be able . . ." She paused, her thoughts jumbled and overwhelmed by the passion of the moment, the heat rising between their bodies. "Tell me you love me."

"I love you," A. G. said raggedly, unable not to as he cupped one of her breasts in his right hand.

It was just past midnight when A. G. shifted his car into neutral, turned off the lights and the engine, and coasted gently to a stop in front of his house. He sat in the car for several minutes, listening to the engine ticking and creaking as it cooled and contracted. *Much like my heart,* he thought rather cynically as he opened the door and got out. On the porch he let Pearl out of the house and then walked over and sat heavily on the glider. Lighting a Chesterfield, he heard more than saw the cat walk slowly past him to the edge of the porch. "Good Lord," he said out loud, his voice heavy with fatigue and regret, "I'm thirty-four years old." He looked with sudden distaste at the cigarette he had just lit and flicked it angrily out into the yard, the glowing ember flaring briefly as it fell to earth. "Thirty-four years old and sitting out here in the dark trying to talk myself into feeling better about something I know is wrong."

Chapter Eight

"He paid for it with cash, well-worn, sweat-stained twenty-dollar bills to be precise."

Spencer Lee, trying to look annoyed but failing, sat down. He wore a tan linen suit, a white shirt with a silk regimental tie, and gleaming wing-tip oxford shoes. The collar of his shirt looked as if it had been starched and ironed not five minutes earlier.

"Furthermore, an exhaustive search of the annotated codes of the Commonwealth of Virginia leads me to the inescapable conclusion that in so doing, druggist Troutman committed no felony and broke no law. Have you ordered lunch yet?"

A. G. nodded. "For both of us." He shook his head in unabashed admiration. "Ninety-five degrees outside and you look like you just stepped out of a bandbox."

"Take my word for it," Spencer replied, settling himself comfortably in his chair, "no one likes to see a public servant perspire, particularly one with lofty political aspirations. It tends to make people think you've done something you shouldn't have. At the very least," he chuckled at his own *bon mot,* waving at an acquaintance at the far end of the restaurant, "it gives the appearance of a guilty conscience, a terrible thing for one seeking higher office. Mr. Truman's clever remark regarding heat and kitchens is as valid today as it was when he first uttered it," he couldn't resist adding as he picked up his fork and wiped it off with his napkin. "Did you listen to the All-Star game last night?"

A. G. shook his head. "No," he said with a slightly forced smile, only too aware that his own conscience would bear little scrutiny, "but I know who the managers were."

"Mildred must have told you," Spencer snorted, aware of his friend's unfathomable lack of interest in baseball. "Well, you missed a good game. All the pundits had predicted an easy National League victory but the American League surprised them." He pointed at the menu board posted above the bar. "Dare I ask what you ordered for us?"

"Special of the day: chicken and dumplings. Margaret," their waitress, "said it was going fast, so, being the man of action that I am, I struck while the iron was hot. And I appreciate your getting me the information on Troutman. 'Well-worn, sweat-stained twenty-dollar bills'?"

"Yeah, that was sort of interesting. The manager at Spellman's Furniture distinctly remembered that the twenties Troutman paid with looked more like they had come from the hands of a sharecropper than a pharmacist." Spencer shrugged. "Maybe he keeps his money in a sock under the bed and likes to count it all the time. And while perhaps simpleminded, such a practice has yet to be declared illegal." He pointed a finger at A. G. "Now comes the part where you tell me why you care so much about how Troutman paid for his new television."

"I don't know yet."

Spencer's look of annoyance was becoming more believable. "I hope you had me send an investigator to Spellman's Furniture for something more than the need to satisfy a vague sense of curiosity about the spending habits of one of your neighbors."

"It's more than that, but, to be honest, I don't know yet how much more. I'll fill you in after I've had a chance to think about it a little." A. G. held up a placating hand. "But I appreciate the information and, believe me, it's not just idle curiosity."

"Like I said, I hope not. Hell, it seems like everybody's buying television sets these days, though God alone knows why. I bought one for Carole and the kids last year, but the stuff they broadcast wouldn't entertain a parakeet. Anyway, you said you wanted to tell me something about the Fitzgerald case."

"I do, but first, have you spoken with anyone at the state attorney general's office about Fitzgerald? Oh," he added quickly, before Spencer could respond, "and also, you were going to try and identify the other players in the weekly high-stakes poker game."

"Yes, I spoke with a colleague at the attorney general's office and, no, I've not been able to come up with any names of fellow gamblers. The attorney general's office has no active file on Fitzgerald, but my friend promised to cross-check the name with their organized-gambling section and see if anything turned up. So far, I haven't heard back from him, but he wasn't real encouraging. It seems that they don't devote many resources to the enforcement of antigambling laws *per se*—they tend to get involved only when a pattern of citizen or police complaints develops around a specific operation or locale."

"I expect your office approaches it pretty much the same way," A. G. guessed.

Spencer nodded. "Given the finite operating resources of the DA's office, it's real easy to consider most forms of gambling to be essentially victimless crimes. And as far as coming up with the identities of Fitzgerald's regular playing partners," Spencer shrugged, "I'd say the odds of success are pretty slim. My investigator is still asking around, but he frankly doesn't expect to turn anything up."

They both paused as their waitress brought large bowls of chicken and dumplings, together with corn bread fresh from the oven and a side order of sliced tomatoes.

"I'm not surprised," A. G. responded after she left their table, "but I'd appreciate it if both he and your friend at the attorney general's office kept at it for a while longer." He paused for a second. "You'll be interested to know that Major Williams thinks he's got the murderer locked up in the Fort Lee stockade."

"What?" Spencer's fork stopped midway between his plate and his mouth.

A. G. chuckled, amused by his friend's almost theatrical reaction. He took several minutes to relate the recent developments and his evaluation of them. "I'm sure you'll agree," he concluded, "that a good deal of work remains to be done before we consign Private Carbone to the state penitentiary for the rest of his life."

"I'm not sure I would agree to any such thing. Listen, A. G., despite the fact that you're the sheriff and I'm only a lowly assistant district attorney, we both know that I've had a lot more experience in criminal matters than you have. A whole lot more. Hell, I've tried seven murder cases in the past three years alone. And, believe it or not, I've learned the hard way that evidence trumps intuition every time."

"I'm working on more than intuition," A. G. objected.

"No, you're not. Look, with Carbone, based on what you've just told me, you've got what we in the prosecution business modestly refer to as the Big Three: motive, opportunity, and murder weapon, all tied up in an unusually neat package. One of our summer clerks could get a conviction in this case for Christ's sake. Hell, I wouldn't even waste any office resources trying Carbone—his lawyer'll jump at the chance to plead him down to second degree, maybe even manslaughter, take twenty years, and he's out in seven or eight max."

"All of the evidence is circumstantial," A. G. pointed out.

Spencer laughed. "I wish I had a dollar for every man sitting in prison based solely on circumstantial evidence. Every *guilty* man." He shook his head at what he obviously perceived to be A. G.'s naïveté. "Hell, boy, how many convictions do you think I've gotten based on eyewitnesses?"

"What does that say about Fitzgerald? The decedent? Who's going to speak for him? If Carbone did kill him, shouldn't the penalty be a little stiffer than a manslaughter conviction and eight or ten years in jail?"

"To put it bluntly, *Captain* Fitzgerald shouldn't have been screwing an enlisted man's wife," Spencer sniffed, emphasizing the word *captain*. "I'm certainly not saying he should have been killed for it, but," he shrugged. "I don't have much sympathy or respect for a man who can't control his own zipper. Particularly around someone else's wife. And worse, not just someone else's wife, but a *subordinate's* wife, for God's sake. Furthermore, in my considerable experience, neither do juries in this state, which is why I'd be inclined to plead him down and avoid a trial. A first-rate defense lawyer might even get him off on a temporary-insanity plea, particularly given the timing of the sequence of events."

"How do you mean?"

Spencer finished the last of his lunch and, signaling their

waitress for a cup of coffee, laid his knife and fork carefully across the plate. "Well, for one thing, there doesn't appear to be any premeditation here. From what you've told me Carbone got the anonymous telephone call and almost immediately thereafter did the good captain in. If the right jury gets impaneled, from the defense point of view, who knows what verdict they might bring back? And getting back to the subject of wives, if all the evidence, circumstantial or not, wasn't pointing at Carbone, any good DA or homicide detective would tell you to look closely at Fitzgerald's wife. In a case like this, you can almost make book on the likelihood of the spouse being the guilty party."

A. G. irritably shook his head. "Mrs. Fitzgerald had nothing to do with the murder."

Spencer raised an eyebrow at the vehemence of A. G.'s assertion but decided not to comment on it. "A minute ago you said a good deal of work remains to be done. What have you got in mind?"

"I'm going to finish interviewing Carbone's wife, for one thing. This afternoon. Then, I'm going to interview Fitzgerald's coworkers, see whether or not any of them knew about the affair with Mrs. Carbone. Also, to the degree I can, I want to follow up on his gambling. If none of that yields anything useful," A. G. shrugged, "well, I guess I'll deal with that when the time comes."

"Get ready to deal with it, because, believe me, you aren't going to turn up anything. I'll admit that the poker angle was an interesting one, but it's clear to me that Carbone's your man." Spencer pushed back from the table. "I've got to get back to the office. Listen, why don't you and Dolores come over to the house for a cookout this Sunday? Carole and the kids haven't seen either one of you in months."

"Lunch is on me," A. G. said, grabbing the check. "For

the information on Doug Troutman, not to mention the added benefit of your keen intellect and powers of observation." He stood up. "Oh, and Sunday sounds fine."

"Keep all these favors in mind when it comes time to write a check to my election committee. And while you're at it, sign up the pharmacist, too." He winked at A. G. "I'll need all those sweat-stained twenties I can get my hands on."

Audrey Barnes, Mildred's older sister, was sitting at Mildred's desk studying her horoscope in the latest issue of *True Crime* magazine and shelling red pistachio nuts when A. G. walked into the office.

"Sheriff," she cried out, startled by his sudden appearance. "Mildred asked me to watch the phone while she was at the dentist this afternoon. She didn't know when you might be back from Richmond." Audrey put down the magazine and picked up her official stenographer's pad, tangible evidence of her completion the year before of a mail-order shorthand course. "You've got two messages," Audrey proudly informed him, flipping back the pad's stiff cardboard cover the way she had seen it done countless times in the movies. "The first one is from a lieutenant out at Fort Lee." She squinted at the pad, clearly unable to decipher her own shorthand. "He said his name so fast I don't think I got it down, at least not exactly." She looked up at A. G., a frown on her face. "Who do you suppose it was?"

Suppressing a smile, A. G. picked up a pistachio nut and neatly shelled it. "Could it have been a Lieutenant Giles?"

"Yes," Audrey exclaimed. "I believe it was. Anyway, he said for you to call him." She looked up, the frown reappearing. "He hung up before I could get a number."

"Not to worry, I think I may have it. Who else called?"

"A Mrs. Fitz-something." Again the frown. "I think she and the lieutenant are from up north—they both talked so fast."

"I wouldn't doubt it," A. G. agreed. "Did Mrs. Fitz-something leave a message?"

"I think she wants you to call her back." Audrey stared fixedly at the hieroglyphics penciled on her steno pad, clearly in need of a personal Rosetta stone. "She didn't leave a . . ."

"That's okay," A. G. interrupted. "I think I have her number as well." He picked up another pistachio and walked into his office, carefully closing the door behind him. He sat down and lit a Chesterfield, taking a moment to collect his thoughts before picking up the telephone.

"It was much sadder than I thought it would be," Theresa said, pulling the sheet up to cover her breasts as she reached for the pack of cigarettes next to the bed. "I don't mean to imply that Marty's death wasn't a tragedy, but I hadn't anticipated that the graveside service would be so emotional, so *moving*." She lit two cigarettes, giving one to A. G. "It's difficult to articulate, but perhaps you know what I mean."

Although A. G. did know, or at least thought he knew, what Theresa meant, he elected to say nothing. In fact, having just made love to her, in the middle of the afternoon, he wasn't entirely certain he could say anything that would make the least sense, and in any event the last thing he wanted to discuss was the funeral of the recently deceased Captain Fitzgerald.

"And now this," Theresa continued, shaking her head. "To come home and learn that Marty was killed by the husband of a woman with whom he was having an affair." She looked at A. G., disbelief on her face. "It seems so tawdry, so cheap."

She hadn't known. He knew that, saw it in her face, as

soon as he told her about Wanda Carbone, and the arrest of Private Carbone. *"What?"* she had said, her eyes rounded in astonishment, her mouth open in disbelief. The obviousness of her dismay, and the relief it brought him, made A. G. realize how important it had become to him that she not have known, that there be not even a hint of suspicion regarding her presumed lack of involvement in her husband's death. She had started to cry and, without thinking consciously about it, he had taken her into his arms, held her face against his chest, as she sobbed, his own breath catching in his throat as he felt the heat of her body on his chest and stomach and thighs. Then, she had lifted her tear-streaked face and they had kissed. Now, lying next to her, he found himself wanting to laugh out loud, to share with her the joy that coursed through him as he contemplated a future that mere days earlier he couldn't possibly have even guessed at.

"I won't have to meet her, will I?" Theresa asked suddenly, concern clouding her face. "I mean, with the investigation over and all—the investigation *is* over, isn't it? Now that the killer has been put in the stockade?"

"Almost. There are still some loose ends I need . . ."

"Almost?" Theresa sat forward suddenly, dislodging the sheet and exposing her breasts. "What do you mean, 'almost'? I thought you just told me that Private Carbone was the guilty party. My God, you even caught him with the gun."

"Not exactly. Clearly the weight of the evidence we've gathered so far implicates Carbone, but because we're dealing with murder, we need to be certain beyond a reasonable doubt before we can say the investigation is over."

"I'm not a child," she said with growing irritability. "I understand the standards of proof required in a criminal case. It's just that I presumed you wouldn't have locked Private Carbone up in the stockade if you hadn't concluded that he was in all likelihood guilty of Marty's murder."

A. G. sat up and caressed her back with his left hand. "Please don't be upset," he said in a quiet voice. "I hadn't intended to tell you this way, that is, tell you about your husband and Wanda Carbone, and then almost immediately . . ." A. G. paused, unsure of how to put into words the fact that their frenzied and unexpected lovemaking had kept him from sharing with her his very strong reservations about Carbone as the prime suspect.

"And then almost immediately take me to bed?" Theresa teased, finishing his sentence for him. Her irritation appeared to dissipate as quickly as it had arisen.

Chagrined, A. G. smiled and nodded. "Exactly. I should have told you in a much less disjointed fashion." His eyes dropped unconsciously to her exposed body and then immediately back to her face. "I'm sorry if I . . ."

"Hush," Theresa whispered, drawing her fingers across his lips. "Don't explain. Not now." She pulled the sheet away from both of them, drawing his face down to her breasts and smiling as she felt him stir once again with passion.

A. G. came slowly and reluctantly to the surface, rising as if from a great and comforting depth. He lay alone on the bed, the lower half of his body covered with a light cotton sheet, a feather pillow gathered under the back of his head. He could hear someone rustling in the kitchen, and without opening his eyes he knew it must be Theresa. *So this is what it's like,* he thought, *to love and doze and love again, the passage of the sun across the sky of no more consequence than leaves fluttering in a gentle breeze.* The intense heat of the afternoon, radiating down from the uninsulated roof and only slightly mitigated by the laboring air conditioner, left a glowing sheen of perspiration on his body, even as it accentuated and compounded a sense of sexual satiety akin, he presumed, to the exquisite lethargy of an opium smoker.

"Are you going to lie there the rest of the afternoon?" Theresa's teasing voice came from the kitchen.

"I believe I could without a great deal of difficulty," A. G. said quietly, more to himself than in answer to Theresa's question.

"What did you say?" she asked, standing in the doorway.

A. G. smiled and swung his legs out of the bed.

> "In Xanadu did Kubla Khan
> A stately pleasure dome decree:"

he began to recite,

> "Where Alph, the sacred river, ran
> Through caverns measureless to man
>   Down to a sunless sea."

"Let's see," Theresa said, tapping a finger in mock concentration, "that means one of two things: Either you're my demon lover and I'm the gifted and talented Abyssinian maid, or, worse, and probably more likely, you think of me as the unknown person from Porlock."

"A fellow devotee of Samuel Taylor Coleridge," A. G. exclaimed with delight.

"I don't know if I'd go so far as to call myself a devotee of Coleridge," Theresa responded, "as much as merely the end product of an exceedingly liberal education."

A. G. stood up, modestly turning away from her to pull on his trousers. "Whatever you're cooking smells great."

"Coq au vin. I started it before you got here. Come out to the kitchen and pour yourself a glass of wine."

In the kitchen A. G. picked up the bottle of red wine and tried unsuccessfully to decipher the label. "French wine," he commented, pouring himself a glass and refreshing hers. "We don't see much of this around these parts."

Theresa laughed. "One of the first things I discovered when Marty and I moved to Fort Lee was that a sign of high culture south of the Potomac is serving iced tea with dinner instead of Coca-Cola."

"You're probably right," A. G. admitted ruefully. "I'm afraid the Baptists have done a good job of keeping wine both out of the sacrament and off the dinner table." He took a sip of the wine and was much too self-conscious to say that he didn't find it all that appealing. "Did you learn about wines in Washington?"

"Earlier than that, actually. The father of one of my college roommates was in the Foreign Service, and she was always bringing pilfered bottles of wine back to school. A small group of us would sit around the dormitory drinking it out of water glasses, feeling very sophisticated and pretending we knew what we were doing. Eventually, probably as much by accident as intent, our palates became more or less educated."

"Where was this?"

"Smith."

"I'm impressed," A. G. said, taking another sip of the wine and finding it no more appealing than his first. *Surely it will grow on me,* he thought but did not say.

"Indeed." She was busy at the small stove, putting the finishing touches on the main course and a green salad. "I would have preferred the University of California, but when I was sixteen my parents moved to New York."

"You were born in California?" Saying it, A. G. realized that, for him, California represented as foreign and exotic a locale as any place he could imagine. He leaned against the counter and tried to picture himself living easily in a land of palm trees and ocean on one hand and the Sierra Nevada mountains on the other. *Not in this life, I'm afraid,* he thought wryly.

"San Francisco. I had my heart set on going to school in Berkeley but," she shrugged and smiled, "in that event we might never have met." She tucked a strand of blond hair behind one ear and handed A. G. her wineglass for a refill. "Have you been to San Francisco?"

"As an educated and admittedly privileged member of the southern aristocracy, such as it is . . ."

"Able, as no doubt few in the Commonwealth of Virginia are, to recite Samuel Taylor Coleridge from memory," Theresa interjected with a laugh.

". . . I'm ashamed to admit that I've never even been out of Virginia in my life."

"What?"

"Never."

"Good God, you mean to sit there and tell me that you've never even been to Washington? Or New York?"

"I haven't," A. G. confirmed. "I told you, the only member of my family who ever traveled was my aunt. And she made up for the rest of us by sailing to England, Europe, you name it. I even got a postcard from her once that came from Friedrichshafen, Germany, on the *Graf Zeppelin.*" A. G. smiled and shook his head, taken with the sudden memory of a child's delight. "Imagine. I used to follow the zeppelin's travels around the world on a map in my bedroom."

Theresa turned quickly from the small stove, her eyes shining with excitement. "I've got a wonderful idea—let's go this weekend." She snapped a finger. "Just like that."

"Where?"

"To New York. We can catch the train in Richmond. Oh, A. G., there are so many wonderful things I can show you, so much we can do together."

A. G. laughed, taken with her sudden enthusiasm. "We can't just go to New York . . ."

"Why not?" she interrupted. "We're both adults—we can do whatever we want, can't we?" She took both of his hands in hers. "We'll go first class, stay at the Waldorf-Astoria in Manhattan. It will be my treat."

"No, no, it's not the money. It's . . ." A. G. paused, realizing that he was saying no for the simple reason that that was what he had always done. *What am I afraid of?* he asked himself. He pulled her into his arms. "Not this weekend, but we'll do it soon, I promise."

Pearl was waiting for him in the foyer when he opened the screen door and switched on the light. It was only minutes away from full dawn, and the morning birds—titmice and chickadees—were already at the feeder hanging off the end of the porch. She glared at him accusingly for several seconds and then, summoning up all of her dignity, she turned and walked slowly toward the kitchen.

"Yes, I know," A. G. admitted, following the old cat into the kitchen, "I stayed out all night again. Lord," he added, "this old house never saw such comings and goings." He got some chicken out of the refrigerator for Pearl and poured himself a glass of buttermilk. "Don't worry," he assured her, "I'll get Mildred Tatum to look in on you when Theresa and I go to New York."

He and Theresa had talked until early morning before falling asleep, much of their conversation to do with the planned trip to New York. They had finally decided to go in September, after the worst of the summer heat had broken. Carrying his glass of buttermilk, A. G. walked back out through the foyer, turning off the light as he passed, and onto the porch. *And not just New York,* he thought. *We'll take the train to San Francisco,* she had said, *and from there we'll fly to Honolulu.* A. G. chuckled and lit a cigarette, watching as the top of the sun began to break over the eastern horizon. Other than soldiers during the war, he doubted that twenty-five people in the entire state of Virginia had ever been to the Hawaiian Islands. Sitting down on the glider, he watched a pair of bats, wonderful creatures he normally saw only at dusk, put on an astonishing display of aerial acrobatics as they dined on flying insects attracted by the house lights. His mind quickly returned to thoughts of Theresa, and he realized how effortless it had been, lying in the darkness, in her arms, to indulge in sweet fantasies of the two of them checking into a hotel in Manhattan, listening to after-hours jazz in Harlem, or walking, hand in hand, on a moonlit beach in Hawaii. What had not been easy, and what he had ultimately been unable to do, was ask her, now that her husband was buried in Arlington National Cemetery, where she would go, what she would do when she left Fort Lee.

"Soon," he promised Pearl, who had come out on the porch to watch the feeding birds. The bats, he noticed, had disappeared as silently as they had arrived. "We'll talk about it soon." *But what am I going to tell Dolores?* he wondered, the smile fading from his lips even as the sun rose above the eastern horizon. *And when?*

Chapter Nine

"Boy, where the hell you been spending your nights?" Bud Taylor's voice boomed through the Easy Street Cafe.

A. G., who had stopped in for a quick cup of coffee on his way to the office, felt an icy hand grip his heart and with effort kept a smile on his lips. *Bud can't know anything about Theresa Fitzgerald,* he thought, his composure only momentarily shaken. *Nobody can.* "Hey, Bud," he responded in a hearty manner, sliding into the booth. "What are you talking about?"

"I was trying to get hold of you on the telephone last night." Bud folded the copy of the Richmond newspaper he had been reading. "I finally gave it up around ten o'clock and went to bed." He paused for a second. "You ain't been sleeping over at Dolores Anderson's house, have you?" he asked, his voice dropping to a conspiratorial whisper. "Just kidding," he continued before A. G.

could respond. "Still, you two ought to be getting married before folks start to talk."

"I was over in Petersburg late yesterday afternoon doing some follow-up work on the Fitzgerald matter. I decided to stay for dinner and then took in a movie just to enjoy the air-conditioning. I saw that new Marlon Brando motorcycle movie everyone's talking about." He shrugged. "I must have just missed your call." He caught Casey Bartlett's eye and signaled for a cup of coffee, realizing unhappily that he was becoming quite adept at lying, a skill he had never anticipated acquiring.

"You'll have to get your own," Casey yelled, busy with several breakfast orders at the large grill. "Jenny's out today, and I've got my hands full."

A. G. got up, went behind the counter, and poured himself a cup. "I'm glad I ran into you this morning," he told Bud when he got back to the booth. "I've got something I want to talk to you about." He paused and took a sip of his coffee. "But first, what's on your mind?" he asked Bud.

"Nothing much," Bud grunted, shaking his head. "I just hadn't talked to you for a while, and I wanted to know what was going on with the dead soldier."

A. G. spent several minutes bringing Bud up-to-date, including his concerns about the circumstantial nature of the evidence against Private Carbone.

"Sounds to me like you're trying too hard," Bud opined, sipping his coffee. "It's always been my experience that where there's smoke, there's fire. And anyway, Hopewell ain't got the money to be having you running around cleaning up after the army's mess. Have you got any idea what the state's charging us for the autopsy on that soldier?" He shook his head, appalled at what he considered to be an unnecessary and wasteful expenditure of scarce taxpayer resources.

"You can bet I'd have never had it done if the law hadn't required it. Hell, any fool could see that the bullet hole in his head is what killed him." He looked closely at A. G. "Is something the matter with you, boy? You ain't been looking too good lately. You been having trouble sleeping in this heat, or what?"

"I expect everyone's having trouble sleeping this time of year, but I'm fine, Bud, really. And I appreciate your asking." He smiled and paused for several seconds, trying to ease into the subject of the circumstances of Julie Brown's death as delicately as possible. Finally he decided that with Bud the direct approach was probably the only way that made any sense, particularly with such an unpleasant topic. "Speaking of autopsies, like I said a minute ago, there's something I want to talk to you about." He reached into his breast pocket and took out the list of three names he had culled from the county death certificates. "What do you think of this?" he asked, handing the piece of paper across the table.

"What am I supposed to think?" Bud asked, shrugging as he looked at the names. "I knew all three of them, or I should say I knew their families." He pointed at the first name on the list, Susan Anderson. "I don't recall the girl, of course, but her daddy's share-cropped and worked for Jim Jamison all his life." He pointed to the next name, Cissie Jackson. "This girl's daddy is Roscoe Jackson. Roscoe's worked for me off and on for years, and preaches at some little church he put together out off the county road up near Jubal Bishop's place. As I recall, both Jim and Roscoe always had about eight or nine young 'uns running around. And of course you know all about Julie Brown and her daddy." Bud laughed. "Hell, the state and federal agents been trying to put Sam Brown behind bars since he was sixteen years old." He pointed at the list. "What's *septicemia*?"

"A fancy way of saying blood poisoning."

Bud shrugged again and handed the piece of paper back to A. G. "So what about it?"

A. G. took a deep breath. "I think it's possible that all three of these girls died after having illegal abortions performed," he said, his voice low and guarded. "I'd like to have the Brown girl disinterred, as soon as possible, so an autopsy can be performed. I doubt Sam and Leona will consent to having it done, so we'll probably have to get a court order authorizing it."

Bud looked at him as if he thought he had taken leave of his senses. "We? You want me to help you get a court order to dig up the Brown girl and then, on top of that, pay for the state to come over here and do an autopsy because of this?" He pointed to the piece of paper in A. G.'s hand. "Have you lost your mind, or what?"

"I know it's something of a stretch right now, Bud, but I feel strongly about this." He told him of his conversation with Paul Graham in Petersburg. "It's just not right, these girls all dying like this—there's got to be more here than meets the eye."

"What got you started on all this?"

A. G. told him about his visit out to Dorcas Craige's house and her enigmatic comment about Julie Brown not being the first to die under such circumstances. "And after talking to Miz Craige, I started asking around—it seems that Julie had been developing quite a reputation, running around with soldiers from out at Fort Lee, drinking, whatever. And," A. G.'s voice dropped even lower, "rumor has it that she was pregnant when she died."

"That's it? That's all you have? Good God, A. G., you know as well as I do that Dorcas Craige's been half crazy ever since she lost her boys in the war, and then what with her husband, Percy, getting killed and all. Hell, she's liable to say anything." He shook his head for emphasis. "You can't rely on anything Miz Craige might say, not about something like this. And as for the Brown girl's reputation," he waved a hand dismissively, "if you listen to any group of young men hanging around a filling station drinking beer, you'd have to conclude there isn't a virgin in the county over the age of twelve. None of that kind of talk means a thing—you should know that. And even if it was true, even if she was getting a bad reputation, so what?" He thought of something. "What does Doc Maple have to say about all this? As far as I know, he tended the Brown girl before she died, and probably these other two as well."

A. G. shook his head. "I haven't talked to him about the Anderson and Jackson girls yet."

"What about Sam Brown's daughter?"

A. G. sighed, knowing what Bud's response was going to be. "He didn't see anything unusual or suspicious about her death."

Bud slammed a hand down on the table, causing several men in the crowded diner to look in their direction. "Then how in the hell do you think you're going to get a judge to . . ."

"Medically speaking, Doc Maple can't see his hand in front of his face," A. G. interrupted, his tone of voice caustic. "You know that as well as I do."

"Wait a minute. You're not thinking that old Doc Maple's the one doing these"—Bud lowered his voice—"these"—he gestured with his right hand, unable to bring himself to utter the word *abortion*—"these, you know."

"Of course not," A. G. assured him. "I'm just saying that Doc Maple wouldn't know a suspicious death if he saw one. That's why we have to disinter the Brown girl and have an autopsy done."

"No." Bud's voice carried an unmistakable tone of finality. "In the first place, all you've got is some vague suspicion based on what is probably no more than," he pointed again to A. G.'s list, "a downright coincidence. You'd be laughed out of court, rightfully so, and, worse, folks would think I was a fool for letting you do it. Second, you go telling Sam Brown you think his daughter died from an illegal operation she got because she was pregnant, and he'll shoot you deader than a doornail in about two seconds." Bud snorted. "Maybe quicker." He stood up and tossed some change on the table. "Do both of us a favor and put this nonsense about these girls out of your head. Oh, and one other thing—I want you to keep me posted on your investigation about the dead captain. From what you've told me, I don't see any reason that thing can't be wrapped up and turned over to the district attorney PDQ. After that," he paused for a second, working a toothpick around to the corner of his mouth, "maybe you need to think about taking a few days off."

A. G. drove slowly from the Easy Street Cafe, vastly annoyed with himself for the manner in which he had raised the issue of the girls' deaths with Bud Taylor. *The only thing I managed to accomplish,* A. G. thought, *other than making myself look like a fool, was to gratuitously antagonize him and, worse, predispose him against anything new and significant I might turn up.* "I have without question confirmed," he said ruefully to the world at large, "Major Williams's worst suspicions about my shortcomings as an investigator."

Working his way through the light midmorning traffic in Petersburg, A. G. tried to put his aggravation with himself out of mind in order to focus on Wanda Carbone. *I'll deal with the roadblock I've created with Bud later,* he promised himself.

Before leaving home that morning he had telephoned Lieutenant Giles. A. G. explained that he was going to make a surprise visit to the Carbone apartment to continue their interrupted conversation with Wanda. *There's no need for you to be there,* he had told Giles, *and in fact she may be a little more relaxed talking to just me, a civilian, particularly since Major Williams locked her husband up in the stockade.* Inasmuch as Wanda hadn't struck him as a young woman very able to make up convincing lies on the spur of the moment, *unlike myself,* he thought ruefully as he turned onto her street, an unannounced visit was more likely to lead to truthful answers.

Parking in front of the Carbones' triplex apartment, A. G. got out of his car and strolled slowly up the sidewalk, struck again by the depressing grimness of the neighborhood, the absence of even a modicum of color, whether natural in the form of flowers or artificial in the form of paint, to brighten the sepia-toned environment of low wages and a dearth of hope. What little grass and shrubbery had been originally planted had long since been burned to a uniform shade of brown by a combination of the unrelenting summer heat and the willful neglect of an absentee landlord and apathetic tenants. As he approached Wanda's apartment, accompanied by the jarring sound of a young mother screaming at a crying child somewhere in the immediate vicinity, her screen door opened and a tall, handsome black man stepped out. He was dressed casually but expensively in a white knit shirt, crisply pressed trousers, and gleaming oxford wing-tip shoes. Definitely not, A. G. realized when he thought about it later, a typical wardrobe for that particular neighborhood. Startled, A. G. said, "Good morning," and began to explain that he was there to see Wanda Carbone. The other man wordlessly nodded toward the apartment and, stepping around A. G., quickly walked away. A. G. turned and watched until he rounded a corner of the opposite triplex apartment building and disappeared. A. G. thought briefly of following him but, beyond a vague sense of unease, could think of no immediate reason why he should. He knocked on the screen door.

"Now what?" Wanda's voice rose in pitch and volume as she approached the door. "If you think I'm going to change my . . ." She stopped, startled to see A. G. on the other side of the screen.

"Hello, Wanda," A. G. said, smiling. "I was passing through the neighborhood and thought it might be a good time to visit with you again. May I come in?" Without waiting for an invitation, A. G. opened the door and stepped forward, forcing Wanda to back into the apartment.

"Actually," Wanda stammered, "it's not, I mean I was just planning to, well, I don't . . ." Her voice gradually ran down, much like an automobile engine sputtering as it ran out of gasoline. Realizing A. G. had her trapped, she shrugged and abruptly sat down. "You wouldn't happen to have a cigarette, would you?" Although her swollen cheekbone had gone down considerably, the blackened eye, in the normal course of healing, continued to exhibit several rather gaudy shades of yellow, red, and purple.

A. G. handed her a Chesterfield, put one in his own mouth, and lit both with his lighter, realizing as he did so that, absent the black eye, she was really quite pretty. A couple of empty grocery-store cardboard boxes sat on the threadbare, three-legged sofa, and five or six others were scattered haphazardly about the living room. He moved one of the boxes off the sofa and sat down, his eyebrows raised in a silent interrogatory.

Wanda shrugged again and glared at A. G. "I got a call from the Quartermaster School telling me I been fired, probably no thanks to the lieutenant that was out here with you the first time."

"I'm sorry to hear that, Wanda. I'm sure Lieutenant Giles had nothing to do with it, and in fact I'll bet he'd be more than happy to make a call for you, see if . . ."

"Forget it. I don't think anybody out at the fort feels too sorry for me, not with Joey behind bars. Anyway, now that he's locked up, I've got to find another job PDQ, if you know what I mean." She sighed. "Nobody around here's going to hire me, that's for sure, so," she nodded toward the empty boxes, "I guess I'll have to start over again somewhere else. I ain't planning on going anywhere right away, leastways not before Joey's court-martial, but I figure it never hurts to get stuff ready."

"You think he's going to be in the stockade for a long time?"

She laughed, a short bark of amusement. "Don't you?" She started ticking things off on her fingers. "Murder, beating up that sergeant, stealing the gun." She laughed again. "Yeah, I think he's going to be there a while."

"Actually, I'm not at all sure he killed Captain Fitzgerald. That's why I'm back here to talk to you again today."

"You think I done it?" she asked sarcastically.

A. G. smiled. "No, but perhaps we, you and I, can figure out a way to keep Joey from spending the rest of his life in jail."

"I doubt it. Anyway, from what I hear from friends at the fort, that asshole provost marshall, pardon my French, is going to throw the book at Joey for beating up the MP sergeant and for the stolen pistol they found in his locker. The one they're saying was the murder weapon." She shook her head. "You're going to have to get in line to get to Joey for killing Marty."

"Where's home?" A. G. asked, suddenly changing the direction of the conversation. "I mean, where are you and Joey from originally?"

"Detroit."

"Are you thinking about returning there?"

Another laugh, this one evidencing no humor whatever. "Not hardly. I don't have any family there anymore, and

Joey's people think I'm nothing but a dumb Polack. They tried everything they could think of to keep him from marrying me, not that it did them any good, the bastards. No, I'm thinking maybe California. I saw in one of those Hollywood magazines where there's lots of jobs out there, good jobs, for people that want to work."

California, A. G. thought, suddenly seeing himself lying next to Theresa the evening before, the two of them spinning dreams of California and beyond. "Have you got enough money to get out to the West Coast?" he asked, putting aside the uncomfortable thought that the three of them, he, Theresa, and Wanda, might well have in common the need to start their lives over again elsewhere. "And to live on," he added, "once you get there?"

"Maybe," Wanda answered shortly. She finished her cigarette and nervously stubbed it out in the ashtray on the battered coffee table. "It don't cost much to ride the Greyhound out there, and after that," she shrugged again, "I don't guess I'll have too much trouble finding a job."

Noticing her sudden nervousness and the obvious nexus between it and his question about money, A. G. paused for several seconds, allowing an uncomfortable silence to build. When she started shifting in her seat, A. G. leaned forward to put his own cigarette out. "Who was that leaving just when I arrived?" he asked in a casual tone of voice.

"What?" she asked, almost yelping, the question clearly frightening her. "Oh, him. He, well, that was nobody," she said, emphatically shaking her head, trying and failing to think and talk at the same time, "just a friend from, uh, somebody who brought me some stuff from the store 'cause I don't like going out looking like this." She waved a hand vaguely in the direction of her bruised face and smiled. "I get tired of explaining to people how I walked into a door or something."

"Is he a soldier?"

Another emphatic shake of her head. "Um, no, he's a, he lives around here, he's a friend of Joey and me, just someone who heard I wasn't doing too good and came by to help out."

"A neighbor?"

"Yeah, that's it, a neighbor," Wanda agreed, relief washing over her face like a wave as A. G. provided her with what she perceived to be a plausible explanation. "Yeah, just someone from around here. I don't know exactly where he lives—he's just someone Joey knew and was friends with." She leaned forward as if to share a sudden sociological insight with A. G. "Sometimes these colored people can be real nice, you know what I mean?"

"Indeed I do." A. G. stood up. He handed her his half-full pack of Chesterfields. "Why don't you keep these—I've got more in my office."

"You leaving already?" Startled at A. G.'s abrupt departure, Wanda struggled to her feet. "Don't you want to ask me any questions about Marty?"

A. G. nodded. "I do," he looked at his watch, "but I've got a couple of things I have to get to this afternoon. Why don't I drop by again tomorrow?"

"Well, if you think so. Listen, Sheriff," she unconsciously lowered her voice as if afraid someone might hear her, "I've got to be honest with you—I think Joey did it. Killed Marty, I mean."

Somewhat surprised, A. G. raised his eyebrows. "Really? What leads you to believe that?"

"Well, I mean, you know he's got a terrible temper, and if he didn't do it, well, who did?"

"Lieutenant Giles, please. Sheriff Farrell calling." A. G. leaned back in his chair and looked out the open window. He had been back in his office only half an hour and had already made several calls. Through the plate-glass window of Doug Troutman's drugstore he could see several diners sitting at the lunch counter. "Yes, Lieutenant Giles, A. G. Farrell here. Have you had lunch yet? . . . Well, if you can get away for a little while, I'll buy you a sandwich and fill you in on my visit this morning with Wanda Carbone. . . . Yes, something interesting came up that I'd like to discuss with you. . . . Good. I'll see you here at my office in a few minutes."

He reached into his pocket for his Chesterfields and remembered he had left the pack with Wanda Carbone. Walking out to Mildred's desk, he picked up her pack of Pall Malls and shook out two cigarettes.

"You going out for some lunch?" she asked, taking the cigarette he offered.

A. G. shook his head. "Not yet. The lieutenant's dropping by in a few minutes, and I'm going to take him across the street for a sandwich at Doug's." He leaned over the edge of the desk to light her cigarette.

"Speaking of your lieutenant, guess who took Mary Frances O'Brien to the movies over in Petersburg last night?"

"No."

Mildred nodded affirmatively, a smug look on her face.

"That's the best news I've heard in a while," A. G. declared, a broad smile breaking across his face. "That young man may be her last good chance to get out of Prince George County."

"Where's he from?" Mildred asked suspiciously.

"Milwaukee. He got his army commission through the ROTC program at the University of Wisconsin."

"Milwaukee," Mildred repeated, rolling the word gingerly around her palate as if it were wrapped in barbed wire. Other than north, she had no idea and, what's more, no interest in where the city might be situated geographically. "I doubt Lorraine O'Brien would be any too pleased to see her daughter carried off to such a place." *Place* was pronounced as if it were a synonym for *prison camp*.

"You know as well as I do that any man attempting to *carry off* Mary Frances O'Brien would be in for a long and unprofitable day." A. G. shook his head, pleased at the prospect of Giles and Mary Frances getting together. "No, if she decides she wants to go with Giles, my advice to anyone idling in the vicinity would be to get out of the way." He started to say something else but paused at the sound of someone opening the outer-office door. "Well, speak of the devil. Lieutenant Giles, I believe you met Mildred Tatum the last time you were here?"

"Yes, how are you, Mrs. Tatum?"

"I'm fine, except that when someone calls me Mrs. Tatum it always makes me think of my late mother-in-law." The look on her face made it plain that it was not a memory she particularly cherished.

"In other words," A. G. laughed, "call her Mildred. Come on, Lieutenant, let's get a sandwich."

Outside, on the sidewalk, Giles asked A. G. rather diffidently where he had in mind to go to eat.

A. G. motioned across the street with his thumb. "I thought maybe we'd get a grilled pimento cheese sandwich and a milk shake over at the lunch counter at Troutman's Drugstore. Did you have something else in mind?"

"Well," Giles said, tugging at his garrison cap, "I wondered if we might try the Little Acorn. You know, where we ate the other day."

"Indeed I do know," A. G. said. He had already decided not to let Giles know that he knew about his date with Mary Frances. If the young man wanted him to know about it, he would tell him. If not, it was in fact none of A. G.'s business. "The Little Acorn's a good idea," A. G. said, thinking how eager he himself had been to see Theresa yesterday.

"Hello, A. G.," Lorraine O'Brien called out from the kitchen as the two of them walked into the small diner. She came out to the front counter, wiping her hands with a clean dishtowel. She smiled at Giles. "It's good to see you again so soon, Barry."

"You two know each other?" A. G. asked, feigning mild surprise.

"We met last night," Giles confirmed in a slightly embarrassed tone of voice.

A. G. craned his head around. "Mary Frances not working today?"

"We ran out of change, so I sent her across the street to the bank," Lorraine said. She gestured toward an empty booth. "Have a seat—she'll be back directly."

"What's cooking today?" A. G. asked over his shoulder, shooing Giles to the booth.

"Meat loaf with mashed potatoes and gravy, served with fresh snap beans simmered all morning with a big piece of fatback."

"Sounds good to me," A. G. said, looking to Giles for confirmation. "In fact, make it two." He smiled at the younger man as the two of them sat down. "So you went calling on Miss Mary Frances last night?"

"We went to a movie over in Petersburg," Giles confirmed sheepishly, looking at the door for a sign of the young woman in question. "I really like her," he added rather needlessly.

"I hate to let business intrude on our dining pleasure," A. G. said with a smile, wiping at a water spot on his fork with his napkin, "but as you know, I met rather briefly this morning with Wanda Carbone."

"Yes," Giles said, reluctantly turning his attention from the front door to A. G. "How did it go?"

"To begin with, as I approached her apartment, a colored man happened to be coming out of it."

"Really?" Giles leaned forward, his curiosity suddenly piqued. "Who was it?"

"I don't know. When I asked her about him, Wanda got exceedingly nervous and tried to slough him off as nothing more than a neighbor, someone her husband knew, who had stopped by to see if she needed anything."

"But you don't think so."

"No." A. G. shook his head. "For one thing, he was far too well dressed to be living in that neighborhood. His clothes were expensive and his shoes were polished. Another thing was his demeanor. He didn't speak, but I got the distinct impression that he was an educated man. Nothing I could put my finger on, you understand, just the feeling that he was too intelligent to be a friend of the Carbones. And finally, there was Wanda's nervousness. She clearly didn't want me knowing who he was or what her relationship with him might be. When I knocked on her screen door, immediately after the other man had left, she came to the door clearly thinking it was him, because she was saying something to the effect that she wasn't going to change her mind." He shrugged. "As soon as she saw it was me, she clammed up, but what little she had already said didn't exactly comport with what you would expect if he had been just a friendly neighbor."

"But you have no idea who he might have been?"

"I don't know his identity, but I have a clue as to where we might find him." A. G. straightened his right leg out from under the table and pointed to his foot. "Remember," he prompted, smiling at Giles's perplexed look, "what I said about his shoes: They were polished, almost, in fact, to the point of being, what does the army call it, spit-shined."

Giles snapped his fingers. "A soldier," he said excitedly, just as Mary Frances walked in the door. His eyes went to her so quickly that A. G. almost laughed out loud. "Hello, Mary Frances," he said, his voice suddenly tentative.

"Hello," she said, obviously pleased to see him. "What brings you in to Hopewell?"

"Lunch," A. G. said. "I asked the lieutenant over to lunch to discuss matters of grave military and civilian importance, and he immediately suggested that we dine here." A. G. lowered his voice to a conspiratorial level. "Between you and me, I think he rather enjoys your mother's cooking."

"Orders up," Lorraine yelled from the kitchen. She poked her head out and pointed at Mary Frances. "Put the change in the cash register and get an apron on. You can visit with Barry after everyone's been served."

"I'll talk to you in a few minutes," she assured Giles. Thirty seconds later she was back at the booth with two servings of meat loaf, mashed potatoes and gravy, and fresh snap beans. "I told Momma to give you each an extra slice," she whispered as she put the plates down and hurried away

"Proof that no good deed goes unrewarded," A. G. said, winking at Giles. "I'm already reaping unexpected benefits from having introduced you two the other day."

They both fell silent for several minutes, attacking lunch with enthusiasm. Midway through the large portion, A. G. pointed his knife at Giles.

"You haven't forgotten the polished shoes, have you?"

Giles shook his head, his mouth full. "No, sir," he managed to say between bites. "You think the man might be a soldier because his shoes were spit-shined."

"More than that," A. G. mused, pausing for a second in his assault on the meat loaf and mashed potatoes. "He had a military bearing, a presence I guess you could call it. Most folks from around here, particularly working men like you'd expect to find in the Carbones' neighborhood, are pretty casual in how they stand or act when they meet someone, even if the meeting comes as something of a surprise. They'll kind of slouch, probably put their hands in their pockets, mumble something, maybe not quite look you in the eye, that sort of thing. And the clothes match the man."

"How do you mean?"

"Well, for one thing, in a hard-luck neighborhood like Joey and Wanda's, a man's shirt is almost certainly not going to fit as if it were tailor-made—it's going to be either a little large or a little small. For another, a button or two is probably going to be missing, one side of the collar may be a little higher than the other, the cuffs will most likely be frayed. His shoes are going to be work shoes, badly scuffed and run down at the heels. The man I ran into this morning, on the other hand," A. G. shook his head, seeing him clearly in his mind's eye, "even though he was surprised to see me, stood up straight, looked me right in the eye. He wore his clothes like they were a uniform, and he went about his business like he had a purpose." He moved a piece of meat loaf around the plate. "Everything about him said *soldier*."

"If he *was* a soldier from Fort Lee, say a friend of her husband's who was just stopping by to see if he could help out in any way now that Joey's in the stockade, she shouldn't have been so nervous about you seeing him," Giles pointed out. "Certainly not to the point of lying about it." He thought for a second and then whistled. "Say, you don't think . . ."

"I don't *think* anything," A. G. interrupted. "If he's a soldier, and stationed at Fort Lee, we need to find him and ask him some questions."

"That could be easier said than done. Fort Lee's a big post."

"If we proceed with the assumption that he knew either Captain Fitzgerald or Private Carbone, we can considerably narrow the odds of finding him, can't we?"

"Of course," Giles said sheepishly when he realized what

A. G. was suggesting. "We can concentrate our efforts, at least initially, on the Quartermaster School and the post motor pool. I should have thought of that."

"That's why two heads are almost always better than one. Particularly," A. G. nodded toward Mary Frances, "when one of them has something else occupying its attention." He laughed. "And in any event, keep in mind that you were the one who found Wanda Carbone for us in the first place."

"I suppose," Giles agreed, nonetheless annoyed with himself for being so slow on the uptake. "Can you give me a good physical description?"

"Tall, perhaps six feet or six one, athletic build with a trim waist," A. G. thought for a second, "perhaps one hundred and seventy pounds. Handsome, regular features, neither light- nor dark-skinned, more in between. Oh," A. G. remembered something he had wanted to say, "and he's not a raw recruit. I'd say he was my age, perhaps thirty-four or thirty-five."

"That makes it even easier," Giles said. "If he's that old and still in the army, he's almost certain to be a sergeant of one grade or another."

"Good. I now leave it in your capable hands. As soon as you have him identified, let me know—I think it would be best, from the point of view of hopefully obtaining his active cooperation, if we approach him with some discretion."

Giles nodded, remembering the manner in which Major Williams and Sergeant Dickey had corralled Private Carbone. "I agree," he said simply. "I have to finish a report for Major Williams this afternoon, but I'll start on the job of identifying our mystery soldier first thing in the morning."

"One last thing," A. G. added. "Wanda had empty grocery-store boxes all over the apartment."

Giles whistled. "You think she's getting ready to take a powder?"

A. G. shook his head. "I don't think so, at least not immediately, but we'd do well to keep a fairly close eye on her all the same. She said she felt that she was going to have to relocate to start her life over again, which makes a great deal of sense given all that's happened—and by the way, she told me that she got fired from her job at the Quartermaster School."

"That's too bad," Giles said, "although I guess I'm not surprised to hear it. I'm sure the school commander felt there was no way she could stay once the affair with Captain Fitzgerald became public knowledge, particularly after her husband got thrown in the stockade." He shook his head. "Still, it seems like she's being unfairly penalized."

"I agree. Wanda's clearly paid a heavy price for getting involved with a married man, but it's my experience that most folks seldom think about the consequences of what they're doing until it's far too late. Anyway, she admitted that she's planning to leave the state but said that she wouldn't do so until after her husband's court-martial."

"When are you going to see her again?"

"I told her I'd drop by tomorrow, but I'm thinking now I'll give her a day or two to worry about my having seen the mystery man coming out of her apartment. His visit might well have been completely innocent, but until I know for sure, a little pressure on Wanda might just be the ticket. Now," A. G. smiled, "how about a piece of Lorraine's homemade pie for dessert before we both have to get back to the office?"

"Claire Biddle called," Mildred said with a tight-lipped smile when A. G. walked in the door. "She said Doug Troutman never showed up at the drugstore this morning and doesn't answer the telephone at home." The smile broadened. "She wants you to do something about it."

"He's probably just sleeping one off," A. G. said, not eager to listen to Claire Biddle whine about having to work all by herself. Doug was known to occasionally overindulge in Kentucky bourbon when Angie was out of town visiting her family. "Nonetheless, I guess I'd better go over and talk to her," he said unenthusiastically, not quite sighing. He walked quickly across the street, the extreme heat of the asphalt, soft and tacky in the blazing midday sun, uncomfortably apparent even through the soles of his shoes.

"Mornin', Miz Biddle," A. G. said with as much cheer as he could muster as he entered the drugstore. "I understand that . . ."

"It's afternoon, Sheriff, not morning," Claire interrupted, her tone of voice making clear what she thought of anyone who was unable to distinguish between the two. Stout and middle-aged, she was abrupt and impatient in her dealings with the public and had a voice to match—harsh and high-pitched, it brought to mind fingernails drawn across a blackboard, or a handsaw hitting a nail buried in a piece of lumber. "I've been here, on my feet, since eight-thirty this morning without a break," she added, lest there be any doubt as to the cause of her present and obviously growing irritation. "Doug Troutman doesn't pay me enough to put up with this kind of nonsense." She stood planted on the floor in front of A. G. like the Rock of Gibraltar, hands on hips, chin thrust forward pugnaciously, daring him to contradict her.

"Doug's probably not feeling well," A. G. said quickly, hoping to forestall further gratuitous complaining. "Why don't . . ."

"Not feeling well, my foot," Claire snapped before A. G. could continue. "I expect he's either drunk or badly hung-over—it happens every time that wife of his goes out of town, and I don't mind telling you I'm getting good and tired of it." She pronounced *wife* as if it were synonymous with *whore*. "I had to open up the store by myself, serve the whole lunch crowd by myself, and, on top of that, deal with the telephone the whole time. Mrs. Magruder's called four times already, wanting her prescriptions filled, and she's not the only one. I'm so mad I could spit." Claire pointed a finger at A. G. for emphasis. "He won't answer the phone, so you're going to have to go roust him out and get him down here."

Doug and Angie lived in a pleasant brick house little more than walking distance from downtown Hopewell and the drugstore. A. G. parked in the driveway and walked up to the front porch, taking a second to admire a small patch of sunflowers Angie had planted on one side of the porch. On the other side was a showy stand of zinnias and marigolds, their variegated blossoms drooping in the heat. Although the front door was closed, A. G. could hear what sounded like Doug's new television blaring away inside. He smiled and knocked loudly.

"Doug," he called out, trying unsuccessfully to peer through the door's small window. "Doug, it's me, A. G. Farrell." He knocked again and, after a second or two, opened the screen and tried the front doorknob. It was open. "Doug," he said in a loud voice, opening the door partially and putting his head through, "Claire Biddle asked me to come get you."

When no response was forthcoming, he pushed the door completely open and stepped across the threshold. Having never before been in the Troutman home, he paused in the vestibule another few seconds, trying to orient himself to the house's layout. The sound of the television was coming from the rear of the house and, as he started back, he continued to call Doug's name. Two corridors ran off the living room, one leading, he could see, to a small dining room and, beyond that, the kitchen. He took the other corridor, following it and the sound of the television until, after a short distance, it opened into a small parlor room or, as such rooms were now being called, a family room. Against one wall stood the new television, its black-and-white picture rolling continuously from top to bottom on the small screen. In front of it, with his back to A. G., Doug sat motionless in a fabric-covered easy chair, his head slumped down onto his chest. An almost-empty bottle of bourbon sat on the floor next to the chair, and the smell of whiskey permeated the room.

"Lord, he must still be dead drunk," A. G. murmured, and then, louder, "Doug, it's me, A. G. Farrell." He walked up behind him and put a hand on the druggist's shoulder. "Wake up, now. Claire needs you down at the store."

A. G. stepped around the side of the chair and, as if struck at by a poisonous snake, involuntarily leaped back in shock. Blood-soaked from his chest to the tops of his thighs, Doug stared sightlessly at the pool of blood on the floor between his legs, a distinct look of shock and dismay frozen onto his face.

Chapter Ten

"If folks keep getting murdered around here, me and the old lady'll be able to do that addition on the house she keeps nagging me about," Henry Beal said, as he went about loading a fresh roll of film into his camera.

"What's that?" A. G. asked distractedly, running a worried hand through his hair. He had been out in the Troutman living room waiting for Bud Taylor to arrive. "What did you say?"

Henry nodded toward the body of Doug Troutman, still slumped in his easy chair exactly as A. G. had found him twenty minutes earlier. "I said, if folks keep . . ." He paused for a second and then shook his head. "Never mind, it wasn't very funny anyway." He licked the back of a flashbulb to ensure a good contact and put it into his flash attachment. "If it's okay with you, I'll go ahead and start taking pictures."

"Yeah, fine, just watch where you step, and don't touch anything." He heard steps on the porch. "Oh," he added, turning to intercept whoever was coming into the house, "and get several shots of the room itself from various angles."

"A. G.?" Bud Taylor's voice boomed through the house. "You back there?"

"Here I am," A. G. said, hurrying out to the living room.

"What the hell's going on?"

"Bad news," A. G. murmured, almost more to himself than to Bud. He raised his voice and looked the older man in the eye. "Real bad news." He nodded toward the rear of the house. "Doug Troutman's dead."

"What?"

"Murdered from all appearances. His throat's been cut. He didn't show up at the drugstore this morning, so Claire Biddle called me after lunch. We both figured he was sleeping off a bender, what with Angie out of town, and I came over to see if I could rouse him." A. G. took out his handkerchief and wiped it across his forehead. "It was a shock to find him in there, I don't mind telling you." He turned and, with Bud cautiously in tow, started back down the corridor to the family room. "I mean, it's one thing to have to deal with a murder victim you don't know, like Captain Fitzgerald from out at the fort, and another thing entirely when it's a neighbor, someone you've been knowing for five years." A. G. knew he was talking too much but could not help it—the obviously unexpected discovery of Doug's body, compounded by the hideous wound at his throat, had greatly unsettled him.

"Damn." Bud took a quick look at Doug Troutman's body, and the mess he had made in dying, and turned away. Back in the living room he, too, in an unconscious mimicry of A. G., took off his straw hat and mopped his brow with a handkerchief. "Who knows about this besides the two of us?

And of course," he added quickly, looking back toward the rear of the house, "Henry Beal."

A. G. shook his head. "No one else. As soon as I discovered the body, I called you and then Henry. I wanted to get photographs before anything was disturbed."

"Good. You know who this boy's daddy is?"

A. G. shrugged. "I know he's a surgeon over in Richmond, and I've been told he's a big wheel with the state medical association."

"More than just a big wheel," Bud grunted. "A lot more. He's been president of the association at least half-a-dozen times over the past twenty years but, more important, he sits on the association's board of trustees and directs their political-coordination efforts."

"Political coordination?"

"Money. A lot of it. More than you can imagine. If you're a politician and you want election money from the doctors in this state, you get right with Bill Troutman. Nothing, and I mean *nothing,* having to do with the practice of medicine, and a lot of other things besides, gets through the state legislature until he's approved of it. The governor, the speaker, the congressional delegation in Washington, they all play ball with Troutman." Bud again wiped the perspiration from his brow and then ran the damp handkerchief over his bald head. "Damn." He thought for a second. "What are you going to do with the body?"

"Just like I did with the captain's—call Bob Creech and have him store it until we can get someone from Richmond to come over and do an autopsy."

"But you haven't called him yet?"

"No."

Bud looked at his watch. It was just past three o'clock. He thought of something and snapped his fingers. "I almost forgot—what about Angie?"

"As far as I know she's still in Norfolk, visiting her family. I'll have to run down their telephone number and get in touch with her as soon as possible." A. G. shook his head, wondering how he was going to break the news.

"No, you better let me take care of that," Bud said, surprising A. G. "I'll call John Doyle," the state Democratic Party chairman, "and we'll figure out how best to break the news to Bill Troutman and then let him decide how he wants to inform Angie."

"We'd better do it quickly," A. G. said. "This is going to make all the newspapers, and I sure don't want Angie finding out that Doug was murdered from some reporter."

Bud started to leave and turned quickly around. He motioned back toward the family room with a wave of one hand. "Have you got any idea why someone would have wanted to kill him?"

"You mean a motive? No. Although . . ." his voice trailed off as he thought of something.

"What?" Bud asked impatiently.

"It has to do with Doug's new television." He quickly described how he had discovered that the television had been paid for with cash. "Well-worn twenty-dollar bills, to be precise. Maybe Doug and Angie made it a habit to keep large sums of money around the house," he said. "If so, and someone found out about it . . ." He shrugged, letting his sentence finish itself without words. "And, while it's true that most thieves aren't necessarily murderers, whoever did it may not have expected to find Doug at home on a workday, sleeping off a drunk with his wife out of town."

"Well, whatever the motive, you're going to be on the hot seat until the case is solved. My guess is that Bill Troutman is going to be lighting fires under everyone who's anyone in Richmond to get whoever did this tried, convicted, and into the electric chair PDQ." He pointed at A. G. "You'd better plan on putting that soldier's murder on the back burner for the time being, if you get my drift."

Henry Beal walked into the living room just as Bud was going out the front door. "I shot three rolls of film," he informed A. G. "Like you said, I got the entire room from every angle, as well as the body." He shook his head, knowing that it would be some time before he would be able to forget the images he had seen through his camera's viewfinder. "I can think of a whole lot better ways to die than gettin' your throat cut." He pursed his lips and exhaled. "Did you happen to notice the look on Doug's face?"

"What do you mean?"

"Well, it looks almost as if he was surprised—like maybe someone he knew stepped up and did it before Doug had time to do anything but be," Henry shrugged, "surprised."

"I'm going to want those pictures first thing in the morning," A. G. said, choosing not to dwell on the significance, or lack thereof, of Doug Troutman's postmortem facial expression, "so I'm afraid you're going to have to develop and print them tonight. And you better let me have the negatives, too. I'll probably have to send them over to Richmond sooner or later, so I might as well keep them locked up in my desk for the time being."

Henry nodded and started back to the family room to pack up his gear.

"Oh, and Henry," A. G. added as he picked up the telephone to call Bob Creech, "don't be talking to anyone about this, okay? It's going to get out soon enough, but until we get in touch with Angie, I want to try to keep a lid on things."

Forty minutes later Doug's body was zipped up in a black rubber bag and on its way to a stainless-steel embalming table at the Creech Brothers Funeral Home.

"Whoever did this had a sharp knife," Bob Creech had said after he and A. G. had lifted Doug's body out of the easy chair and placed it on the funeral home's gurney. "Look." He pointed at the edges of the gaping wound on Doug's throat, clearly visible to the two men for the first time as they laid the body flat on the gurney. "The cut is clean, with no tearing of the skin, almost like it was done with a surgeon's scalpel."

After helping Creech load Doug's body into his van, A. G. went back into the house. He stood for several minutes in the doorway to the family room, arms crossed, smoking a cigarette, the smoke curling slowly up and around his face and head. Something underneath the easy chair, at its side, caught his eye and he stared at it without moving, trying to figure out what it was. At first he thought it was a cleaning or dust rag of some sort, inadvertently dropped and then kicked under the side of the chair. He continued to smoke his cigarette, leaning against the door frame, his head still, but his eyes, hooded against the smoke rising from his cigarette, moved carefully across the room and its furniture, lingering on first one thing and then another, yet always coming back to the barely visible piece of cloth under the easy chair. Finally, he went to the chair and knelt down beside it, careful not to disturb the whiskey bottle that had not yet been dusted for fingerprints. From that vantage point, mere inches away, what had appeared from across the room to be nothing more than a cleaning rag now resolved itself into a pair of women's cotton panties, once red or pink, faded almost completely to white.

A. G. knew it was going to be another unpleasantly hot day well before the sun rose. He had had a fretful night on perspiration-dampened sheets, and what little sleep he had managed in short, interrupted segments had been restless and troubling, full of anxiety dreams. The high temperature and humidity had not been the least assuaged by either ceiling fan or open window, and so finally at four A.M. he threw in the towel and sat up on the edge of the bed. Feeling as if his body were coated with oil instead of perspiration, he padded quietly downstairs for a glass of buttermilk, followed shortly by Pearl, who was awakened by the hall light. He poured a dollop of milk into a saucer to make up for waking her in the middle of the night and, glass of buttermilk and pack of Chesterfields in hand, walked out onto the porch. Not the slightest breeze could be felt as he sat down on the glider and, glancing sky-ward, he realized that the night air was so full of moisture that the stars appeared smudged and indistinct, their light seemingly able to make its way through the atmosphere with only the greatest of difficulty. Pearl joined him after drinking her milk and walked slowly down to the far corner of the dark porch. A full moon, quite low in the sky, cast a wan, spectral light over the house and yard, turning her into something of an apparition as she sat grooming herself.

"You might be annoyed that I woke you up," he informed her in a soft voice, "but to be perfectly honest, your company out here on the porch is not completely unappreciated. I sup-pose my insomnia shouldn't come as much of a surprise— not only have I had Doug Troutman's murder thrust unex-pectedly upon me, but I'm afraid that falling in love with Theresa Fitzgerald still has me turning around in circles."

A. G. knew that in entering into a sexual relationship with Theresa he had forfeited the moral high ground he was so used to occupying, a forfeiture made all the more disturbing by virtue of how little struggle he had put up to avoid it. He had tried to call her last night when he got home from Doug Troutman's house and had been unable to reach her at her quarters at Fort Lee, despite trying a number of times.

"Perhaps," he said aloud, feeling not the least bit foolish talking to a cat, "she's feeling a little guilty, too," although, even as he said it, he thought it unlikely. He took a sip of buttermilk. "But I wish I could have been with her last night nonetheless."

He turned his body sideways and stretched out full-length on the glider, putting both hands behind his head as his mind began to drift. Suddenly, just as a pleasant image of Theresa was forming, another thought muscled it aside and he sat bolt upright.

"Of course," he said out loud, snapping his fingers once as he fumbled in the dark for a Chesterfield. "It's the only thing that would make sense about the murder." The sudden flare of his match startled Pearl, and she looked back at at him, clearly annoyed. He shook his head, oblivious to her disapproval. "I can't imagine why I didn't see it right away."

An owl, unsettled first by A. G.'s unexpected presence on the porch at four o'clock in the morning and then by the sound of his voice, hooted twice and soared out of one of the tall pines in the field opposite the house. Both A. G. and Pearl tried to follow its flight but were unable to see it in the low light of the waning moon, and its feathers made no sound as it slipped through the heavy, predawn air. An atavistic fear tickled at the back of Pearl's mind, and she instinctively moved from the edge of the porch to the side of the glider where A. G. sat. He reached down to reassure her.

"Lord, we're something, you and I," he told her, "sitting out here like a pair of fools waiting for the sun to come up and chase away the principalities of the night."

"You're going to burn up in that suit," Mildred observed tartly as A. G. walked into the office.

"I don't doubt it," A. G. agreed, "but I figured I'd better spruce up a bit, what with all the VIP traffic from Richmond we're liable to be getting through here in the next few days." He had told Mildred about Doug's murder the evening before, knowing she would undoubtedly hear about it herself before morning anyway, his warnings to Henry Beal and Bob Creech notwithstanding.

"It's handsome, I'll grant you that. One of your daddy's?"

He nodded. The suit, a navy, double-breasted tropical-weight worsted wool, was a little large across the shoulders but otherwise fit reasonably well. "I doubt he wore it three times."

"That hat will certainly come in handy."

A. G. smiled and held up the broad-brimmed Panama hat. "With any luck it'll save my life." He yawned and sheepishly apologized. "It's been too hot to sleep lately."

"You should get one of those window air conditioners for your bedroom," Mildred admonished. "They've got them over at Sears, Roebuck in Petersburg."

"If I wait until October they'll be on sale," A. G. pointed out. "Winter's the time to buy an air conditioner. Besides, I've managed to live thirty-four years without one, so another month or two shouldn't make a bit of difference." He offered her a Chesterfield. "You hear anything last night?"

"Are you kidding?" She smiled sardonically. "Four people called me before nine o'clock with the news, all wanting to know if I knew anything specific. I hope someone got to Angie before her friends and neighbors did."

A. G. nodded, not the least surprised. "I talked to Bud last night and again this morning before leaving home. Dr. Troutman, her father-in-law, broke the news to her last night."

"She coming back today?"

"No. Bud told me this morning that apparently she became hysterical and had to be put under sedation. I doubt she'll leave Norfolk before the funeral."

"When will the funeral be?"

"I don't know. Bud told me that a pathologist is coming over from Richmond this morning to do the autopsy."

"That's fast."

"Considerably faster than we got poor Captain Fitzgerald's done. Anyway, since today's Friday, my guess is they'll bury him Monday or Tuesday. The fingerprint technician is scheduled to be here this afternoon, so I've got Warren Elam sitting outside the Troutman house this morning making sure no one goes in before then."

Mildred leaned back in her chair and looked at A. G. over her cigarette. "Why would anyone want to kill Doug Troutman?"

"Maybe whoever did it didn't want to," A. G. said, shaking his head. "Maybe it was an accident."

"An *accident*? How do you get your throat cut by accident?"

A. G. smiled. "Well, I'll grant you that *accident* probably isn't the best descriptive word when murder is involved. But suppose someone had been planning to burglarize Doug's home. Someone who knew, as did most of the county, that Angie was out of town visiting her family in Norfolk, but *didn't* know that Doug often took advantage of such absences to get drunk."

"So you think whoever killed him stumbled on him unexpectedly."

"It's possible."

"But why would anyone undertake to burglarize Doug's house?" Mildred asked skeptically. "Doug and Angie aren't exactly the richest people in Prince George County."

"Perhaps whoever did it thought they were. After all, within the past month or two Doug purchased not only a new Buick but also a television set." A. G. told her about Doug paying for the television in Richmond with well-worn twenty-dollar bills. "So the question in my mind is, did he have some sort of reputation, regardless of how silly or ill-founded it might have been, for keeping a lot of cash on hand?"

"And you want me to ask around," Mildred surmised.

"Indeed I do. If he had such a reputation, whether it might have had some basis in fact or not, I want to know about it."

"And if he didn't?"

A. G. shrugged. "Then I'll have to think of something else," he said, not wishing to tell her yet that he already had.

"What are you doing this morning?"

"I'm not exactly sure yet," A. G. said, putting his cigarette out in Mildred's ashtray. "I've got to make a couple of calls, see who's in, that sort of thing. And, Doug's murder notwithstanding, I've still got a few loose ends to wrap up on the Fitzgerald thing before turning it over to the district attorney."

"You're still not convinced that that private killed him," Mildred said, her comment more a statement than a question.

"No, I'm not," A. G. answered, almost more to himself than to her. He wanted to talk to Lieutenant Giles as soon as possible to see if he had made any progress identifying the man he, A. G., had seen coming out of Wanda Carbone's apartment.

He walked into his office, opened the window and turned the ceiling fan to its highest setting, and sat down with a sigh. Although he had dozed on the porch he had never really gotten back to sleep after getting up at four o'clock that morning, and he felt tired and mentally sluggish. He looked at the telephone on his desk and thought about calling Theresa but decided not to, knowing it would only make him feel worse if he called and she wasn't home. He sighed again and quickly dialed a number.

"Dr. Graham, please," he said when the call was answered. "Sheriff A. G. Farrell calling. It's very important. . . . Yes, thank you, I'll wait." He closed his eyes and yawned, stretching both arms over his head. "Paul, A. G. here," he said when his friend came on the line. "Listen, Paul, I have to talk to you this morning, as soon as possible. Yes, I know you're busy, but this is important. I've got a situation over here that I don't want to talk about over the telephone. I wouldn't ask if . . ." He broke off as Paul interrupted him, looking at his watch. "I'll be there in twenty minutes." He hung up and quickly dialed again. "Spencer? Listen, I've only got a minute but . . ."

"Let me guess," Spencer joked, interrupting. "Someone there in Hopewell bought a new refrigerator in Richmond and you want to know whether or not they paid cash for it."

"Doug Troutman was murdered yesterday," A. G. said, getting right to the point. "His throat was cut while he was sitting in front of that new television. The one he just bought with cash."

"You're kidding," Spencer said after a second of shocked silence.

A. G. shook his head as if Spencer could see over the telephone line. "I kid you not. Bud Taylor thinks that we're going to get a lot of attention from Richmond on this one. . . ."

"You know who his father is, don't you?" Spencer interrupted again.

"That's why I'm calling. I may need to talk to you about a thing or two, and, in any event, I'd like to know who's saying what over there as this thing develops."

"I'll do what I can," Spencer said cautiously, "but you've got to understand that Dr. Troutman's an important man, a *real* important man. When he gets unhappy, a lot of people run for cover, if you know what I mean."

"I think I do. I've got to run, but I'll call you this afternoon—see if you've heard anything, okay?" A. G. hung up and walked out to the front office. "I've got to run over to Petersburg," he said to Mildred, who stopped typing long enough to look up at him. "If Bud Taylor calls, tell him I'll be back in no more than an hour."

"I hope this is important," Paul Graham said as his nurse ushered A. G. into his office.

"Doug Troutman was murdered yesterday," A. G. said, thinking he was going to have to get used to saying those words, at least for the next day or two, until everyone knew about it.

Paul inhaled with a dramatic hiss of breath. "You know who his father is, don't you?"

"If I hadn't known, you're about the third person in the past twelve hours who's been eager to tell me," A. G. responded good-naturedly.

"Do you have a suspect or a motive?"

"No to the first, and as to the second, that's why I'm here."

"You don't think Troutman *fils* was your abortionist, do you?"

"It's possible," A. G. said cautiously, pleased that his friend had connected their last conversation and this visit so quickly. He told Paul about his four A.M. epiphany on the glider. "I know how busy your schedule is this morning, so rather than take up your time with a recitation of the various things that have raised at least an inference in my mind, let me just ask you a medical question or two, okay?" When Paul nodded affirmatively, A. G. began. "First, how difficult would it be for a nonphysician to learn how to abort a pregnant woman?"

"The stock answer any doctor would give you is that it takes years, literally, to learn even the simplest surgical procedure, and a D & C is far from the simplest. However, I would guess that a reasonably intelligent person, with basic reference materials to . . ."

"Such as?" A. G. interrupted.

Paul shrugged. "A medical school OB-GYN textbook, a basic surgical text, those sorts of things. Anyway, with things like that to go by I don't see why someone couldn't learn enough to at least try." He shook his head, a grim expression on his face. "Of course, such a person is going to run a high probability of killing a few women in the course of perfecting his technique." He thought of something and snapped his fingers. "The good news for someone like Troutman would be his access to prescription drugs, both narcotic painkillers and antibiotics, although, as may well have happened with the three girls whose death certificates you showed me, certain infectious-disease problems can't be controlled by anything in the pharmacological arsenal once they gain a foothold in the body."

"How could Doug have gotten access to prescription drugs, particularly narcotics? I thought the FDA controlled those things pretty tightly."

"Unfortunately, he could have gotten them as easily as buying an ice cream sundae. All he would have had to do was find a detail man . . ."

"Detail man?"

"The pharmaceutical sales reps are called detail men. All Troutman would have had to have done was find a detail man who was buying back free samples of drugs from the physicians in his territory."

"The physicians sell drugs back to these so-called detail men?" A. G.'s tone of voice betrayed his surprise and skepticism.

"It happens all the time. Keep in mind that the detail men and doctors spend a great deal of time together. The detail men pay for golf, drinks, dinners at the country club, things like that. At the big professional meetings in New York and Chicago and San Francisco the pharmaceutical companies and their reps spend even more lavishly, entertaining the docs and their wives like you wouldn't believe. Money flows like water." Paul chuckled, a not altogether humorous sound. "It can be pretty impressive to a small-town doctor with a run-of-the-mill general practice and not much opportunity to visit the big city. So, it's a relatively easy thing for the detail man to periodically buy a doctor's entire stock of sample drugs as a way to get cash into the doc's hands and make him even more beholden to a particular pharmaceutical company."

"Lord," A. G. murmured, "I had no idea."

"Few people outside the business do. So, anyway, back to Troutman *fils*—he gets friendly with a detail man or two and places orders with them for off-the-record drugs he needs for his little private practice."

"What about the government? I thought drugs, particularly narcotics, were regulated in such a way as to prevent this sort of thing."

"They are, but the free-sample trade is the weak link in the chain."

"So Troutman could have taught himself to do abortions, and, as a pharmacist, would have been able to provide illicit prophylactic antibiotics and painkillers as part of his 'service,' " A. G. said.

"Who else have you discussed this with?" Paul asked.

"No one, yet," A. G. answered, shaking his head.

"Then take my advice and don't, at least not until you have some sort of concrete evidence. Dr. Troutman, Doug's father, is an exceptionally powerful man in this state, and, believe me, is unlikely to want to hear that his son was a criminal. Particularly if such a charge is based solely on inference or speculation. He would make a very dangerous enemy." Paul made sure he had A. G.'s undivided attention. "Very dangerous. Do you understand?"

A. G. nodded. "I understand. Have you got any suggestions regarding evidence I might look for?"

"First and foremost, look for surgical instruments. If Dr. Troutman's son was doing abortions, he would have had to have had at least a basic surgical kit. Also, look for gyneco-logical literature—textbooks, notes, that sort of thing. Things you wouldn't necessarily expect a pharmacist to have in his possession."

By the time A. G. got back to his office his collar was limp and the back of his shirt was wet with perspiration. "This tie may have been a big mistake," he muttered, loosening the knot with one hand and fanning himself with the other as he walked into the building. "Any calls?" he asked Mildred when he got to her office.

"The fingerprint technician from Richmond called and said he was coming over this morning," she answered. "He said he knew he told you it would be this afternoon and hoped it would be okay with you."

"Sure," A. G. said casually. "Do I need to call him back?"

Mildred shook her head. "He's on the way. Sounds to me like Doug's daddy's got everyone in Richmond moving this up to the front burner."

"I wouldn't disagree with you." A. G. snapped his fingers as he thought of something. "I'd better get word over to War-ren Elam to let . . ."

Mildred held up a hand. "It's already done. I sent Lester," one of the city's two maintenance men, "over to the Troutman house to make sure Warren was awake and to tell him what was going on."

"I declare, I don't know how this office would get along without you. Who else called?"

"Bud Taylor wants you to call him." She snorted. "My guess is that he's going to want to hear from you a couple of times a day until this thing is solved. And you got a call from Jubal Bishop." She looked at A. G. suspiciously. "What do you suppose he wants?"

A. G. shrugged noncommittally. "Hard to say." He re-commenced fanning himself with his hat and turned to go into his office. "Lord, it must be at least ninety-five degrees and it's only," he looked at his watch, "ten o'clock." After making sure his ceiling fan was on and the window open, A. G. picked up his telephone and called Bud Taylor. "Yeah, Bud, A. G. here." He listened for a second. "No, nothing at all. I was over in Petersburg checking out a few things. I'll give you a call later this afternoon. What's that? . . . No, but I've got a feeling that a few things are going to fall into place pretty quickly." He hung up and immediately dialed another number. "Jubal, A. G. here. What's up?" He looked at his watch as he listened, unconsciously nodding his head. "Yeah, give me twenty minutes. I'll see you out there." Hanging up the telephone, he leaned back, putting one hand behind his head and tapping out a syncopated rhythm on the arm of his wooden swivel chair with the other. He yawned and knew if he closed his eyes it would take no effort whatever to doze right off. In-stead, he jumped up and walked out to the front office. "I should be back by noon," he said on his way past Mildred's desk, moving quickly to avoid having to tell her where he was going. "If anybody calls, tell them I'll get back to them after lunch."

After a quick stop at the Troutman house to make sure that Warren Elam was indeed awake and expecting the fin-gerprint technician, A. G. drove out to the Club St. Louis. One of Jubal's sons, busy picking up trash in the gravel parking lot, gave him a surly look as he pulled in and parked. Jubal, dressed in only a T-shirt and boxer shorts, was seated at a table near the screen door, struggling to balance his accounts and stay cool at the same time. He had a small dishtowel in his lap that he used periodically to wipe the perspiration from his face.

"Dern, Jubal," A. G. teased as soon as he saw him, "the

least you could have done is put on a pair of trousers when you knew I was coming to visit."

"I don't know how you can wear a suit, as hot as it is today," Jubal countered.

"I'd be a sight driving around in my underwear." A. G. smiled, unable to imagine such a thing. "Folks around here would think I'd plumb lost my mind."

"If this heat wave don't break soon, I swear I'm going to close for a week and go up to the mountains," Jubal assured him. "You want an iced coffee?" Without waiting for an answer, he waved at another of his sons, wiping down the long bar. "You, Mason, bring us a couple of iced coffees."

"As much money as you're making in here, it seems like you could air-condition the place," A. G. said, pulling up a chair and sitting down across the table from Jubal. "And, yes, an iced coffee would hit the spot." He took out his Chesterfields, offered one to Jubal, who declined, and settled back.

"God only knows what it would cost to air-condition this barn," Jubal said, looking around the cavernous room. "Besides, folks like to sweat when they're drinking." He chuckled. "Leastways, folks that come here do." He fell silent as his son arrived with two glasses filled with ice and coffee. "I heard about Doug Troutman getting killed," he said obliquely when the boy returned to his cleaning chores.

"I don't reckon there's anybody in the county who hasn't heard about it," A. G. said, taking a careful sip of the cold coffee. He looked at Jubal contemplatively. "As my daddy used to say whenever he knew or suspected that I had done something wrong, 'Boy, it's time to come to Jesus.' " A. G. smiled, pleased with the memory. "It's not that he was a particularly religious man," A. G. added, more to himself than to Jubal. "I think he just like the way it sounded." He took another sip of coffee and the smile faded. "What have you got for me, Jubal?"

"Sam Brown knew his daughter had gotten herself pregnant," Jubal said quietly. He wiped his brow with the dishtowel.

"You make it sound like there wasn't a young man involved in the process," A. G. said dryly. When he realized that Jubal had no idea what he was talking about, he waved a hand. "Never mind. Tell me something, did you know that Sam knew about it when we talked the last time?"

Jubal shook his head. "No, I didn't. Like I told you then, at that time it was only a rumor as far as I knew, and I had no idea what Sam may or may not have known."

A. G. nodded. "Go on."

"Well, two nights ago, one of Sam's boys was in here, pretty liquored up."

"Which one?"

"Virgil. Anyway, he was in here running his mouth and making a nuisance of himself. If it wasn't for his daddy, and the fact that we've done some business together over the years, I'd have thrown him out and been done with it. Instead, I tried to calm him down, get some coffee into him to sober him up, that sort of thing. He wasn't having any of it, though. He sat over there," Jubal nodded toward one of the booths, "telling whoever would listen that Sam knew who had caused Julie's death and that he, Sam, was going to kill him. Crazy talk." Jubal shook his head and wiped his face again with the dishtowel. "Finally, he was making too much of a fuss to tolerate so we had to throw him out." He smiled sardonically. "He was so rowdy that Mason," Jubal nodded toward his son, now back behind the bar, "had to get a little physical in the process."

"Did Mason hurt him?"

Jubal shook his head. "Nah, blackened an eye, probably bloused his lip, not much more than that. Anyway, Virgil brung it on himself. He just kept talking about how his daddy was going to kill the man."

"They knew who got her pregnant?"

"See, that's what I thought at first, that Virgil was talking about the soldier, or whoever, that got her pregnant. But as he kept talking, I understood differently." He paused for a sip of coffee. "I didn't think too much about it at the time. When folks get really drunk, they're liable to say anything. But then, this morning, when I hear about Doug Troutman . . ."

"How does Doug figure into all this?" Even as he asked, A. G. suddenly knew what Jubal was going to say.

"That's just what I'm trying to tell you, Sheriff. It was Doug Troutman that Virgil was talking about. He kept saying that his daddy was holding Doug responsible for Julie's death." Jubal sighed, a long, drawn-out exhalation of breath. "He said Sam was going to kill him."

Chapter Eleven

The steering wheel of A. G.'s Ford was almost too hot to touch as he turned onto the county blacktop road out of the gravel parking lot of the Club St. Louis. Heat radiating off the macadam surface of the road rose in waves, distorting the hazy sunlight and creating the unsettling illusion that the painted white lines were twisting and writhing slowly in the foreshortened distance, bringing to mind a Hieronymus Bosch rendering of souls burning in hell.

"I need to check on something before I head back to the office," he had told Mildred, using the telephone behind Jubal's bar, "and I'll probably stop by the house for a quick change of clothes as well. Any calls?"

"Nothing that can't wait until you get back," she assured him, unable to resist adding, "I told you you'd burn up in that suit."

"You did, indeed," he confirmed, smiling. "Listen, do me a favor, would you?" he asked just before hanging up. "Call Claire Biddle and have her drop her key to the drugstore off with you sometime in the next hour or two."

The drive out to Sam Brown's place took only fifteen minutes. Briars and wild berry vines reached out for the Ford as A. G. worked his way down the long, badly rutted dirt lane that led almost a mile from the county road to the house. At one point, about halfway in, the drive crossed through a broad, graveled streambed, little more than a mud hole in July. Sam's dogs, mostly coonhounds, hearing the car approach, started baying well before the house came into view, and they, together with the fact than any car coming down the long lane at more than the pace of a man walking risked breaking an axle or puncturing an oil pan, guaranteed that no one, particularly law-enforcement officials, could sneak up on the house.

Three or four junked cars and pickup trucks in various stages of demolition littered what could only charitably be called the front yard, and a large, Cyclone-fenced pen to one side of the house held the dogs, eight or ten of them by A. G.'s quick count. The house itself, a frame structure that had been haphazardly added onto over the years, sat baking in the sun, not a blade of grass nor a shade tree within fifty feet in any direction. A. G. stopped fifteen feet from the house and turned off the engine, waiting for someone to come out onto the porch. After several seconds the screen door opened and Sam's son Virgil appeared, looking at A. G. with overt suspicion and hostility. He walked down the three steps to the hardpan, dusty yard and sidled over to the car, moving in an odd, slightly sideways crablike gait, almost as if he were suffering from some sort of inner-ear problem.

"Hello, Sheriff," he said without a trace of cordiality, bending slightly from the hips to look in through the driver's-side window at A. G. "What brings you out this way?" Although he tried to keep the left side of his face turned away from the car, he could not hide his blackened left eye and badly swollen lower lip.

"Is your daddy around?" A. G. asked, pointedly ignoring Virgil's question.

By way of answer Virgil shook his head, obviously intent on not volunteering any information that might somehow prove useful to A. G.

"Where is he?"

Virgil looked at A. G. for a second before answering, clearly trying to think of a plausible lie. "He and Willis"—another of Sam's sons—"went to look at a truck."

"You expecting him back this afternoon?"

Another shake of the head. "Maybe tomorrow."

"Must be a complicated transaction," A. G. said dryly. "When did they leave on this extended commercial expedition?"

"Couple of nights ago, I guess. I wasn't paying no attention."

"How's your mother doing?" A. G. asked, pointing toward the house. "Is *she* home?"

"She's been right poorly since the funeral," Virgil responded, shading his eyes with one hand to better see A. G. "The doctor had to come out day before yesterday and give her some pills. She's sleeping now."

"I'm sorry to hear she's not feeling well." A. G. nodded toward the passenger side of the car. "Why don't you and I have a little chat out here, and that way we won't have to go in and disturb her."

Virgil walked around and got in, slouching low in the seat.

"It's too hot to be beating around the bush," A. G. said, "so I'll get right to the point. I understand you were doing a lot of talking a couple nights ago out at Jubal Bishop's place."

"Who told you that?"

"It doesn't matter who told me. What matters is what you were saying."

"I was drunk," Virgil said, shrugging his narrow shoulders. "I might have said anything."

"Let me refresh your memory: What you said was that your daddy was going to kill Doug Troutman."

"I never said nothing like that," Virgil protested, a look of serious concern on his face.

"I thought you just said you were too drunk to remember what you said," A. G. pointed out.

"I can't remember, not exactly, but I know I never said nothing about daddy killing nobody."

"Tell me why you said it," A. G. pressed, ignoring Virgil's worried denial. "It had something to do with you sister Julie's death, didn't it?"

"I tol' you I never said it." His voice took on a distinctly unpleasant, whiny quality. "Whoever tol' you I did was lying to you." He picked at a scab on the back of his hand, refusing to meet A. G.'s eyes. "It's hot in here."

Indeed, the inside of the Ford, even with all the windows open, was heating up like a wood-burning stove stoked with dry kindling.

"And fixin' to get hotter," A. G. assured him. He paused for several seconds, letting Virgil squirm. Finally, he spoke. "Here's what I want you to do—are you listening to me?"

Virgil nodded, still staring at the back of his hand as if written on it he would find a complete set of directions out of the unpleasant predicament he found himself in.

"When your daddy gets home, whether it's tonight or tomorrow or Sunday, you tell him that I was out here today and that I want to talk to him in my office in Hopewell at nine o'clock Monday morning. Have you got that?"

Another surly nod.

"Look at me," A. G. commanded. When Virgil complied, his narrowly set eyes squinting in the bright sunlight reflecting off the car's dash, A. G. continued. "Nine o'clock, Monday morning, in my office," he repeated slowly, tapping his finger on the steering wheel for emphasis. "No ifs, ands, or buts."

Stripping off his clothes as soon as he got home, A. G. stepped into a cool shower, sighing as it mercifully lowered his body temperature several degrees. Although he hadn't planned to, he lay down on the bed after toweling off, thinking that a short nap would complete the process of recovery started by the shower. Almost immediately he fell into a troubled sleep, too shallow for the release of dreams, too short to refresh. Finally, after almost forty-five minutes, he rolled out from under the mosquito netting with a sigh and, dressing quickly, returned to the office.

"Any calls?" he asked Mildred as he walked in.

"Two. Lorraine O'Brien wants to talk to you, and you got a call from Mrs. Fitzgerald." Mildred looked at A. G. as if she were going to make a comment about something but remained silent.

"Either of them say what they had in mind?" He knew Mildred was getting exceedingly curious about Theresa's telephone calls.

She shook her head. "I told them both I expected you back around two o'clock."

"Did you get any lunch?" A. G. asked, turning to walk back to his office.

"Audrey brought a tomato salad by, and we ate here in the office. Did you eat anything yet?"

A. G. shook his head. "I'll go see what Lorraine wants in a minute and grab a quick sandwich then." A. G. walked into his office, closing the door behind him. Sitting on the edge of his desk, he dialed Theresa's number and fanned himself with a sheaf of paper while he waited for the call to go through.

"Hello?"

Her voice sent a thrill through A. G.'s body. "Hello," he said. "I'm sorry I wasn't here when you called earlier." Then, without thinking, he added, "I missed you last night."

"I missed you, too. I spent the evening in Petersburg. I got back here late and thought about calling but didn't want to wake you." She paused for a second. "I'm going to have to stay at Fort Lee tonight. Some friends of Marty's on the post are having a dinner—you know what those things are like. Anyway, could we get together tomorrow afternoon? In Petersburg?"

"Of course. Around five o'clock?" *Who were you with in Petersburg last night?* he wanted to ask but did not.

"That would be perfect. We'll open a bottle of Chianti, and I'll make something Italian for dinner. See you then."

After hanging up, A. G. sat still for several seconds, recalling without conscious thought the sweetness and warmth of her breath as it washed over his face when they lay together. Startled at the strength and clarity of his memory, and its immediate effect upon his body, he stood up and moved around the desk to his chair, adjusting himself sheepishly inside his trousers as he sat down. He took a Chesterfield from an open pack in his top drawer and lit it, inhaling deeply as he quickly dialed Lieutenant Giles's number at Fort Lee. When he identified himself and asked to speak to Giles, Sergeant Dickey's gruff voice informed him curtly that the lieutenant was out. "Would you be so kind as to ask him to call me when he returns," A. G. countered, quickly hanging up before Dickey could refuse. He tapped his index finger on the desk for several seconds, annoyed with himself for letting Dickey aggravate him so. Realizing suddenly he was hungry, he breezed out of his office.

"I'm going to get a sandwich at Lorraine's," he reminded Mildred as he passed her desk. "If anyone calls, tell them I'll be back in half an hour or so."

Mildred nodded her head, not bothering to look up from the Underwood.

"Good afternoon, Lorraine," he said, sliding onto a stool at the Little Acorn's counter. "Got any pimento cheese left?"

"Sorry, A. G., the lunch crowd cleaned me out. How about a BLT? I've got some sugar-cured bacon left from breakfast."

"Sold." A. G. carefully extracted a toothpick from the dispenser next to the cash register and chewed it for several seconds. "Mildred told me you called earlier."

Sliding two pieces of white bread into the toaster, Lorraine nodded. "Let me get this sandwich made, and I'll sit down and chat with you. What do you want to drink with it?"

A. G. thought for a second. "A glass of milk sounds good." Glancing around the empty diner, he noticed that most of the booths had not been bused from lunch. "You working by yourself today?" Then, before she could answer, "Where's Mary Frances?"

"Just a minute." Lorraine finished the sandwich and put it on the counter in front of A. G. "Move over to one of the tables, and I'll join you," she said, taking a bottle of milk out of the dairy case. She followed A. G. to a table and sat down. "Lord," she said with a deep sigh, "it feels good to sit down. I've been on my feet since five o'clock this morning."

"Is Mary Frances out sick?"

Lorraine shook her head, a smile on her face. "Mary Frances and your young lieutenant ran off to get married early this morning. To Myrtle Beach, South Carolina."

"What?" A. G. froze in shock, his sandwich midway between the plate and his mouth.

Lorraine laughed. "Eat your sandwich," she advised, "and I'll tell you all about it. But first, give me a cigarette. I left mine at the cash register, and now that I'm finally sitting I don't think my feet are going to let me get up right away."

A. G. fumbled for a Chesterfield and lit it for her. "Married?" he asked, a foolish grin on his face. "That scoundrel," he added, referring to Giles. "And after, what, only two or three dates?"

"He's a sweet young man. They went out on a date last night, and when he brought her home he came in and asked for my permission to marry her. I didn't have to ask her if she loved him—any fool could have seen that from a mile away."

"Is she old enough to be getting married?"

Lorraine laughed. "I know it's hard to believe, but she turned twenty this spring. I married her daddy when I was barely seventeen."

"Do you think he can support a wife? I mean, what's he going to do when he gets out of the army?"

Lorraine shrugged. "Who knows? Listen, A. G., I told her the same thing my momma told me. You don't get too many second chances in this life. If you love him, and he loves you, forget everything else. If you spend your life waiting around for guarantees, the only thing certain is that you'll end up an old maid." She winked at A. G. and stubbed out her cigarette. "Or an old bachelor," she teased, cutting closer to the quick than she realized.

A. G. tossed his hat onto the hat rack and turned to Mildred's desk with a smile on his face. "I'll bet you didn't know that Mary Frances O'Brien and Lieutenant Giles ran off to get married this morning, did you?"

Mildred looked up from the Underwood, a noncommittal look on her face. "That's what Lorraine wanted to tell you?"

A. G. nodded, knowing from her look that she was annoyed he had heard about it before she had. "Just now." His smile broadened. "And I'm tickled to death about it."

"Where'd they go to get married?"

"Myrtle Beach." He turned to go back to his office. "Oh, by the way, did Claire Biddle drop off a key to Doug's drugstore?"

"She wasn't too happy about leaving it," Mildred said, reaching into a desk drawer for the key. "She went to some length to explain to me that it's the only one she has."

Good, A. G. thought but did not say. "She won't be needing it anymore," he said, taking the key in his right hand. He had not told Mildred, nor did he intend to tell her, that he already had Doug's keys, taken from the body before he and Bob Creech had loaded it onto the gurney. "Besides, I don't want anybody rooting around in there for the time being."

"I hardly think Claire would be doing any 'rooting around,' " Mildred pointed out.

"Well, you never know," A. G. said, smiling, "she might mess up some evidence without even knowing it."

"What kind of . . ." Before she could finish her question, the telephone rang. She answered it and, after listening for a second, held the receiver up. "It's Bud Taylor. Do you want to take it here or in your office?"

A. G. answered by walking quickly to his office. "Hello, Bud?" He listened for several seconds, absently nodding his head. "Yeah, I've turned up a couple of things, but nothing I want to talk about over the telephone." He looked at his watch, somewhat surprised to see that it was already almost three o'clock. "I need to get over to Doug's house and let Warren go—he's been over there most of the day, keeping an eye on the place for me. Now that the fingerprint technician from Richmond's been there, I want to get in and give the house a thorough going over myself, particularly before Angie gets back in town. Why don't I stop by your office at the warehouse and fill you in when I'm done?"

The first thing A. G. noticed was that someone, probably the fingerprint technician, had stepped in the blood around Doug's easy chair and tracked it back down the hallway, through the living room, and into the vestibule, where the track gradually petered out. He stopped suddenly, and Warren Elam, who had been right behind him as he entered the front door, almost bumped into him.

"You're not squeamish, are you, Warren?" he asked. "I mean at the sight of blood."

Palpably nervous but not wishing to be thought unmanly, Warren shook his head.

"Good, because the first thing we need to do is get you started on cleaning up the blood, here and in the family room. Angie Troutman's probably going to be coming back sometime this weekend, and we don't want her seeing a mess like this, do we?" Without waiting for a response, A. G. pointed back toward the rear of the house. "Why don't you go back and see if you can find a mop and some rags."

After getting Warren started on the cleanup, A. G. quickly and efficiently worked his way from the front of the house to the rear, looking for anything that one might consider to be out of the ordinary. Although the house yielded nothing in the way of surprises, he had not expected it to, not really. There was no sign of a forced entry by whoever had killed Doug, but he assumed that the Troutmans, as was the case with everyone in Hopewell, seldom if ever locked their doors or windows. Further, there was no sign of a hurried search for money or valuables by a would-be burglar—the mattresses and bedding had not been tossed, clothes had not been pulled from the dressers and flung to the floor, nothing in the den or any of the other rooms seemed to be out of place or in disarray.

"Sheriff?" Warren Elam's voice reached A. G. in Doug and Angie's bedroom.

He walked quickly back to the front of the house. "Yes, Warren?"

"I'm all finished cleaning up. Do you want me to do anything else?" Warren's tone of voice made it clear that he sincerely hoped not.

A. G. looked into the den and along the hallway to the vestibule, noting with pleasure that Warren had indeed carefully eradicated the last traces of Doug's messy demise.

"No, that will be all," A. G. said, shepherding the young man out onto the front porch. "I appreciate your help, and I'll see that you get paid for the time you spent here today," he promised.

Back in the house, alone, A. G. lit a cigarette and leaned against the doorway into the den. He had found neither surgical instruments nor medical literature, nor indeed anything that would have supported an inference that Doug had led a secret life as an abortionist. "He wouldn't have kept anything here," A. G. said quietly to himself, "not where Angie could have found it and asked questions." He finished his cigarette and, just to satisfy himself that he hadn't missed anything, did one more quick walk-through of the house before leaving.

"I didn't learn much at the Troutman house," he told Bud Taylor as he settled into a chair in the older man's office after the short drive out to the warehouse, "but to tell you the truth, I hadn't expected to." The thought suddenly entered his mind that the last time he had met Bud here at the warehouse, Martin Fitzgerald had been slumped behind the wheel of his DeSoto with a large-caliber hole in his head.

"You said you had something to tell me," Bud said impatiently.

A. G. nodded as he fanned himself with his hat. "I got a call earlier today from Jubal Bishop." He spent several minutes telling Bud about his visit out to the Club St. Louis and his subsequent conversation with Virgil Brown.

"Damn," Bud muttered, more to himself than A. G. He thought for a second and then looked at his watch. "It's after five o'clock," he said, taking a pint bottle of sour-mash bourbon out of his desk, "do you want a drink?"

"No, thanks, but I will take a Coca-Cola," he said, pointing at the cooler sitting just outside Bud's office.

"Get me one, too," Bud said, taking a big slug of whiskey directly from the bottle. He shuddered once and cleared his throat, blowing out his breath in a long, whistling exhalation. "Damn," he said again, shaking his head as the bourbon, followed closely by several quick swallows of cola, worked its way toward his stomach. He belched indelicately and pointed at A. G. "You may have been right about that business with Sam's daughter." As was the case during their previous conversation, Bud did not seem to be able to use the word *abortion*. "Should we call the state police to be on the lookout for Sam?"

A. G. shook his head. "I don't think so, Bud, at least not right away. Virgil'll tell him pretty quickly when he gets home that I was out there, and even if Sam did in fact kill Doug, I don't think he'll run." He shook his head again. "Where would he run to? Other than when he was in the army, Sam's never been out of Virginia in his life." *Like me,* A. G. thought but did not say.

"What are you going to say to him on Monday?"

"The truth. That his boy Virgil was telling everyone who cared to listen that he, Sam, held Doug Troutman responsible for Julie's death and was going to kill him. If he denies it, which I expect he will, at least at first, I plan to tell him that I'm going to ask the district attorney's office in Petersburg to prepare an affidavit to file with the court seeking an order to exhume her body and perform an autopsy." A. G. took a drink of his Coke and shrugged. "If that doesn't get his attention, nothing will."

"You got anything else, any evidence, linking Troutman to this business with the young girls?"

"You mean abortions?" A. G. asked, wondering if Bud would ever use the word. "No," he continued, having already decided not to say anything yet about the panties he had found under Doug's chair. "I'm going to search the drugstore first thing in the morning." He told Bud about his visit that morning with Paul Graham. "If Doug had any surgical instruments, or medical literature, my guess is that he kept it locked up at the drugstore. If it's there, I'll find it." He also planned to talk to Dorcas Craige that evening, but, again, was disinclined to tell Bud about it ahead of time.

"I hate to take this to Bill Troutman with nothing more than suspicion and Sam's boy Virgil mouthing off, drunk, to back us up." Bud shook his head. "He's not apt to be pleased to hear it."

"Then don't," A. G. advised firmly, finishing his Coke and leaning down to put the bottle into a wooden crate sitting on the floor next to Bud's desk. "As a matter of fact, I'd rather you didn't say anything at all just yet. We'll know a whole lot more by this time on Monday, so if I were you, I'd tell him that we're following up on a couple of leads but don't expect to have anything to report for the time being. He'll just have to wait."

Dorcas Craige was sitting at her kitchen table when A. G. knocked on the screen door.

"Don't get up, Miz Craige," A. G. called out, "I'll let myself in." He stepped into the kitchen and smiled, genuinely pleased at how much better she looked than the last time he had been out there. He held up a paper bag in his right hand. "I brought you some barbecue and Brunswick stew, and," he held up a smaller bag in his left, "two cold bottles of beer."

"Bless your heart, Sheriff," Dorcas said, motioning for A. G. to join her at the table. "Put that barbecue and stew over there on the counter—I'll eat a bite later this evening when it cools off some."

A. G. did as she asked and, after putting one of the bottles of beer in her icebox, he opened the other and gave it to her.

"Mmmm," she murmured after taking a sip, "don't that taste good on a hot evening." She looked at A. G. "Aren't you going to join me?"

Shaking his head, A. G. took out his cigarettes and lit one. "I've still got some work to do yet and, besides, you'll want to enjoy that second bottle with your dinner."

They both sat quietly for several seconds, A. G. enjoying his cigarette, Dorcas her beer. Finally, when he deemed enough time had passed that it wouldn't be considered impolite to get to the business at hand, he spoke.

"I expect you've heard about Doug Troutman getting murdered."

Dorcas nodded and pointed at the label on her bottle. "What does that say?" she asked.

"Pabst Blue Ribbon," A. G. answered, knowing that she could not read.

"Percy used to love to drink a beer in the evening, but I've gone and forgotten what kind it was he used to drink." She fell silent and, for a second, A. G. wondered if his comment about Doug Troutman's murder had registered. Just as he was about to repeat it, she looked up from her beer bottle. "Mr. Troutman was a bad man."

"I believe it," A. G. said. "I surely do. He was performing abortions, wasn't he?"

"He was, for girls all over the county, and some folks would say he was pretty good at it, if you don't count the three or four girls he killed," Dorcas said sarcastically, shaking her head. "I knew little Cissie Jackson," one of the girls whose death certificates A. G. had culled, "ever since she was born. She wasn't no bigger than a minute, even when she was grow'd, and Lord," she looked away and shook her head sadly, "that child was pure as the jest of God." She smiled, suddenly remembering something, and looked at A. G. "That's what your momma used to say about you when you was just a baby. 'Pure as the jest of God,' she used to say, picking you up from your cradle to show all the folks that came around to see you." She fell silent and took a sip of beer. When her eyes finally came back to A. G.'s face, the smile was gone. "As far as I know, Mr. Troutman only did colored girls—they said the white folks' daughters had a for-real doctor over in Richmond to take care of them. That Julie Brown was the first white girl I heard of him operating on." Dorcas shrugged. "Maybe she couldn't go all the way to Richmond."

"Her father, Sam Brown, is a prime suspect in the murder." He told her about Virgil's bragging about how his daddy, Sam, was going to kill Doug.

"Sounds to me like you got your man," Dorcas observed quietly.

A. G. reached into his pocket and took out the panties he had found under Doug's easy chair. "I think somebody, possibly another young girl wanting an abortion, was there the night Doug was killed," he said, holding them up for Dorcas to see. "I doubt whoever these belong to did it, but she might have seen whoever did."

"I don't know anything about that," she said firmly.

A. G. smiled. "I didn't think you would, Miz Craige, but I was sort of hoping that you might be willing to ask around, see if you could find something out. Believe me, I don't want to get the young woman in trouble, I just want to talk to her, privately, to find out if she saw anyone or anything that night." He leaned forward in his chair, the smile gone from his face. "Like you said, Doug Troutman was a bad man, Miz Craige, there's no doubt about that. If I had known what he was doing, I would have put him in jail, or at least tried to, for killing those girls. It wouldn't have mattered to me that he was white and they were colored. Not a bit it wouldn't have. And I don't doubt that whoever killed him, whether it was Sam Brown or someone else, thought they had a good reason for doing it, but that's not for us to decide. You know as well as I do that we can't have folks running around taking the law into their own hands."

"I'll think on it," she allowed, taking on no commitments and making no promises. "I will."

"That's good enough for me," A. G. assured her, rising from his chair. "I'll visit with you again in a day or two."

Although he started for home when he left Dorcas Craige's house, A. G. changed his mind and decided instead to conduct his search of Doug's drugstore. Although he had planned to do it in the morning, he didn't feel like going home just then, knowing that Dolores Anderson was expecting, at least, a telephone call from him. He knew he had to tell her about Theresa Fitzgerald, about falling in love, but could not bring himself to do so, at least not that evening, not that weekend. "Monday," he said to himself as he parked in front of the drugstore, "we'll talk on Monday."

The front door yielded easily to Doug's key, and A. G. carefully locked the door behind him. Claire Biddle had left the blinds drawn on the front windows, giving him ample privacy from the curious eyes of passersby as he moved through the small store. Ignoring the lunch counter, A. G. walked quickly to Doug's private office, behind the prescription counter at the rear of the store. Although the nonprescription medications and nostrums were openly displayed on shelves behind the counter, the prescription drugs and narcotics were secured in a separate room, little larger than a closet, adjoining Doug's small office. A. G. first went through Doug's unlocked desk, checking the contents of each drawer in turn, finding nothing out of the ordinary save a so-called French postcard at the back of one drawer featuring a rather buxom young woman clad in what was no doubt an unintentionally modest corset and black stockings. He spent only a minute or two trying to decipher the inventory ledgers, quickly realizing that they would be better audited, if it became necessary, by an accountant from the state pharmacy board.

Flipping through Doug's key ring, A. G. found the key to the prescription drug and narcotics storage room after only three tries. He opened the door and the first thing that caught his eye was a box of condoms. Although he had not thought about it before, since he had never bought any, he realized with some surprise that anyone wanting to purchase condoms had to ask Doug personally, something many men, married or single, would be extremely reticent to do, particularly if other customers were within earshot. *Doug might have had less business as an abortionist if these things were more readily available,* he thought as he moved on, his eyes sweeping the shelves. Although he had originally planned to look for evidence of an illicit trade in free samples such as Paul Graham had mentioned, he realized that, as with Doug's ledgers, it was a job for the state pharmacy board.

At the rear of the small room, sitting on the floor under a shelf and so inconspicuous that A. G. almost missed it, was a small, two-drawer, metal filing cabinet, locked. It took A. G. several tries with various keys on Doug's key ring before he was able to unlock it. The top drawer was filled to capacity with a disorganized jumble of pill bottles and boxes, most labeled as FREE PHYSICIAN SAMPLE—NOT FOR RESALE. The names of the various drugs listed on the labels were, not surprisingly, unfamiliar to A. G., but he had no doubt that they were antibiotics and narcotic painkillers. He pushed the drawer closed and opened the bottom drawer. Unlike the top one, it contained only a single item—a small, pebbled-leather physician's bag, of the sort doctors carried when making house calls. Even without opening it, he knew what it would contain.

Chapter Twelve

A. G. was in the kitchen on Saturday morning, still in his pajamas, when Bud Taylor knocked on the front screen door.

"Come on in, Bud," he called out from the foyer when he saw who it was. "Let me run upstairs and throw on a pair of trousers and a shirt. There's a fresh pot of coffee on the stove," he added over his shoulder while climbing the stairs. "Help yourself."

Bud was still standing in the foyer, holding a hand-tinted color photograph mounted in an ornate metal frame, when A. G. came back downstairs, hurriedly tucking a short-sleeved white shirt into a pair of rumpled tan trousers.

"I remember when this picture of Herbert and Mary Elizabeth," A. G.'s parents, "was taken," Bud said, holding it up for A. G. to see. "It was in late 1918—a year or two before you were even born—and your daddy had just opened his law office in

Hopewell." He put it back on the foyer table with a sigh. "Now here you are the sheriff, and I'm an old man."

"Not *too* old, Bud," A. G. said with exaggerated cheerfulness, wondering what in the world Bud was doing there at eight o'clock on a Saturday morning. "Come into the kitchen—I'll pour us a cup of coffee."

"I didn't think you drank coffee," Bud said as they walked back together.

"I guess I've taken more of a liking to it recently," A. G. said lightly, already looking forward to seeing Theresa Fitzgerald that evening. "What brings you here this morning?"

"They got Sam Brown," Bud said without a preamble as soon as he sat down at the kitchen table. "That's what I came out to tell you."

"Whoa, just a minute," A. G. exclaimed, almost spilling the coffee he was pouring. He carefully handed the cup to Bud. "What do you mean they got Sam Brown? Who is *they*?"

"The state police." Bud paused and took a sip of his coffee. "I decided that I had to tell Bill Troutman about our conversation," he muttered, looking at his coffee cup as he put it back on the table. "I didn't feel right about him not knowing, so I drove over to Richmond yesterday afternoon, right after you and I talked."

"Bud, I thought we agreed that we were going to wait until we had . . ."

"I know we talked about not saying anything yet," Bud interrupted, holding up a hand, "but I had to tell Troutman *something*. He doesn't have what you might call a *waiting*-type personality, if you know what I mean. If he found out we knew something we hadn't told him . . ." Bud paused for a sip of coffee and then looked at A. G. "Believe me, we don't need that kind of trouble. Anyway, after I told him, I tried to get him to not do anything, but he immediately called the governor, who in turn had the state police put out an all-points bulletin."

"Where are they holding him?" A. G. asked with a sigh, knowing there was no point in further argument about the pros and cons of prematurely revealing his, A. G.'s, suspicions to Doug Troutman's father.

"He's dead," Bud said, still refusing to meet A. G.'s eyes.

"Dead?" Bud's response was so unexpected that A. G. was momentarily confused. "Who's dead?"

"A highway patrolman spotted Sam's car over near Richmond about one o'clock this morning," Bud said, indirectly answering A. G.'s question. "He tried to pull him over, but Sam took off. During the chase, Sam lost control of his car and rolled it. The patrolman said Sam was thrown from the car and killed instantly."

Stunned, A. G. sat down at the table.

"The state police are saying that the fact that Sam tried to run points to his guilt in Doug's murder," Bud added.

"He could have been running for any number of reasons, Bud," A. G. protested. "Half the time he was on the road he was carrying whiskey, you know that. Plus, he was just plain ornery—he could easily have taken off for no reason other than that he didn't feel like getting a speeding ticket."

"Have you searched the drugstore yet?" Bud asked, changing the subject.

"Yesterday evening, after I talked to you." A. G. shook his head. "I can't believe Sam is dead."

"Believe it," Bud advised, his tone of voice clearly indicating that he was beginning to lose patience with A. G. "What did you find at the drugstore?"

"Proof that Doug was doing abortions," A. G. said. He told Bud about finding the locked filing cabinet with the drugs and the surgical kit. "I haven't had a chance to show the surgical instruments to Paul Graham yet, but I already know what he's going to say."

"Did you leave everything at the store?"

"I left the drugs there, of course, but I locked the surgical instruments up in my office. Monday I'll call the pharmacy board and have someone from their office come do an inventory and take possession of the drugs. Maybe they can trace where they came from, who Doug was buying them from, that sort of thing."

Bud shook his head. "Don't do anything until you talk to me first, including showing those instruments to Dr. Graham," he ordered. "I need to run this by a couple of people in Richmond before we go making a federal case out of things."

"What do you mean, a 'federal case'? The drugs and surgical instruments are a clear indication that Doug was involved in an ongoing criminal activity." He leaned forward in his chair, agitated that the older man seemed not to appreciate the magnitude of the crimes that had been committed. "Bud, at least three young women, maybe more, died as a result of what Doug did to them. That's murder. This community needs to know exactly what he was doing and whether or not other people were involved—particularly people, whether doctors or drug salesmen, who were illegally selling him prescription medications."

"This community doesn't *need* to know anything," Bud said heatedly. "Doug Troutman paid in full for whatever crimes he committed. He's dead and, as far as I'm concerned, so is the man, Sam Brown, who killed him." He pointed at A. G. "What we've got now is a political problem, not a legal one. So, unless I tell you differently, we're going to wrap this thing up as quietly as possible because there's absolutely nothing to be gained by dragging Doug's name, his *father's* name, through the mud." He suddenly thought of something. "Have you talked to anybody else about this? I mean, other than Jubal Bishop and Sam's boy Virgil?"

A. G. shook his head slowly, unwilling to tell Bud about his visit the prior evening with Dorcas Craige.

"Good." Bud nodded with satisfaction. "Let's keep it that way. I'll drive out to Jubal's place later this morning and have a little talk with him. He'll keep his mouth shut if he knows what's good for him, and as for Sam's boy Virgil, I think we can convince him that if he doesn't want to find himself in jail as an accomplice to murder, he'll keep quiet." Bud chuckled mirthlessly. "In fact, we can probably even convince him to leave town if that's what it takes." He stood up from the table. "Remember—don't do anything and, even more important, don't *say* anything to anybody, until I've got this mess straightened out in Richmond."

"I'm sorry, but I agree with your boss," Theresa said. She and A. G. were reclining against the headboard of her bed in the warehouse apartment in Petersburg.

"Actually, Bud Taylor's not technically my boss," A. G. responded, "although I suppose that, given our relationship, it amounts to the same thing." He shifted his weight over to his side so he could look more directly at her. "But surely you don't think it's right to just sweep the whole thing under the table, do you? I mean, doesn't the public have the right to know that crimes were committed, that abortions had been conducted by the town's pharmacist?"

"What possible good would it do?" Theresa asked. "The abortionist is dead, killed by the father of one of his victims, who in turn is now himself dead." Her finger traced a circle in the air above them. "The loop is closed—there's no one left to punish."

"We don't know that Sam Brown killed him," A. G. pointed out. "I have neither confession nor murder weapon."

"What you have is a compelling motive, the fact that, according to his own son, he knew the druggist was responsible for his daughter's death. You also have intent, based again on the son's public statement that his father intended to kill the druggist. Lastly, you have a convicted felon for a suspect, a man not unaccustomed to violence."

"None of which means he necessarily did it. An alternative theory is that it could have been . . ."

"Please," Theresa said, holding up a hand as she interrupted him. "We could speculate endlessly. Tell me, have you ever heard of Occam's razor?"

"Of course," A. G. confirmed. "It stands for the notion or the rule that, given the existence of competing explanations for an unexplained phenomenon, the simplest explanation is always preferred over the more complex."

"Exactly." She playfully poked him in the chest.

"Strictly speaking," A. G. pointed out, "Occam's razor was intended to be applied to scientific problems. I would submit that in the realm of human relations there is no such thing as a simple explanation."

"Why is it that men always have to get the last word in?" she asked, feigning annoyance with him.

"Because highly educated, good-looking women like you make most men feel inadequate."

She leaned into him, one hand dropping mischievously underneath the sheet that covered them both to the waist. "*Inadequate* is hardly a word I would use when describing you, my love."

A. G. had woken up on Sunday morning with the smell of freshly brewed coffee tickling his nose as he stretched under the light cotton sheet. He looked at his watch and, with a fleeting pang of conscience, realized he would have, in a prior life, been putting on one of his daddy's suits right about then in preparation for teaching his regular Sunday-school class. He smiled though, a second later, when Theresa Fitzgerald walked into the bedroom, carrying a tray with a pot of coffee, two cups, and a plate with two sweet rolls. Her hair had been quickly brushed and pulled back into a ponytail, and she wore only an olive-drab, army-issue T-shirt that fell not quite to the tops of her thighs.

"I doubt anyone at the Pentagon ever imagined such a sight," A. G. teased, alluding to the T-shirt as he sat up in bed.

Theresa dimpled with pleasure and put the tray on the floor beside the bed. She knelt down and poured two cups of coffee, handing one to A. G., together with one of the sweet rolls. "These rolls are just appetizers," she said, sitting on the floor and crossing her legs Indian fashion. "After you're up and showered and shaved, we're going out for breakfast."

"Where did you have in mind going?" A. G. asked, taking a careful sip of coffee while he tried, unsuccessfully, to avoid noticing that the T-shirt had ridden up to Theresa's waist.

"The Country Kitchen, here in Petersburg. They've got the best . . ."

"As a matter of fact, I've eaten there many times," A. G. interrupted, a smile on his face. "The owner was a good friend of my daddy's."

"Would you rather go somewhere else?"

"To be honest, when you mentioned it, my first reaction was to say no, and before Friday afternoon I probably would have."

"What happened Friday?" Noticing that his gaze was wandering, she smiled and, before A. G. could answer her question, she asked another. "Do you like looking at me?"

"Excuse me," A. G. stammered, embarrassed, his eyes returning to her face. The sudden heat rising into his cheeks told him he was blushing violently. "I'm sorry . . ."

"Don't be sorry," she said. "I like being looked at." She uncrossed her legs and looked down at herself. "It makes me feel attractive. And I've been meaning to ask you, would you like me to shave my pubic hair? It's a very common practice among French women, according to my father. We talked about it one evening at dinner, my father and mother and I, while I was still in college. To be honest, it's a bit of a nuisance," she continued, seemingly oblivious to the shock on A. G.'s face, "but I'd be happy to do it if it would please you."

"It is? I mean, you would?" A. G. managed to say, certain that he sounded like an unsophisticated bumpkin, if not a complete idiot. He could not imagine how such a topic would have come up at the dinner table, particularly between a father and daughter, notwithstanding the fact that the father had been a physician. After several seconds of silence he realized he had not answered her question. "Well, perhaps later, after we've . . ." His voice drifted into silence as he realized he had absolutely no idea what he was saying.

Theresa laughed and patted his arm reassuringly. "We'll talk about it later. Now, you were going to tell me what happened Friday to change your mind about being seen in public with me."

"You remember Lieutenant Giles, don't you?" A. G. said with sudden animation, grateful for the change in subject. "In the course of assisting me in my investigation, he met, quite by chance, a young woman in Hopewell. I found out yesterday that, after only a couple of dates, they decided they were in love and they've driven down to South Carolina to get married." A. G. shook his head, a smile on his face. "I realized that I would never have done something so spontaneous, so . . ." he paused for a second, searching for the right word, ". . . so absolutely, wonderfully *reckless.* I thought about your idea of going up to New York this weekend and how my immediate reaction had been to say no, let's think about it, plan for it, et cetera, et cetera, until, ultimately, we would never go." He paused again and held her eyes with his own. "I'm tired of living my life according to everyone else's expectations. If folks see us out together and don't like it," he shrugged, "it's their problem, not mine."

"I think I like the *new* A. G. a lot better than I would have liked the old one," Theresa said, jumping to her feet. "Let's go to breakfast and shock the world."

"Has a date been set for Private Carbone's court-martial?" Theresa asked casually. "For possession of the stolen pistol and assaulting the MP sergeant?" She was sitting with A. G. in a booth at the Country Kitchen, finishing a breakfast of eggs, sausage patties, cheese grits, and biscuits with molasses poured over them.

"Not that I'm aware of," A. G. replied. He smiled. "Of course, I doubt Major Williams would voluntarily keep me advised of anything he considered to be primarily a 'military' matter."

"Have you gotten any closer to having the district attorney charge him with Marty's murder?"

A. G. smiled again and shook his head, the gesture more one of irony than a negative response to her question. "If you had asked me that question yesterday, I probably would have said no, but this morning," he paused for a second, signaling their waitress to bring fresh coffee, "this morning I feel differently."

"How so?"

He waited until the waitress had filled their cups and left

the table before responding. "Believe it or not, your reference to Occam's razor yesterday had me thinking all night."

"That's not all you were doing last night," she teased, and A. G. actually blushed, delighting her. "But back to Occam's razor," she continued. "Does this mean I might have the final word in that argument, after all?"

"I think so. See, I remembered that you aren't the only one I've talked to who's made the point about simplicity being preferred over complexity." He told her about Spencer Lee's contention, based on his experience as an assistant district attorney, that when all the evidence points to a particular suspect, as it pointed in this case toward Private Carbone, the smart money bets in that direction. "I think I've been guilty of unnecessarily complicating things in both Doug Troutman's and your husband's murders. Interestingly, in both cases the suspects, Private Carbone and Sam Brown, had motive and opportunity and, while Carbone was apprehended with the likely murder weapon, Brown's own son told the world at large that his father intended to kill the victim." He lit a cigarette for each of them and started to tell her about the un-identified man he had seen coming out of Wanda Carbone's apartment, but quickly decided against it, not wanting to spoil what was starting out to be such a nice day with details that might upset her. "There's only one or two small details I need to get cleared up when Lieutenant Giles returns from his honeymoon, but I fully expect to turn the matter over to the district attorney within a day or two after he gets back."

"To Occam and his razor," Theresa said, holding up her coffee cup in a mock toast.

"To Occam and his razor," A. G. echoed. "And to Theresa and A. G. And the future."

Her eyes shining with tears, she reached across the table and took A. G.'s hand in her own. "Take me back to the apartment," she whispered huskily, "and make love to me."

―――――

"A. G., it's good to see you," Carole Lee said, hugging him tightly. A large woman, she wore a bright yellow sundress and a red ribbon in her hair. "And you smell good, too." She drew back, a twinkle in her eye. "That's a woman's perfume— you and Dolores must have done a little necking after church this morning." She looked over his shoulder, in the direction of his car. "Where is she?"

"Dolores couldn't make it this afternoon," A. G. said.

"I'm sorry to hear that. She's not sick, is she?"

"No, she's fine." A. G. smiled. "Where's Spencer?"

"Out back, trying to light the barbecue." She rolled her eyes as she led him by the hand into the house, a large, four-bedroom colonial design surrounded by half an acre of turf grass. "Men and barbecues—I don't know what it is about cooking outdoors that makes every man think he's some sort of French chef." She waved a hand dismissively. "How about a drink? Go on back," she continued, not giving A. G. a chance to answer, scarcely pausing to draw a fresh breath, "and I'll bring it out."

"Spencer." A. G. walked through the kitchen and screened-in back porch, and continued out onto the patio. Several pieces of lawn furniture and a wooden picnic table were grouped around an enormous brick barbecue grill. His friend was leaning over and vigorously waving a folded magazine over a large pile of smoking charcoal briquettes. "Careful you don't catch yourself on fire."

"The great American Sunday-afternoon ritual," Spencer snorted with mock disgust, unwittingly echoing his wife's sentiment. "Whoever thought this crazy idea up should be shot. Still," he pointed at a platter holding four large porterhouse steaks, "nothing like thick, juicy steaks cooked outdoors." He looked toward the house. "Dolores in with Carole?"

"Dolores couldn't make it."

Spencer looked up from the grill, obviously surprised by the tone of A. G.'s voice. "You two didn't have a fight or anything, did you?"

A. G. shook his head. "No, nothing like that. I'll tell you about it later," he said quietly, hearing Spencer's wife opening the screen door behind them.

"Fresh drinks," she called out, carrying a silver tray with three highball glasses and a small bowl of mixed nuts. "Bourbon and Coke all around."

"Where are the kids?" A. G. asked.

"Church camp," Carole said gleefully. "It's only for two weeks, but thank God for small favors!" She laughed loudly and took a big sip of her drink. "I've got to finish making the salad." She turned and walked a little unsteadily back into the house. "Just yell if you need more ice or anything."

A. G. took a cautious sip of his drink and winced at the overpowering taste of bourbon. "I don't believe Carole did much more than pass the bottle of Coke in the general direction of my glass," he joked, putting the drink down on the picnic table. "If I drink all of that I'll have to spend the night here."

Spencer cast an annoyed glance in the direction of the house and shook his head. "Carole had a couple of drinks before you got here," he said rather curtly by way of explanation. "Not, I'm sorry to say, an unusual occurrence. How about a cold beer?"

"Maybe in a few minutes." He nodded toward the house, concern on his face. "Carole doing okay?"

Spencer shrugged. "Who knows?" He smiled, an expression that communicated little humor. "About the only time we talk anymore is to argue about one thing or another, usually her drinking."

"I'm sorry to hear that." A. G. looked back at the house

and then at Spencer. "I was going to wait until dinner to tell you and Carole this, but maybe I'd better do it out here first." He lit a cigarette and waited somewhat awkwardly while Spencer rearranged the glowing briquettes in the barbecue in preparation for putting the steaks on the grill.

"I'm sorry," Spencer, suddenly realizing that he was being rude, looked up, "what were you going to say?"

"I've decided to get married."

Stunned, Spencer stared openmouthed at his friend for several seconds before extending his hand. "Congratulations," he exclaimed, clearly delighted despite his own present marital difficulty. "This is the best news I've heard in a while. When are you and Dolores tying the knot?"

"Actually, it's not Dolores."

"Not Dolores?" Puzzled, Spencer repeated his question. "You're not marrying Dolores? Well, who else do you know? I mean, who is it?"

"Theresa Fitzgerald." A. G. smiled at his friend's confusion. "I haven't actually asked her yet, but . . ."

"Wait, wait, wait," Spencer interrupted, waving a hand. "Theresa Fitzgerald? The dead officer's wife? From Fort Lee?"

A. G. nodded, a broad smile on his face. "I know it sounds sudden . . ."

"It doesn't sound sudden," Spencer said, interrupting again, his voice suddenly harsh, "it sounds crazy. Have you lost your goddamned mind?"

The smile left A. G.'s face.

"Jesus H. Christ, she's the widow of a man whose murder you're still investigating. Where the hell do you think you are, New York City or something?"

"Now wait a minute," A. G. said, his voice tight. "You don't have the . . ."

"No, *you* wait a minute. Listen," Spencer, pausing to take

a deep breath, lowered his voice to a normal, conversational level and motioned downward with both his hands, trying consciously to lower the tension level, "I'm sorry I spoke the way I did, but, good God, A. G., think about what you're saying. You and Dolores have been an item for what, five years? Folks in Prince George County expect you to marry her."

"All my life I've been expected to do certain things, and I'm sick and tired of it. It's *my* life, Spencer, no one else's, and I've decided that from now on I'm going to live it in a fashion that pleases *me*."

"You can wipe your ass with a pinecone if you want to," Spencer said sarcastically, "but it's still going to hurt. Listen," he snapped his fingers, "I've got an idea. Let's you and me take a couple of days off and go fishing. What do you say? We haven't been off together like that for years. We'll take a few bottles of whiskey, get drunk, and look at this thing backwards and forwards. Then, if you still want to go ahead, hell, I'll stand up for you and be your best man."

A. G. shook his head. "I appreciate it, Spencer, I swear I do, but I've already looked at it backwards and forwards, and I'm still going to marry her."

"How in the hell can she love you enough to marry you?" Spencer asked, his annoyance returning. "A. G.," he shook his head, exasperation getting the better of him, "her husband was just *murdered,* for God's sake. She should be mourning him, not out running around with you. And another thing." He pointed a finger at A. G. "You told me that you don't believe that the main suspect, this Private whatever-his-name-is, committed the murder. If you're right, if he didn't do it, then who did?"

A. G., his face flushed with sudden anger, held up a hand. "Don't say it, Spencer."

"Somebody's got to," Spencer retorted, caught up in his own anger. "If she killed her husband, what better way to throw you off the track than take you to bed?" He looked at A. G. and shook his head again. "What the hell's come over you? This is . . ." Spencer paused for a second, searching for the right word, ". . . this is *lunacy,* talking about marriage to some woman you barely know, and who may well have murdered her own husband."

A. G., his face red and his hands shaking, turned and, without a word, walked away, disappearing around the corner of the house. A second or two later Spencer heard his automobile start and pull out of the driveway, tires squealing in protest.

"The salad's ready," Carole called out through the back-porch screen door. "How about a quick refill on those drinks before we sit down?" She stepped out onto the patio and stumbled, almost falling before she caught her balance. "Where's A. G.?"

Regret had replaced anger long before A. G. got home. He ran through the brief conversation with Spencer a dozen times, trying each time to understand how he might better have gone about it, all to no avail. *I'm a fool,* he finally realized, *to have thought that there was any way Spencer, or anyone else for that matter, would have, first, understood and then, second, approved of what I'm about to do. Everyone I know,* he thought, *everyone I've ever known, wants to see me in one way and one way only: thirty-four years old, only child of Herbert and Mary Elizabeth Farrell, graduate of the University of Virginia, sheriff, and, lastly, husband-to-be of Dolores Anderson, music teacher and church organist. Nothing else will do, no other persona will be accepted.*

"The fact is," he said out loud, pointing at the speedometer for emphasis, "I'll go crazy if I have to live the life everyone in Hopewell expects me to live."

He held one hand out the open window, letting the onrushing wind play through his splayed fingers. The extreme heat and humidity seemed to give the air a feeling of substance, a sense that it could be sliced and weighed, packaged and sold as a commodity.

"But who'd buy it from me?" he asked, as if he were planning to sell such a thing. He brought his hand back inside the window to get it out of the scorching sun. "Who in his right mind would buy anything from a fool?"

He saw Dolores sitting on his front porch well before he turned into the circular gravel driveway. She was still dressed in her Sunday dress, pushing herself back and forth on the glider, and fanning herself with that morning's church program. He turned off the engine and shifted into neutral as he always did, as his father Herbert had always done, and the car coasted to a dead stop precisely in front of the steps, bringing a smile of satisfaction to his lips that vanished almost as quickly as it appeared. For an instant, A. G. wished he could just sit in the car, wished that if he were to do so Dolores would simply not be there when he got out, that the heartbreak she was suffering, and would further suffer upon hearing that he intended to marry another woman, would not have to be borne, would not have to be endured.

"I've been waiting for you," she said when he climbed the steps and came up onto the porch. "I borrowed Julie Carpenter's car," she pointed to the old Hudson sitting just off the driveway, "and came over right after church." She nodded toward Pearl, who, ill used by the heat, lay sleeping in the shade of the sofa. "The door was open, so I let her out. And, I hope you don't mind, I went in for a glass of water for myself."

A. G. put his right hand on his forehead as if he had a migraine headache and slowly nodded. "Of course I don't mind—I'm just sorry you've had to wait out here in this heat."

"I wouldn't have come over, but you said on Friday you were going to call me. When you didn't, I . . ." Her voice trailed off to a whisper and then died altogether. She took a deep breath. "You didn't come home last night either."

"I should have called like I promised. I'm sorry." He sat down in the chair next to the glider. "Dolores, I don't know what to say other than I'm sorry."

"It's that woman, isn't it?" Tears began to gather in her eyes and were soon coursing down her cheeks. "That murdered officer's wife."

A. G. nodded, staring at his hands as if they, and not him, were somehow responsible for breaking Dolores's heart. "Yes," he finally said, looking up at Dolores. "Theresa Fitzgerald." He spread his hands apart and then brought them together again. "I've fallen in love with her."

Dolores stood up, clutching the church program to her breast. "I wish we hadn't . . ." She stumbled on the words as her breathing broke down into sobs, her grief and pain suddenly overwhelming her. "I wish we hadn't made love," she finally managed to say, holding up a hand to indicate that she didn't want him to respond. "I wish we hadn't."

She walked quickly past him and down the steps and, seemingly in a heartbeat, was gone.

Chapter Thirteen

"Wanda Carbone was murdered yesterday?"

A. G.'s incredulity was apparent in the tone of his voice.

"She was strangled." Tug Benson, Petersburg's chief of police, brought his fists together and rotated them in opposite directions as if wringing a chicken's neck. "Hell, even a fool could see the thumb marks on her throat." He shook his head. "Take my word for it, it wasn't a pretty sight. Whoever did it must have had hands like a blacksmith. The doc thinks she died sometime yesterday afternoon, maybe early evening. No evidence of rape, the apartment didn't appear to have been burglarized, and the neighbors say they didn't hear or see anything out of the ordinary." He leaned back in his wooden swivel chair and began to roll a cigarette. "Of course, in that neighborhood 'out of the ordinary' may mean something a little more extreme than, say, where you or I live." Tall and lanky, he was as bald as a billiard ball and, though he struck many who knew him only superficially as somewhat slow and dull-witted, he came to Petersburg after the war with almost twenty years' experience as a special agent of the Federal Bureau of Investigation. He had been summarily dismissed from the bureau after having been overheard joking that the director, J. Edgar Hoover, harbored a suspicion that the Girl Scouts of America was in reality a secret Communist-front organization.

"Needless to say, my first thought in such cases is almost always the spouse, but unfortunately," he looked at A. G. and smiled, "so to speak, I come to find out that the victim's husband," he leaned forward and looked at a paper on his cluttered desk, "one Joseph Carbone, an enlisted man in the United States Army, makes an unlikely suspect inasmuch as he was incarcerated in the stockade at Fort Lee at the time of the murder. Under suspicion," he looked up from his papers, his eyes squinting with amusement, "and I think this is a nice touch of irony, of the murder of a Captain Martin Fitzgerald." He neatly licked the glued edge of the cigarette paper, rolled it deftly between the thumb and forefinger of his right hand, and put it in the corner of his mouth, where it dangled, unlit, for the remainder of A. G.'s visit. "With whom *my* decedent, Wanda Carbone, apparently had been having an extramarital affair. Naturally," Tug's voice no longer carried a humorous tone, "I had heard all about that captain's body being found over in Hopewell but," he paused long enough to make sure he had eye contact with A. G., "I never knew you were talking to folks here in Petersburg about it. In *my* jurisdiction. Imagine my surprise when the provost marshall out at the fort filled me in on the whole thing this morning. He said that you and a . . ." he leaned forward again to consult his notes, "here it is, a Lieutenant Giles, visited with Mrs. Carbone at her apartment on one or more separate occasions."

"That was my fault, Tug, and I apologize." A. G. was not having a particularly good Monday morning. After Dolores left his home the night before, he had been unable to reach Theresa by telephone and had spent the night tossing and turning, unable to sleep. He had not been in his office ten minutes when Tug called with the news of Wanda Carbone's murder and asked him to drive over to Petersburg right away. "I only talked to her on two occasions, but I should have advised you as soon as I made the connection. It won't happen again."

Tug nodded, clearly satisfied with A. G.'s response. "That's good enough for me. Now, back to Wanda Carbone. I take it I was correct when I said that she was having an affair with the late Captain Fitzgerald? Major Williams told me a little this morning, not a great deal, and I got the distinct impression that you and he haven't been seeing eye to eye on the conduct of your investigation." He smiled. "He's not exactly what I'd call a big fan of civilian law enforcement, is he?"

A. G. nodded. "Indeed, he's not. Fortunately, his assistant, Lieutenant Giles, has been extremely helpful. As a matter of fact, Giles discovered Wanda Carbone through a telephone call Captain Fitzgerald made at the officers club on the night he was murdered. We, Giles and I, followed up with an unannounced visit to her apartment, where she admitted to having an affair with the captain."

"How did they meet?"

"She was a civilian employee at the Quartermaster School on the fort. He was an instructor at the school."

"Was her husband at the school, too?"

A. G. shook his head. "No. Private Carbone worked as a mechanic at the motor pool."

"How did he find out about the captain and his wife?"

"An anonymous telephone call. After Giles and I interviewed her, we went back to Fort Lee and informed Giles's boss, Major Williams. He decided to bring Carbone in for questioning, and the MP sergeant picking him up discovered a stolen army .45 automatic in Carbone's locker at the motor pool."

"The murder weapon?"

A. G. shrugged. "My guess is that it probably is, but there's no way of knowing for sure. Carbone claims that it was planted there. Frankly, at first I didn't think he murdered Captain Fitzgerald, the pistol notwithstanding, but now I'm not so sure. In any event, Williams has him locked up for the time being on assault and stolen-weapon charges."

"Infidelity is often a sufficiently compelling motivation for murder," Benson observed. "What else have you got?"

"Gambling. I've discovered that Fitzgerald was a big-time poker player who frequented both high-stakes games in Richmond and smaller, though not exactly insubstantial, games at Jubal Bishop's place outside Hopewell."

"You talk to Jubal?"

A. G. nodded. "He confirmed that the captain was a weekly player."

"Was he a loser? Could he have welched on a bet?"

"Not according to Jubal. In fact, just the opposite. Almost always won, but in any event, Jubal thinks the stakes involved wouldn't have justified a murder."

"Depends on your point of view," Benson said cynically. "I've seen men cut down for less than a dollar. A lot less." He paused, organizing his thoughts. "Major Williams said you had interviewed the dead captain's wife." He looked at his notes for a second. "Mrs. Fitzgerald. Theresa. Anything there?"

A. G., knowing of and respecting Benson's keen powers

of observation, developed over his many years as a special agent, tried consciously to maintain a casual tone of voice. "Nothing. She was visibly shocked when I told her about her husband's affair with Wanda Carbone."

Benson shook his head and sighed. "Until Mrs. Carbone turned up dead, I'd say you had yourself an open-and-shut case against her husband. The gambling angle, I'll admit, added a small element of uncertainty, but experience tells me," he said, unwittingly echoing Spencer Lee's words, "that when the preponderance of the evidence points overwhelmingly in a certain direction, that's usually the way to go. Unfortunately, just when things were looking neat and tidy for you, somebody ups and strangles the main suspect's wife." He sighed again. "You said you talked to Mrs. Carbone on two occasions."

"I wanted to follow up on a few things from our first conversation, so I went back to visit with her several days ago."

"What did she tell you?"

"Not much. She seemed resigned to the fact that her husband was going to be in the stockade for a long time, regardless of whether he had actually murdered Captain Fitzgerald, and so was planning to leave the area in the not-too-distant future."

"Did she say where she was going to go?"

"I doubt she knew herself, although she did mention the possibility of going as far away as California to try and start over again. Something interesting did turn up, though." A. G. sat forward in his chair. "On the way in I encountered a man coming out of her apartment, a Negro. Tall, well dressed, clearly out of place in the neighborhood. When I asked her about him, she became extremely nervous and said something about his being a neighbor, a friend who was helping her out while her husband was in the stockade. She could have been nervous about my seeing the man for any number of reasons, all of them innocent, but then again, you never know. The more I thought about it, the more convinced I became that the man was a soldier—the way he was dressed, the way he carried himself. And that made me think that if he *was* a soldier, why wouldn't she have said so when I asked who he was? I told Lieutenant Giles about the encounter and gave him a description of the man. He was going to check out both the motor pool and the Quartermaster School to see if he could identify him."

"Any luck?"

"Unfortunately," A. G. said somewhat ruefully, "Giles took off to get married late last week. I'm not even sure when he's due back."

"Well, I don't think we can wait, not with another dead body to deal with. Like you said, even if he is, or was, just a friend of the Carbones, I'd like to talk to him sooner rather than later." Tug picked up a tablet and a pencil. "Give me a description of the man, and we'll put Major Williams to work on it." He smiled. "You better let me call him, though—I don't get the feeling he's a big fan of yours at the present time. Anyway, if the man *is* a soldier, with a little luck we'll know his identity before lunch and can be talking to him this afternoon. I trust you'll want to sit in on the questioning."

A. G. nodded and stood up. "I'll be back at my office," he said, not quite successfully stifling a yawn. "You can reach me there all day."

Tug looked up, a mixture of curiosity and concern on his face. "I'll be honest with you, A. G.—you don't look so good. You feeling okay?"

"Yeah, it's just been a tough couple of days, what with Doug Troutman's murder and all."

"That's right. I heard about it over the weekend. How's your investigation coming along?"

"Actually pretty well—I should have it wrapped up this week with any luck at all." He shook his head ruefully. "Knock on wood. Then, if this heat wave would only break, maybe we could all get a good night's sleep."

A. G. got out of his car and walked into Bud Taylor's warehouse. Inside, out of the sun, the temperature differential made it seem at first a good deal cooler than it actually was, a pleasant illusion that would soon be dispelled. A. G. removed his hat and wiped the perspiration from his brow with a clean, white handkerchief.

"Mildred said you wanted to see me."

"Yeah," Bud grunted from behind his desk. "Where you been?"

"In Tug Benson's office, over in Petersburg. The wife of Private Carbone, the soldier the provost marshall has locked up in the stockade at Fort Lee, was murdered yesterday. Strangled."

Bud looked up, surprised. "Hell, I thought that case was all but settled."

"I'm afraid not. Unless it was a heck of a coincidence, I'm thinking that whoever killed Wanda Carbone was involved in the killing of Captain Fitzgerald. And, since Carbone was in the stockade when his wife was murdered, it clearly wasn't him."

"What does Benson think?"

"I doubt he has an opinion yet. Right now we're trying to identify a man I saw coming out of Mrs. Carbone's apartment the last time I was over there to talk to her. I'll let you know if anything interesting turns up." A. G. sat down and fanned himself with his hat. "What did you want to see me about?"

"I spent a good bit of yesterday over in Richmond with

Wilbur Marshall and Bill Troutman," Bud said, "talking about this business with Doug and Sam Brown."

"What's Wilbur doing in Richmond in July?" A. G. asked casually, although he had a feeling he knew pretty well where the conversation was headed. Wilbur Marshall was a state legislator and tobacco farmer from near Danville, on the North Carolina border. He was also a Democratic Party leader in the legislature and an old friend and drinking buddy of Bud Taylor's. "What with the legislature in recess, I mean."

"He went back home this morning, but he was up here most of last week tending to some business." Bud pronounced it *bidness*. "I wanted to take advantage of the fact that he was here to see if we couldn't get things resolved with Bill Troutman." Bud leaned back in his chair and regarded A. G. like a father about to give a child an unpleasant dose of medicine. "An agent from the attorney general's office, together with one from the state police, spent several hours interrogating Virgil Brown yesterday." He raised a hand to forestall interruption from A. G. "Now, damn it, just wait a minute and let me finish. The attorney general knows this is your jurisdiction, but as a personal favor to Dr. Troutman, and with *my approval*"—Bud stressed the words *my approval*—"he agreed to assist you in your investigation. After some initial resistance, young Virgil finally admitted that his daddy had indeed vowed to kill Doug Troutman for his alleged role in Julie Brown's death. Based on Virgil's statements, Sam's criminal record, and his actions when the police tried to stop him, everybody, including the attorney general's office, agrees that all the evidence overwhelmingly points to Sam Brown as the one who murdered Doug."

"You said 'alleged role' in Julie Brown's death. Does that mean there is some doubt in Richmond as to whether or not Doug was an abortionist?"

Bud, with an unpleasant expression on his face, paused

for a second before continuing. "Everyone also agrees that Sam's death, caused by his own unlawful flight, effectively closes the case," he said, ignoring A. G.'s question.

A. G., hearing Bud use the expression "unlawful flight," and knowing he must have seen it in the state police report of Sam's fatal accident, resisted the urge to smile. He decided to come at things from a slightly different angle. "I'll admit it's likely that Sam was the guilty party, but given the fact that Doug probably caused at least two other deaths that we know of, clearly there are other people with a motive equally as strong as Sam's. Shouldn't we at least eliminate all the other possibilities, even if they're admittedly remote?"

Exasperated, Bud shook his head. "Those other girls you're talking about died, what, over two years ago? Don't you think that if their kin were going to do something to hurt Doug they'd have done it by now? Besides, they were colored girls—I frankly don't see much likelihood their daddies or whatever other kin they had would be killing a white man, even if they had known what Doug had done, which they probably wouldn't have in the first place." He pointed at A. G. for emphasis. "You start talking to folks about this and all you're going to do is stir up a hornet's nest, worrying people about something that might not have even happened. Those girls are dead, and I say let them rest in peace."

"So we're going to sweep Doug's criminal activities under the rug," A. G. said, shaking his head with anger. "What about the evidence—the surgical instruments and the drugs I found? Don't you suppose the district attorney will want to know about what was going on here?"

"The district attorney has already agreed that nothing further needs to be done," Bud countered with a look of distinct pleasure. "I talked to him yesterday when I got back from Richmond."

"You weren't exaggerating when you said that Doug's

daddy is a powerful man," A. G. observed, his demeanor and tone of voice misleadingly calm. "I guess I just didn't expect you to cut bait the minute he started throwing his weight around in Richmond."

"Then you're a bigger fool than some folks around here think you are," Bud said cruelly, his face flushed with sudden anger. "And what you call 'cuttin' bait' happens to be the way business gets done around this state." He paused for several seconds, trying to control his temper. "What the hell's come over you lately? You been actin' queer since that captain got himself murdered out here. And here's another thing: Jimmy Morton told me that Dolores Anderson quit her job as church organist this morning."

"What?" A. G.'s jaw dropped in shock at the unexpected news.

"That's right, quit. She's leaving Hopewell, for good, moving down to Raleigh. She wouldn't give Jimmy a reason, but I'm thinking it's got to have something to do with the way you been acting lately."

Back in his office, A. G. closed the door and lit a cigarette with still-shaking hands. The confrontation with Bud Taylor had disturbed him deeply, and his attempts to resolve his anger had been largely unsuccessful. *I don't care,* he kept telling himself, uncomfortably aware that he was not willing to delve too deeply into what exactly it was that he didn't care about. He picked up the telephone, intending to call Spencer and talk to him about it, but, chagrined, hung up immediately when he remembered that he had all but burned that bridge not twenty-four hours earlier. Suddenly eager to hear her voice, he tried to call Theresa at her quarters on Fort Lee, but after the sixth ring he gave up and slowly replaced the telephone in its cradle. *At least,* he thought, *I'll see her tonight in Petersburg.*

He got up from behind his desk and paced across the small office, stopping after several passes at the open window that looked across to Doug Troutman's drugstore. In the mid-afternoon heat few people were on the street, and the green awnings cast deep shadows across the plate-glass windows of the now closed store. A. G. sighed and sat down again at his desk, looking at his telephone and wishing he had someone, anyone, he could call. He stood up again and walked out to Mildred's desk in the outer office. From the look on her face, he knew she already knew all about Dolores leaving town and, unlike Bud Taylor, likely knew the reason why.

"I think I'll walk around the corner and get a Dr Pepper," he said to her, getting his hat off the hat rack by the door. "Would you like anything?"

Before she could reply, the telephone rang. She answered it and looked up at A. G. "It's Chief Benson."

A. G. walked back into his office and sat down. "Tug, A. G. here. What have you found out?"

"Your man is named Robert Stevens, and he worked at the Quartermaster School," Benson replied. "You'll note my use of the past tense. Unfortunately for us, he mustered out of the army one week before Fitzgerald was murdered, and no one out at Fort Lee has any idea where he might be."

"Mustered out?"

"That's what I said. Major Williams sent me over a copy of his personnel file. He was born in Chicago in 1927, enlisted for four years in 1946, then signed up for a second four-year hitch in 1950. That second term of enlistment expired, like I said, a week before Fitzgerald's murder. Stevens was promoted to buck sergeant almost two years ago, and the school commandant had promised to promote him to staff sergeant if only he would reenlist for another four-year stretch."

"And he turned it down. I'm surprised."

"You aren't the only one—apparently lots of people at the

school were shocked when he refused to reenlist. Everyone seems to have assumed that, particularly since Truman desegregated the armed forces six years ago, Stevens was a twenty-year man."

"He must have been a good sergeant if his commander promised him another stripe for reenlisting," A. G. mused. "It just doesn't make sense for him to throw away eight years of service, not when he was getting promoted like that. Did he give any reason?"

"Not much of one. Told several people he had to get back to Chicago, his home of record, to take care of family matters. Wouldn't say what they were, and turned down an offer for a full thirty-day leave."

"Did he and Captain Fitzgerald work together at the school?"

"You'll love this: Stevens served with Fitzgerald at Fort Myer, and Fitzgerald apparently pulled some strings at the Pentagon and had him transferred to Fort Lee shortly after his own transfer there. Fitzgerald was his immediate superior at the Quartermaster School and was the one who approved his promotion to sergeant while they were both still at Fort Myer."

"Any indication Stevens might have known Private Carbone?"

"None whatever. Major Williams sent a man to the motor pool to check on that, but no one there knows Stevens or can remember seeing anyone of his description in the area." Benson paused for a second. "My guess is that if the two men knew each other, or were friends, it was, for whatever reason, an off-the-base friendship."

"*If* they were friends," A. G. said, emphasizing the *if.* "What next?"

"Obviously, we try to find ex-sergeant Stevens. Since you saw him coming out of the Carbones' apartment less than a week ago, there's a chance he's still in the area. I'm having copies made of a recent ID photograph of Stevens—by the way, I'll send over several for your use—and if he is still around, we shouldn't have too much trouble corralling him. On the other hand, Mrs. Carbone was still alive when you saw him, and if Stevens had anything to do with her murder, he may have since taken a big powder. If that's the case, about all we can do is get a warrant and hope for the best."

"None of this seems to make a great deal of sense," A. G. said slowly. "I mean, if Captain Fitzgerald was actively furthering Stevens's career as an NCO, there would seem to be no motive there for murder. I suppose that if Stevens thought Private Carbone had murdered Fitzgerald in a jealous rage, he, Stevens, might be tempted to seek revenge, but why kill Mrs. Carbone?"

"Who said murder had to make sense? Maybe he killed her because she had the affair that led to Fitzgerald's murder."

"And that's assuming Fitzgerald was killed by Carbone," A. G. said. "Keep in mind that we don't have proof of that yet."

"We may not have proof yet, but we have the three next best things."

"What are they?"

"Weapon, motive, and opportunity," Benson pointed out dryly. "Based on those three, I'm perfectly willing to assume that Private Carbone murdered Captain Fitzgerald, at least for the time being," he continued. "But first things first. Let's get our hands on ex-sergeant Stevens and see what he knows."

A. G. showered, changed clothes, and was putting out fresh food and water for Pearl when someone knocked at the front screen door.

"Now what?" he muttered, annoyed to have a visitor just

as he planned to leave the house to drive over to Petersburg to be with Theresa. His annoyance turned to surprise when he saw who it was. "Miz Craige, what in the world are you doing out here?"

"I came to visit," she answered primly. "Earl Jackson brought me over." She gestured toward the car sitting in the drive. "He's going to wait and take me home."

"Sit down," A. G. invited, pointing to the chair next to the glider. "It's cooler out here on the porch. Would you like a glass of tea or anything?"

"You weren't fixin' to leave just now, were you?" Dorcas asked, noticing A. G.'s freshly pressed shirt.

"No, ma'am. I'm going over to Petersburg in a little while, but you don't need to rush." He sat down on the glider and smiled. "I don't believe you've visited out here before, have you?"

"Not out here on the front porch," she answered, no more than a hint of a smile tickling the corners of her mouth. " 'Course I been *in* the house lots of times, helping your momma with the wash and cleaning when you was just a boy." She looked around, admiring the view from where she now sat. "But I ain't never been out here on the porch before, not sitting down."

"Times can change, can't they?"

"Not much they can't," Dorcas responded, shaking her head. "I don't expect I'll see too many colored folks sitting on white folks' porches sipping tea." She laughed, a not altogether humorous sound. "Not in my lifetime, anyway."

"No, Miz Craige," A. G. replied honestly, "now that I think about it, I don't guess you will."

"Folks is saying that Sam Brown killed Doug Troutman," she said after a brief silence. "They sayin' that with both of them dead the whole thing just going to go away." She looked at A. G. "That what you think?"

"What I think doesn't much matter, Miz Craige," A. G. said, amazed at how quickly the news of Sam's death had circulated. "You and I both know that Doug Troutman was performing illegal abortions and that he caused several deaths over the past five or so years, including, in all likelihood, Julie Brown's. A certain amount of credible evidence points to Sam as the killer, and Doug's father, a very powerful and important man in Richmond, wants the matter wrapped up with as little publicity as possible."

"What do *you* want to believe?"

"I don't *want* to believe anything, Miz Craige. I want to know the truth, and I want the people in the county, white and colored both, to know the truth, not only about who killed Doug Troutman but also why he was killed." He shrugged and smiled. "But, as my daddy was fond of saying, 'If wishes were horses, beggars would ride.' "

"The woman that belongs to those panties you showed me, she the one killed Mr. Troutman," Dorcas said abruptly. She shifted in her chair, clearly anxious to be done with conversation and back on her own porch. "What I heard was that she went to him for . . ."—Dorcas paused, clearly uncomfortable, as Bud Taylor had been, with the word *abortion*—"she went to him for help, and he tol' her she had to have sex with him before he would help her get rid of her baby." Dorcas looked away from A. G., embarrassed to have to be saying such things, particularly to a man young enough to be her son. "That's what he tol' all the girls that came to him." She shook her head, disgusted. "All the colored girls, anyway. After she did what he wanted, he tol' her he'd think about it, and she'd have to come back again in a few days." Dorcas looked back at A. G., her face grave. "I guess she was the wrong girl for him to be trifling with, 'cause folks say that quick as he said it, she took out a straight razor and cut his throat. Said she didn't even blink an eye."

A. G. nodded, an odd feeling of closure, if not outright contentment, settling over him like a fine mist. "Do you know who she is?"

Dorcas shook her head. "What I heard, she's not from around here. She's got a man over around Petersburg, a married man, and was down here visiting him from up north someplace. I expect he's the one got her in trouble in the first place." Dorcas looked at A. G. one last time. "She's gone now, back up north."

Chapter Fourteen

A. G. approached the chilled martini glass with an excess of caution and took a tentative sip, not quite closing his eyes. He swallowed, inhaled, and smiled at Theresa. "I think I could develop a taste for these," he allowed, taking another, slightly larger sip, knowing that his words would please her. In fact, the gin tasted worse to him than medicine.

"I still can't believe you've never had a martini in your life," Theresa said, shaking her head. "My father used to say that a dry martini, or, better yet, two, is the only civilized way to mark the end of a day well spent." She laughed. "He was never one to let his angst for the great, unwashed masses interfere with his love of creature comforts."

"What other creature comforts was he fond of?" A. G. asked, trying not to make a face as he drank. *Angst* was still another word he had never before heard used in everyday conversation.

"Beautiful women, primarily. Oh, he loved big houses, expensive automobiles, bespoke suits from Savile Row in London, things like that, but more than anything else he loved beautiful women."

"That must have pleased your mother no end," A. G. teased, assuming that Theresa had been joking.

"My mother was a weakling," she said with a vehemence that startled A. G. "My father was an extraordinary man, a man of larger-than-life accomplishments, both professional and social. He loved life, and he made no secret of it, certainly not from my mother."

"He sounds like he was an interesting man," A. G. murmured, somewhat taken aback.

Theresa laughed, and A. G. thought he heard a hint of derision in her laughter. "*Interesting* hardly begins to describe him," she said, taking one of A. G.'s cigarettes from the pack on the low table in front of the sofa.

"I'm sorry," A. G. said, lighting her cigarette, "I guess that sounded somewhat, I don't know, superficial." He smiled. "I wish that I . . ."

"You said you had a surprise for me," she said, interrupting and changing the subject. Settling back on the sofa with her martini and cigarette, she shook a strand of hair out of her eyes. "I love a good surprise."

"Then you'll like this one," A. G. assured her. He proceeded to relate the story of Doug Troutman's murder as told to him by Dorcas Craige not an hour earlier.

"That's wonderful," Theresa said, putting her martini glass on the table and clapping her hands when A. G. finished. "Particularly the part about the straight razor, although I suppose the entire story could be apocryphal. You know, a way for the Negro community to take 'credit' for Troutman's murder and deal psychologically with what it must perceive as the white community's failure to protect it from his predations." She picked up her glass and finished her martini. "Do you think it could be true?"

Predations? A. G. thought but did not say. "I'm sure Miz Craige didn't make it up, if that's what you mean. As to whether or not the story itself, as it was told to her, is true," he shrugged, "I have no idea. And," he quickly added, "I *am* quite concerned about how both the white and Negro communities view my performance as sheriff."

"I'll bet it is true," Theresa said. "The story has the ring of verisimilitude, if you ask me. Also, don't forget the panties you found under his chair—they certainly lend credence to the overall picture. I *hope* it's true," she added mischievously. "What are you going to do about it?"

"There's not much I can do," A. G. admitted rather reluctantly. "Bud Taylor made it pretty clear that the powers that be have decided that by selecting the conveniently deceased Sam Brown as the perpetrator of the murder, they can close the book on the crime without having to get into the unpleasant question of Doug Troutman's activities as an abortionist. Now that they've done this I'm reasonably certain that nobody in Richmond wants to hear that someone else, particularly a Negro woman who had just been raped by Doug, might have done it."

"I hope she did it," Theresa repeated, surprising A. G. with the passion with which she said it. "The bastard deserved to die like that, choking on his own blood."

"I wouldn't go so far as to say that he deserved to die," A. G. said carefully, disturbed by her words. "He certainly deserved to go to jail for a good many years, but . . ."

"I don't want to talk about it anymore," Theresa said

abruptly, finishing her martini with a single gulp. She stood up and looked down at A. G. "I want you to make love to me now."

It was a different Theresa Fitzgerald than he had known. She began undressing on the way to the bedroom, pulling her silk blouse free of her skirt and unbuttoning it quickly, letting it drop carelessly to the floor behind her as it slid free of her arms. Her skirt followed, falling soundlessly to the floor as she stepped free of its encumbrance, kicking it from around her ankles even as she approached the bed. She wore no undergarments and lay on the bed touching herself with a complete lack of self-consciousness as she waited impatiently for A. G. to join her. When he did, she bit and scratched him, demanded that he do things to please her, cursed him while at the same time urging him on, all the while refusing to allow him the slightest degree of pleasure in the coupling. She cried out at the moment of greatest passion, a guttural sound from the low reaches of her diaphragm that communicated fully as much pain as joy, and held him tightly afterward, her shoulders convulsing with sobs, her face streaked with tears. A. G., helpless, stroked her hair and whispered words of love until, obviously emotionally exhausted, she fell asleep in his arms. Uncomfortable yet unwilling to move and chance waking her, he lay quietly and listened to the beating of their hearts, watching the shadows of the approaching night lengthen across the small room's walls. Her breath was warm and moist against his chest, and the rhythm of his own breathing unconsciously slowed to match hers. Presently, without even realizing it, he too fell asleep.

Although he could not see them in the inky, predawn blackness, A. G. woke up feeling as if the small room's walls were inexorably pressing in on him. For several frighteningly claustrophobic seconds he did not know exactly where he was, only knew for sure that he wasn't in his own bedroom at home and, heart pounding, he sat up quickly, swinging his feet over the side of the bed. His sudden movement woke Theresa, and she drowsily reached up and put a hand on his back.

"You're soaking wet," she exclaimed, sitting up herself as she fumbled for the switch at the base of the table lamp on the nightstand next to the bed. "What's wrong?"

"Lord," A. G. shakily ran a hand over his face, "I woke up feeling like I'd lost my way or something." He turned his head to look at her and, even in his still-confused, rather frightened state of mind, he was stirred by the sight of her naked body next to him. He tried to smile and mostly failed. "I must have been having a bad dream." He tried to look over her shoulder at the windup clock on the nightstand. "What time is it?"

"Almost five o'clock. What were you dreaming?"

A. G. shook his head. "I can't exactly recall—I think I was being chased by something." *Probably my conscience,* he thought ruefully but did not say.

"Well, whatever it was, it was just a bad dream." Yawning, she stood up and put on a kimonolike silk wrap. "I'll go put on a pot of coffee."

A. G. sat quietly on the edge of the bed, absently listening to Theresa first grind coffee beans and then draw water for the pot. As he thought about it, he felt certain the bad dream was the direct result of his confrontations with both Spencer Lee and Bud Taylor. Thinking about the two of them somehow brought Dolores Anderson to mind, and that in turn made him feel distinctly guilty about being in Theresa's bedroom, his clothes in disarray on the floor at the foot of the bed. Guilt turned quickly to anger at the notion that he, an unmarried adult, should feel answerable to anyone about his private life. Almost as quickly as it came, his anger left, leaving behind

only a sense of personal loss, the very same feeling, he realized, that had troubled him so when he woke up. *And it's not
just Bud or Spencer or Dolores,* he thought, running a hand
wearily across his face, *but some part of me that's gone for-
ever.* Finally, he stood and gathered up his clothes and began,
ever so slowly, to dress.

"Would you like me to make some toast or something?"
Theresa asked when A. G. joined her in the kitchen.

"No, just coffee will be fine. I'll get a bite to eat downtown later this morning." He smiled at her. "Even at five A.M.
you manage to look good." He hesitated a second and then
added, "It wouldn't take a great deal of effort to get used to
waking up next to you every morning." When the hoped-for
response to his compliment and implied suggestion of cohab-
itation was not immediately forthcoming, he mentally
shrugged, his relatively limited early morning experience with
Theresa having already demonstrated to him that she was seldom at her best before midmorning. "I didn't get a chance to
mention it last night," he continued, "what with telling you
about Dorcas Craige's revelation and," he smiled sheepishly,
thinking of Theresa's sudden passion, "other things, but I
think there's been something of a break in the case." He could
not bring himself to use her husband's name, not with the two
of them so recently out of bed.

"If you mean the murder of Private Carbone's wife, I
heard about it yesterday, Monday, from a neighbor at Fort
Lee. It's all over the post." Her voice was flat, emotionless.
"Are you sure it was related to Marty's murder?"

"No, we can't say for sure, but . . ."

"We?"

"Tug Benson, the chief of police here in Petersburg. She
was murdered in Petersburg, so it's his jurisdiction. Anyway,
we can't say for sure that the killings are related, but there is
an interesting connection. The last time I visited Wanda Car-

bone, to ask her some additional questions about her, um, relationship with Captain Fitzgerald . . ."

"I don't think he would mind if you called him Marty," Theresa interrupted, sarcasm evident in her tone of voice.

"I'm sorry if I've annoyed you," A. G. said quietly. "It wasn't very thoughtful of me to bring this up with no warning."

"Don't be sorry." Theresa smiled weakly. "It's my fault, not yours—you know what a bitch I can be in the morning." She took a sip of her coffee. "Please go on with what you were saying."

"The last time I went to see Mrs. Carbone I saw a man coming from her apartment, a Negro. Although we didn't speak, I was sure he was a soldier—his bearing, the way he wore his civilian clothes, that sort of thing. Mrs. Carbone was extremely nervous about the fact that I had seen him and would only say that he was a friend of her husband's, a neighbor. Anyway, I told Lieutenant Giles about it with the thought that if the man really was a soldier at Fort Lee, he could be found rather easily. Unfortunately," A. G. smiled ruefully, "as you know, the young lieutenant ran away to get married before he could institute a search of the post. I was going to wait until he got back from his honeymoon, but the murder of Mrs. Carbone made it clear that . . ."

"Sergeant Robert Stevens," Theresa interrupted casually, pouring herself another cup of coffee.

A. G. sat stunned, his mouth open. "How did you . . ." His voice trailed off into astonished silence.

"I take it from your expression that it *was* Sergeant Stevens you saw at Mrs. Carbone's?"

"Yes, but how did you know?"

"He served with Marty at Fort Myer," she explained. "When we moved to Fort Lee, Marty called in a favor he was owed by someone at the Pentagon and had him transferred to the Quartermaster School shortly after we arrived here. I met him on one or two occasions, when he brought paperwork to our quarters. When you said the man you saw at Mrs. Carbone's was a soldier, and a Negro, I put two and two together and took a guess. When you think about it, and know the relationship between Marty and Sergeant Stevens, who else could it have been?"

"Do you know him well? Do you know where he might be? I mean, his present whereabouts?"

Theresa shook her head. "No to both questions. As I said, I met him only a couple of times. As I recall, he was well-spoken and respectful. And as to where he might be," she shrugged eloquently, "I haven't a clue. I understand he got out of the army shortly before Marty's death, for reasons I never understood. I remember that Marty was quite upset about it. I guess I just assumed he had left the area, returned to his home, wherever that might be."

"Chicago," A. G. said, "but he didn't go there, at least not right away, because I saw him at Mrs. Carbone's apartment less than a week ago." He shook his head, amazement still evident on his face. "This is astonishing, I mean your knowing . . ."

"Why is it so astonishing?" Theresa asked, interrupting him again, a slight edge to her voice. "I told you that Sergeant Stevens and Marty had served together for several years before he came to Fort Lee. And as to the fact that I had met him on a couple of occasions, most of the officers' wives have occasion to meet the NCOs that work closely with their husbands." She shook her head, clearly annoyed. "You make it sound somewhat sinister that I was able to guess the identity of the man you saw."

"That is the last thing I intended," A. G. said quickly, holding both hands up. "Knowing what you know, it was perfectly natural that you would come up with Sergeant Stevens's name." He leaned back in his chair and smiled. "You have to understand, though, that it was quite a surprise to hear you say his name before I could." He leaned forward again. "Would you have any idea, any at all, why Stevens would have been visiting Mrs. Carbone?"

"None. I assume that because she worked at the Quartermaster School he would have known her, but I can think of no connection beyond that."

"I can't either," A. G. admitted. "Not yet, anyway. Of course, there may well have been no connection between Sergeant Stevens's visit and Mrs. Carbone's murder either."

"It sounds to me, from what I've heard of her, that the woman was little better than a common whore," Theresa said angrily. "She could have been killed for any number of reasons, none having anything whatever to do with Marty's murder."

"You may well be right," A. G. said quietly, taken somewhat aback by Theresa's vehemence. Still, he reminded himself, she just recently found out about her late husband's infidelity, so perhaps her anger toward Wanda Carbone was understandable, if not particularly charitable. Realizing that this was neither the time nor the place for further speculation regarding Wanda Carbone's murder and its possible connection to Captain Fitzgerald's, he took the last bitter sip of coffee in his cup and stood up. "I'd better head back to Hopewell. I need to clean up and change clothes before I go in to the office." He reached out and took her hand. "I'm sorry if all this has upset you. Let me take you out to dinner tonight." He paused, wishing desperately he could let her know what was in his heart without having to say it. "I want to talk about," he shrugged, feeling awkward and stupid, "other things, you and me, and perhaps make a few . . ."

Theresa rose and put a finger to his lips, silencing him. "It may not be possible tonight," she said quietly, leaning in to kiss him gently. "I'll call you this afternoon."

Lieutenant Giles sat in A. G.'s office and whistled, the long, low note bringing a broad smile to A. G.'s face.

"She was strangled?" Giles asked, his tone of voice clearly communicating his incredulity.

A. G. nodded, his stomach growling audibly. It was just nine-thirty in the morning, and he was very hungry. When he left Theresa before dawn he had gone straight home, where he had quickly showered, changed clothes, and, just before leaving the house, fed the cat.

"Sweet Miss Pearl," he had said quietly, watching her eat, "I'm afraid I haven't been much company for you lately."

Other than having a glass of buttermilk, he himself had not eaten anything, thinking to stop at the Easy Street Cafe for a quick breakfast on his way in to the office. However, Bud Taylor's car had been sitting in the parking lot, and A. G. felt strongly disinclined to face the older man after their recent unresolved unpleasantness.

"She was," he confirmed, plainly delighted to see the lieutenant again. "Tug Benson, the chief of police in Petersburg, called me right after he talked to Major Williams and learned that we, you and I, had questioned Wanda Carbone in connection with the Fitzgerald murder."

Giles shook his head. "Poor Wanda," he murmured. He and his new bride had gotten in late the night before and had stayed with her mother, Lorraine. He had decided, on a whim, to stop in at A. G.'s office on his way out to Fort Lee. "I have to wonder if I had identified Sergeant Stevens earlier, perhaps she might still be alive."

"Absolutely not," A. G. said forcefully, meaning it. "Stevens had already gotten out of the army even before Captain Fitzgerald's murder, so he wasn't just sitting around Fort Lee waiting to be picked up and questioned. And we still don't know if his visit to Wanda was just a coincidence as far as her murder is concerned."

"But you don't think it's a coincidence, do you?"

A. G. shook his head. "No, I don't." He stood up. "Listen, I'm about to starve to death. Let's you and me step around the corner to your mother-in-law's diner and get something to eat."

Breakfast consisted of three eggs, grits, two sausage patties, and three of Lorraine O'Brien's homemade buttermilk biscuits dressed with butter and molasses. Giles, who had eaten earlier, had only a cup of coffee and a sweet roll.

"I swear, A. G., I don't know how you can eat like this and still be as skinny as you are," Lorraine said, joining them at the table for a cigarette and coffee. "You must have a secret nightlife that none of us knows anything about," she teased, winking at Giles.

"Where's Mary Frances?" A. G. asked, sitting back and lighting a Chesterfield.

"She drove over to Richmond first thing this morning with a friend," Giles said. "To look at furniture."

"I thought the army provided furnished quarters for married officers," A. G. said, remembering the Fitzgeralds' Quartermaster furniture.

"They do," Giles confirmed, "but it's always nice to have something you can call your own, even if it's just a piece or two. Besides, I'm only going to be in the army for another year, and Mary Frances wants to find a bedroom suite we can take with us."

"It's going to be my wedding present to them," Lorraine said, stubbing out her cigarette and standing up. "Back to the salt mines for me," she said, nodding toward the kitchen. "Unlike you two, if I don't work, I don't get paid."

"What next?" Giles asked A. G. as soon as Lorraine left the table.

"Certainly the next development of any significance will be getting our hands on the elusive ex-sergeant Stevens," A. G. replied. "As you surmised back in my office, I don't hold much to the notion of coincidence in this case." He held up his right hand, fingers and thumb splayed apart. "Five things, or if you recall from one of our first conversations, five snapshots to keep in mind: First, Stevens, in an act completely out of character based upon what we know of his career, decides against all advice to get out of the army. Second, Wanda Carbone, a low-level clerical employee at the Quartermaster School, at some point in the relatively recent past begins an adulterous affair with Captain Fitzgerald. Third, shortly thereafter, Captain Fitzgerald is murdered. Fourth, we know that Stevens, on at least one occasion, paid a visit to Wanda Carbone at her apartment. Fifth, shortly thereafter, Wanda is murdered. Although, of course, anything is possible, it strains my credulity, not to mention my imagination, beyond its natural limits to believe that those five events are totally unrelated."

"Don't forget the mysterious telephone call to Private Carbone while he was on duty, and the murder weapon that was found in his locker," Giles added.

"Six and seven," A. G. said, holding up two more fingers. "And number eight, the snapshot of Fitzgerald as a gambler, a poker player who played in weekly high-stakes games in Richmond."

"I had almost forgotten about the poker angle," Giles admitted somewhat sheepishly.

"Understandably. I myself have about concluded that Fitzgerald's gambling habit was unrelated to his murder."

"A coincidence," Giles said, smiling mischievously.

276

"Just so." A. G. stood and patted his stomach. "Breakfast came in the nick of time, believe me." He put money on the table for the bill, and the two men walked outside. "Lord, it must be ninety-five degrees already," A. G. muttered, putting on his hat. "Let's talk this afternoon, after you've had a chance to get caught up on things from Major Williams's point of view."

"Do you think Stevens is still around?" Giles asked.

A. G. shrugged. "I wouldn't be if I were him, certainly not if he was the one who murdered Wanda Carbone, but who knows? For the time being, we'll just have to wait and see if Tug Benson can flush him out. Like I said, we'll talk again this afternoon. Oh, and," he reached out and shook Giles's hand, "congratulations again on getting married. I'm tickled to death for you and Mary Frances."

Mildred looked up from her Underwood when A. G. walked into the office. "You got a call from Chief Benson in Petersburg," she said. "He wanted you to call him back as soon as you came in. And Gladys Arthur called again."

A. G. tossed his hat on the hat rack and closed his office door behind him. "Tug?" He balanced the receiver on his right shoulder as he lit a Chesterfield. "A. G. Farrell returning your call."

"Yeah, A. G., thanks for calling back so soon. I was wondering if you might have any idea how I might get in touch with Theresa Fitzgerald, the murdered captain's widow."

A. G. sat up a little straighter at the mention of Theresa's name. "I would assume you could reach her at Fort Lee," he said. "It's my understanding that she hasn't moved off the post yet."

"I'm not so sure about that," Tug replied slowly. "When I kept getting no answer on her telephone, I had Major Williams send someone over to see if anything was wrong. The neighbors told him that she hasn't been staying there, at least not overnight, since she buried her husband up at Arlington." Tug paused for a second. "When was the last time you talked to her?"

A strong feeling of apprehension surged through A. G. He had always assumed that whenever he and Theresa weren't spending the night together in her warehouse apartment in Petersburg she was staying at Fort Lee, keeping up appearances.

"Are you still there, A. G.?"

"Yes, Tug, sorry, I was just trying to remember when she and I spoke the last time." A bead of perspiration ran down his back, between his shoulder blades. "I'm, uh, not exactly sure, but it's been a while," he lied, instinctively not wishing to divulge anything that would make the police chief suspicious of his relationship with Theresa.

"Was it out at the fort?"

"No." A. G. shook his head as if Tug could see him. "I believe it was by telephone, although she would have been in her quarters at Fort Lee when we talked." He paused and, holding his palm over the receiver, cleared his throat. "If you don't mind my asking, what did you want to talk to her about?"

"Not much in particular. I thought it might be interesting to get her take on this Sergeant Stevens thing, see if maybe she knew him, or had an idea why he got out of the army so unexpectedly. Like that."

"Any word on Stevens's whereabouts?"

"Not yet, but I've got his picture out and a lot of people asking around about him. If he's anywhere in the Petersburg area, I'll know about it sooner rather than later. Listen, A. G., I've got to go. Be sure and let me know right away if you hear from Mrs. Fitzgerald, will you? And if she does call you, tell her that I want to talk to her as soon as possible."

"I'll do it, Tug," A. G. promised. He hung up the telephone slowly, his heart pounding with anxiety over the lie he had just told. Why had Theresa misled him about where she had been staying, he wondered. What possible reason could she have had for such a thing? Feeling suddenly trapped behind his desk, he stood up and walked out to the front office.

"I'll be out for a while," he told Mildred. "Oh, and if Gladys Arthur calls back, tell her I'll call her in the morning," he added, hurrying out before she could ask any questions.

A. G. peered through the kitchen screen door and tapped softly on the jamb. "May I come in?" he asked.

Dolores walked over and pushed the screen open. Dressed in a pair of patched cotton work trousers and a man's long-sleeved, white shirt with paint stains on it, she carried a mop in her right hand.

"It's a little late for spring cleaning," A. G. teased, trying unsuccessfully to make her smile.

"I wouldn't want anybody to think I'd leave behind anything but a clean house," she explained, "although Lord knows it was dirty enough when I moved in." She pointed to the stove. "If I remember correctly, it took me two days to get that clean enough to cook on." She shook her head at the memory. "I can't imagine letting anything get as filthy as it was when I first saw it."

"When are you leaving?" A. G. had wanted to ease his way into the question, ideally working it in at the end of a broader conversation, but found himself asking it immediately, as almost the first thing out his mouth.

"Tomorrow afternoon. I'm catching the Greyhound in Petersburg."

"Do you need a . . ."

"No," she interrupted, shaking her head. "Francine Baker is giving me a ride over to the bus station. What little furniture I'm moving is going to be picked up tomorrow morning."

"I wish . . ." A. G. paused for a second, suddenly unsure of how to express what he wanted to say. "I wish you didn't feel you had to leave," he finally said, shrugging.

She started to say something and stopped. "You *wish*," she finally said, shaking her head at the irony of the word. "As if all this were somehow out of your hands, not your responsibility."

"Dolores, I . . ."

"I think it would be better for you to leave now," she said, nodding toward the screen door. "As much as you would like to, you can't make this any better by talking about it."

She turned and walked into the bedroom, closing the door behind her. A. G. stood quietly for several seconds, and then, moving as if being sent to his own hanging, he turned and left.

The first thing A. G. did when he got home at five-thirty was try Theresa's telephone number at Fort Lee once more. Although she had promised when they parted early that morning to call him, he had not heard from her and, particularly since Tug Benson's query regarding her whereabouts, he had grown increasingly concerned. He had tried reaching her several times that afternoon to no avail and finally decided that if he had not heard from her by seven-thirty he would drive to the warehouse apartment in Petersburg. After putting out fresh food for Pearl, he showered and changed clothes, relishing the short-lived pleasure of clean, dry fabric next to his cool skin. Barefooted, he padded downstairs and out to the kitchen, where he heated up a light supper of stewed tomatoes and turnip greens. He had barely finished eating when the crunch of automobile tires on the gravel of the driveway alerted him to an arriving visitor. For a brief, giddy instant the thought that Theresa had driven over to be with him flashed through his mind, until he remembered that she didn't even know where he lived, much less how to get there. Still wearing only the pair of light cotton trousers and a sleeveless white undershirt he had put on after his shower, he stepped out onto the porch and saw a gray, 1947 Plymouth sedan with Michigan license plates. Not recognizing the car, he bent down to see who the occupants might be. He saw Gladys Arthur, a small, middle-aged Negro woman who taught third grade in the county's segregated elementary school.

"I've been trying to call you, Sheriff," she explained as she got out of the car, reproof plain in her voice, "but you haven't returned my calls." She looked back into the sedan. "Get out," she ordered the driver peremptorily, "and come around here." Looking back at A. G., she began vigorously fanning herself with a palm-leaf fan. "You remember Titus, don't you, Sheriff, my youngest boy?"

"Yes, I do, Miz Arthur." A. G. nodded toward the handsome man as he got out of the car. "Titus, it's good to see you again. If I recall, you moved up north about the time the war started, didn't you?" He and Titus were approximately the same age, and he vaguely remembered hearing that Titus had left Virginia for work in the automobile industry in 1940 or '41.

Gladys nodded, pleased that A. G. remembered. "He did," she confirmed, speaking as if her son weren't standing there. "Went up north and got married. He and his wife never had any children, and she died of cancer last year."

"I'm sorry," A. G. murmured.

"He moved back down here almost four months ago," Gladys continued, "staying with me and working over in Petersburg as a mechanic at the Buick dealer." She paused to pat her brow and face with a small, lace-trimmed handker-chief.

"Please, come up on the porch," A. G. said, still mystified as to the reason for the visit and embarrassed to be standing there in his undershirt. "Excuse me for just a second while I run into the house and put on a shirt." He paused briefly at the screen door and turned back toward his visitors. "Would either of you like a glass of iced tea?" he asked. "Or perhaps a glass of fresh buttermilk?"

"A glass of tea would be nice," Gladys confirmed, fanning nonstop.

Several minutes later A. G. reemerged from the house, sporting shoes and socks, a fresh, white shirt, and a tray bearing three glasses of tea. "I'm sorry to keep you waiting," he said. "Won't you have a seat?" He motioned Gladys and Titus onto the glider, and sat himself in one of the wicker chairs. Taking a pack of Chesterfields from his trouser pocket, he offered one to Titus, who politely refused. "I have to apologize for not calling you back," he said to Gladys, lighting his cigarette. "It was impolite, and I hope you'll forgive me."

Gladys nodded, clearly pleased to accept A. G.'s apology. "Titus has something he wants to tell you," she said, turning to her obviously nervous son. "Tell the sheriff what you told me," she ordered bluntly, her tone of voice leaving no doubt as to her unquestioned authority.

"I've been working over in Petersburg since I got back from Detroit," Titus began, sitting stiffly on the edge of the sofa and looking down at a spot between his feet. "It's been about three months now, maybe a little longer."

"The sheriff's not interested in all that," Gladys interrupted, impatient for him to get to the heart of his story. "Tell him about the club you go to."

"Take your time," A. G. soothed, trying to relax Titus and deflect Gladys's impatience. He was struck by how young

Titus looked, to be a widower. "You wanted to tell me something about a club?"

Titus nodded. He was a handsome man, slightly built, with closely cut hair and large, expressive eyes. "A club over in Petersburg, a nightclub. It's called Grey's Tavern." He paused for a second. "For colored folks," he added.

"Where you go drinking," Gladys inserted indignantly. "With loose women."

A. G. suppressed a smile and nodded at Titus. "Take your time," he repeated. He knew the club Titus was talking about, or, more accurately, knew of it.

"You know that captain that was killed here in Hopewell a couple weeks ago?" Titus asked.

A. G. nodded, slightly confused by the apparent unrelatedness of the nightclub in Petersburg and Captain Fitzgerald's death.

"His wife." Titus stopped, suddenly a good deal more nervous, and licked his lips. "His wife," he began again in a rush, "has been coming to the club."

"His wife?" A. G. asked, even more confused. *Captain Fitzgerald didn't have a wife,* he almost said, when the image of Theresa came to him. *How can that be?* "She's been coming to the club since the captain was killed? Is that what you're telling me?" he managed to ask, shaking his head. "I'm afraid I don't understand what you're saying."

"And before he was killed," Titus confirmed. "I've been seeing her out there, off and on, ever since I came back to Petersburg." He took a deep breath and plunged ahead. "She's been coming with a man from out at the fort, once a week, sometimes more." He looked over at his mother and then back down at his feet, unable to meet A. G.'s eyes. His voice dropped, and both A. G. and his mother had to strain to hear what he was saying. "A colored man. I don't know his name, but folks at the club say he's a sergeant or something. At Fort Lee."

Chapter Fifteen

Long after the sun had finally disappeared below the western horizon, the glowing tips of A. G.'s cigarettes could be seen tracing a red parabola from the glider's armrest to his mouth and back. He smoked one after another until his throat was raw and his heart beat rapidly from the nicotine racing from his lungs to his brain.

"Titus was afraid to say anything to you, her being a white woman and all," Gladys had said quietly, pausing briefly at the door of her son's Plymouth. She and her son had both been palpably relieved by A. G.'s low-key response to Titus's stunning revelation, and they had left shortly after Titus finished telling his story. "I don't know what it means, whether it has anything to do with that woman's husband being killed, but quick as I heard it, I knew you should know about it."

"I know what it means," A. G. said to

Pearl an hour after Gladys and her son had left. "It means I'm a fool." He shook his head. "A damned fool. And worse." The cat looked up at him from where she sat in the darkness next to the glider as if nothing he did, or failed to do, would ever again surprise her. He stood up and walked into the house, taking care to hold the screen door open for Pearl, following slowly behind him. In the narrow hallway between the dining room and kitchen he passed the telephone and almost picked it up, but instead continued into the kitchen. He put down fresh food and water for Pearl and, standing at the sink, drank a glass of water from the tap to quiet his own hunger temporarily. "It's funny," he said, carefully drying his water glass before putting it back into the glass-fronted cabinet opposite the stove, "how much time we spend in the kitchen without ever realizing it." Pearl looked up at him, a drop of water clinging to her chin whiskers. "I used to think I'd miss living in this old house, but now," he shook his head, "now I'm not so sure."

The drive to Petersburg seemed to take no time at all. A. G. had no trouble finding Grey's Tavern, although he had never been there before. He parked where he could see the front door and lit another cigarette, wondering what exactly he was going to do if he found Theresa inside with Stevens. *I should have called Tug Benson,* he told himself, knowing that that would have been the proper thing to do. *This is his jurisdiction—I have no authority to be doing anything here, much less making an arrest.* He laughed, a hollow sound devoid of humor, and got slowly out of the car. He could hear music coming from the club, from a jukebox he assumed, since he doubted they would have a band on a weeknight. At the front door he paused for a second, knowing he was about to make a mistake and yet no more able to do anything about it than a falling man is able to reach out into thin air and somehow arrest his downward flight. He opened the door and walked in.

"Sheriff!"

The man's voice, though not particularly loud, carried an unmistakable tone of authority. The club was almost empty, just two or three tables of social drinkers who looked up with open hostility when A. G. entered. He smiled, thinking that if looks could kill he'd be lying dead on the floor. Originally a single-story shotgun row house, the long, narrow building had been gutted to create a single room, some eighteen-by-thirty feet in size, with a low, sagging plywood ceiling and a stained and scuffed wooden floor. Two large industrial floor fans at the front and rear circulated hot, humid air redolent with the smell of stale beer and cheap perfume. A long bar, complete with shiny red leatherette stools, occupied most of one wall, and a bandstand and small dance floor was located against the back wall. Neon beer signs on the wall behind the bar hummed with all the colors of the spectrum from infrared to ultraviolet. They provided much of the room's illumination, creating an atmosphere of artificial bonhomie in the immediate vicinity of the bar that faded quickly away to an uneasy darkness the farther back in the room one went. The voice that hailed him came from a table two thirds of the way to the rear. A. G. walked back.

"Sergeant Stevens," he said, inclining his head in greeting to the sole occupant of the table. "I see you remember me from our brief encounter outside the Carbones' apartment."

"Oh my, yes," Stevens replied, a chuckle from deep within his chest rumbling to the surface. "Not only do I remember you, I expect I know as much about you as there is to know." He stood up with mock politeness and pointed to the chair opposite his. "I have to say, though, that it took you long enough to find me." Impeccably dressed in a worsted wool, tropical-weight sport coat, starched white shirt with an open collar, and pressed linen trousers, he looked cool and dry, as if the evening's heat and humidity did not affect him as it did other men. "But now that you have, you're not in a hurry, are you?" Without waiting for an answer, he nodded A. G. into the chair across the table and waved a hand at the bartender. "Leon," he called out, "bring us two cold Blue Ribbons and a shot glass for the sheriff." A bottle of Ancient Age bourbon and a single shot glass sat in front of Stevens. "You'll join me in a social drink, won't you, Sheriff?" he added, sitting down and turning his attention back to A. G. "I mean, before we turn to *business*." He emphasized the word *business*.

"A glass of beer never hurt anybody," A. G. allowed, settling into the chair.

The bartender walked over with their beer.

"You want a glass with that beer?" he asked A. G. in a surly tone of voice, holding up a water glass.

Even in the low light A. G. could see that the proffered glass was filthy. "No, thank you," he demurred, "I'll drink it out of the bottle."

The bartender grunted and took a shot glass out of his shirt pocket, putting it on the table in front of A. G.

"Pay the man," Stevens ordered peremptorily. "Nobody drinks for free around here."

A. G. reached into his pocket and took out a five-dollar bill. "How much is it?" he asked.

"Five dollars," the bartender said, taking the bill from A. G.'s hand and walking away without another word.

"You'll have to excuse Leon," Stevens said, referring to the bartender's rudeness. "It's not that he's prejudiced against white folks in general," he said, smiling sardonically, "he just doesn't like having to serve them in his establishment." He picked up the bottle and poured each of them a shot of bourbon. "You can understand his feeling that way, I'm sure. In any event, I propose a toast."

"I'll stick to the beer," A. G. said, holding a hand up. "I've never been much of a drinker to tell you the truth and, in any event, technically I'm in here on official business."

Stevens looked at him for a long second and then, reaching behind himself with his right hand, drew a Colt .45 automatic from his waistband at the small of his back. "You misunderstand me, Sheriff—I wasn't *asking*," he said, calmly thumbing the pistol's hammer back. The sound, by no means loud, could be heard throughout the room. The patrons at the other tables finished their drinks and hurriedly exited the premises.

A. G. immediately put both hands on the table, palms down. "I'm not armed," he said.

"Then you're a fool," Stevens opined.

"You won't get an argument on that from *me*," A. G. said lightly, hoping to make Stevens smile. "In fact, you'd have a hard time getting almost anyone I know to disagree with you."

"Pick up the glass," Stevens directed, motioning with the pistol as he picked up his own glass with his left hand. "To Theresa Fitzgerald," he toasted mockingly. "The woman of our dreams."

A. G. picked up the shot glass and took a tentative sip, grimacing at the unpleasant taste.

Stevens laughed derisively. "Drink it all at once," he ordered, demonstrating with his own. "You can chase it with the beer."

A. G. complied, gagging slightly before he could force down a swallow of Blue Ribbon. He took out his pack of Chesterfields and offered one to Stevens, taking no small comfort in the fact that his hand was steady and his heartbeat slow and rhythmic.

"You were right when you said you weren't much of a drinker," Stevens said dryly, taking one of A. G.'s Chesterfields. He put the big Colt down on the table and struck a match, lighting both cigarettes. "I thought drinking was something you white fraternity boys learned your first year of college."

A. G. shrugged. "Sorry to disappoint you, Sergeant, but . . ."

"Actually I'm not a sergeant, not anymore." Stevens's voice was flat, conveying an obvious undertone of bitterness at the recent loss, whether voluntary or not, of his military status. "But since we, you and I, aren't exactly going to be friends, you may continue to use my former rank in addressing me." The sardonic smile reappeared. "It will help to keep things a little more . . ." he paused for a second, searching for the right word, ". . . a little more formal between us."

"Actually, much the same can be said for your calling me Sheriff. By this time tomorrow, assuming you don't shoot me tonight," A. G. smiled, frankly amazed that he was able to joke about the fact that another man, a man who, as far as he knew, had already killed two other people, was holding a gun on him, "I won't be a sheriff any longer."

Stevens raised a single eyebrow. "Somebody going to fire you?"

"I doubt it, but I intend to resign in any event. My conduct ever since Captain Fitzgerald's murder has been, continues to be," he smiled without humor, "deplorable."

"I'm surprised you're honest enough to admit it," Stevens murmured, almost more to himself than to A. G. He looked with renewed interest at A. G. "Particularly since I suspect you could get away with it if you really wanted to."

"Perhaps, although 'getting away with it' at this point in time would be, at best, a Pyrrhic victory." A. G. shrugged and decided not to beat around the bush. "You and Theresa are lovers, aren't you," he said, more as a statement of fact than a question.

"Almost from the start," Stevens admitted, not the least angered by A. G.'s words. "Of her marriage, I mean." He took a drink of his beer and shifted in his chair, always keeping his right hand near the Colt. "Captain Fitzgerald was not a very smart man. Not at all. In fact, in many ways he was quite stupid. Nonetheless, he was not mean-spirited, particularly toward the Negro soldiers serving under him, unlike many, if not most, of his fellow white officers. I was his orderly at Fort Myer, and when he found out that I was taking night and weekend classes at Howard, in the District, he arranged my schedule so as to make it more convenient for me to go back and forth." He smiled. "Never having been to college himself, he simply could not understand why I wanted to go, but, to his credit, he did what he could to make life a little easier for me."

"How did you and Theresa meet?"

"The good captain himself introduced us. Not two weeks after they were married." He laughed at the irony. "A man's got to be careful about who he goes around introducing his wife to, particularly a wife like Theresa. After he'd learned that she had been raised in a very liberal home environment, I suppose he thought it would impress her to see how civilized he could be around a colored man. They had just moved into their quarters behind the main parade ground up on the North Post at Fort Myer, and he brought me over to help her hang pictures and move furniture around. He was quite complimentary, telling her how impressed he was with me, going to college and all, how I was a credit to my race and what a fine soldier I was, and, oh yes, how wonderful everything was going to be in the new, integrated army. Meanwhile, I was standing there at attention in my starched fatigues like a house nigger meeting the master's new wife for the first time." He shook his head. "Not ten minutes after he left me there alone that first time she had me in bed." He paused for another sip of beer. "I hear you're something of a liberal thinker, Sheriff, particularly for a Southerner," he said, his voice sarcastic. "Tell me, what do you think about that, your sweet Theresa in bed with a colored man?"

"Did Captain Fitzgerald find out about you and his wife?" A. G. asked, ignoring Stevens's question. He was surprised to realize that he found it difficult to say her Christian name. *Theresa.* "Is that why you had to kill him?"

"Shit." Stevens reached for another of A. G.'s cigarettes and lit it with a flourish. "He could no more imagine the two of us together than he could have imagined flying to the moon. She kept an apartment over in the District of Columbia—just like the place here in Petersburg. You didn't know she owns that warehouse, did you?" He looked at A. G. with a gleam in his eye and laughed with obvious delight. "Lock, stock, and barrel. And what's more, you didn't even bother to wonder who did own it. 'A friend,' she told you, and you were only too happy to believe it. One call to the county recorder's office and you would have found out she owned it—her name's the only one on the title—but then you would have had to ask yourself why she lied to you about it. Some sheriff you are." He nodded, the blue smoke from his cigarette curling up and around his face. "Anyway, a couple of times a week I'd meet her at the apartment in the District, before or after my classes. It got to the point that I even stopped going to classes altogether, just to be able to spend more time with her." He smiled, remembering something. "She loved going out with me, to clubs and such. In Washington, we'd go out dancing and drinking at least one night a week, often more. Up there, it wasn't too unusual to see white women in our clubs. Down here, though," he shook his head, "man! These Petersburg niggers never saw anything like Theresa Fitzgerald. You know how she can dress when she wants to. We'd come in here," he waved his right arm to encompass the entire room, "and this whole place would go crazy. Leon, there," he nodded toward the bartender who was still watching them, apparently unconcerned about the gun on the table, "used to serve us free drinks, not charge me a dime for anything, just to be sure I'd bring her back. She loved it, loved being the center of attention like that."

"Weren't you afraid someone might see you? Someone who knew the two of you?"

Stevens laughed. "Who? Not some white officer, that's for sure. Fort Myer was just across the river from the capital, and yet Washington might as well have been on the dark side of the moon as far as an officer venturing off it for culture or entertainment was concerned. Their idea of a fun evening is pretty much limited to getting drunk on the cheap booze at the officers club. Fort Lee, the same. And you think a Negro soldier's going to say anything? I'll bet half the colored GIs at both Fort Myer and here knew all about us. No, there was no danger of him finding out, not really. And even if there was, let me tell you," he leaned forward, tapping on the table to emphasize his words, "she wouldn't have cared. That woman's got a craziness about her, almost like she didn't care if she got caught or not. In fact, at times I thought she almost *wanted* to get caught. When we were still at Fort Myer she'd get bored during the day and call over to his office at the battalion, tell him to send me over to their quarters to do something for her. Once, she called to tell him to send me over to open a pickle jar!" He shook his head in wonder at the outrageous duplicity. "Can you believe that shit? Anyway, I'd go over, and we'd jump right into bed. Their bed. Fitzgerald walked in unexpectedly one day and caught us coming out of the bedroom. She told him I was in there moving furniture around for her. The only thing that saved us was the fact that he literally could not imagine her fucking a black man. She thought it was funny, but it scared the shit out of me, I don't mind telling you. The army might have been recently integrated, but I had no doubts about how they'd treat a black GI caught in bed with his commanding officer's wife." He shook his head again, still shocked at the memory of the incredible risks they had taken. "If I was lucky I'd have gotten twenty years at Leavenworth and a dishonorable discharge. More likely, Fitzgerald would have shot me deader'n a fucking doornail and gotten a letter of commendation from the President for doing it." He laughed at the absurdity. "And probably a promotion into the bargain."

"I assume then that she, Theresa, convinced Captain Fitzgerald to have you transferred here to Fort Lee with him."

Stevens waved a hand dismissively. "She didn't have to do much, believe me. Everything the captain signed—letters, reports, whatever—I wrote. Once he got past the comics section in the newspaper, the fool could barely read. He knew that down here, at the Quartermaster School, he'd have to have someone like me to cover his ass if he ever wanted to get promoted again."

A. G. decided to ask a dangerous question. "You did kill him, didn't you?"

Anger passed quickly across Stevens's face, leaving behind only a sense of resignation and, perhaps, A. G. thought, melancholy.

"What do you think?"

"I think you did," A. G. said quietly, "although to be honest I'm not exactly sure why."

"Nor am I," Stevens admitted, "strange as that may sound." He toyed with his shot glass and then picked up the bottle of bourbon and filled both it and his. "Another toast," he proposed. "To uncertainty." He drained the glass in one swallow, motioning with his hand for A. G. to do the same.

A. G. managed it without gagging and was able to smile after a quick sip of beer. "It was a little easier that time," he said.

"It always is with bad habits," Stevens observed without humor. "First few times are hard and then, before you know it, you're having fun." He waved at the bartender. "Two more Blue Ribbons."

Leon walked over slowly and put two bottles on the table, looking pointedly at the big Colt lying on the table.

"My round," Stevens said, holding up a five-dollar bill.

"You payin'?" Leon asked. When Stevens nodded affirmatively, Leon shook his head. "On the house," he muttered, turning and walking back to the bar.

"You see?" Stevens asked A. G. "I could shoot you right now and it wouldn't mean shit to him."

"He might lose his business license," A. G. responded, trying hard to keep his voice light, his manner nonchalant.

Stevens shrugged. "A small price to pay to be able to tell everyone he saw a white, southern sheriff shot and killed by a colored man." He picked up the weapon and hefted it in his hand, sighting it over A. G.'s shoulder at the door behind him. "Not many men, black men in particular, can say such a thing." He chuckled, pleased at the thought. "I expect that'd be more than worth losing a business license over."

A fresh bead of perspiration broke out on A. G.'s forehead, and he felt his scrotum tightening.

"And speaking of white men getting shot, I'll tell you something else your little investigation never turned up: There was a witness out there the night I killed Captain Fitzgerald. An old man." A broad smile spread across Stevens's face. "An old colored man." He told A. G. about whirling around at the sound of the old man dropping the whiskey jar. "He was sure I was going to kill him, too, but when I saw that he was a Negro, and half drunk into the bargain," Stevens shook his head, "I just left him standing there. I knew he'd been called nigger by too many white men to send me to the electric chair for shooting one." Sighing, Stevens put the Colt back down on the table and took a sip from the fresh bottle of beer. "We, Theresa and I, were going to go to Paris together. To live. That was the plan." He reached into the breast pocket of his jacket and took out a passport. "Hell, I even got a passport." He held it up for A. G. to see and then dropped it on the table next to the pistol. "Just as soon as I finished up my hitch and got out of the army," he snapped his fingers, "we were going to take off."

"You could have done that without killing her husband," A. G. pointed out.

"And should have," Stevens agreed, nodding his head slowly. "I didn't have any more thought of killing that man than I did stepping in front of a train. But Theresa got to talking about how we'd need money to live in France, lots of it, and how he had these insurance policies." He looked at A. G. "You know how it goes—one thing leads to another."

Indeed I do know how it goes, A. G. thought but did not say. "What about Wanda Carbone? I take it you somehow got her involved so you could set up her husband."

"I knew her from the Quartermaster School. Little cracker girl whose husband regularly beat her up whenever he got drunk. She was always coming to work with a black eye or a split lip, telling everyone some foolish story about how she had walked into a door, or tripped on something. I paid a little attention to her, gave her some sympathy, and then offered to show her how she could earn enough money to leave her husband before he finally went too far and killed her." He chuckled. "Easiest thing I ever did. Told her that the captain's wife needed grounds for a divorce and was willing to pay her two hundred dollars to have an affair with him. Shit." He shook his head. "Wanda'd never seen two hundred dollars in one place in her entire life. It would have been more than enough to get her on a Greyhound out to California and away from her worthless husband. Then I went to the captain and told him that Wanda had a big crush on him. Next thing you know, they're going at it like a couple of high school kids. The captain thought I was the greatest idea he'd ever had— not only was I doing all of his work at the Quartermaster School, I was now out procuring women for him."

"Was it difficult to arrange?" A. G. asked, curious in spite of himself.

"You mean killing him?" Stevens shook his head. "Easiest thing in the world—all it took was a little patience. I kept an eye on the motor-pool duty roster and waited until Carbone pulled CQ. Then I told Captain Fitzgerald that Wanda was hot to meet that night, what with her husband stuck on the post. When he called her from the officers club, she told him to meet her out at that warehouse in Hopewell."

"Why Hopewell?"

Stevens smiled. "Theresa made that decision. You see, killing him on Fort Lee would have involved the military police, and Major Williams struck her as too much of a bull-dog for comfort. Plus, as a crime on a federal reservation it might have pulled in the FBI. She did a little research and discovered that the Petersburg chief of police was ex-FBI and ran what was considered to be a very efficient operation, so Petersburg was out, too." He tilted his beer bottle in a mock salute to A. G. and laughed delightedly. "That left you."

A. G. nodded silently, his ears burning with shame.

"Anyway, the rest was simple. I made an anonymous call to Carbone at the motor pool and told him that Fitzgerald was fucking his wife. I then told Wanda not to go to Hopewell after all because someone had wised her husband up about the affair and I was afraid he might try to follow her and catch the two of them together." He paused for a long sip of beer.

"Later, after it was done, I slipped the pistol I had used into Carbone's locker at the motor pool."

"So Wanda didn't have any idea you were planning to kill Fitzgerald?"

"Of course not. Since Wanda knew her husband had a violent temper, Theresa and I figured she'd fall for the setup just like we assumed the authorities would."

"What tipped her off?"

"Wanda wasn't quite as stupid as I had thought. After I paid her the two hundred we'd agreed upon, she called me back." He shook his head, appalled at his own miscalculation. "She told me she'd been thinking about it and was pretty sure her old man hadn't done it, which, in her mind, could only mean one thing."

"How much more did she want to keep quiet?"

"Ten thousand. Can you believe that shit?" He smiled and shook his head. "That was the time you ran into me coming out of her apartment. I threatened her, but she could already smell the money. I told her we'd get back to her. I wasn't even that worried about having run into you, because as long as Wanda stuck with the story, we could claim I was just a friend from the Quartermaster School, helping her out with groceries or whatever. I went to see her again last Sunday, tried to reason with her, tell her we didn't have ten thousand dollars." His face hardened. "She called me a nigger. Said she knew I was probably fucking Theresa and laughed at me." He looked at A. G., his eyes narrowed with anger. "That's the way it always works, doesn't it? I mean, first, when she was grateful for the chance to get enough money to get away from her husband, when I was helping her out, then I'm a nice guy, a good Negro, a credit to my race. Then, things turn around a little, Wanda feels she's holding all the cards, got me over a barrel, now I'm a worthless, white-woman–chasing nigger. I'll tell you something, Sheriff." He picked up the pistol and slowly brought it to bear on A. G.'s chest. "I may have some regrets about killing Captain Fitzgerald, but I had no problem whatever strangling that little ofay bitch."

A. G., convinced that he was about to be killed, thought suddenly of his mother. "I'm sorry," he whispered.

"I'll bet you are," Stevens said sarcastically, angrily. "Sorry as hell you came in here tonight looking for me." He laughed, bitterly. "Even sorrier you didn't bring a gun with you."

"Actually," A. G. said quietly, "I wasn't talking to you." He smiled, amazed at how calm he felt with the end of his life just seconds away. *Probably the whiskey,* he thought. "Don't get me wrong, I am sorry about this . . ." he waved a hand vaguely, "this whole thing, but there's nothing I can do, or say, about it now, is there?"

Stevens looked silently at A. G. for what seemed like an eternity and then slowly put the pistol back down on the table. "No, there isn't," he said, picking up his bottle of Blue Ribbon and taking a long swallow. "I'll bet you're wondering why I stayed here, in Petersburg, after killing her," he said, taking another of A. G.'s Chesterfields. He leaned forward, across the table, accepting a light from A. G. "Thanks. I mean, you might have thought I'd have taken it on the lam, as they used to say."

A. G. nodded. "Actually Tug Benson, the police chief here in Petersburg, the one Theresa," he smiled, "was so impressed with, did wonder if you might not have left town by the time we got around to identifying you. I had a feeling you were still here, though why I can't say. I assume now it was because of your relationship with Theresa." *Perhaps you thought she would hide you,* he also thought but did not say. *Perhaps she has been.*

"It had nothing to do with her," Stevens responded, shaking his head. "And everything." His words were beginning to slur ever so slightly from all the alcohol he had been drinking. "She knew as soon as I told her that you'd seen me at the Carbone apartment that it was all over. For me, anyway. See, Wanda had never seen Theresa, never talked to her. Only me. So, whatever Wanda might say, Theresa could just deny everything as it pertained to her. She, Theresa, knew you'd eventually identify me," he smiled, "though it took you a lot longer than either of us figured it would, just like she knew that, when push came to shove, I wouldn't turn her in, wouldn't testify against her. At that point Wanda, and what she did or didn't know, or would or wouldn't say, didn't matter anymore, not really. I went over on Sunday just to talk to Wanda one last time, maybe scare her a little, try to get her to leave town." He shrugged. "I didn't go over there intending to kill her, but," he laughed humorlessly. "when a colored man kills a white woman, it doesn't much matter to a jury of white men whether he planned it a year ahead or did it on the spur of the moment, not here, not in Virginia. After that, after I killed her, Theresa and I both knew there was no point in me running away—the police would catch up with me sooner or later."

"It's not right, her getting away with this," A. G. said. "You could testify . . ."

"Shit," Stevens interrupted. "You *are* a fool. Even if I wanted to, and I don't, no jury's going to listen to me, a black man that's admitted to killing two white people, one of them a woman. All she's got to do is get up there and say I'm lying and that's it. And besides, whatever I do or say, I'm still going to the electric chair."

"Maybe not," A. G. said. "Life in prison is better than execution, and I could . . ."

"You could what? You aren't even going to be a sheriff when all this's over—you said so yourself. Shit." He took a quick sip of beer. "The district attorney's not going to give you the time of day when he finds out what you've been up to, who you've been sleeping with."

"But you've got no choice," A. G. insisted heatedly. "You might as well . . ."

"No choice?" Stevens asked rhetorically, picking up the pistol. In a movement that was almost too fast for A. G. to follow, Stevens raised the gun to his right temple and pulled the trigger.

Chapter Sixteen

"You look nice," A. G. said.

"You sound like you mean it," Theresa responded lightly, not quite smiling.

"I do mean it."

"You're lucky you caught me," she added, looking at her watch. They were standing just inside the door of her converted warehouse in Petersburg. She was wearing an ivory linen suit and, despite the withering heat, looked fresh and cool. A small, leather suitcase sat on the floor next to the door. "I was about to call a cab."

"I heard you were leaving," A. G. said, turning his straw hat over in his hands. "Moving back to Washington. I thought . . ." His voice trailed off into silence.

She looked at him curiously. "The district attorney told me you had resigned as sheriff. Frankly, it struck me as a rather . . . ," she paused for a brief second, searching for the right word, "a rather *extreme* gesture. Clearly I misjudged you."

"How so?"

"I had no doubt you would ultimately come to disapprove of me, probably even dislike or resent me, but your penchant for self-destruction took me completely by surprise. I suppose your anger at finding out about my relationship with Robert Stevens explains your attempt to have the district attorney indict me as an accomplice in the murders of Marty and that wretched Carbone woman, but why in the world did you feel the need to reveal your own affair with me? Nobody, certainly not the DA nor that pompous ass of a provost marshal, would have found out about it if you hadn't felt the need to confess." She shook her head disapprovingly. "And, at the risk of sounding ironic, I can only imagine what your friends and neighbors in Hopewell must think of you." She paused briefly to take a cigarette out of her purse, leaning forward slightly to accept a light from A. G. "Thank you . . . and did you honestly think," she continued, turning her head and exhaling a cloud of smoke over her right shoulder, "that the district attorney would move to indict me on the basis of poor Robert's suicidal confession? A confession unwitnessed and unheard by anyone but you?" She laughed. "Southern gentlemen are so predictable. Truly, all the district attorney wanted to hear, after you gave him Robert's confession, was my indignant denial that I had ever gone to bed with a colored man, much less conspired with him to murder my poor, ignorant husband."

A. G. nodded. "Tug Benson showed me the sworn deposition you gave. He also told me that everyone in the DA's office felt that our involvement, yours and mine, would have seriously complicated the case in any event. Which," he held her eyes firmly with his own, "I suspect was what you planned all along."

"I wouldn't be too sure of that if I were you," Theresa responded, a smile tugging at the corners of her mouth. "Your rather understated gallantry that first time you came to see me at Fort Lee was quite irresistible." The smile disappeared. "Then again," she flicked the ash off the end of her cigarette and shrugged, "you may be right. The only thing we can be sure of is that it doesn't matter now, does it?"

"Actually it does—to me, at least. You did conspire with Sergeant Stevens, didn't you? At least with regard to your husband's murder. I mean, the two of you planned his murder and the implication of Private Carbone just as Sergeant Stevens told me, didn't you?"

Theresa dropped her cigarette to the rough wooden floor and ground it out with her foot. "Surely you don't think you're going to get some sort of a last-minute confession, do you? Fueled, I can only imagine you hope, by the same middle-class guilt and self-flagellation you exhibited in telling a salaciously curious district attorney all about our relationship and then, wholly unnecessarily, resigning from your office of public trust. No," she shook her head emphatically, "I don't think so." She paused and smiled rather cruelly. "If you haven't lost your sense of humor altogether, I suggest you reread the deposition I gave the district attorney. If that doesn't . . ."

"Stop it," A. G. said forcefully, not quite shouting. "Just," he ran a trembling hand across his face and lowered his voice, "stop it. All right? Despite what you or anyone else in Petersburg or Hopewell might think, I'm not entirely a fool. I didn't come here expecting a confession or . . ."

"Why did you come then?" Theresa interrupted brusquely. She slipped out of her linen jacket and draped it over the leather suitcase.

"I don't know," A. G. started to say, and then stopped, shaking his head. "No, that's not true." He drew in a deep, shuddering breath, as if that could calm the sudden racing of his heart. "I came because I wanted to see you again."

She laughed and shook her head. "You're too honest for your own good—a trait you share, or shared, if you don't mind my saying, with Robert Stevens."

"He told me you were planning to go to Paris together—to live."

"We talked about it, but the trip, at least in my mind, was by no means a certainty. Robert was becoming increasingly possessive," she shrugged, "and, frankly, boring." She took a small Japanese silk fan from her purse and unfolded it, looking at him with sudden curiosity. "Why did you mention Paris? Were you thinking about *our* planned trips to New York and California? And Hawaii?"

A. G. nodded. "Among other things." He felt a bead of perspiration run down his back. Although the apartment to the rear of the warehouse was air-conditioned, the warehouse itself was not, and he guessed that the temperature where they stood was at least ninety-five degrees. He could see a fine blush of moisture on Theresa's face and, incongruously, suddenly remembered something from what now seemed like a past life: *Southern ladies don't perspire,* Dolores Anderson used to be fond of telling him, *they glow.*

" 'Among other things'?" Theresa repeated teasingly. She smiled and fanned herself. "As I mentioned a moment ago, you shouldn't automatically assume that my attraction to you was merely a matter of . . ." she paused for a second, searching for the appropriate words, "calculated self-interest. Or at least not entirely." She unbuttoned the top two buttons of her silk blouse and fanned her neck and throat, holding the blouse away from her body with her left hand. "Before we met I had frankly expected Hopewell's sheriff to be little more than a stereotypically dull-witted southern policeman. Imagine my surprise when you showed up on my doorstep at Fort Lee, a devotee of Dürer, Vermeer, and Coleridge. And a virgin, no less. As you might expect, poor Robert had the most difficult time dealing with your seduction." She laughed delightedly. "I must confess, I had to tell him the most outrageous lies about your . . ." she paused briefly for dramatic effect, "about your *performance* to keep him under control."

A. G. felt the back of his neck flush with anger and embarrassment. "What else did you tell Robert?" he asked, his voice shaking as he realized that he suddenly wanted to hurt her as badly as she was hurting him. "Did you tell him I cried the first time we made love?" He unconsciously clenched his fists, digging his fingernails into his palms.

"You still want me," Theresa marveled, a distinct tone of triumph and pleasure in her voice as the full realization came upon her. "That's it, isn't it? My God, that's the *real* reason you came here today." Without waiting for a response, she stepped boldly toward him. When their bodies were almost touching she reached out and put a hand intimately on his chest.

A. G. took her roughly into his arms, covering her mouth with his. She came willingly, surprising him, and immediately answered his kiss with her own, her sweet breath washing over his face.

"Yes," she said, her voice strained and urgent, "yes." She reached down with one hand and began to roughly stroke him through his trousers, biting him almost painfully on the ear and neck.

A. G. fumbled unconsciously with his belt and zipper, lowering her to the floor as she pulled up her linen skirt. A searing heat rose between them, soaking them both in perspiration as they lay on the rough pine planks, their bodies coming together with an electric urgency. Theresa cried out with passion, her voice guttural and explosive as she arched her body to meet his thrusts. Suddenly, as if an unexpected eclipse

307

had fallen over the room, A. G. felt a darkness descend upon him. His movements took on a violent, crazed quality as he began to use his body to batter hers. He rose partway and, like a man possessed, ripped her silk blouse open with his left hand.

"No," he gasped through clenched teeth, his eyes fixed and staring at Theresa's face. "No," he repeated even more harshly, his breath ragged and panting as his right hand grasped her about the throat.

Theresa's passion turned quickly to fear as she heard the almost demonic quality of his voice, and her fear turned to panic when she realized that he was strangling her. Using his tightening grip on her throat for leverage, A. G. continued to pound his body into hers until pinpoints of light flashed behind her eyes and she slipped into unconsciousness. As her body began to jerk spasmodically, it was the frightening, terminal nature of her convulsive movements that finally registered on some part of A. G.'s rational brain, and he immediately loosened his grip on her throat.

"Theresa," he whispered, almost more to himself than to her, startled by the rapid twitching of her eyelids and the gasping quality of her breathing as she struggled to fill her lungs with air. He stood up and walked quickly to the apartment at the rear of the warehouse where he filled a glass with water, his hand shaking as he hurried back to where Theresa lay on the floor. "Here," he said, lifting her head up to the glass. "Drink this."

The first sip caused a small spasm of her bruised esophagus, and she coughed for several seconds. Finally, as her breathing came more under control, she was able to take another sip, and then a third. Sitting up, she made a futile attempt to cover her breasts with the remnants of her silk blouse. A. G. remembered her jacket and retrieved it from the top of the suitcase by the door.

"Get out," she said, her voice hoarse and raw as she threw the jacket over her shoulders and stood up unsteadily. Her skirt had twisted around her waist, and she struggled with it for a second or two before giving up with a curse of frustration. "I said, get out," she repeated, much louder, near hysteria, as A. G. made no move to leave. "Get out, now."

"Calm down," A. G. said, his voice quiet yet firm. He took the time to tuck his shirt into his trousers, carefully centering his belt buckle before looking back at Theresa. "Just calm down."

A snarl twisted her lips. "You son of a . . ."

"Stop." A. G.'s voice rose in sudden anger as he interrupted her. "You don't have the right to call me, of all people, names," he said, pointing an accusing finger at her. "In fact," he paused, a sardonic smile flickering across his face, "as far as I'm concerned, you don't have any rights at all." He shrugged and rolled his shoulders twice, releasing tension in his neck and upper back. "I honestly hadn't intended for that," he nodded toward the floor, "to happen, but let's not kid ourselves about your being the suddenly aggrieved, innocent party. If we want to talk *aggrieved,* we can talk about your husband, or Wanda Carbone, or," again the hint of a sardonic smile, "me." He lit a cigarette, taking a second to savor the bite of the bright-leaf tobacco on his tongue. "But certainly not you, Theresa Fitzgerald, and not Sergeant Stevens, remorseful as he might or might not have been when he shot himself in the head."

"If you don't leave," Theresa said quietly, avoiding looking at him as she buttoned her jacket and straightened her skirt, "I'll call the police."

A. G. laughed, genuine amusement evident in his voice. "Believe me when I tell you that short of murder," the smile vanished from his face, "neither the district attorney nor Tug Benson would go so far as to cross the street to hear your complaint. They might both think *me* a fool, and with some justification, but despite what you may believe, neither one of them was misled for a moment by your protestations of innocence. In short, while there may not be enough evidence to prosecute you, they know exactly, even as I do, who you are and what you've done."

Theresa looked at him for a second, clearly struggling to control her anger. She bent slightly forward and hiked up her skirt, exposing her legs to midthigh. Reaching down, she straightened first one, then the other seam of her silk stockings, her movements slow and deliberate. That done, she smoothed down her skirt and looked back at A. G., once again in control of herself. She took a cigarette from her purse and, as she had before, accepted a light from him. "Thank you. I think it's fair to say that we've both made mistakes. For one thing, as I've already said, clearly I misjudged you." The barest hint of a smile tugged at the corners of her mouth. "But why burn bridges that don't need to be burned?" She stepped closer to him. "Come with me to Washington."

A. G. laughed again, humor less evident than before. "You still don't get it, do you? That," he nodded again at the floor, "wasn't love. At best it might have been . . ."

"You'll miss me," she pointed out, hurriedly interrupting him, as if not wanting to hear what he might say. Her voice changed subtly, the confident tone undercut by what could only be described as a sudden, and unexpected, note of insecurity. "You know you will."

A. G. shook his head. "It's funny you should say that. Before I came over here today I thought I would, I thought I'd miss you terribly. But now," he shook his head again for emphasis and turned to leave, "I don't think so."

"Damn you," she said angrily, flinging her cigarette to the floor, "what makes you . . ."

He stepped through the warehouse door and closed it

firmly behind him, cutting off the flow of Theresa's invective. He took a deep breath and, walking down the sidewalk to his car, he realized that, for the first time in months, the afternoon sun felt good on his face.

Chapter Seventeen

"Hurry up or you'll let all the cold air out," A. G. said impatiently, holding the screen door open for Pearl. She had followed him from the kitchen and now, ignoring his facetious entreaty, she walked slowly and deliberately onto the porch, pausing briefly at the threshold to sniff the air suspiciously, as if she suspected a trick of some sort. *Hurry up or you'll let all the cold air out.* In spite of himself, he smiled, remembering Theresa's explanation that the expression was a small joke she and her husband had used to lessen the discomfort of un–air-conditioned army housing. October was only three days away, and the long summer heat wave had finally broken the week before. The days were still warm, but the evenings had begun to cool nicely, and a light cotton blanket on the bed felt good toward morning. A. G. sat on the glider, sipping a glass of buttermilk and watching the clouds moving in from the west. "We could use the rain," he said to the cat, "but I doubt we'll get any." He pointed to the west. "I'm afraid those clouds are moving too fast to do us any good."

Before Pearl could respond, had she been of a mind to, the crunch of tires on the gravel driveway leading up to the house caught both her and A. G.'s attention.

"Lieutenant Giles," A. G. said, pleased to see the young man. "What a nice surprise. We haven't talked in, what, almost a month now."

"I heard you were leaving," Giles said somewhat sheepishly as he climbed the steps up to the porch.

"Yes," A. G. confirmed, "it's true."

"For good?"

"For good. Have a seat. Would you like a glass of buttermilk?" A. G. pointed to his own glass on the table next to the sofa. "Or iced tea?"

"Nothing for me," Giles said. "I can't stay but a minute—I've got to pick Mary Frances up at her mother's café. She's going to continue working there until I get out of the army next spring." He sat down on the edge of the sofa. "Are you selling the house?"

"It's already sold. A lawyer over in Richmond, a man who knew my daddy quite well, bought it. He'd always admired the place, and when I called and told him I'd be willing to let it go," A. G. snapped his fingers, "he bought it just like that." He paused and lit a cigarette. "I was born in this house," he said quietly, more to himself than to Giles. " 'Borned and raised,' as folks around here would say." He pointed toward the second floor. "Of course, most women these days go to a hospital, but I was born right up there, in my mother's bedroom." He smiled and shook his head. "I should have sold it years ago."

"How do you mean?"

"Well, take yourself for example. You left home to go to

college, then into the army, and you haven't looked back, have you? Now you've gotten married, and you and Mary Frances have started a new life. At each stage of your life you've grown and moved on. I didn't do that. I let myself get talked into coming back here during the war and taking the sheriff's job. It was only supposed to be temporary, until after the war, but twelve years later here I am, right where I started." He shook his head. "If all I was going to do was stay here, I might as well not have wasted four years in Charlottesville."

"It hasn't necessarily been a bad life for you," Giles pointed out.

"That's what I thought, too, but I was wrong. You see, coming back here, to this house, to this life, was like," he paused, trying to think of the best way to articulate what he was thinking, "was like wrapping myself in gauze, if you can picture that. Things were too comfortable, too easy. There was no challenge and, like water just sitting in a pond, I stagnated. I'll give you an example: How could I have been so blissfully unaware of the activity, in such a small town, of Doug Troutman, our drugstore abortionist? Obviously I knew that the white and Negro communities lead relatively separate existences, but for me to have missed so many clues that something was terribly wrong means that I simply wasn't looking. And I wasn't looking because, again, things were too comfortable." He remembered something and shook his head. "Sergeant Stevens told me as much before he killed himself."

"The witness to Captain Fitzgerald's murder," Giles murmured. He had read A. G.'s report to the district attorney of Stevens's confession.

"Exactly. Stevens knew instinctively what I would never have guessed: that the witness, an old Negro gentleman, could be counted on not to come forth and give evidence against him in the murder of a white man."

"Did you ever find out who it was?"

"No, and now it really doesn't matter. The point is, I was blissfully ignorant that such a divide, such enmity and distrust, existed, and I was ignorant because my life here was so comfortable, so womblike, that I never developed truly critical faculties. Look at yourself." A. G. smiled. "Your boss, Major Williams, might be a fool and a hard man to work for, but he's kept you light on your feet, and when you leave here, the last thing you'll be able to say is that you stagnated on the job."

"Which reminds me, I wanted to tell you that Private Carbone was released from the stockade yesterday."

"I'm glad to hear it. Were all the charges dropped?"

Giles shook his head. "Everything but the assault charge. I tried to get Major Williams to take Mrs. Carbone's murder into account and give him a break, but no such luck. He was sentenced to time already served and reduced in rank one grade from PFC to private."

"That's unfortunate. I think it's fair to say that Private Carbone did not deserve to be treated in such a fashion," A. G. mused. "Not by a long shot."

"Speaking of treatment, I think it's terrible the way people around here have treated you," Giles blurted out. He knew from his wife and mother-in-law that A. G. had been shunned by the community since his resignation as sheriff and the details of his relationship with Theresa Fitzgerald became common knowledge.

A. G. smiled. "I appreciate your concern, I really do, but to be honest with you, I think folks around here have a right to be upset with me. What I did was wrong, pure and simple."

"But to have to resign . . ."

"I didn't *have* to resign," A. G. interrupted, "not in the sense that Bud Taylor or anyone else told me to resign. I resigned because it was the right thing to do."

"I'm not sure the punishment in this case fits the crime, so to speak," Giles persisted.

"Think about it for a moment," A. G. responded. "Putting aside the unrelated murder of Doug Troutman, three people are dead," he held up three fingers for emphasis, "two of them murdered and one a suicide. Additionally, a completely innocent man, Private Carbone, was very effectively framed and thereby subjected to what amounts to extreme psychological abuse, including the murder of his wife, while he was wrongfully incarcerated in the stockade. Last, and worst of all, the person most responsible for all of this, Theresa Fitzgerald, has been allowed to go scot-free, at least in part because of my shortcomings."

"Have you," Giles paused, afraid he might be getting too personal, and then, curiosity overcoming concern, plunged forward, "heard anything since she left?"

A. G. shook his head. "I wouldn't expect to, of course, but no, nothing. I'm pleased to be able to say that Tug Benson, in Petersburg, believed Sergeant Stevens's confession as fully as I did, despite the district attorney's disinclination to pursue an indictment against her. Tug told me he was going to try to have her kept on the law-enforcement radar screen through his contacts with the FBI, but he doubted, as do I, that she'll ever be held to account for either her husband's or Wanda Carbone's murder." He shrugged and sighed. "So as regards my resignation and unofficial public censure, not only does the punishment very handily fit the crime, I think it could be argued quite convincingly that, given the magnitude of the harm done, and its irreversibility, I got off easily indeed." He smiled, suddenly thinking of something. "Besides, George Scott," the interim sheriff appointed by Bud Taylor, "wears a uniform with a Sam Browne belt and a Colt pistol. Another thing I didn't realize was how uncomfortable most folks around here were with the fact that I never wore a uniform or carried a gun."

"When are you leaving?"

"Sometime in the next day or two. I've got one or two things left to clean up, and then I'm off." He looked down at the cat and smiled. "Miss Pearl's going to go live with Mildred Tatum." He reached down and affectionately stroked her between the ears. "I'm afraid she's too old and set in her ways to be up and moving and, in any event, she was my mother's cat and never had a great deal of confidence in my judgment." He chuckled. "I'm afraid she would worry if I took her along."

Giles looked at his watch and stood up. "I've got to go pick up Mary Frances," he said awkwardly, not knowing how best to say good-bye. "By the way," he added, realizing he had not asked, "where are you moving to?"

"California," A. G. said casually, as if going to California was of no greater significance than walking across the street.

"California?" Giles repeated, as if unsure he had heard correctly. "But what will you do? I mean," he stammered, realizing that his question could be interpreted to mean that he thought A. G. unqualified for meaningful work, "after you get out there."

"Wanda Carbone told me that there are lots of jobs in California for people who want to work," A. G. answered, a broad smile on his face. "She said she read it in a Hollywood fan magazine, so of course it must be true."

"Wanda Carbone?"

A. G. nodded. "In our second, and last, meeting at her apartment, when she told me she was preparing to leave Petersburg. She thought California would be a good place to start over and, having given it some thought lately, I've come to the same conclusion."

"Where in California do you think you'll go?"

"Hard to say. I've been doing some research, and San Francisco sounds awfully nice, but I'm going to give Los Angeles a long look, too. Something about palm trees, just the idea I guess, tickles my fancy." A. G. extended his right hand. "I plan to keep Mildred Tatum posted on my address, so you and Mary Frances stay in touch, you hear? Who knows, when you get out of the army, you may want to come west yourself."

They shook hands, and A. G. waved as the younger man drove off. He stood on the porch, watching, until the car was out of sight.

"California," he again said out loud, liking the way the syllables rolled off his tongue. He opened the screen door and walked into the house, imagining a perfect golden Pacific sunset.